The
Devil's Tears

M. C. Dutton

The
Devil's Tears

Matador
9 De Montfort Mews
Leicester LE1 7FW, UK
Tel: (+44) 116 255 9311 / 9312
Email: books@troubador.co.uk
Web: www.troubador.co.uk/matador

ISBN 978 1906221 638

A Cataloguing-in-Publication (CIP) catalogue record for this book
is available from the British Library.

Typeset in 11pt Stempel Garamond by Troubador Publishing Ltd, Leicester, UK
Printed in the UK by TJ International Ltd, Padstow, Cornwall

Matador is an imprint of Troubador Publishing Ltd

As a new author there were times of self doubt. It takes special people to carry you through these times. I should therefore like to dedicate my book to those very special and important people.

Special thanks to my children and grandchildren:

Helen, Ben, Isabella and Kiera
Richard, Amanda, Rebecca, Josh and Thomas,
Andrew, Nansel and Bradley
LUA xxxx

Special thanks to Richard Charles for his valuable and motivational creative help

Special thanks to Pam Cumberworth for her explosive, expletive enthusiasm

CHAPTER ONE

Capture

The Guardians peered down intensely at him, they tried unsuccessfully to sit back and wait until he had calmed down but each were agitated and their tutting and groaning and mutterings of oh dear just increased the tension around. They asked each other why he was panicking so much and why he just didn't sit still and wait. He was like a wasp in a jam jar, all fury and posture but nowhere to go, he was beaten, they asked why he couldn't see that for himself. They found it so frustrating; Their hands were tied, and they were not able to help him at that moment. They were desperate to calm him down to make him feel at ease and safe, this was too horrible to endure. The Guardians questioned their role, over and over again in bringing him here. That, alone, had been a difficult and scary time in the no mans land of the lost. They were considered experts in this line of work but each time was different and held perils not experienced before. The anguish of seeing him so scared and fighting made them wish they had an easier role.

After what seemed ages, and to their immense relief,

they could see he was beginning to calm down. He had used up all his energy and stood slightly swaying and breathing deeply and fast, they were fearful he was on the point of collapse and they could do nothing for him. They knew in the end it was for the best, that he would be all right, but they hated seeing any being in such distress. They were the Guardians and mistakes were rare, but they wondered if he would be up to the challenge. It was a deep worry for them. They would help him as best they could but, and it was a big but, they were very aware that he had to succeed. Again they questioned if he was the man for the job? It required that he felt a deep bond with her, that was not a concern to them, but a calm, clear head, and an understanding of events was definitely going to be a problem. Looking at him fighting every inch of the way, exhausted now, but still defiant, swearing and shouting at thin air, they were very sceptical, and a little depressed at the thought that he may not be up to the challenge.

**

He was in a strange room and he couldn't remember how he had got here. Where he was before he couldn't remember, all he knew with certainty was it wasn't this place. He was scared and panicking and all his senses were geared up ready to fight, but there was nothing to fight. After rushing round and raising enough adrenaline to fuel an army, he ran out of breath, energy and hope. He was sick of never feeling in control, never quite knowing what was going to happen next.

Now he had stopped rushing around he realised the saying "*blind panic*" meant just that, he had seen nothing, knew nothing. He looked around and tried to note where he was, to see if anything was familiar. He had never experienced a place like this. It could only be described as white but that was not right. It was stunningly bright but it did not hurt his eyes. He had to make some sense of all this. Something, someone, wanted him to stay here and he was going to have none of it. He was no sheep to be led to the slaughter. He was confused about everything but he was sure about one thing, this was not right. He wasn't sure what he wanted or where he wanted to be, but it certainly was not here. Whatever might be trying to disorientate him he would fight it and keep control. He was Michael Angelo, Angel to his friends and these bastards would not get their way. He stood still, fists clenched, legs apart he was ready for anything.

He closed his eyes and forced himself to start again, slowly and calmly. This area, he knew it must be a room but the light didn't give it any shape. There were no corners or angles and his vision wasn't able to penetrate further than 4 metres in any direction. It was spookily still, his heart pounded loudly jostling for sound space with his breathing. He shouted "Hello" but nothing bounced back at him. Like a thick fog it absorbed the sound. At this point he fought again for control of his senses, as he started to descend into that state of panic which made the hairs on his body stand to attention. He badly wanted to scratch his arms. Again he looked around and he knew this place was all wrong. His breathing, which had nearly returned to normal, was descending again into that deep and fast rhythm which would trigger the dizzy feeling.

He moved forward, fists clenched, his legs screamed at the command to run faster, they wobbled and strained at the weight they had to carry. After what seemed an age, he stopped, his legs buckling through exhaustion and his lungs losing the battle to get enough air. He looked around and saw nothing had changed. He knew he had run for longer than he had ever run before, but everything still looked the same. His hands extended out in front of him, but there was nothing to touch and the room, damn it! He knew it was a room, had no edges. Just as he was about to be overwhelmed with more fear than his brain could hold, he saw a chair. It was the first solid thing he had seen and it had the effect of relaxing him. He went to the chair, touched it and felt how thick and firm the wood felt. Memories of people, sounds and smells hung in a hazy mist, tantalisingly and frustratingly just out of his reach. His eyes pricked and he could feel tears very close to spilling.

He thought he heard but realised he felt someone tell him to sit down. He was hot and tired and surprisingly emotional and for a second all he wanted to do was sit and rest. But then, of course, that was how they wanted him to feel, he was getting angry now; and wanted to know why They were playing games with him. He looked around and shouted at the fog, "Who the hell do you think you are telling me to do anything you, fuck you and go to hell."

He could feel the rage boiling inside him and the last thing he was going to do was sit down for those scum suckers. He stood swaying for sometime, then a warm, yellow cloud engulfed his senses and a sense of calm overtook him. The rage dispersed and he decided, on reflection, he was tired, "so what the hell", he told himself he could do with the rest, he knew that was his decision not theirs. He needed his strength to fight them and he chose to sit down. The chair felt good, the ache in his back and legs felt easier. He felt mesmerised and comfortable his eyes focussed ahead and all he could hear was his own urgent breathing.

Something was going to happen. The tension in the air and a muffled quiet sound in the distance, like an orchestra tuning up for the start of a show made him alert and ready for what was to come. His frustration was that with knowledge of everything so close he could almost taste it, but with every snatch it sidestepped him just out of reach. Acceptance was part of his new existence. He still had a problem with that. Everything had to be learned the hard way. He looked around, took a deep breath and shouted defiantly, "Fuck you!" He knew it wouldn't make any difference but it made him feel good. He promised himself that they, whoever they were, would not have everything their own way.

The Guardians watching him sighed. This all felt so unnecessary, they wanted to tell him everything but he would never cope with it at the moment. There was so much to learn, all they could hope for was that in time, he would understand and work with them. The inner film would start playing soon. He must watch, learn and remember. With his resistance on hold, he waited as the film rewound and started over a lifetime ago.

He sat up straight and looked at what was a big screen ahead of him. A buzzing feeling surge through him. The face, big and close up on the screen, was someone he thought he recognised, a mist curled around her face obscuring her features then clearing again. It was tantalising and infuriating. He knew her, and spat at the screen, "Goddam it! Let me see her clearly." He agonised and stared hard hoping the mist would clear. They heard him and made the picture clear. He fidgeted, peering closer his forehead knitted as he struggled to remember. She was familiar, he had been close to her, maybe even loved her, but who was she? He licked his lips and concentrated trying to remember more, trying to see right into her to find the answers he wanted and needed. The beautiful young girl he saw on the film was skipping across a field. He leaned forward to look more closely, craning his head this way and that trying to see into her eyes, to catch a mannerism that would give him her name. "God!" he thought, "she was so beautiful and carefree."

It came to him in a sudden unexpected moment. "Maria." She was called Maria. He felt excited and fidgeted on his chair, repeating her name like a mantra. "Maria, you're called Maria, who are you Maria? Are you the person I am searching for? Maria, Maria." The more he said her name the more something was stirring in his head. He could not take his eyes off the screen in front of him, the answers were there and he knew he would have to be patient. The tears were waiting in the wings again, as he realised this was the first time in all his memory that he did not feel afraid or quite so lonely. The thing he was searching for was here and Maria was part of it.

CHAPTER TWO

The Beginning

Maria Angelo was not her real name. She didn't know who her parents were and it was not something she had lost sleep over. She had been left at the orphanage as a baby and was given her name after the nuns decided she would be blessed with the Holy Mother's name and Angelo after a Roman Catholic prophet. Maria was one of eight girls with the Holy Mother's name.

The Nunnery had been built in St. Josephs town, Kansas. The rich and fertile land had been claimed as church property at the beginning of 1800. In 1860 thirty nuns and a priest were sent from Ireland to set up a self supporting Nunnery in this strange and heathen land. Over the years 200 acres of land that adjoined the church was turned into a thriving farm at an unacceptable cost to the order. Unused to such harsh physical labours, the nuns were susceptible to any infections that regularly swept across the country. With no strength to resist the ravages of infections passed to them by the many immigrant wagon trains, which would stop for religious sustenance on their travels across the country over four years, the order lost six nuns to infection and many more were regularly unfit to work. Those 200 acres tilled and worked by the nuns made them self sufficient in food, with enough to barter in the small town shops for the additional items of clothing and food necessary to live. The cost was high and all surviving nuns became fitter and tougher than any group of women in America. When younger nuns regularly joined them sent from England and Ireland the order was increased to forty nuns. It would take many months of prayer and tears to adapt them to the hard life. The regime of the day was waking for early morning prayers at 4.30 a.m. and after a simple breakfast of gruel and bread they would work in the fields from 6 a.m. sowing and reaping the land until 6 p.m. at night with evening prayers ending the day at 9 p.m. There was no retirement for these women. The elderly, frail nuns were allowed by the Priest to stay in the nunnery where their life was a little easier, but with an average age of 60 years the washing, cooking, and cleaning kept them busy until exhaustion and illness gave them merciful release in death.

The Priest, a colourless man with greying hair and grey features lived his life in the nunnery. His role was to oversee the running of the nunnery in a spiritual and practical way. He had been plucked from the town of Galway where his life had been predictable and regular, and dumped in this godforsaken place at the age of 40 years. He bore the burden of this by praising God and drinking whiskey. He was often found slumped in the vestry by nuns attending evening prayer. He never toiled in the fields. The nuns cherished him and looked after him as their Priest who tended to their spiritual needs and was their earthly father.

The Nunnery was a tough place to live and only the strong and fit survived. There was not much room for sentiment in their lives. Working for God was their only goal. Over the years the odd baby and child had been left at the Nunnery. When wagon trains passed by their land, occasionally someone would leave a baby orphaned through death from disease or the harsh life of the settlers. The old nuns brought up these few children and they in turn helped on the land when they became old enough to dig and sow.

As if these poor women did not have enough to cope with, the Catholic Church ordered them to take in babies and children orphaned. The flood gates had been opened and people poured into America. All the poor people in the free world who had nothing, wanted to come to America. Everyone knew that the land in America was free and there was gold in the hills for the picking. The migration to America was at its height in the 1870's and with so many people came children and babies. Death walked hand in hand with birth and many children were left orphaned in a strange country with no one to look after them.

The Catholic Church paid the Holy Order of the Sacred Cross a small sum of money each year to help with the clothing and feeding of 50 orphans. In reality they had 100 children shipped by train and coach from various towns and cities from New York to Atlanta. The Nuns understood their role in life. They were used to adversity and hardship and they would cope somehow with these children as decreed by the Holy Church and the Pope.

The rules and order of this remote nunnery were reflected in the upbringing of the 100 children in the care of women who had never married, let alone had children. Discipline, prayer and hard work was the tenet of the Holy Order of the Sacred Cross. The children grew up knowing little of any other life and accepted the harsh discipline of the orphanage as normal.

Maria's life at the orphanage was a colourless existence that did not encourage the sort of individualism she wanted to express. The nuns found her a cunning wilful child who did not want to work. Unbeknown to them Maria had found ways of getting the little extras in life without working for it. It had started with allowing boys to look at her knickers for a piece of pumpkin pie. This delicacy was on the menu once per week as a treat. There were many boys who saved their piece of pumpkin pie to tempt Maria to show those areas of a girls body that boys had never seen. At 13 years old Maria was experimenting with sex. There was a resourceful boy who managed to earn a few cents by selling some apples from the orchards on visits to town, when he helped the nuns collect supplies. He bought bows and bits of lace in the store and gave them to Maria. In the austere surroundings of the orphanage, Maria had never seen such fabulously gorgeous pieces of beauty. The first bow was bright red. It was brighter than any sunset and when she put it in her hair she felt magnificent and beautiful. For that first wonderful piece she let the boy, Dougal, do whatever he wanted. He spent an hour exploring her naked body. It would be two or three more glitteringly colourful presents before Dougal had sex with her. She thought it was a perfect swap, her body for lovely presents. The boy was willing to do anything to please her and she found lots of work for him to do on her behalf to make her life a little easier. She engineered the field rota so they worked together, Dougal was very happy working twice as hard in the fields doing her work as well as his own knowing she would be very grateful.

Despite the perks Maria was enjoying, the orphanage was still a bleak experience and at 14 years old she was glad to leave, ready to move on to better pastures. Maria was a pretty young girl with thick dark hair, lips that were full and promising and a figure that looked on the verge of blossoming into something interesting. She managed to catch the eye of Mr. Henderson. The orphanage arranged for her to live in at Mr and Mrs Henderson in exchange for cleaning duties etc. It was considered a respectable job for a young girl. Mr Henderson was a Councillor for the small town of St. Joseph, Kansas. He was a patron of the Orphanage and was well known in the community for his charitable work. His wife was a pleasant but timid woman who spoke quietly and kept in the background. The gossip was that Mrs Henderson came from good stock and her quiet manner was the way refined ladies were supposed to act. Mrs Henderson's pointed thin nose always looked as if it had a very nasty smell under it, making her lips purse in a disagreeable fashion. Her demeanour was thin and ungenerous. Mr Henderson on the other hand was considered rather robustly vulgar, but he was blessed by the nuns because his heart was in the right place. He occasionally bought a side of beef for the nuns to have which was a special treat for them and they were grateful. Unlike Mrs Henderson, Mr Henderson was a large-framed man whose clothes always looked as if they valiantly struggled to stay seamed together.

Maria was given a room of her own, it was in the basement where it was quiet and the room was all hers. She loved it; enjoying the first bit of privacy in her short life. Her bed had a patchwork cover that had bright colours in it and she sat and stared at it, stroking it and fingering the blues, greens and reds, she thought it the most beautiful thing she had ever seen. The work was hard but it was indoors for the most part. She now had to get up at 6 a.m. to clean the grates and start the fire for cooking, by 9.30 p.m she was allowed to return to her room. Mr Henderson's first visit to her room was not a shock to Maria, she found it quite interesting. He found her a willing participant in his sexual fantasy and oh so easy. Most girls who had passed through his hands had struggled and cried and made it very difficult for him, but Maria was something else and very receptive and accommodating. His mouth watered at the thought of her, he had watched her at the orphanage and recognised the come on look from her. Despite the nuns arguments of how lazy and sly she was, he insisted on having her, to help his wife.

As a young girl who had never owned anything or been allowed to make any decisions about her own life, she found out quite quickly that sex was power and freedom. The boys had been just boys, Mr Henderson was going to be much more rewarding and she was busy working out what she wanted. Maria was an intelligent girl but it would take time to work out what life had to offer her, because she had never seen much of life outside of the orphanage to know what to aim for. There was one thing she had and that was time.

Mrs Henderson was a Christian and a good respectable wife. Sex was, unfortunately, a blessed requirement in a marriage and as a good Christian Mrs Henderson would never complain. To this end, the missionary position was the only method she would suffer and as infrequently as possible. Mr Henderson, on the other hand, enjoyed a variety of sinful pleasures not practised with his wife and he enthusiastically instructed his willing pupil into all his fantasies.

Maria discovered she had an imagination and many new games were tried out, much to Mr Henderson's delight. Maria was rewarded for her efforts with small gifts of money every now and then. This mutually satisfactory relationship was to continue in Kansas City. Many maids had passed through the Henderson household over the years but Maria was the best, so keen, so talented, Mr Henderson would not let her slip through his fingers. He lusted after her and told her he loved her.

Mrs Henderson had never liked her. She found Maria a lazy good for nothing creature who looked at her with almost contempt. Mr Henderson, she concluded, was too good a person to realise that some girls would always be bad whatever you try to do for them. Mr Henderson said she must be given a chance and who was she to argue with him.

The subtle change in Mrs Henderson's attitude

towards her made Maria realise she had power. Maria had flexed her muscles with Mr Henderson and realised as long as she did what Mr Henderson wanted and needed she could make her life easy and get Mrs Henderson off her back. Quite quickly, she realised staying with the Hendersons was not enough. She could not believe how easy it was to get things going her way. On the face of it, she was no freer with the Hendersons than when she was at the Orphanage, but, oh she was far more in control than they realised. The pregnancy could not be excused and Maria knew this. She was fed up with the Henderson household. She was doing very little housework but that was too much. She wanted to spread her wings and live a little. A place of her own and some money to buy pretty dresses and trinkets was her goal. So according to her plan, Mr. Henderson found her a small apartment in Kansas City and used his contacts to arrange an abortion.

Maria left the Henderson household at 16 years of age. The extra duties Mr Henderson insisted on left her pregnant and sacked. Mrs Henderson had always known what type of girl she was and with a self-righteous stance, made sure Maria left her home. She could not resist her parting words to Maria, "You're an evil whore who never did deserve help. May God forgive you." With these words ringing in her ears, Maria went to Kansas City with just a small bag and $5. It was easy to work as a prostitute in this thriving farming town.

Mr Henderson was comfortably off but didn't have the sort of money to keep a mistress full-time. He told her she would have to get a respectable job in the town to pay for her keep, but he would pay for the apartment. He held her hand and sadly told her he would only be able to make the journey and visit her once per week. He hoped she would not miss him too much. Maria had kissed him and almost in tears, told him she would count the hours between his visits. She was actually working out her own plans. He left her feeling very happy and contented. He had decided that his life would not be worth living without Maria and this way, he could see her in privacy every week. He thought he was quite clever to have arranged this. He knew Maria could not survive without him, and he looked forward to receiving her gratitude.

Mr Henderson paid the rent on her small apartment and during the week Maria saw her customers. She was very popular. She looked young and fresh but had the experience of an old whore, which proved very lucrative. She enjoyed the variety of men and the power of having her own place that allowed her to invite her chosen clients into her home when she wanted to. She was in control, no more midnight visits, or being pushed into the barn for sex while Mrs Henderson was baking or distracted in the house, or just being mauled on the stairs, in the kitchen, or anywhere it took Mr Henderson's fancy. He was in love with her, he told her often, as he drawled, licked, pawed, fondled and pushed himself all over her. She found it increasingly difficult to cope with him, he had got more frenzied as time went on. Given only a few minutes of Mrs Henderson being distracted he would leap on her, abuse her, touch her and often hurt her in the panic of quick gratification. She was fed up with being attacked all the time. She had no control over her life and it was tiring never knowing when he would pounce on her.

She liked her new life in Kansas City. She loved her apartment, her freedom, the money. She had a few abortions on the way but for three years life was fair. All good things come to an end. The weather changed, the crops failed and business for Maria started to drop as slowly farmers gave up the fight with the elements left their farms and moved to large towns to start again. Maria decided to move on to better pastures. Kansas City was a big town but there were bigger and more exciting places to live. She had heard people talk about Chicago, a big city up North, and the train that stopped at Kansas City station would take her straight there. She had made a very nice living and saved enough money for the fare and accommodation when she got there. She was sick of Mr Henderson and he was getting possessive. She didn't need him anymore. A new start with no ties would suit her fine. Who knows she mused, she might even find herself a really rich and handsome customer who would provide her with fine clothes and a fancy apartment.

This was the most exciting thing she had done for years. She was still just 19 years old but she felt as if she had lived a long life in Kansas and now she was ready for a big city with new and exciting prospects. Living in a big city up North would be so thrilling and had possibilities undreamed of. She had heard somewhere that there were cars that were so sleek and polished you could use their chassis like a mirror. Fine ladies would travel in the back of those sleek vehicles with handsome, rich men. She had heard that there was wealth beyond her imagination in big cities up north. She knew she would do alright in Chicago and couldn't wait to arrive and make her fortune.

She arrived in Chicago with determination and optimism born of a certain amount of naivety. This was a big city. She asked at the station where the cheapest end of town was. The conductor looked at her, he could see what she was, and told her downtown Chicago would suit her down to the ground. She travelled on a trolley car. She'd never seen one before. She knew she had made the right decision, Chicago looked good and the buildings amazed her, they were so tall. Kansas had one storey buildings but these were six or seven storey buildings. She wondered how they did not fall down. Everything she had heard about Chicago was true, the streets were so noisy with more cars on one road than she had ever seen. She wondered if she would ever get used to the noise or how she would ever cross a road and reach the other side alive. She had arrived in September and the weather was hot. The landlord showed her the basement apartment and was busy looking her up and down while she surveyed the small but cheap apartment. He laughed when she asked if it was always this noisy. Chicago in the summer was a hellhole. Every window of every stinking apartment was open letting the world into the sights of sweating people. The rotting vegetables in the road from the daily market mingled with the smells of cooking permeated into every open window, crack and crevice and hung like a low, still, cloud over this part of Chicago. Tempers were always frayed in the summer and violent arguments would scream across alleyways into open windows to amuse or scare neighbours. Everywhere within three blocks of the apartment was crowded with screaming kids, barking dogs, drunken men, babies crying in perambulators, women gossiping while hanging out clothes or shouting at kids. He laughingly told her she wouldn't notice the deafening and invasive noise after the first five years and the smells got better in the winter. This would do temporarily she thought, when she found her feet things would change.

Downtown Chicago was tough and her customers were not wealthy. Although she was working long days and earning fair money it was not what she had hoped for. Maria being Maria she just sort of stayed put. The most ambitious thing she had done was to get to Chicago and that had used up any get up and go she had. She got complacent and settled in and life was quite good.

CHAPTER THREE

Michael

Maria had been pregnant before but got rid of the babies. Michael's birth was an accident. When she became pregnant with Michael she visited the local woman dealing with abortions. She had a lot of pain and bleeding and thought as usual the blight had been taken away. By 6 months her nagging doubts were confirmed when she felt the child kick. She decided to go through with the pregnancy. Why on earth she wanted to keep the baby she did not know. It could have been fear of terminating such a late pregnancy, she had heard stories from others about crippling infection, terrible pains and death. It could have been loneliness, who knows. At the time she was earning regular money. She was in the same rented one-room basement apartment she took when she arrived in Chicago. It was plenty big enough for her and a baby. She was a striking looking girl with black thick hair and blue eyes, the product of Irish descendants. She would have been considered beautiful except for the scar that ran from her ear to her mouth, the result of a drunken bad tempered customer. He left her bleeding profusely in a dark alley and staggered off not a second thought about what he had done. Life's experiences teach you lessons, and Maria made sure that situation would not be allowed to arise again.

Surprisingly perhaps, she carried on working until she was 8 months pregnant. She was nothing but skin and bones. Her regulars approved of the increased size of breasts and a bit more meat around the hips and stomach, but quite honestly it didn't matter much to most of them what she looked like. At 8 months she had enough money, if careful, to see her through her pregnancy and for one month after, her rent was paid up for 2 months so she had a roof over her head and enough money for food. She found a local woman willing to birth the baby. They were always old, mind you it felt safer to use an old woman, experience and all that with no distraction of young kids of their own. There were always women around who quite cheaply got rid of babies and birthed them. These were brutal times. Contraception was still a hit and miss affair. These midwifes were often the most important person in a woman's life. Unmarried girls were the regular customers for abortions, that's not to say married women didn't avail themselves of this confidential service. Over the years the midwifes had aborted, birthed and buried enough babies and women to fill a small town. They had seen most of nature's dirty tricks and were not above helping a deformed baby on its way to peace. Poor little mites no good to themselves or anyone else. Such was the power of the midwifes, women put their trust and their bodies in the hands of a midwife knowing she will do what's right . This could sometimes be very misguided but who would know? The workings of the body were still a mystery to most people and deaths were common.

Maria went into labour on 1st September 1901 at 5 p.m. It started slowly and comfortably. The fear of giving birth subsided a little. She thought, "It's not so bad." By 5 a.m. 2nd September she was feeling tired and unwell and it was hurting. The midwife sat knitting and, watching, she knew what was going on. No sense in telling the girl.

By 7 a.m. all hell let loose. From timid beginnings the pain started strongly and reached a crescendo of mindnumbing agony. The pain, which started in her abdomen, rose tortuously up into her throat and came out as a piercing continuous scream, which seemed to those in the street to be endless. Women crossed themselves and shuddered with knowledge, men quickened their pace. When the contraction had subsided, Maria gasped, sucking air in at a rapid rate, "I can't take any more of that, I want it to stop now."

The midwife told her quietly but firmly to calm down and behave. As she said that, another contraction began. For 6 hours each contraction ebbed and flowed and the pain crashed through her and over her they reached heights of pain unimaginable to Maria. She would pass out only to be lifted and shot out of oblivion into a new and unspeakable contraction. They followed relentlessly one after another with no rest in between. By 1 p.m. Maria was almost lifeless, she did not scream any more, she was hanging on by a thread. Each contraction brought a low moan and her eyes projected the wide-eyed look of terror and agony so deep she fair gave the midwife the shudders.

The midwife stopped her knitting. Now was the time to start preparation. Thank God the screaming had stopped. She had heard some screamers in her time, but this one fair gave her a headache. By 1.30 p.m. the bearing down started. It was a merciful release for Maria, the pain had stopped. Through dry lips she mumbled "Thank God, thank God. Is it over?"

The Midwife at this point was preparing Maria for birth.

"No my dear, but you are nearly there."

Maria managed a short gasp then she started to bear down. The pain had gone but it was replaced with an automatic biological primeval need to push down. She was totally out of control, her body was working without her consent, forcing her to push harder than she had ever pushed. She was clinging to her life force, her body was collecting and consolidating all the small reserves of energy which make the heart pump, the lungs breathe and channelling it to assist with the birth. Her own body had made the decision that she was not important, and would be sacrificed for the sake of the baby. She felt this and didn't care. Death was something she had been frightened of. Now she welcomed it, wanted it. Peace and calm and to be left alone. There was an explosion of pain and light and then darkness.

The baby was born after 22 hours 30 minutes. The midwife cut the cord. It was a boy. She looked at Maria unconscious. She cleaned the baby and Maria. With a few more hours to wait and watch, the midwife heated some broth on the stove for herself and she would save some for Maria who would need nourishment, she had a baby to feed now. For now she would wait, so Maria could sleep for a few hours.

Maria woke to the sound of clicking. The midwife stopped knitting and felt her head. You will be fine. You have a son who will need feeding soon. The midwife propped her up and gave her some broth to eat. Feeling stronger, Maria thanked her and paid the agreed sum of money. When the door had closed and she was alone she turned to looked at the baby boy. She thought she would automatically love him, she felt nothing for this sleeping baby. She decided to call him Michael, there was no particular reason for the name, just that she thought it was nice.

Michael Angelo was hers. The first living thing in the world that was hers. She reconciled that she would love him as time went on, and he would always love her because children love their Mothers.

Maria and Motherhood parted company very quickly. Constant sleepless nights, dirty nappies feeding and crying, continuous bloody crying she'd had enough. After 2 weeks she was ready to start work again and dumped the kid on a neighbour during her working hours at a suitably bartered price. She could have left him at an orphanage where he would have been looked after. Maria could not do that. She asked herself on many occasions why not. Her own experience of an orphanage had been bleak, just enough food, just enough clothes, and just enough warmth. No love, no Mother or Father just religion, morning, noon and night. She must have loved him a little she had supposed, why else would she keep him. People can make decisions that make no sense, on what looks like a whim, and stick with a disaster that looked planned all along.

CHAPTER FOUR

Angel

With more luck than judgement Michael reached 10 years old. Without the drawbacks of a stable home life, with mealtimes, clean clothing and loving parents, Michael grew to be a resourceful and impish lad. He cashed in on his cherub looks. He was small for his age with thick curly black hair and large dark eyes that could melt the hardest heart. His round face and chubby body belied his real age, he always looked at least 2 years younger and at 10 years old to look 8 years old with the mind of a 10 year old going on 30 years was a lucrative bonus. The crying act worked for quite a while, as his Mother's visitors left he would stand blocking their exit crying for his Mother. Invariably a few cents were pushed his way to keep him quiet. When his Mother was doing well, so was he. By the time he reached 12 years old he had to rethink his earners. Maria had never enjoyed anything involving real work and had never to his knowledge done any proper cooking or housework but now he noticed that she had become a fat, slovenly, drunken whore who just laid around most of the day. Business was not doing well and it seemed to Michael that he would have to increase his methods of earning money to keep a roof over their head and food on the table.

At 12 years old he learned the power of charm as a way of conning money out of the uptown people. He practised first on the people in his street. It was a painful experience, causing him a few clips round the ear. Charm did not go down well in downtown Chicago but he was learning his trade. His cherub looks would not last much longer, he found all the local kids his age were growing taller than him and leaner. He was staying small and getting fatter. His cute little nose was developing an ominous looking bump in the middle of the bridge and the end seemed more pointed with a slight hook on the end. Jesus he thought, what did my Father look like, but the eyes were his main feature. He could tell a lie and his eyes would tell you this is the honest truth. So blatant was the power of those eyes he could point to something black and tell you it was white and you would believe him.

His latest con involved using a neighbour's baby. He would carry it to the better end of town, he called it the goodies end of town. Once there, a suitable benefactor was spied and set upon. "Mister, excuse me Mister. I am terrible sorry to bother you, I don't actually know what to do," (slight anguished sob as he paused for breath).

"What's the matter Sonny?"

"Got him!" Michael thought, chuckling inwardly. He proceeded to spin a yarn about his poor darling Mother, who was unwell, Father had died recently in a mining accident. He added, hoping it was not too much, that he died a hero saving other men trapped in a mine. Father, he explained always sent money home with a letter and now his beloved sister (kiss on the forehead at this point for the baby) had no food, a quick hidden pinch of the baby's arm started a howl of anguish followed by sobs. Looking straight into the stranger's eyes with a totally innocent look maintained all the time.

"How old are you?" asked the stranger.

"I'm a big boy, I'm 9 years old," Michael wondered if he had pushed his luck on his age, he might have got away with 10-11 years but not 9 years, not since the nose had started sprouting. The man offered him $3.

"Mind you go straight home to your dear Mother, she will be worrying about you." "Yes Sir, thank you very much indeed Sir, I do not know what to say, I will call the Doctor for my Mother, and we can eat. Thank you Sir. God Bless you!"

This was the best taking he had managed so far. $3, gee that was a fortune, a fucking fortune. He told his Mother he had $1 otherwise it would go in the usual way. He returned the baby to a grateful neighbour.

"You are such a good boy for looking after Rosy for me. Here, have a piece of cake." He had done well, money and cake what more could he want.

"Poor but Honest" has to be the most ridiculous saying ever. If you are poor, you can't afford to be honest. No one gives you anything for nothing. and nine times out of ten the only way to get what you need is to steal it, con it or barter for it. Up until 12 years old Michael had only stolen what he needed to survive. When he hit 12 years two things happened, he realised you take more than you need because the need had changed. Now he saw the advantage in selling stolen items for money or bartering for items you would like but not need. He had realised that some days were better than others for earning; steal more today in case tomorrow is a bad day. The other thing that happened was his Mother gave up work. Well, rather the work gave her up. She was only 33 years old but by now the ravages of infections, drink, and just pure laziness had turned her into a fat, filthy, drunkard. She had developed an irrational temper and she would, regardless of the situation, fly off the handle lashing out, and cursing at whoever was nearby. She had a particularly nasty infection a while back. Michael had forgotten what it was called but she wasn't supposed to see men anymore because of the infection, well she did anyway. Since then she was getting odder and odder. Michael could handle most situations. He could move fast and she couldn't.

He never went home until the evening, as usual the place stunk. He had got used to the smell of urine but the other smell was taking over. His Mother was lying in bed as usual in a drunken stupor. Gees, he thought what a sight. She was losing her teeth and what were left were going black. Her hair was a matted mess and she stunk to high heaven. He couldn't think why or how she had got like this without him noticing. She stirred, "Michael have you brought me …"

"Yeah Ma got a bottle here."

She grabbed it with her left hand. The right hand was not working again. "You are a good lad."

God knows what gut rot this home brew gin was he thought. The rich could buy good stuff, but all those around here could get hold of was a few dubious sellers who sold undercover a liquid that was supposed to be gin. He had never tasted the "real thing" so wouldn't know the difference, but he once had a small swig of his Mothers and promptly spat it out, it tasted like bitter piss.

"Got my cigarettes Michael?"

"Oh shit, I forgot Ma." He screwed his face waiting for the tirade to start. She didn't let him down and screamed, "You Bastard! I don't ask for much, you have ruined my life, my figure has gone. I had plenty of money before you arrived. I would have had a big house by now, lovely clothes, one of my gentlemen callers would have married me because I was beautiful before you ruined my figure. I would be riding round in a carriage in my finery instead of living in this dump, you ungrateful little fucker!"

As he left he mouthed exactly the words she was saying with all the inflections, and all the pauses. When you have heard the same thing every day of your life it goes over your head. "I think I will put it to music."

Michael was now the chief breadwinner, cook, cleaner and recipient of his Mothers ravings. He was doing well. The baby scam was working well. He found the best place to hang out was the clip joints and gambling clubs. A winner would be quite generous. Once he got $10 dollars, an unthinkable amount of money because the guy he approached had just won a nice bit of money and the girl with him, obviously not his wife, was so taken with Michael and his story she wanted to take him home with her. The guy had different ideas on what was going to happen when she got home. He gave the kid $10. In gratitude Michael went over the top in his thanks to the man, which left the girlfriend in tears and with a very warm passionate feeling for her knight in shining armour. "Well," thought Michael, "he made my day and I reckon I made his."

But Michael was stupid, really stupid. He worked the same patch for 3 months. OK he was careful to pick different times, sometimes until midnight – tricky with the kid but he handled it. He hid from faces he remembered but there comes a time when you forget faces and times because there were so many. It had to end sometime.

"OK Sonny, so you say your Mother is ill and your Father is pushing up the daisies, and your sweet little sister here is hungry."

Michael felt uneasy. This was sarcasm, best leave now before there was problems, this guy was not wearing any of this. The brush off he could handle the clip behind the ear fine, but the sickly sweet sarcasm had an undertone he recognised, trouble. Just as he was about to leg-it he felt a huge hand grab his arm, he nearly dropped Rosy. Rosy by the way was screaming, and hollering, and kicking. She was 8 months old but boy was she big. He couldn't run with Rosy and the guy had his arm anyway so his backup plan would have to do.

"Mister, Sir, my sister is really upset I think I best get

her home." Michael adopted his nearly, hardly ever, except under exceptional circumstances knock 'em dead look of sweetness and eye contact. Looking him straight in the eye, blinking very occasionally, Michael said, "I think you have mistaken me for someone else sir. I am taking my Sister home. My Mother will be so worried if we arrive back late."

"Kid, it is late – you have some nerve! You worked a scam on me. Do you know who I am?"

"No Sir, but I am sure you are someone really important because you dress so well." "Cut the crap. This ain't working on me so stop the pathetic look." He said quietly, and with quite a degree of self-importance, "I am Johnny Sabetti, I own this area." "My God," thought Michael, "now what." Michael asked "What do you want me to do Sir?"

"For a start, who are you, and where do you live?"

Michael thought for two seconds and decided to come clean. This guy was not losing his rag too much and he was not the sort to lie to.

After Michael telling him about the scam, his Mother, and anything else he wanted to know, Johnny said "If you live that far away I'll give you and the kid a lift, we can talk on the way."

"Gees," thought Michael, "when he knows where I live, I will have had it."

He gave a false address but Johnny knew his game.

"Try again, don't screw with me, one more lie and I'll knock your fucking head off. Don't tempt me, I'm close now."

So Michael, out of his depth, and definitely out of his

league, took Johnny home. "My God! you live in this dump and it stinks." Johnny screwed his face in disgust. "That you Michael?" his Mother was calling from the bed.

"Fuck me, is that your Mother?"

"Yes Sir, you see, she is ill."

"Drunk more like and copped a nasty dose of Syphilis if I'm not much mistaken." "You a customer sweetheart?" she said using her come and get me smile which a few years ago got her a bit of trade, today she just looked grotesque.

"Go to sleep Ma, I want to talk in peace to your boy."

While this interesting little tête-à-tête was going on, Michael had a chance to look unobserved at Johnny Sabetti. He was tall, well at least 6 foot, slim and wearing clothes that must have cost a fortune, silk shirt, shoes you could see your reflection in, and the cut of his suit was exquisite, well Michael would have said fucking brilliant. His hair was immaculate, not one hair out of place. But it was his nails that Michael could not stop looking at. They were perfect, each nail was the same length, clean, no not just clean but white and they had a shine like polish. He had never seen a man with nails like that. His hands were huge but perfectly proportioned with long fingers that tapered delicately. Men's hands he thought had only sores, redness and chipped dirty nails from work or living in dirt. This man was elegant, this man was something else. What did he want?

"Ok you little bastard, I ain't no charity, you have taken up more time than I want to give you. I can offer you a job. I am not Father Christmas so don't think your line has taken me in. I know you, I know you well, come see me tomorrow at the KitKat club 11 a.m. sharp. Fuck with me and you're dead."

"Yes Sir, thank you sir. What do you want to see me for?"

"I'll see you tomorrow." With that Johnny left, glad to get out of the stink.

"Who was that Michael?"

"Shut up Ma, I don't know yet. I'm seeing him tomorrow."

"Got my cigarettes Michael?"

"Yeah Ma."

Michael was tough but every ounce of life seemed to have left him. He laid down and fell asleep, frightened to think about tomorrow, he was just a kid, why did this man want to see him. He fell asleep thinking of shootings, floggings, meat hooks, and beatings. A boy's imagination is a frightening thing.

CHAPTER FIVE

Alfredo Tarrantinni

"Well Boss, I found just the person we are looking for."

Alfredo Tarrantinni sat back in his brown leather chair , which swamped him. No one would dare suggest it, but he looked faintly ridiculous sitting in an oversized chair behind a desk which would accommodate a dozen men. The room was designed for an extra large ego and was nearly the size of a theatre. Filled with the latest in leather suites and lamps, statuettes and pictures, the whole scene was quite frankly a mess. Alfredo's wife Serena was an ex-dancer, beautiful but dumb. With all this access to money she reckoned she was an interior designer. She loved Alfredo's room and insisted she design and choose everything for her honey. Who was going to tell them it was a mess, trust me on this, no-one.

"So tell me about your find Johnny. Want a drink?"

"No thanks Boss. I found this kid called Michael Angelo."

"That sounds familiar."

"Not from around here boss. Well this kid is 12

years old and he is real cute. He looks about 9 years old and he could charm the birds out of the trees."

"Ok, Ok this ain't no baby competition Johnny."

"I have been watching him pull scams on punters leaving the clubs. He's real good. I leaned on him a bit and he held his own. He has a nice patter."

"We need someone we can trust Johnny."

" Well Boss, I went with him to his home. What a dump. His Mother is not long for this world she looks halfway gone with Syphilis, no Father. He is earning the money to keep both of them. He's a loner. He needs money, I think he will be perfect. I told him to get here at 11 a.m."

Mr Tarrantinni was getting a bit more interested. "So you think he has the nerve to bluff his way past cops or whoever and get our work through?"

"I'd lay bets on it Boss."

Michael slept in fits and starts and finally gave up about 5 a.m. He washed in cold water and put on his cleanest passing for best clothes. By downtown standards he was a fastidious boy. He always made sure he cleaned himself and his clothes regularly but there is only so much you can do with old clothes. His clothes stank of his Mother. She was smelling worse. He changed and put on some old clothes and hung his what passed for best clothes out of the window to air. Early it might be but the market was open and he slipped out for bread, a bit of cheese and some milk for both of them. He made his Mother a drink of hot milk and gave her some bread and cheese. He actually didn't know what to do about his Mother. She seemed just drunk and lazy before but now, he wasn't sure what was wrong. He didn't have enough money for a real Doctor and anyway no one went to see a real Doctor unless it was absolutely life threatening. He would ask Mrs. Arkinshaw to look at her. Mrs. Arkinshaw was the local woman who saw to most medical ailments for a small sum of course. Michael decided to wait until after he had seen Mr Sabetti this morning. Perhaps she will know what to do. For the time being he opened all the windows and the door to blow some of the smell out. After cleaning the dishes and cups he got ready, told his Mother he'd see her later and left. It was 9 30a.m. and the walk uptown to the KitKat club would take him at least 45 minutes. He did not bunk a lift on a tram as a lot of boys did. He had seen and heard of too many boys falling off or being pushed off the back of trams and being killed. Michael knew he was not agile or particularly strong and he certainly was not stupid enough to put himself in that sort of danger. He also wanted time to spend alone preparing his nerve for 11 a.m. Perverse as it sounds, he was quite looking forward to the meeting. This morning he remembered Mr Sabetti saying something about a job. He bristled with fear and excitement and his confidence was growing by the minute. By the time he got to the KitKat club he was flying. His bravado had gone into overdrive.

He knew the outside of the KitKat club well. He had stood there often enough over the past 3 months, but he had never been inside. He entered through the front door. At 10.45 a.m. the club looked a sorry sight. the main lights were off and intermittent voices and clattering of metal buckets disturbed the air. Michael looked around not knowing where to go. He suddenly saw a movement in the corner of his eye and he turned quickly to see a man, no more than 20 years leaning against a wall idly looking at him through a haze of cigarette smoke. The man slowly removed the cigarette from his lips and screwed his eyes up as the smoke stung.

"What do you want snot nose?"

"I'm here to see Mr. Sabetti."

"Oh no you ain't."

"Oh yes I am," replied Michael.

"Don't get lippy with me, you little lump of shit."

"Mr. Sabetti asked me to call here at 11 a.m. to see him, go check and see." Michael felt a little nervous, sure that he said that. Yesterday a red mist of fear was surging through his head, did he get it wrong? The man eyed the little insect with disgust.

"Mr. Sabetti wouldn't want to see a dirty little irk like you, he wouldn't lower himself."

"I must see Mr. Sabetti now, he is expecting me, go and ask him." Michael looked at this jumped up streak of nothing. He was a joke, his shirt collar hung out from his scrawny neck and his suit couldn't find the shoulders to hang the jacket from. Just a lump of spit and bones thought Michael. Call his bluff came to mind and Michael started walking firmly down the nearest corridor. Spit and bones moved fast and grabbed him, gee he was strong. Michael did the only thing he could under the circumstances he started hollering for Mr. Sabetti and then promptly bit spit and bones as hard as he could on the back of the hand that was holding him across the chest. With a roar spit and bones dropped

Michael and looked at his hands. Michael took off without looking back and headed down the corridor shouting "Mr. Sabetti! Mr. Sabetti!" He was more afraid of Mr. Sabetti's wrath than that streak of nothing. He hadn't got more than 3 yards before doors opened and 4 of the biggest men piled out and grabbed him, none too carefully I might add. One carried him kicking and hollering into the end office. A quiet voice from the back of the room said, "Ah, Mr. Michael Angelo I presume."

Michael breathless and pumping more adrenaline than is good for a little fellow, stopped in mid gouge of the neck of the ape holding him which in turn saved Michael from a hefty slap across the head. The quiet voice sounded faintly amused.

"What on earth is going on here Jimmy?"

"Little fellow here got a bit carried away boss." Jimmy was laughing, not much got to him, no brains you see, just brawn, and he enjoyed the scrap with the little fellow. At that point spit and bones entered the room, breathless with temper.

"Leave him to me Uncle, I'll teach him a lesson he won't do this again in a hurry." Pointing at Michael he said, "See if you can bite me without any fucking teeth."

"Out, everyone out now, not you Michael, come over here." Johnny had been amused by all the commotion but was bored with it and wanted to get on. "Out! Now!" They all left in an orderly pile and closed the door very quietly behind them.

It was silent, all Michael could hear was his heart thumping and his own heavy breathing. After all the shouting, swearing, pushing, shoving now the room was empty except for Mr Sabetti, who sat coldly observing the boy who was shakily trying to tuck in his shirt and pulling his clothes into some sort of recognisable shape. The adrenaline was still pumping and he did not know what to say or do. The stare did not tell him anything, if he had to make a guess he would say Mr Sabetti was not best pleased. Without taking his eyes away from Mr Sabetti, Michael cocked his head towards the door, his fingers were shakily trying and failing to button his jacket, Michael said, "I'm sorry about all that. Who is that streak of nothing I met at the door?"

"That's Tony and I will ask the questions, sit down kid and stop fiddling with your clothes." Johnny looked at the dishevelled boy standing in the middle of the room. He was still trying and failing to do up the buttons on his jacket.

"Kid sit down and listen. I'm going to introduce you to a very important man, his name is Alfredo Tarrantinni, Mr Tarrantinni or Sir to you. We may have some, shall we say, messenger jobs for you to do. If you are given a message you will hide the sealed envelope inside your jacket and only, I repeat only, give it to the person we have named. Got that?"

"Yes Sir," Michael was trying hard to concentrate.

"This message is not to be seen by anybody else, you are not to mention my name, you have nothing whatsoever to do with us. Got that?"

"Yes Sir."

"Mr. Tarrantinni will fill you in on the rest. Now do that fucking jacket up and come on." With that Johnny strode out of the office and up the corridor with Michael running behind still finishing the buttons. Johnny came to an abrupt halt outside double doors, Michael just skidded to a halt before colliding with Johnny.

"OK kid buttons done, thank God for that. Be respectful and only speak when spoken to. Got that?"

"Yes Sir."

Johnny knocked on the door and entered immediately. Michael had never seen such a big room it was wonderful. It had lots of nude fat women paintings on the walls and skinny white statues of women holding lamps or balls or things. It was crammed with leather furniture and old wooden ornate furniture and little tables. Michael was overawed by the size of the chair the man was sitting in and the desk in front of him was big, everything was so big and it belonged all to that man. He must be real important.

Tarrantinni looked at the scrap of a boy, he was none too impressed. Michael was breathing hard again and shifting from one leg to the other, his eyes were everywhere. "So you reckon you can deliver messages?"

"Yes Sir."

"It is vital the messages get to the right person. We need you to do whatever you have to, to get the message through."

"Is it dangerous Sir?"

"Nah, you just got to be a bit cunning. Mr Sabetti thinks you can talk your way out of any situation." With pride Michael confirmed he could.

"OK I have a letter here. Don't even think of opening the envelope, if ever I get reports that you are unreliable Mr Sabetti is instructed to deal with you. Get my meaning?"

Michael, ashen-faced and totally rigid nodded far too much. Alfredo softened and dropped his voice, "But young fella, you do a good job for me and I will see you are O.K." Michael relaxed a little. Alfredo thrust the envelope across to Michael.

"Take this to Gekko Stores on 5th and 23rd Street and give it to Mr. Gekko personally. Make sure no one sees you give it to him. Mr Gekko will confirm he has read it and send a message back, which you will bring back here. Got it?"

"Yes Sir."

"I want you to go now and be back within 1 hour. Any problems with that? "

"No Sir."

"Well get going then."

Michael almost ran out of the KitKat club. He went from hot adrenaline floods to stone cold fear and awe. He just wanted to get out into the fresh air. In the same place near the entrance stood Tony Pirrelli. Michael stopped in his tracks and looked. Tony shifted position and walked slowly towards him his eyes flashing with venom. "I'm going to get you snot nose. When you least expect it, I will get you." Michael deftly swerved away from a punch and ran out of the door. In a mad thrilling moment Michael stopped and turned. "That's twice you've missed me don't reckon much on your chances." He ran off laughing. He didn't realise this was no child's game of catch, it was a deadly game that would be played to the bitter end.

Michael found his way to Gekkos Store no problem. He went into the shop and found Mr Gekko, no problem.

He waited until the last customer left the shop and gave the envelope to M Gekko carefully checking no one was looking. It was easy. Mr. Gekko went out the back of the shop and returned with a paper bag. Make sure Mr. Tarrantinni gets this straight away, was that a twinkle in his eye or just a reflection, Michael didn't know.

He hurried as quickly as he could back to the KitKat club, "Oh shit, have I got this everytime I go in or out of there!" He could see spit and bones hovering in the doorway smoking a cigarette and trying to look tough. He hadn't spotted Michael yet, too busy posing for the chorus girls arriving for rehearsal. Michael ducked towards the girls entering and got in the middle of a group of 4. Tony saw him and could do nothing. He followed Michael in with hateful brooding eyes.

The girls thought he was cute. "What's your name honey?"

"I'm Michael Angelo."

"Hey what do you know, isn't there a famous bandleader called that?" They all couldn't agree but Michael was wafted in to the KitKat club on a breeze of perfume and giggles. As the girls went into the backroom area they waved goodbye and blew him kisses. Bye bye Angel, see you later. Wow, they were something else. His face was a little warm, he was blushing.

The lights were on now, and Michael could see the place in all its glory. Deep, dark, rich red. Everywhere. It was breathtaking. In the background he could hear the sound of someone idling fingers over a keyboard, life was good here.

"You back again kid? Want another scrap?" He

looked like an ape in an evening suit. Whoever made him wear a bow tie was having a laugh, it looked like a pimple on a boil. Jimmy Cane stopped strolling and went into prize fighter mode, his head bobbing from side to side and his huge body weaving with his giant fists in front of his face tightly punching the air, making hissing noises through his nose in time with the punches. Michael stood and watched, not sure what to make of him. Jimmy ducked and dived his way up to Michael and gave him a few imaginary punches to the head and one playful punch that connected on his shoulder knocking Michael against the corridor wall. God this man was powerful. If he had meant it, I would be dead.

"You OK kid?"

"Yes thank you Sir."

" Call me Jimmy, everyone does."

" I've come back to deliver something to Mr Sabetti, could you tell me where he is?"

"He's in that room over there," Jimmy pointed to the next door down the corridor on the right. "Just knock and go in." With that, Jimmy ruffled Michael's head in a good-natured fashion and walked off to watch the dancers rehearsing for the evening show. As he was about to close the saloon door, Jimmy poked his head through the opening and said in a high pitch voice "Bye bye Angel." Laughing he closed the saloon door. "Oh God, he saw me with the girls." Michael flushed with embarrassment, thought about it, and laughed. He thought Jimmy was a nice guy.

Michael knocked and opened the door when he heard "Come in." Johnny Sabetti sat on a leather chair talking to a very attractive woman. She was sitting opposite Johnny with a carefree elegance, one arm draped across the back of her chair. Long thin white fingers came to a violent end with blood red talons. If you had told Michael this woman was 50 years old he would not have believed it. The gawking boy amused the woman, she was getting older and admirers whatever age were welcome these days.

"Excuse me Sonia, I'll be back in a minute." With that Johnny grabbed Michael by the sleeve and pulled him out of the room. "Well?" Johnny seemed a bit distracted. Michael took a deep breath and gabbled excitedly. "It was easy Sir, no one saw me give the envelope to Mr Gekko and I wasn't followed on the way back. I took precautions to make sure I was alone." Michael looked around in an exaggerated way and when he saw it was all clear, gave the paper bag to Johnny. "Did you look inside kid?"

"No way Sir, I brought it straight here." In fact Michael wasn't curious at all, the threat of Mr Sabetti "dealing with him" if he was unreliable killed any curiosity.

"You did well kid." Johnny took $5 from his wallet and gave it to Michael. "Come back tomorrow at 10 a.m. sharp, might have other jobs for you. Now scat! I'm very busy at the moment."

Michael walked home very satisfied. Such an easy job and $5. He felt real good and very relaxed. Life was looking up. If he had thought about it, he would have been worried about how his Mother and he were going to survive in the coming years. But he didn't think about it and now this had turned up. He had never consciously thought it but he had always relied on the instinct that "something will turn up," and you know, it always had. He arrived home in time to see his Mother being sick on the floor.

CHAPTER SIX

Mrs A

Michael knocked on Mrs Arkinshaw's door. She lived 1 block down from him. The door opened and 6 kids piled out and pushed past him. The eldest was about 5 years, a boy, was the last to leave. He was awkwardly holding a writhing baby of about 6 months. Michael heard the familiar voice of Mrs Arkinshaw shout, "mind you put that baby in the pram outside and wheel her up and down the road for a bit."

"OK Mrs Arkinshaw," the boy shouted back as he held on tightly to the baby. Michael felt old. He remembered when he was doing exactly the same thing for her. He found Mrs Arkinshaw in the kitchen. To someone else it would have looked a mess, but not to Michael. She had obviously just fed that lot. There were plates and cups all over the table. Mrs A was scrubbing clothes in the big stone sink. There were clothes in a neat pile ready for ironing and other piles of clothes ready for washing. Her washing line was always full of clothes drying from early morning until nearly dusk. He suddenly felt bad, wishing he had maybe visited her before now. He had been quite fond of her when she looked after him. He'd wished his Mother was like her. When her husband, "The Bastard," as she always referred to him, left her with 4 small children and no money coming in, she put on her best clothes which was the summer dress and jacket she married in and walked to the nicer part of town and knocked on doors. She took in washing. To start with she collected and returned it the same day herself for next to nothing. She got recommendations and was soon washing morning noon and night and she got by. Then she added childminding and this helped pay for her children to have an education. Mrs Arkinshaw was a saint, well this is what she told everybody. She was in fact an honest, hardworking woman who had survived. Mrs A was an unbelievable 40 years old. Surviving takes its toll. "Hi Mrs A, long time no see." Mrs A looked up surprised, her eyes, at first quizzical then illuminated with recognition.

"Michael, what can I do for you?"

She stopped scrubbing for a moment, straightened and using both hands rubbed the small of her back. A clump of grey long hair fell across her face. As she brushed it away, she gave him a tired smiled and plonked down in a chair by the table. She was glad of an excuse to sit for a moment, her back and feet were killing her. Michael sat next to her, he paused before saying anything, wondering if she would have any spare time. He didn't want to ask her for help straight away, it didn't feel right. In his best conversational voice he asked, "How are your kids Mrs A, haven't seen them lately."

That was a mistake. She tensed her body and spat out, "Bastards the lot of them. Just like their Father, they left me. I scrimped and saved for them, I worked my fingers to the bone for them, and I went without for them. Now I'm not good enough to be their mother. They have got themselves posh jobs and just left me. No thank you, or how can we help you now ma. They left and never contacted me since."

She looked at Michael and prodded him none too softly in the chest.

"I would understand it if I was like your Mother, but oh no, I was too good to them. All that education did for them was make them high and mighty. Curse them, curse the lot of them."

With that she slumped back her mighty bosom heaving. She looked at Michael,

"Well what do you think of that!"

She had arms like a man, muscle hard. Michael watched fascinated as she tried to fold the huge arms across her mountainous chest and was failing. Michael let the comment about his Mother pass. Well it was true. Looking straight into her eyes he said what she wanted to hear. She was a saint. They were not fit to walk in her shadow. She was the most wonderful Mother in the whole world, etc. He actually meant some of them. Mrs A moist eyed thanked him, and added, "What a perceptive boy you are, and so young."

Suitably placated, Mrs. A pulled her considerable self together.

"Let's get down to business. This is not a social call, am I right?"

"As ever Mrs A. you know everything."

She liked that.

As arranged with Michael, Mrs A. arrived at the basement apartment at 7 p.m. to look at "the problem." Before the door opened she could smell the stench. Michael let her in. The place was surprisingly clean and tidy. She looked at Maria and knew. Syphilis had taken hold. Nothing could be done for her but make her comfortable. She spotted the bottle of hooch by Maria. Gently Mrs A. whispered, "Hallo Maria, remember me?" Maria looked up but her eyes didn't register recognition. She was stone drunk. With great effort she slurred "go away." Mrs A. bustled and straightened the sheets and in her crisp businesslike voice said, "Now you hush up and close your eyes and sleep Maria and I'll take this." Mrs A. grabbed the bottle, too quick for Maria to stop her. Maria groaned and gave up arguing. In the same crisp voice Mrs A. said, "I'll talk to you outside Michael." With that she swept out of the door.

They both sat on the steps, heads together, bartering on what Mrs A. could do, was prepared to do, and how much it would cost. Mrs A. suddenly realised she was talking to a 12 year old. Easy to forget. Head on his shoulders this one. Gently she asked, "How long has your Ma been like this?" Michael thought for a bit. It had been so gradual. "Well she's been drinking heavily for a year or so, since her work went down the pan and then she had to give it up." Mrs A. bit her tongue, work he calls it. She doesn't know what work is, but not his fault. Michael deep in thought added, "I thought she was just drunk. God knows I've bought enough booze for her." He thought harder. "She's been throwing up and smelly for about one year, and yeah – she started getting really moody and ranting and raving for no reason, that started about six months ago. I thought it was the drink." Michael paused and looked at Mrs A. "Do you know exactly what's wrong?" Mrs A. tried to explain in a kindly way the horrors of Syphilis. "Well, Michael, it's most probably one of your mothers customers who gave it to her. Probably years ago. Have you noticed any sores on your mother?" Michael shook his head, "What sores, never noticed any?"

"Well, the reason your mother smells rather bad is because she will have sores on her body. Do not touch them Michael, what she has is contagious and the sores will be passed on. Anyone who looks after your mother must be careful of getting infected. She finished by saying, "The drink has been making it worse although it would have helped to ease the pain she must be in. I can get her laudanum, it will keep her out of pain and help her sleep. No point calling in a Doctor, he'll be expensive and he can't do anything more than I will do."

"Will she get better?" Michael asked in a little voice. Mrs A patted his hand

"No my dear, but she will be with us for a bit longer." Mrs A. sat up, took a deep breath and changed the atmosphere to a more business like one. "Right! I'll get the laudanum, a bottle should last for a few weeks if we are lucky. I know a man but I'm not sure of the price, could be up to $5, don't know till I see him." Michael trusted her and gave her his earnings for today. He figured in the long run the cost won't be much more than the drink he'd been buying. Mrs A. went on "I'll come in twice a day to give the laudanum and wash your Mother and make her comfortable – I'll wash her clothes and bedding every day. Has your Mother got changes of night clothing and bedding?" "Yes," said Michael, feeling his burden was being shared and feeling more business like. "So to the price," said Mrs A. "It'll cost $3 per week – it's a nasty job and no-one will look after your Mother like I will." He knew this to be true. She always did what she promised. Michael looked at the floor and weighed up the cost. "I'll pay $2 per week, week, I can't afford more." She looked long and hard at him. There was a silent stare that went on for what felt like ages. Finally with a huge intake of breath Mrs A. said "I'll settle for $2.25 and not a nickel less." Michael said, "Done." Both felt satisfied that a good deal was struck. When Mrs A. had gone, Michael went into the basement and looked at his Mother. He felt a strange mixture of emotions, none of which he recognised or understood. His eyes filled with tears. He decided he must be tired and went to bed.

CHAPTER SEVEN

Work

Johnny saw Sonia to the door. She looked at him through hooded eyes. God! he was still very attractive. 10 Years ago had been a good time. Although he had filled out since then, he was firm and muscular and the grey at his temples contrasted with his still thick black hair, slicked back now making him look quite distinguished. She sighed inwardly, oh well, life goes on. In a sultry voice that vibrated through him and made his finger tips tingle, "Maybe I'll see you later Johnny? Johnny smiled, "The same old Sonia." He looked into her eyes and whispered "You are still a beautiful and fascinating woman. You know I'll always be fond of you." He offered, "Maybe a drink sometime for old times sake eh?" She never failed to stir something in him. She gave him a deep slow nod, never taking her eyes from his, her hand gently brushed his arm down to his hand and then glided out of the room leaving her perfume hovering around him. The air had been filled with sexual tension and now Johnny started to relax. "Wow, what a woman," he breathed. He liked his women young and firm these days but she still had something special. Maybe one visit for old time's sake would be good. Every time he saw her, it was the same, he'd forget her within hours, out of sight, out of mind. Down to business. He went straight to Alfredo's office.

"We need to talk Boss, Sonia has been in." They had been talking for the last few weeks about the problem of runners. Alfredo Tarrantinni was an astute businessman who sometimes fell short of being legal. It amused and massaged his ego to think he was a gang leader, yes he surrounded himself with hefty minders, although their job titles were, security specialist, bouncers, and chauffeur, it looked good, he got respect, and that was the name of the game. He was a very big fish in a kiddies paddling pool. The real sharks ran the North, South, and West of Chicago. They hadn't ventured into the East so far. There were 3 large gangs in Chicago and an assortment of affiliated groups. Over the last few years as the gangs had become more powerful, time honoured boundaries were being crossed. Gang fights were fought in deadly pursuit of the winner takes all. Tarrantinni and Johnny had watched from a distance and so far, the three largest gangs, and they were the ones that counted, had been totally involved with watching and fighting each other and had no time or inclination to look farther afield. East Chicago was poor and as yet not first choice to move into. This suited Tarrantinni. He wasn't stupid, He had carried on regardless, mindful never to overstep the mark from small time comfortable to anything worth challenging. Until lately. They had been aware for a few weeks that some of the pickup points for their runners were being watched. Until now they weren't sure if it was the cops or others. They were sure it was Tarrantinni's men they were watching. So far nothing had happened, no one was touched, talked to or intimidated. It was a tense time.

Business had suffered recently with runners getting cold feet and missing four of the best pickup points because they were being watched. Tarrantinni looked on his businesses as a service to his customers, suitably rewarded of course. When you offer such a service you need a reputation that says reliable, regular and trustworthy. Tarrantinni couldn't afford to lose his reputation, it was worth good money to him, and growing. That was the problem, he hadn't read the signs.

Al Capone was a rising star. His style was very noticeable. Shoot first and ask questions later. The waiting game being played was not his style. The Leone gang were North of Chicago so they were neighbours. He had been interested in Tarrantinni for some time. He was like a spider, he had built his web and was just waiting and watching for the right time, if ever, to pounce. Tarrantinni's numbers were growing steadily and would, if all was well, be worth having. The club and gambling house at the back were building trade nicely. Customers were getting sick of all the raids in the city by cops and rival gangs. Although the KitKat was not quite as plush as some of the joints, it was an acceptable alternative and more than anything you could be almost certain, at the moment, of a relaxing evening. Tarrantinni was small time but had nice little businesses working for him. His stable of girls were small, clean and quite classy. It turned over enough to keep him comfortable. Leone was always a forward planner. He had seen the plans for the City. The Eastside would in the next so many years be rebuilt and would attract a better class of residents. Time was on his side. He had no wish to rush into the area, there were bigger fish to fry at the moment.

Leone thought he knew all of Tarrantinni business but he didn't know about Sonia. Sonia was one of the best girls in the Tarrantinni's stable. She worked for him for 10 years. When she approached him about setting up on her own and running a small stable she wasn't surprised by Tarrantinni's reaction. They had been quite close and he trusted her. He had an almost family attitude to his employees, it made him feel good, and it made excellent business sense. Loyalty and a core of long term staff was more cost effective. The Mafia may have the Godfather but Tarrantinni was the Dutch Uncle. Mind you, he was no pushover, to cross him was a mistake. If you were with him for a number of years and showed loyalty, he looked after you. Anyway, Tarrantinni funded setting up Sonia in a different part of town with a small talented group of girls. He took 10% of the takings as his interest. Over the last 10 years his money was well repaid and the money was still coming in regularly. Both parties were satisfied. The spin off for Tarrantinni was any useful gossip that came Sonia's way was, out of friendship, passed to him.

Tarrantinni was trying to light a cigar with a huge 2-foot long replica of the statue of Liberty. It wouldn't light. Exasperated, he threw the statue on the floor, careful not to hit any of the ornaments or furniture.

"Goddam! give me a light Johnny. All I want is a lighter not a fucking piece of shit that doesn't work." He kicked at the lighter. "Where does she get this crap from? If I didn't know better, I'd say she was sleeping with the prick that sells all this garbage to her."

Tarrantinni sat down and asked, "So what did Sonia have to say?"

"Sonia has been looking after a customer called Carlo Tramolta, one of Leone's lads. She says there is talk about your numbers racket. Interest has been expressed by some people in what you are doing. We've been picking up some big money lately. Sonia reckons our numbers would slot in nicely with their business. It's well known that the Bertrolli, Giovanni and Leone gangs have their own problems so haven't been giving too much time to looking at us."

Tarrantinni sat deep in thought for a while, weighing up the pros and cons. Suddenly he sat forward and thumped the table. Johnny jumped. "No! this cannot go on, it must be contained now." Johnny sat forward, "What can we do?"

"Okay, go with this for a minute Johnny" Tarrantinni sucked on his cigar, "We can't give up the numbers. One it brings in good money, and two, if any of them get an inroad into my area, it's over, they'll have everything. So!" He paused for breath and took another suck on his cigar. "They haven't moved on us yet. I don't think they are sure, they're scouting. Our original plan was to use the kid for the more lucrative pickups. We wanted to keep anybody who was curious away from the real money. We know now they are interested.

If the kid goes undetected they will concentrate on our other more visible runners. They are going to grab one soon to see what he's got. They'll find nothing much. We are looked on as small time and the snatch will confirm it. It won't be worth their while taking over, well not at this time anyway. What do you think Johnny?"

Johnny said, "Sounds very simple but what we need is another gang bust to take their mind of us."

Tarrantinni sucked on his cigar and said, "See what I can do. Now back to this kid. I would have liked to try him out for a bit longer but we are gonna have to use him now. Do you think he's up to it?"

Johnny nodded, "He is our best bet."

Tarrantinni trusted Johnny's judgement, "Okay, I'll leave the details to you, you know what to do?"

Johnny handed the package to Tarrantinni. "Well the kid delivered your message and brought this back. He followed your instructions to the letter. What did you get him to do?"

Tarrantinni opened the bag and took out a box of cigars. He looked at them and said "My favourite. Did you know these are rolled on the thighs of dusky maidens?" They both laughed.

He woke at 5.30 a.m. It was getting light. The thin curtains had given up the fight and let everything in. Michael was immediately awake. Money was the only thing on his mind. He crawled under his bed and found the special place in the wall hidden by the bed leg. He brought out a small tin. His Ma was still asleep. He counted the cents and bills. He had $10. It would have been a lot more but the booze cost him. He figured he had just enough, if careful, to buy food, pay rent and Mrs A. for 2 weeks. Hopefully Mr Sabetti will have work for him and his nest egg will not be touched. For the time being, he would need some, he would replace it, and he took $1 from the tin to get food today. He carefully hid the tin. He would go to the market at 6.30 a.m. There would be a lot of traders setting up then. First things first, he put a bowl of water on the stove to heat. He wanted to wash his spare clothes and sheets.

At 6.30 a.m. he left for the market. Maria was still asleep. He left her like that. It was going to be hell today. No booze to keep her quiet. He went straight to the butcher and bought a piece of beef to stew and the butcher gave him a marrowbone. "Can I have that put in a bag mister, my Ma doesn't trust me to carry it in wrappings only." The butcher should have known him by now, but so many kids in the neighbourhood, you only remembered when there was trouble. "Okay sonny, just this once." Michael thanked him and left. As he walked through the market he bumped and swerved to avoid stallholders unloading their goods. He started in the middle aisle of the market and went round again on the outside of the stalls. As he did, he took a carrot from one, an onion from another, a potato here, a potato there and a cabbage that was asking to be taken and any other bits as he passed. He never took more than one item as he passed. You don't get caught if you are quick. He'd seen kids piling bits from one stall. Of course they are gonna be noticed and get caught. Michael had never been caught. By the time he got to the deli he had a bag that had everything for a stew and more. His final purchases of bread, milk and a small piece of sausage for breakfast left him enough for his Mother's cigarettes from his $1. He would have enough to make a stew for 3 days with vegetables and potatoes for the following days.

By 9 a.m. he'd got the stew cooking, had breakfast, hung out his washing to dry and cleaned up a bit. Maria was sitting on the edge of the bed. She had drunk the warm milk and eaten a bit of bread and sausage. She had been watching the boy go about his business through vacant eyes. She got back into bed with effort and said, "Michael I feel awful."

"It's the hangover Ma."

"Yeah you're probably right." Maria felt sick and her head was throbbing. The pains in her stomach were dull at the moment but she knew that would get worse as the day went on. Suddenly she looked around her and then called "Michael! What have you done with my gin?" She wasn't quite panicky but getting there. Michael sat down and explained about Mrs A's visit last night, Maria didn't remember. He told her Mrs A. knew all about what was wrong and that the drink was making it worse. How Mrs A. would be getting something for the pain and was coming in every day to make her comfortable. Don't worry Ma we'll take care of you. Maria went quiet. She was trying to sort out these new bits of information and make some sense of them. It slowly dawned on her and she couldn't believe it at first, and then she knew it was true. In a low and frightening voice she drawled, "You Mother Fucking Bastard. I know your game. You and Mrs Arkinshaw are trying to kill me. You're poisoning

me – Yeah! that's why I'm ill. Get me some gin now!"
Her voice rose to screaming pitch " You bastard, I don't
ask for much. You have ruined my life, my figure has
gone, I had plenty of money before you arrived."
Michael left the house carrying on the standard raving,
mimicking her screaming monologue under his breath. "I
would have had a big house by now, lovely clothes, one
of my gentlemen callers would have married me, etc, etc!
They wouldn't have married you anyway because you
were a fucking whore." Someone in the street turned and
looked at him and he realised he was shouting.

Michael hurried a bit. The morning discussions with
Mother had made him late in leaving. He didn't want to
be late. He arrived with 5 minutes to spare. He licked his
fingers and slicked his hair quickly, adjusted his
clothing, it didn't make any difference – still looked a
mess, and went into the club. It seemed noisier today, he
could hear voices and laughter, and all the lights were
on. In the main foyer were the four henchmen he'd seen
yesterday including Jimmy with Tony 'Spit and Bones'
Pirrelli in the middle. Michael stayed where he was by
the door. The object of their interest was his good friend
Tony. He could afford to watch for a few minutes.
Everyone was having fun except Tony. He was bright
red with rage and humiliation and the more he
spluttered to speak, the more they laughed. One of the
men sarcastically said, "So you reckon you're going to
ride shotgun today toughman?"

"Did you hear that," said another of the group,
"Reckons he is tough, he can fight anyone they put in
his way, I'm scared." He said in a shaky voice.

Someone else added with zeal, "Yeah this boy is tough, but there is one giant of humanity that even he can't control."

"Who's that?" another asked, much too innocently.

"Why the horror of horrors the little boy."

"Ooh," they all squealed in a high pitched voice. Tony was beside himself with rage and started lashing out at anyone within range. Two of the hulks grabbed an arm each. Jimmy said, "You've got to lighten up a bit Tony. It's all a bit of fun." Tony's answer was to give a hefty kick connecting on Jimmy's shin. A hard slap round the head calmed Tony in an instant. The four henchmen, bored with Tony, moved off. Tony was feeling very sorry for himself. He wanted to kill the lot of them. His head hurt. Then he spotted Michael. "This is all your fault, I will get you for this." Michael who enjoyed the spectacle, laughed. He mimicked one of the men and said in a shaky voice, "Ooh, I'm scared." Spit was all talk and uncoordinated, and that couldn't hurt you. Tony got up and lunged towards Michael. Michael saw his condition and knew there was nothing to worry about. As Tony got close, arms and hands outstretched to squeeze and rip whatever flesh he could get hold of, Michael ducked forward and head butted Tony in the stomach. Tony stood still for a moment, his eyes crossed temporarily and he fell to the floor trying to catch his breath. He brought his knees up to his chin and lay holding his crotch rocking back and forth. Michael obviously missed the stomach. That's the trouble when you are small, no sense of aim and this low blow he knew, would be repaid in full. Michael ran towards the corridor where Mr Sabetti would be, he passed the 4 henchmen who appeared to be doubled over. One, coughing and laughing said, "Kid you crease me up, that's the best show we've had since the strippers. Little Dick! needed teaching a lesson." The others nodded and carried on laughing and choking. Michael seemed to be given the nickname Angel from that day, Jimmy most probably suggested it. Anyway it appealed to them all. A sweet little boy with a deadly aim. They also said if Tony gets you, you'll be an Angel very quickly.

Michael walked to Johnny Sabetti's door. He was enjoying the laughter of the men and wasn't watching where he was going. A hand grabbed him and Michael jumped. "Why is it everytime you come here there's a riot?" It was Johnny standing in the opening of his room. "You look a mess kid."

Johnny showed him into the room and told him to sit down. "Want a lemonade?"

"Yes please sir."

"OK I'll get you something to eat as well."

This was good. Michael was feeling quite comfortable. While Johnny organised this Michael looked around his room. It was very tasteful. It had just enough furniture and tables to make it functional without cluttering. Johnny worked and lived on the basis that a little said a lot. The drink and food came Michael sat and eat and drank while Johnny went outside to speak to Jimmy, coming back after a suitable time. "Finished kid?"

So much rich food and not being used to it Michael replied with a burp.

"Jesus kid, no-one teach you any manners?"

Michael was embarrassed and knew he was not making a good impression today.

"Let's get down to business. I want you to make some calls today. I'll give you the contact name and address. This is very important. You will give the envelope only to the name I give you. You will have this hidden in a pocket or somewhere. You will collect an envelope and hide this in a pocket, down your pants, anywhere out of sight. Look natural, if approached, talk your way out of it. Don't under any circumstances give up the envelope. When you have got the envelope take it to this address and give it to the name on this piece of paper. Watch you are not being followed. Remember you don't know me or Mr Tarrantinni, or anyone else from here."

"Yes sir."

"First things first, Jimmy is taking you out to get some new clothes, nothing fancy, just clean looking and not worn. You've got to blend. Get the clothes and come back here, you've got just over 1 hour. Don't say a word to anyone about our business. Get going."

Jimmy was waiting outside. "Get in the car Angel, we're meeting Stella at the shop in 10 minutes."

This was the second time Michael had been in a car. This was the first time he felt relaxed and quite excited. Life was looking good. "Who's Stella?" Michael asked as he twiddled with the door handles and opened the glove compartment. Jimmy gave him a slap across the arms, it stung and Michael sat still.

"Don't touch anything. Stella is my wife."

Michael hadn't thought about Jimmy being married.

Well let's face it, he didn't know too many people who were. They arrived at the shop and Stella was waiting outside. She was not what Michael expected at all. Small, quite frumpy with a school marmish look. Her glasses made her nose look thinner and more pointed. She had one of those faces that looked as if the character had been bleached out of it. Apart from the nose the rest of her face was bland like a child's drawing no depth of eyes, no cheekbones, structured chin, just surface with mousy hair. Stella saw Jimmy and she smiled. Wow, what a change, her whole face became quite beautiful. "Sorry to drag you here Stell, but Johnny wants him back in about 1 hour and I don't know anything about choosing clothes for him."

"No worries, we'll get this done in no time." She looked at Michael and screwed her eyes. "What are you doing with a, what, 9 year old kid?"

Michael piped up, "I'm 12, nearly 13 years old mam."

This annoyed Stella. "Who's talking to you, speak when you are spoken to please." Jimmy could see an argument developing and wanting to get moving, "Stell the kid is known as Angel, Johnny wants him to have new clothes now. We have got to get a move on."

Stell gave a compliant grunt, grabbed Michael's hand and started into the shop. Michael couldn't believe this, no one held his hand. He wasn't a kid, and he felt stupid. The woman was not going to be easy so he just went along with it. Stella chose underwear, socks, pants, shirt, jacket, and hat for him. Michael saw a pair of shiny shoes he really wanted. They were patent black with laces and they were smart. He asked for those, Stella said no, they had a few exchanges and Michael caved in. She was not to be argued with. The items were duly bought, paid for and in no time Jimmy had kissed Stella goodbye and they were on their way back to the KitKat club.

Johnny approved of the clothes, well he said. "He'll do." He went through all the details again and Michael repeated what he had to do. Within 10 minutes he was on his way to his first pick up. He made 4 pick ups all together. He deposited the envelopes with the man named by Johnny at the address given to him and made sure he wasn't followed. Then he went back to the KitKat club once again making sure he wasn't followed. There were no problems, it was so easy. Michael hadn't had so much fun for a long time, if ever, pretending he was being followed and ducking behind walls, diving down alleyways, and watching who was behind him. He felt really good in his new clothes. I mean he really, really, felt good. He had never had clothes of such quality that fitted so well. They smelt wonderful. Brand new, who would think it. How did he get to be so lucky, and he was going to be paid for the work. He arrived back at the KitKat with a level of confidence and self-assuredness that blunts the survival instincts. Johnny was pleased all had gone well. "Kid, who named you Angel?

"The lads did sir," replied Michael mystified, so what! he thought, he was feeling a bit too cocky for his own good.

"Well Angel, nice name, lets get down to money. I'll give you $3 for today plus $4 as a bonus for doing so well. You will get $3 every day. After a while, if all has gone well, there will be a bonus in it for you. "

Michael was busy counting. "Does that include Saturday and Sunday Sir?"

Johnny smiled "It does so that is $21 per week. That's more than you would ever earn. But if you screw up, mess me around, or don't turn up every day you will be singing with the fucking angels, do I make myself quite clear?"

Michael was beside himself with indescribable joy and well being and in a state of not believing. Even threats didn't dampen his excitement. "Sir I'll never let you down, even if my legs have been chopped off at the waist, my eyes been ripped out, I'll be here on the dot of whenever you say, even earlier. They can rip my tongue out, I'll never talk." Michael was getting carried away on the tide of overdoing it.

"Leave it kid! Just get back here tomorrow at 9 a.m. Got it!"

Michael's voice was up an octave or two, "Got it, Sir, and Sir, anything, anything you want me to do just name it. I'll do it. Is there anything else I can do for you now?" "Just go kid, now!"

Michael left unable to climb down from this amazing high. Life was good. Thoughts rushed through his mind in an excitable jumble, "Everything was going to be all right. New Clothes, $9 for today and a regular income. I can plan!"

Michael, on his way out of the club, spotted Jimmy in the club area watching the dancers. The girls were going through the motions of a dance sequence for that evening. It was 4 p.m. now and the girls were getting bored with the rehearsals, it had gone on for what seemed like hours. One of them spotted Michael, "Hi Angel." They all looked around and started giggling and coming over to give him a hug. In his new clothes, it has to be said he looked so cute. His black curls framed around his hat and looked like a halo. Michael loved it and lapped up all the glory and hugs and the smell of perfume. "This must be what heaven is like," he thought. The high he was on was getting higher. Michael went up to Jimmy and in a voice that he thought sounded man to man said, "Jimmy, can I buy you a drink? Thanks for today and for Stella helping. It was great." Jimmy laughed. "I'll get you a lemonade." They wiled away an hour talking about this and that. Michael realised this was the longest conversation he'd had with a man. His life had been mainly women with men around as customers or punters, or husbands who only seemed to surface occasionally. Michael liked the company of men, they were different. At about 5 p.m. Michael rose to leave. Got to get home to see how my Ma is and get some food dished up.

CHAPTER EIGHT

Tony

Michael left the club without a care in the world. He thought nothing could ever feel this good again. He had prospects. Michael turned right out of the KitKat club and strutted towards home smiling to himself. He hadn't got more than 20 yards when two hands grabbed him and pulled him into the dead-end alley that ran by the side of the club. No time for fear as a blow to the back of the head knocked him unconscious. When he came round, in bewilderment he wondered why he couldn't move and why his new shirt was ripped open. He wasn't functioning well and it took a few seconds to realise he was tied to the metal fire escape at the bottom of the alley.

"Good you're awake," Tony was leaning against the wall opposite. "I didn't want to start without you."

Michael looked around to see who else was with them, but the alley was deserted. From the fire escape it was difficult to see the street, with all the bins stacked with rubbish from the club almost covering the entire walkway to the street. The alley held its breath. The breeze that had playfully tossed paper into the air was still, and the sun that never quite penetrated the alley had kept its distance and dark, deep shadows cast an eerie black silence. It all felt unreal, and Michael looked at Tony, struggling to understand what was going on. Was this a game? Did Tony just want to frighten him a little? He opened his mouth and in a dry heavy voice asked Tony, "Why?" Tony was frighteningly calm, eyeing Michael as a child would a bug, sort of interested but something that would be stamped on when boredom set in. His voice was matter of fact, as if telling a story, "So you thought you could play me for a fool did you?" Michael, unable to move anything tried to shake his head. "Do you know who I am fuck face. I'm Johnny's nephew. I'm big time. You are a lump of shit that needs to be flushed down the toilet. So I'm going to teach you a lesson, and when you've learnt, you can tell it to your maker. Lesson one," Tony moved forward. Michael's first experience of real fear descended on him like a fire blanket. It started in his head extinguishing hope, thought, survival and worked its way down to his feet stubbing out his vocal chords, his heart beat, his breathing on the way. Every part of him seemed to have stopped, he was held in a nightmare void. All he could do was look with vacant, unbelieving eyes at the knife in Tony's hand. A part of Michael's body was functioning, a puddle was growing on the floor as a trickle of warm liquid ran down his legs.

Tony stood relishing the moment. The tip of the knife searched Michael's cheek and neck, finally resting just below his neck. The tip of the knife punctured Michael's skin, blood trickled slowly down and started to collect on Michael's trouser belt.

"Just so you know and can appreciate, there will be 50 lessons to learn. Lesson 49 will be your balls. When you've finished singing soprano, lesson 50 will be your throat." Tony pushed his face against Michael and, in a mock sympathetic tone, said, "There may be a little pain." Tony thought that was funny and laughed. His breath stunk of smoke and garlic. The knife was pressing harder and cutting deeper. Michael tried to work his mouth but nothing came out. The knife then slowly descended to his navel leaving a thin cut that began almost immediately to turn from white to red. Michael found his voice, a high pitch terror driven scream pierced the stillness and went on and on without breath for a lifetime. Tony stopped to enjoy the scream and then looked at his handiwork and thought – not bad, not too deep, got to keep him aware for 49 more. No time to lose, this is going to take at least one glorious hour. He felt good and powerful. He licked his lips as he felt the rising excitement and pleasure within him. As a sculptor would, he considered his next cut. A pattern would be nice. Michael hadn't felt the pain yet. The knife was sharp but he saw the blood, at first trickling and now building to a slow gush. He hadn't believed it was going to happen. It had. Now he was recognising what was to come. Realisation was more painful that the cut. He looked at Tony and mumbled, "Don't do this Tony. I'm sorry for whatever I have done." Tony laughed, enjoying the look of terror on Michael's face. He was having fun. The knife caressed Michael's face. Tony was getting into the mood, "Now do we cut here?" Tony pressed the tip of the knife into Michael's cheekbone, just puncturing the skin.

"Ooor," The blade wafted inches from Michael's eyes. "We could pop an eye or two?" Michael's heart pumped so hard it's pounding filling his ears and his brain was sending frantic messages of get away, get away. Michael felt dizzy and swooned, he felt a stinging blow to his cheek. "Oh no you don't, you're going to stay awake and keep me company little Angel." The trickle of blood that ran from Michael's nose tasted sour.

In the deafening silence that only terror can bring Michael heard a noise, a door opening followed by someone running down the metal fire escape. Each footfall vibrating through Michael. He saw Jimmy grab Tony and heard the sharp crack of bone as Tony's arm snapped followed by a high pitch scream. Michael was overcome and flooded with unbearable relief and then he fainted.

Michael's first sense as he slowly awakened was the hushed rustling noise of cloth. He felt himself lying on something soft. He opened his eyes slowly and found himself in his bed, Mrs Arkinshaw was sitting close by. Michael remembered and wanted to cry with relief, it was a dream, a nightmare. Then he moved and a pain shot through his chest. His hand touched cloth and he saw he was bandaged. His surprised and enquiring eyes met Mrs A.

"Now you just lay quietly and I'll get you a drink. Hands off the bandage," she scolded. "I've done a good job on that if I say so myself." She sniffed proudly and waddled to the kettle.

After a hot drink Michael felt more in control. Mrs A. told him that Jimmy had brought him home and she was there looking after Maria at the time.

"Do you know that Jimmy was going to send for a Doctor to fix you up. I told him I could do as good a job for less money and I would stay with you." Mrs A. smoothed her hair, averted her eyes and said, "Nice man that Jimmy." Michael saw a hint of red in her cheeks.

"How strange," he thought.

"I asked Jimmy how you got such a terrible cut, but he said he wasn't sure." She added softly, "I'm not stupid Michael, who did that to you?"

Michael tried to think quickly, not easy, he felt giddy and weak. His mind kept trying to play back the terrible evening and he kept pushing it away. "Mrs A. I don't remember at this minute, I'm sure it'll come back to me tomorrow," he lied. Mrs A. looked at him and knew it was a lie. She would not show it, but she was worried about him and what he was getting in to. You could not live in their neighbourhood without either being involved in, or aware of crime and violence. She remembered that Michael even as a young child was different. He collected and delivered washing for her. She paid 6 cents per week for collecting and delivering washing. The eldest kids she minded took on this job and were grateful for the money, but Michael was different. He haggled with her and won 7 cents for collecting and delivering. She smiled in thinking back. Always had a canny way with words that one. Yes, she thought, he was always into some bits of trouble but he was a kind soul and he only seemed to steal, con, or barter for the basics to live. Look how he cares for that mother of his. Mrs A was fond of Michael.

"That stew you made was lovely Michael, where did you learn to cook like that?"

"I used to watch you Mrs A. Who else would I have learned from? You're a good cook. You're good at everything." With that Michael, overcome by fatigue, closed his eyes and slept. Mrs A. chewed over his words contentedly and made herself comfortable, she said she would stay with him and by God, if that meant all night so be it. She looked at him asleep, so sweet, a start of tear appeared in her eyes and she thought sadly, "I wish he was my son instead of the ungrateful bastards that left me." She would not dream of leaving him all night with his mother in his state. Besides Jimmy gave her $5 to stay and he said he was coming back in the morning. She nodded off in the chair beside Michael's bed.

Michael slept fitfully. He replayed the last evening over and over again in his dreams, waking with a sweaty start many times in the night. Each time he woke Mrs A. wiped his brow and he went back to sleep to replay the evening again. He finally woke up to the sound of singing. A high pitched off key voice was screeching out Onward Christian Soldiers. Mrs A. was trying to settle Maria who was now shouting vengeful, fearful quotes from the bible about pestilence, death and damnation.

"Gee," thought Michael, "I thought God was supposed to be good and kind."

Mrs A. settled, cleaned up and fed Maria then gave her some laudanum. Maria went back to sleep. Mrs A. helped Michael sit up and gave him some milky porridge with sugar and some bread to mop it up. Michael realised he was starving hungry. Although the soreness and tight bandages made it difficult, he finished his food in indecent time. Mrs A. washed herself and did her hair while he ate. Michael laid back on the pillow and watched her. She had just managed to put her hair in a plait. Michael noticed her fingers were having difficulty holding the grips to go into her hair. Half a lifetime of hands immersed in hot water and rinsing in freezing water must do something bad to you Michael mused. With a sigh of that's the best I can do, Mrs A. turned to Michael, straightened her apron and busied herself tidying his bed.

"What's all this for?" Michael asked, "Is the President arriving here?"

"Don't know what you mean you cheeky young devil," Mrs A. replied looking decidedly embarrassed. Michael laughed, it hurt and he winced in pain.

"Now see what you've done. Mind you don't undo all the good work I've done." Mrs A. checked his bandages for signs of any blood seeping through, it looked fine.

At 9 a.m. Jimmy arrived to see Michael. Mrs A. opened the door and gave Jimmy her best smile, which vanished quickly when she saw Stella behind him. They were duly introduced, neither knew what to make of the other but instinctively they felt intimidated. Jimmy looked at Michael and asked in a hushed kindly voice

"How are you doing little fella?"

"Okay I guess, bit sore." Michael winced a little as Jimmy sat on his bed. He asked quietly, "How'd I get back here Jimmy and what happened to Tony."

"Later Angel, we'll talk later." Jimmy's eyes told him this was not the right place to talk about this in front of the women. Jimmy looked at the big woman and saw how tired she looked.

"Mrs A, you've done a really good job here. Thank you for staying with Michael. Why don't you go home in a minute, expect you've got things to do."

Mrs A. was a bit put out and felt got rid of but yes, she did have to get going, lots to do. She started collecting and putting together her bags, coat and hat. While all this had been going on Stella had been looking at Michael from afar. Jimmy looked at Stella and remembered.

"Oh Michael, I brought Stell with me. She insisted on coming to see how you are."

Michael looked up and was surprised to see Stella walking tentatively towards him with tears streaming down her face. She sobbed, "You poor little soul. I heard what happened and to see you all bandaged like this is awful." Stella cuddled him gently so as not to hurt him and gave him a kiss. Michael looked wide-eyed and was frankly confused and maybe a little embarrassed. Actually he liked the cuddle and kiss. Stella was soft and gentle and smelt lovely. He didn't think Stella liked him from their last meeting. Stella, full of anguish turned to Jimmy and said, "Oh Jimmy look at him, we can't leave him here in this," she looked around the room and at Maria, "this dump."

Mrs A. by now was put out anyway and bridling with indignation on being dismissed by Jimmy. Now this woman was interfering. With finger pointing at Stella and her back stiff, she boomed, "Now hold on you, you madam, just one minute. This place may not be a palace but I am looking after her," she pointed sharply at Maria, "and I have been looking after him." She stabbed a finger at Michael. Mrs A's voice rose to shouting level. "If you think it is easy looking after her," finger darted venomously in Maria's direction again, "you don't know anything. I have just started looking after them and if I say so myself, I'm doing a damn good job. Now you come along, Miss high and mighty and say I'm no good. Well."

Mrs A. paused for breath, surprised at her depth of anger and not quite sure where it had come from. Stella bristled. If Stella had a fault it was that she could not bear to be challenged, it was a big fault of hers. Jimmy could say and do anything because Stella idolised him and worshipped every hair, curl, wrinkle, words, and breath that he took. But, ever since a child, she would always defend herself against attacks of words. Answering back was a red rag to a bull. In the silence of two women taking a deep breath ready for battle, the shouting had stirred Maria from her sleep.

"Hallo lover boy, come to see me?" Maria's eyes were fixed on Jimmy. Mrs A. and Stella were caught completely off guard as they turned to look at Maria.

"If that's your floozy, get rid of her, I'll give you a much better time. Mrs A, get out, this is business, take the boy with you."

Well Michael just died with embarrassment. He knew Mrs A. would understand but Jimmy his friend, and Stella, what would they think. Jimmy was way out of his depth. Women fighting he never understood. Men would just fight out their disagreement, a good slap and it would be over and they would be friends again but women, gee, they go on and on. Stella and Mrs A. united in their anger at Maria. Stella started.

"How dare you talk to me and my husband in that manner, but worst of all, don't you talk to Mrs A. in that tone. She is a saint, she is a living marvel. She looks and cares for you. No one else would be bothered with such a foul-mouthed whore like you. Michael has been hurt and Mrs A not only tended to him but stayed by his side all night, that's true selfless devotion. A Doctor couldn't do a better job than she is doing, you are so lucky to know her. She does a marvellous job you ungrateful woman."

Stella had gone over the top a trifle but that woman needed answering and she was the one to do it. Mrs A's rigid stance had softened with Stella's words but her anger was now directed solely towards Maria.

"Furthermore Maria Angelo. How dare you talk to this fine lady and gentleman in that gutter talk of yours. Out of the kindness of their wonderful hearts they have paid for your son to have excellent treatment and be looked after by me. They even came back today to this hovel, to see how he is. What thanks do they get, none. You are an ungrateful woman Maria Angelo. They should be blessed by the Lord for their kindness."

Maria who had started the onslaught had fallen asleep ages ago uncaring of what was said. The speeches had fallen on fertile ground, Stella and Mrs A. had called a truce.

"I'm going to make you both a nice hot drink and get you a hot bagel from the Jewish Deli down the Road. Does that meet with your liking?"

Mrs A's generous gesture had come from the heart. Her loss of temper was unexplainable and she was embarrassed. He'd done nothing wrong, in fact he had been very nice, and she, well, got a few too many airs and graces but, well we'll see.

"I'll come with you to the shop my dear," said a warm and caring Stella.

Mrs A bristled at the words "*my dear.*" "Slip of nothing," thought Mrs A, "talking down to me." But she let it pass for now. With that they left uneasily together. . Michael and Jimmy were left with Maria who was snoring.

"I never, repeat, never, interfere in woman's arguments," said Jimmy. "Don't understand them, never will, don't want to try."

They both laughed, partly from relief.

"Now Angel, my little fella, Mr Sabetti has asked me to find out if you can come in today. The jobs you are doing are important and no one else can do them. How do you feel about that?"

"I'll try Jimmy. Mr Sabetti warned me if I didn't come in every day he'd kill me." Michael gave a confused sigh, "Everyone wants to kill me it seems."

Jimmy laughed. "Mr Sabetti won't kill you. He knows what happened and he's asking can you come in."

"I need to go to the toilet, so I'll see if I can walk properly. Can you just help me out of bed."

Jimmy helped him out of bed and watched as Michael shuffled painfully to the back door leading to the outside toilet. When Michael returned he was shuffling better and seemed to cope.

"It's just practice Jimmy, I figure if I don't get out of breath it doesn't feel too bad. I'll keep having little walks before I need to start work and I'll be fine."

Jimmy was full of admiration for the plucky lad. He could see it was more painful than he was letting on. After Jimmy placed Michael back in bed the questions started.

Jimmy told Michael that as Security Officer, he was checking the building as usual. He didn't always bother to open the fire door to check it was working but it was hot in the club and he was going to check the door and have a cigarette at the top of the fire stairs. When he opened the fire door he saw Tony with a knife. He didn't know it was Michael tied to the stairs until he got near the bottom.

"I ran down the stairs two at a time. When I got to Tony he looked ready to use the knife on me. He only dropped the knife when I broke his arm. Mad that one, and dangerous. When I turned to see it was you tied to the stairs, I thought you were dead, there was blood everywhere and you'd passed out. I lost my temper and gave Tony a good kicking. One of the lads got Mr Sabetti. He said to get you home and get you fixed up. He would deal with Tony." Jimmy patted Michael on the head, "You worried me little fella, you didn't come round for ages."

Thankfully Jimmy stopped patting Michael on the head, Michael didn't want a headache as well. Jimmy shifted position and carried on.

"Mrs A. is a good sort and insisted on looking after you herself. You roused a little while she cleaned you up and she said you'd be fine."

"What's going to happen to Tony? He hates me you know," Michael asked feeling a little frightened.

"Mr Sabetti will tell us today. He's not going to bother you again that's for sure."

Jimmy hesitated but decided to fill Michael in about Tony.

"I shouldn't be telling you all this but I reckon you deserve to know what I know. I'm not one for blabbing, but I feel kinda bad about what happened to you. I thought the little shit knew his place but he's a bad'n. Now a lot of what I'm telling you is hearsay but it's backed up from people who know.

You see when Tony's father died in a car accident four years ago, his mother, she's a silly bitch, spoilt him rotten. She'd always given him anything he wanted but when his father died there was no one to keep him in check. She bailed him out of all sorts of nasty situations. When he was arrested for kicking some old tramp dossing in an alley, near to death, it turned out he did it because he didn't like the way the man had looked at him. The silly bitch paid off the cops and the old man so he was never charged. I think he felt he was untouchable.

The final straw, so I heard, was when he fancied this girl about a year ago, she had the sense to want nothing to do with him. So what did the little prick do? He waylaid her one evening and at knifepoint raped her in an empty warehouse. Using the knife, he cut a cross into her stomach and said if she told anyone 'X' marked the spot where he would gut her like a fish. The poor kid was terrified. Somehow the silly bitch of a Mother was told about it. Typically she didn't believe it but she went to see her brother, Johnny Sabetti, and asked him to give the boy a job and be the father figure he needed. So you see, Johnny's fond of his stupid sister and will, I think, always look after Tony. He will not tolerate this sort of behaviour. I know him, he will be very embarrassed that a member of his family would disgrace himself in this way. He'll be kept in check, mark my words, you will be safe, besides, you've got me on your side little fella. He won't touch you again, I'd kill him first."

Michael felt a tear in his eye. He couldn't understand why he was getting so emotional. Perhaps this was the first time he felt someone cared about him. He didn't recognise the feeling of love but he hoped Jimmy would be his friend forever. He just said

"I think I'm becoming a cry baby. I must be tired, I'll have a little sleep if that's OK Jimmy."

"You go ahead little fella. I'll check where those women have got to. If you leave them to chat they'll never get back here."

With a gentle pat on Michael's head, Jimmy got up and went out to look for the women and get some fresh air.

It was 11 a.m. when Michael woke up. Jimmy was gently shaking him.

"Come on little fella time to go to work. Stell got a new shirt, vest and jacket for you, your pants have been cleaned so you'll look fine and dandy."

Michael dressed painfully and walked to Jimmy's car. His Mother looked OK and Mrs A. would be back later.

Johnny Sabetti was waiting in his office and he studied Michael coldly as he walked in. He looked a bit poorly but to someone in passing he wouldn't look out of the ordinary.

"We'll talk when you come back kid but it's getting late and the jobs need doing now. Just for today Jimmy will take you by car and wait in a back street. You're not up to the long walks I can see. But, and this is very important, make sure no-one sees you get out or into the car. It's a big risk but you're new to the job and no one should connect you yet. It's a risk we have to take. Get going."

Jimmy and Michael did the rounds of collection and final delivery mindful that no one noticed Michael getting into and out of the car. For the walks into the various buildings Michael made a special effort to walk in and out of the places as normally as possible. It cost him, and the short car journeys between each building were spent in pain and trying to ease it. When they had finished Michael fell asleep exhausted in the car, the pain and exertion had taken its toll. Jimmy noticed the bandages were seeping slightly with blood. He carried Michael into the club and laid him gently on Johnny's sofa.

When Michael finally woke he saw Jimmy and Mr Sabetti talking in the corner. Johnny looked up.

"Good, you're awake. We'll have to get you home soon and get your dressing looked at. Jimmy will take you. But first, I'm getting you a steak dinner. It'll build you up and some ice-cream to finish."

Jimmy went to get it while Johnny got up to sit near Michael.

"Well kid, it seems you get into trouble every time you come here."

"But sir, it's not my fault." Michael was getting worried, he needed this job. "I was attacked for no reason. I didn't do anything, honest." The tears were forming again and Michael felt annoyed with himself and wondered why he kept crying.

"Okay kid, okay, don't start bawling. I'm proud of you today. I know it wasn't easy. You've got guts and it won't go unnoticed. Carry on like this and you could have a future with this organisation. You've shown loyalty and you can keep your mouth shut. It will be remembered."

Jimmy arrived with the biggest steak Michael had ever seen.

"Eat that all up Angel, it'll put hairs on your chest and make you feel strong."

Michael wasn't feeling that hungry but as soon as he started eating the juicy, blooded steak, his taste buds went into overdrive and he finished it in record time. Jimmy fetched him a large bowl of ice cream. No Michael was not hungry but who has got to be hungry to eat ice cream? Johnny watched Michael eat, he did not enjoy the show, Johnny looked at Jimmy and said, "I'll have to teach the boy some manners if he does stick around." When Michael had finished he laid back and realised he ached like hell.

"So back to business." Johnny was anxious to get the boy home and out of his office.

"No work for you tomorrow, it's Sunday. No betting on Sunday. I want you to rest real good ready for Monday. About Tony. He will never touch you again, you have my word. He won't be around for at least a month. Jimmy gave him a good seeing to and he comes back here under my personal supervision. Now Jimmy has offered to take you to his home for today and Sunday. You need to rest kid. Monday is important and there will be no car to take you around. I'll see you 9 a.m. Monday."

Jimmy carried Michael to the car. He was told to shut up when he protested he could walk. On the drive back Jimmy told a tired Michael who just about heard what he said, that Mrs A. would come to his apartment to redress the bandages.

"You've got to remember, your cut would take some explaining if we got a Doctor and Mrs A. is doing a good job. Stell's made a bed up in the spare room and you can rest and eat well."

Michael grunted a reply and nearly fell asleep when the car stopped and Jimmy carried Michael into an apartment block. Stella fussed and took off his clothes and put him in the pyjamas she had bought for him. They were a bit too big and they covered his feet but he felt good in them. She plumped the softest pillows he had ever laid on and covered him with crisp white sheets and a thick blanket. He contentedly sank into the softest, cleanest, most wonderful smelling sleep ever. Jimmy went straight back to work leaving Stella happily fussing and cooking for Michael. He gave Stella a hug.

"You are loving this aren't you? You'd make a wonderful mother you know. Now give me a kiss you gorgeous creature, I've got to go."

She very happily obliged.

CHAPTER NINE

Family and Friends

Mrs A. arrived at 7.30 p.m. by a cab paid for by Jimmy. Well this event alone was worth repeating over and over again to whoever was around. Her greatest satisfaction was the various neighbours who were sitting on steps outside their apartment blocks enjoying the cool of the evening, bored for the most part, but Mrs A. getting into a taxicab, a sight never seen before, was causing some speculation. To say she milked the part was an understatement. Whoever heard of anyone taking five minutes to get into a cab with only two bags?

Stella showed her into the parlour. Mrs A. gave an appreciative intense glance at everything. "Very nice," she thought, "homely, plush and very tasteful."

Stella kept a nice home with many artistic touches, the fresh flowers beautifully arranged on an oval mahogany table covered with a lace cream table cloth, photos arranged on another small side table. The curtains were breathtaking, heavy green velvet swept back by tasselled green knotted ropes.

"Stella, your home is beautiful," Mrs A. was full of admiration tinged with the merest sigh. She told herself jealousy was not in her nature. The fact she was lucky enough to be married to such a handsome, wonderful man as well was doubly lucky. No, she was pleased for Stella, really, she was.

Stella broke the awkward silence. "Now take your coat off and sit yourself down Mrs A, I've coffee and cakes for us. Angel's asleep and we can talk for a while. You've had another busy day and a small rest will do you good."

Mrs A. felt like a guest of honour, she smoothed the dress she had specially put on for tonight, adjusted her hat and sat down.

Stella genuinely admired Mrs A. Sometimes it was possible to instinctively know someone despite their several layers of protection of a rough and abrupt exterior. Stella could see a good, caring honest woman hidden beneath. She would like to be a friend of Mrs A. Stella did not have any women friends. These two women from very different backgrounds had been deeply hurt in the past. Like magnets they were attracted and repelled by each other. Trust takes time and effort.

Apart from Michael, these two had nothing in common except Stella's business suggestion to Mrs A. They both sat fiddling with their cups, sizing each other up and giving embarrassed smiles. Anxious to break the silence that kept occurring, Stella piped up, "Mrs A. have you thought about my idea, you know you could make your life easier if you employ other women to do some of the washing for you. You would take a small cut of what they're earning but, you know you are doing far too much work yourself. I'll help get more business. What do you think?"

Mrs A. had thought about it since yesterday. She knew she was good at what she did. She knew what to charge for herself but to have to employ women and organise for others and keep books was frightening. She wasn't sure how she would benefit. She hardly charged anything for what she did, let alone farm it out and make money. "Stella the do-gooder," she thought. "Does she think I'm a charity case! I've always managed, I've kept a home and provided four children with a good education and fed and clothed them, not bad for a woman without an education." Mrs A. put her cup down a little too hard but kept quiet.

Stella noticed Mrs A's red cheeked temper but she was only trying to help and it was for her own good. Stella was clever, she had worked it out. She knew Mrs A. did not charge enough money and she had hardly put up the prices in all the years she had been washing. When you are reliant on your customers to survive, fear of losing them makes you undersell yourself. The old customers knew this too. After some discussion it was agreed Stella would find new customers at new rates of pay and Mrs A. would recruit wash and iron women. Mrs A. was doubtful Stella would get new customers willing to pay her new prices, but let Stella find out for herself. Mrs A. felt comfortable that it would not cost her time or money. Her old customers were safe, so why not she had nothing to lose.

After they drank their coffee and ate their cakes, Stella showed Mrs A. into the spare room and woke Michael. The wound was seeping blood and had stained the crisp white sheets. Mrs A. set to work undoing the tight bandages. The wound was actually doing quite nicely but where it had started to knit the exertions of the day had caused the wound to open in places. It looked nasty now. The wound had swollen slightly and blood had congealed in places under the skin turning it a mauve/blue colour. Michael looked at it, colour drained from his face. He immediately felt the pain and soreness. "Am I going to die?" he asked in a small-frightened voice.

"Don't be silly, what a thought," scolded Mrs A. "It looks far worse than it is. It's not very deep and if you had rested all day it would be a lot better now, so behave yourself and let me get you cleaned up and bandaged."

Stella watched, pale-faced. She thought the wound looked terrible. Later she would ask Mrs A. if it should have been stitched by a Doctor. Mrs A. would tell her yes that would have been best but her bandaging, if she said so herself, would knit him together just as well. Besides Jimmy thought it best a Doctor was not involved if at all possible. Mrs A. still did not know what had happened but had the sense not to push it. Michael was cleaned up, re-bandaged tightly and given a hot milky drink and told to sleep. He asked Mrs A. how his mother was and was told, she's still singing hymns and added that she ate some stew left from yesterday and was bedded down for the night.

Mrs A. waited in the parlour with Stella until her return cab arrived. Stella asked how long Maria had got left. Mrs A. shook her head and said, "I don't think she will be with us for many months, maybe weeks. I didn't want to tell Michael but the pains are getting stronger. I've increased the laudanum dose and she's only been on it two days. She must have had Syphilis for many years before the signs began to show. God knows how many people she's infected over the years." On that solemn note the cab arrived and Mrs A. left. Stella washed up the cups and plates, checked Michael was asleep and tried to shrug off the rather dark depressing feeling that seemed to hang in the air. The best way to clear depression was work. She got a pen and paper out of the sideboard and started working on her plan to build Mrs A. a nice little business.

Sunday morning Michael woke to the clinking of china on china. Stella had brought him breakfast in bed. On the tray was a pile of ham, eggs and flapjacks with gallons of syrup, fresh bread and a glass of warm milk. "If I eat all that I'll burst my bandages," laughed Michael. He was feeling much better. He had never slept so much but it had done him good. He had not dreamt about Tony once. Little boys heal quickly. Stella happily watched him eat. She noted his table manners would need attending to at some time but not now. Eating in bed is not comfortable and when he had finished it all, including the bread to mop up any syrup and juice on the plate, he laid back feeling sore. "Stella can I ask how you and Johnny met?" He learnt quickly how to word things for Stella. Stella thought and smiled, that far away look in her eyes. She would give him the abbreviated version, no need to tell him every detail, but she remembered every moment and savoured them.

She had always been a plain looking girl, somewhat of a disappointment to her middle class family. An only child who carried the burden of both parents dreams and ambitions. Their first disappointment was her looks. Both parents were Irish with the striking dark hair, blue eyes and beautiful skin. They realised early on in Stella's life that she would not take after them in colouring, but more likely her looks were on her maternal grandfather's side of the family. It was not until her features settled at about 16 years old did they realise she was not good marriageable stock. She had inherited the famous Irish temper but without the charm and looks that compensate. As a devout Catholic family who regularly attended church, with the local priest often sharing their evening meals it was decided Stella would make a good Nun. An honourable institution for girls of somewhat lesser abilities. This way they could be proud of her and they would have discharged their responsibilities correctly.

Father had a high position in the local bank and mother was respected for her charitable works. Their position in the local community was high and inevitably busy. Stella realised quite early in her teens that they did not really care for her. Yes, she had everything she needed, they were kind to her, but she felt their disappointment. Not pretty, witty or accomplished at anything in particular, her temper really sprouted during this time and caused her parents much embarrassment. Desperate to please her parents, she happily went along with the idea of entering a Nunnery when she was older. Her life followed the path that would lead there. At 16 years her involvement with the Church and their works took most of her time. She loved God, and happily prayed, worked and sung to his glory.

One glorious day, 6th June 1904 when she was 19 years old she was scrubbing the church steps, all 30 of them. This was part of her penance for questioning the priest on his choice of sermon, something she did too regularly. She had stopped scrubbing for a moment to stretch her legs. Jimmy had seen her scrubbing and had asked her why a pretty girl like her was doing this kind of work. She remembered blushing and scolding him for making fun of her, but he had called her pretty. It would not have meant anything much to other girls but to her, she had never, ever, been called pretty. She remembered Jimmy getting embarrassed because she was blushing. He stuttered an apology for being familiar but could he take her for a soda or coffee or something. Well she went and over two years they fell in love, gained respect for each other and they gave each other freely and truly what each needed. Jimmy made Stella feel beautiful and needed and Stella made Jimmy feel intelligent and his opinion always sought. Although their love was kept a secret for one year, stealing hours to meet during the day or evening, it could not go on like that. Preparations were being made in earnest for her to enter a Nunnery on her 21st birthday, which was only nine months away.

She talked it over with Jimmy asking him what she should do and in her own wonderful way, provided him with the answers to her questions and then hugging him for his brilliance. At Stella's subtle prompting Jimmy had decided they must talk to Stella's parents and tell them they were in love and wanted to get married. He would ask for their permission to marry and their blessing. The smile had left Stella's face when relating the potted version to Michael, he could tell he was not being told everything. Stella did not tell him she had spent six months arguing with her parents who did not approve of Jimmy. Frankly they were shocked their daughter would consider someone with no obvious class and with a job that sounded dubious to say the least and to cap it all, he was not even a Catholic. The Priest, Father O'Flaherty, carried on the argument on religious grounds. He culminated his argument with the fact she was going against her parents which was a sin, but his trump card was to bring in the wrath of the Lord together with eternal damnation for her wickedness. This would have floored any other young girl but Stella being Stella rose to the challenge and told Father O'Flaherty in no uncertain terms what she thought of him, and a God who would exact such vengeance. When the red mist had cleared from her eyes she realised she had gone too far in her argument and she was glad. She was excommunicated from the Catholic Church, which saddened her. Her life had revolved around the Church and God. She had made friends who now shunned her. What really hurt was her parents who publicly and ceremoniously disowned her. So with Father O'Flaherty and a congregation praying for her soul, she was told to leave the house and henceforth they no longer had a daughter. She could still feel the intense hurt like a constant pain in her chest. Stella, head held high walked out and into Jimmy's protective arms. She smiled again, they married on her 21st birthday in a registry office with Johnny and Ted who had the job title of Chauffeur at the KitKat Club as their witness. She replaced God with Jimmy. She would love him, cherish him, adore him and her waking moments would be spent honouring him. Powerful stuff!

Michael changed the subject, getting bored with this mushy love story. "Where's Jimmy?"

"He's in bed still, he doesn't get in till late and it's Sunday, his only day off. He'll be up about 11 am. He works long hours all week and I make sure that today is his day."

Michael had a lovely day just resting and being waited on hand and foot. They had a toilet that was indoors and a room with a bath in it, no tin tubs or stand up washes for them. By Monday he was still sore but so much better.

CHAPTER TEN

Payback Time

He did his rounds of collecting and delivery, it was tiring but not too bad, still an easy peasy job. When he had finished he went home. His Mother was being sick again, his heart sank, he was tired but he got down to clearing up the mess. Mrs A. had thoughtfully left a bowl for Maria to be sick into and she had hit the target. He also noticed the place smelled better. Things were not so bad.

Life took on a pattern and for months he did his job, came home, cleared up his Mother's sickness, cooked, washed, and went to bed. He regularly saw Jimmy and Stella and of course Mrs A. His hobby was counting the money he saved. He now had $40 in his tin under the bed and that was after paying Mrs A. and getting new shoes. He was getting through shoes quite quickly with all the walking. He turned 13 years old some time during September, Maria still not sure of the date. The job was easy and although still careful to make sure he was not followed, every contact in the buildings knew him and it became a friendly meet. The odd joke, pleasantry, and good-natured cuff round the ears made life enjoyable.

After three months he noticed the same two people hanging around one particular pick up point. It was O'Malleys bar. A crowded bar frequented by loud, merry drunks whose job seemed to be to out drink and shout everyone else down. A good-natured crowd that could turn nasty for no good reason. Fights seemed to break out regularly but never lasted long. The owner a bulk of a man with rosy cheeks and an amenable good nature that belied his toughness, he had the ability to grab two fighting men one in each hand, bang their heads together and toss them out. He always told them when you get your attitude sorted you'll be welcomed back and they were. Sean O'Malley was Michael's contact.

What brought the men to Michael's attention was they were eyeing him, not intensely but they had obviously twigged that he was there every day and they were curious. Michael told Jimmy who in turn told Mr Sabetti. He was told to be careful and work out how he was going to answer them when he was approached, he was told he would definitely be approached. Michael, full of confidence now, told them there was no worries he could handle them. Johnny was worried, this was the test time. He kept Alfredo informed of ongoing events. They were both tense and very aware that their business was in the hands of a kid.

Michael's reading and writing could do with much improvement but he printed a note to Sean O'Malley saying, "Wotever hapens back me up. I am your basterd son and you dont want me – there cood be truble soon."

He slipped it to Sean on the next day changeover.

Sean read it later but did not question it. He knew the game and could imagine something was going down. This little sideline was worth money to him and he would back Angel to the hilt. Another week went by and Michael saw the men still watching him. It took them a week to even consider the young boy. Michael acted as silly and babyish as he could. He walked like a little child and looked sweet and innocent. He took to carrying a wooden toy soldier, large enough to be noticeable, and he would play with it as he entered the bar.

One day he left the bar and as he turned the corner two hands grabbed him and carried him into an alley. The fear on Michael's face was real, it reminded him of the Tony incident as he now thought of that terrible time. Michael was cornered by the two men he had seen watching him. Nasty characters he thought, as he looked into dead eyes and could see murder. This was the first time Michael had come face to face with real gangsters. They were so far removed from Mr Tarrantinni and those at the club. These men's business was violence and they enjoyed it. He was pinned against the wall and searched roughly, nothing was found but $1 in his pocket. Disappointed they gave him a rough shove and he banged his head on the wall. His chest, although healed, hurt as they pushed him. Tears sprang to his eyes, which helped. He let the tears flow and started bawling loudly. One of them shook him and told him to shut up. Michael was frightened but tried to keep his mind clear. This was why he was paid good money. The men were bored, they had been watching O'Malley's for months and this was the first bit of action they had and were going to get some mileage out of this even if it was a kid. They pushed him from one to the other firing questions with each shove,

"What's your name?"

"Why are you here every day?"

"Who do you work for?"

"Where's the money?"

Michael felt dizzy and battered. He considered fainting, this would give him a break but the purpose of all this was to satisfy the men that he had nothing and was innocently going about his business. When they stopped he started snivelling and threatening to tell his Ma. They laughed. "Here we go," Michael thought and started his prepared yarn. "I ain't got no dad. My ma's sick. She told me Sean O'Malley was my father. We haven't got any money and my sweet ma has worked herself to death so I'd have a reasonable life. He gave us nothing and just upped and left my ma when she was pregnant. Her family disowned her for the disgrace she brought on the family. She can't work and we've got no money so I figure he owes us. I come every day because he never gives me much." He gave them the story looking straight into their eyes. He could soften any hearts with this story and his honest innocent eyes and quivering lip. They had no heart to soften but it seemed believable. Disappointed and still not giving up they grabbed Michael by an ear and pulled him towards O'Malleys. "We'll check this you little bastard, see if O'Malley says the same." They were still hopeful something was going on here. Michael gave a loud cry, "I want my soldier." One of them picked it up off the floor and slammed it into Michael's arms. "Shut up kid before I give you something to cry about."

O'Malley saw the two men pulling Angel into the bar and march up to the counter and stop right in front of him. The men were feeling irritated and mean, one wrong word and they would have O'Malley just for the hell of it. Prodding Michael in the chest, one looked straight into O'Malley's eyes and said, "Who is this kid, and I want it straight." O'Malley quickly considered his answer. The man was on a short fuse and should not be argued with. He put on his most congenial face and leaned forward and in a conspiratorial whisper said, "I can tell you'll not want to be messed about. Please keep this to yourself, my missus mustn't find out. His mother," O'Malley nodded sideways towards Michael, never taking his eyes from the man in front of him, "well, her and I knew each other, if you take my meaning. This kid is my bastard, according to him. This may or may not be true. I'll deny I've said that to anyone else."

"Did you give him any money today?"

Michael held up the $1 and waved it out of sight of the men and quickly put it back in his pocket. It didn't escape O'Malley's attention.

"I might have." That was a mistake, both men leaned sharply forward ready to grab O'Malley.

"Okay, Okay, sorry lads, I'll be straight with you. Yes I gave him a $1."

Michael sensed O'Malley needed help with the rest.

He started snivelling and added quickly, "That's the most you've given me in one visit. I've got to come in every day so my darling ma and I can live. If you were a decent man you'd see us alright instead of making me beg every day. You ruined my ma's life and all you give me is measly cents and the odd dollar, is that fair?" Michael was getting fired up.

"Don't you talk to your elders like that, I'll give you a clip round the ear," O'Malley helped the argument.

"If you touch me I'll tell everyone about you, including your wife, everyone will know what a fine person you really are," Michael was enjoying this.

"I'll swing for you, you fucking little bastard." O'Malley shrieked quietly.

"Hold it, hold it," one of the two men shouted. "We're going. Don't want to listen to your pathetic problems." The two men eased out of the bar and into a waiting car and were gone.

"Gee kid, I need a drink, want one?" O'Malley was quite shook up. He did not know the men, but he recognised the look in their eyes and the bulge under their jackets. He poured a large neat whiskey and downed it in one. He gave Michael a lemonade.

"You did very well Angel, they were nasty pieces of shit."

"And here's to you Mr O, you were brilliant," Michael chuckled. He raised his glass to drink but his hand was shaking so much he gave up.

Michael completed the round of calls quickly but made sure he was not followed. He relayed the details to Mr Sabbetti whose look of grave concern eased as the story was unfolded. Michael gave graphic details of the encounter by replaying each push and shove and throwing himself around the room. Johnny found it a little irritating, but for the sake of getting the story he endured the play enacted for him. At the end of the drama Johnny asked, a little puzzled, "So if they searched you, where was the envelope you'd just collected?"

Michael triumphant and playing his finale, stood and with a dramatic pause picked up his soldier. "My toy soldier is hollow and it was stuffed inside," Michael giggled and took a deep bow. Johnny sat back amazed at this little kid.

"This has earned you a bonus. Fucking ace Angel. You've conned the big boys," Johnny laughed. He thought for a moment and calmed Michael down who was on a huge high. "Now you listen carefully Angel. Tomorrow leave O'Malley till last. The two bastards could still be around. I don't want them following you. O'Malley is your biggest pickup, they were spot on with that, but the others are pretty good and they may turn up at one of those. Check cars and the street before you go near the buildings. Hopefully they've given up on your run."

Over the next few weeks it looked as if the story had held, there was no sign of anyone watching. Tony "Spit and Bones" was now back at work and was assigned a small pickup point by Johnny and he had been pulled by two men who sounded familiar. They had roughed up Tony and taken his envelope containing money and bets. Johnny knew they would pick him. He swaggered into his pickup building looking as inconspicuous as a tart in a nunnery. He argued with the two men and got a severe beating for his trouble. Johnny was pleased. All had gone according to plan.

About one month later Johnny and Alfredo had another Board meeting. Johnny had just spoken to Sonia. The news was Tarrantinni was small meat and all watches had left the area. This was about the same time the three major gangs embarked on another territorial fight. Alfredo told Johnny each gang had heard rumours about infiltration. All had battened down the hatches and were intent on watching each other. The match had been lit, but the wind to fan the flames would be wafted by the many small time hoodlums with grudges to pay and money to make. It only took about two weeks for itchy trigger fingers to start a bloody war.

"Is this down to you boss?" Johnny asked.

"Nah, I can't take all the credit," Alfredo was being modest. "The odd word in certain corners seemed to have been exaggerated and it went from there." Alfredo shrugged his shoulders and took another puff of his cigar. Business was going well. They both discussed staff and Tony was high on the Agenda. Alfredo had promised his sister that Tony would work for him but only if he could exert full control and punishment as necessary. His sister tried to argue but even she was getting worn down by Tony's antics and reluctantly agreed. Both Alfredo and Johnny disliked Tony and found his attitude not conducive to good business. Tony had been swaggering as usual and acting like he was important upsetting staff and some customers, which could not be allowed. When he had returned to work after his assault on Angel, Alfredo had read him the riot act. Tony behaved himself for a short time but then reverted to type. He needed to be taught a lesson in humility. They both decided he would be the kitchen wash up boy. He would be watched closely and kept in line. The cook had a reputation for running a tight kitchen and would not allow any of his staff to step out of line. Angel came up on the agenda and both agreed he was doing a good job and would continue as a runner for the time being.

CHAPTER ELEVEN

Cold Comfort

Michael over the last six months had most of his life under control. He bought clothes to keep up his smart appearance. He could afford good food and was able to save money. Saving money was his protection in case times turned bad, it was his hobby. He still went down the market and lifted the odd vegetable from the stalls, no sense in wasting good money and buying it. He paid Mrs A. regularly every week and paid for more laudanum. Maria was out of his control. She had got a lot worse and seemed in pain all the time. Michael was powerless to help her and it was breaking him up to see her in such pain. He spoke to Mrs A. and she said she would see what she could do. Mrs A. had already been in contact with the local priest to find out if there was a place where Maria could be looked after. She would tell Michael about it when she had some definite news. Mrs A. had seen the disease progress and knew she was at the point where different help would be needed. Despite all the cleaning up and abuse she had suffered from Maria, she could not bear to see her in such pain. Mrs A. marvelled that she had lasted so long, it was now

February and she was still here albeit in a much worsened condition, she was hanging on to life with both hands. Mrs A. knew that was because of the excellent nursing Maria was receiving and the good food. She was cooking for Michael and Maria now, of course Michael paid her extra, but they got the best-cooked food this side of Chicago Mrs A. told herself contentedly.

The definite news came, Mrs A. had a long chat with the local priest and he confirmed the details. Now she had to talk to Michael. When Michael got home late that afternoon he found Mrs A. with dinner cooked and Maria asleep. Mrs A. sat Michael down and explained that the Nunnery which was about one hour walk away had a small hospital and for a small fee per week would take Maria and care for her. Mrs A. explained that she needed 24-hour care and neither she nor Michael could do that. It was kindness because they would make her comfortable and keep her out of pain (Mrs A. was not sure about that), and pray for her. Michael could visit every day. Michael agreed. He could afford the $10 per week, just about, not much left for saving, and yes it would be better for his ma. He knew this was best for her but the guilt he carried was his relief at not having to come home to her being sick, crying in pain, or screaming abuse at him. He did not realise then that he would miss her.

Mrs A. made the arrangements and Maria was moved into the Nunnery the next day. She was taken by cab and Michael gave Mrs A. some money for new nightclothes. Maria was not consulted on the move, she did not care about anything and did not listen to Michael when he tried to explain. She just accepted her new home and treated the nuns to her usual tirade of foul language and abuse. The nuns were good souls, they just crossed themselves and said a prayer under their breath as they tended to her.

CHAPTER TWELVE

Warm Wealth

Mrs A's life had improved. Stella true to her word had gone out and got new customers for Mrs A. at new prices. Mrs A. had five women washing and ironing for her. Stella waited a few months until the new business was established and then, with Mrs A's permission, spoke to all Mrs A's old customers. Stella persuaded and talked them all into paying the new price. She did not tell Mrs A. that she actually said they would have to make alternative arrangements if they did not pay the new price and the high quality of wash would be hard to find elsewhere. Stella had also looked around and found the new prices were no higher than anywhere else. Mrs A. gave up the childminding and some of the washing and ironing. She now had women to do this for her. Stella set up a book-keeping system for Mrs A. and taught her how to work it, although it would be true to say that Stella carried on doing the book-keeping because Mrs A. was not confident to manage this by herself. A recent new addition to the business was a lad employed to collect and deliver the washing. He had been promised a bicycle in the near future to carry the washing to and from the customers. Mrs A. realised she owned her own business and had people working for her. This gave her more satisfaction and pleasure than anyone could possibly realise. She often thought that if only the bastard knew how successful she was becoming. She would love to see him again to throw it in his face.

She found it hard to say thank you to Stella. The woman had been right all along. It had made a difference to her life and she did not have to worry about if she was ill how she would earn money. Her standing in the community had gone up. Women were always respectful of her, after all she had looked after many of their children and helped with illnesses in the past. It was different now, she could offer them work and instead of costing them money for her services she could help them earn money. They were falling over themselves to be nice to her. She liked that.

Yes, she had much to be grateful for to Stella. The woman did not make her feel beholden to her, she was very pleased and excited for her, but she was so darn enthusiastic and wanted more. Mrs A. thought it was funny but now she had less to do she felt more tired. She just wanted enough money to be able to live and to relax a little. Stella kept bouncing in and coming up with more suggestions and ideas for improving business and it was getting on her nerves. But yes, she was grateful and would think of a way to show her gratitude, maybe tomorrow.

Stella had bigger ideas. She had seen the Chinese in another part of town open laundries where people brought and collected their washing. Stella wanted to be different and a delivery and collection service was an added bonus for would be customers. Stella wanted a laundrette and she would keep her eyes open for suitable premises while getting more business and lining up more wash and iron women. She had worked out that if they had a collection and delivery service their premises did not have to be in the main street, which would be dearer. A warehouse type place in the East Chicago area should come cheaply, with the added bonus of cheap labour from the women in the area. She was already investigating the restaurants and hotels in the other parts of town. If she could undercut the prices already being charged for laundry with the added bonus of a night collection with returned laundered items first thing the next morning, the business would survive with this custom. Her long-term plans included a night shift of workers. She reasoned that some women with very young children would prefer an evening job. Husbands could look after the children so no outlay for babysitters. When all this happened Stella wanted a partnership with Mrs A. Her ultimate plan was to earn enough money to allow Jimmy to retire early. She worried about the long hours he worked and by the time Sunday came how tired he was. In maybe 15 years when he would be 50 years old, he might be pleased to give up the club work. Stella would work hard for this to happen. For now, everything was on paper and she ticked each stage accomplished. She would talk soon to Mrs A. about the future and her being a partner but for the moment that could wait.

CHAPTER THIRTEEN

Hospital Visits

Michael visited his mother every day on the way home. For six months he did the two-hour round trip, but as he said, what did he have to get home early for. He found the nuns intimidating, their clothes were quite scary – all black from head to toe. To turn their heads involved swivelling the whole of their bodies, whatever their bodies looked like under the volumes of black cloth. The weather was stifling but he could not understand why they did not look hot and sweaty. He thought it was all very unnatural and spooky, more like the devil's servants rather than brides of Christ. His visits were often boring and mind numbing. His Mother often did not recognise him or was asleep. He avoided eye contact with the nuns, he swore they were putting a spell on him. When his mother first arrived at the hospital he wiled away some time annoying the nuns by calling them just as they had passed his mother's bed, just to see them have to turn the whole of their body to answer him. One day a nun gave him such a long stare that it made him get goosey all over. His spooky thoughts about them stemmed from that encounter and just got wilder as time went on. Now when he saw them walk past he was certain they were floating just inches off the ground, if that was not devils work then he was a Dutchman! He had to admit though that his mother did not seem to be in pain and that made him feel better.

Maria had an odd moment of normality when Michael had been with her. He was to treasure this in times to come. She had told him she was dying and not much longer for this world. She told Michael that she loved him and was sorry for being such a bad mother. She asked him to kiss her, which he did. Through the mist of tears streaming down his face, he saw the remnants of the beauty she had once been. When he visited the following day she lay with a vacant stare. The nuns whispered it was the medication but Michael knew she was leaving him bit by bit.

It was nearing the end of August and Michael arrived at the nunnery hot and sweaty. The priest was waiting at the door to the ward for him and he was led into a side room where he was gently told that his mother had passed away and was now with our Lord. He was nearly 14 years old and alone.

Michael walked home, had a glass of milk and went to bed. Sleep was a good escape, he would think about everything tomorrow. For now he wanted to dream about something good. He would dream about the sea. He had seen pictures but he only imagined what it looked and sounded like. That dream always relaxed him.

In the morning he went to see Mrs A. to give her the news.

"You poor wee soul," Mrs A cuddled him, nearly suffocating him, he reasoned her breasts must weigh at least 14 lbs each. All Mrs A's maternal instincts came to the surface and it was quite awesome. There were kisses, cuddles, cups of coffee, more kisses, scones freshly made this morning, and more cuddles. When she had settled herself down Mrs A. discussed the funeral. She told Michael not to worry about anything, she would go and see the priest, with a bit of luck the funeral might be free but she would find out and let Michael know this evening. Michael decided he would go to work, he could not afford to miss it. Mrs A. thought to herself that it was not right or respectful, but then the poor lad needs to take his mind off of all this, and let's face it Maria had not been a respectable person anyway.

Michael went to work and told Jimmy what had happened. Jimmy was very sorry to hear the news and was anxious to check if Michael was OK. He did his round of collections, it seemed to take longer than usual, his legs felt like lead weights. He arrived home feeling flat, exhausted and numb. Mrs A. bustled in about one hour later with plenty of information. She saw his mood and made it her business to lighten the atmosphere. "Well Michael, everything is arranged. I've done a good job if I say so myself. Your mother is being buried next Monday for free. It'll be nothing fancy but it will be a good Christian service. The priest you met wants to conduct the service. He asked me about your mother and I gave him a potted version of her life as I knew it." Michael turned and looked at Mrs. A sharply, "No don't worry, I didn't mention her sordid, sorry, I mean sad life style. I said she was an unmarried mother who had raised a son by herself." Michael felt better on hearing that.

"I'll provide some sandwiches and sherry for after. I don't suppose many will attend, do you Michael?"

Michael did not think anyone would attend but himself. On the day Jimmy, Stella and Mrs A. attended. The service was attended by quite a few nuns, some strangers who apparently attended the church regularly so the long, boring, and strange service was conducted with half a church full of people. Michael liked that. The priest said some nice things about his mother, none he could relate to her but it was nice to hear anyway. Everyone in the church walked to the churchyard and stayed for the short service as the coffin was lowered. Michael felt quite remote from the proceedings and thought the coffin looked quite nice. He had bought a rose and placed this on the coffin as it was being lowered. He did not cry, he actually felt nothing. Stella kept looking at him waiting for the tears, but all she saw was a sad little boy with a faraway look in his eyes.

The four of them returned to Mrs A's home. The priest was invited but he declined due to appointments already overdue. They were all relieved. After a cup of coffee, glass of sherry and sandwiches Stella was the first to start.

"Michael, what will you do now? You can't live alone."

Mrs A. was indignant "What do you mean Stella, this boy has kept the home together by himself. It wasn't his mother who looked after him, he looked after her and earned the money to keep them going."

Stella sighed. Always an argument with Mrs A. She didn't want to start a row today for Michael's sake. "OK I stand corrected." That took a lot for her to say, each word scratched as it came out. She turned to Michael and held his hand and gently said, "Michael you are welcome to come live with Jimmy and me if you wish. Don't answer now, just think about it, OK?" Michael smiled with gratitude. "Thanks Stella, I'll think about it."

Jimmy and Stella left after an hour. Jimmy had to go to work and Stella had some calls to make. When they had gone Michael and Mrs A. sat across from each other at the table, each holding a cup of coffee. Mrs A. squirmed a little in her chair. Michael could see she had something to say and was having difficulty getting started.

"Michael, if you want to live with Jimmy and Stella that's fine. They've got a wonderful home and I know they will look after you real good. They've got a bit more class than we are used to, but that won't do you any harm." Mrs A. hesitated not knowing how to say the next bit. "This don't come easy to me Michael, I want to say that if, and only if you don't want to live alone and for some unexplained reason that I couldn't understand, you didn't want to live with Jimmy and Stella, I'd be happy to have you here. I like you, you know that. Anyway, its your decision, just let me know what you think." With that Mrs A. folded her huge arms and knocked her coffee over. Michael laughed and got a cloth. He knew Mrs A. was not usually so shy about saying things and wondered why it was so hard for her to say she wanted him to stay with her. Well it was hard. It's always hard to ask for things you really want. More than anything, Mrs A. wanted Michael to live with her. She had more time on her hands now and was lonely, she wanted to cook for someone, she kind of looked on Michael as a son, but she was no great shakes in comparison to what Jimmy and Stella had to offer.

"I'll think about it Mrs A. Thank you very much for your offer. Can I let you know tomorrow?"

Mrs A. got up, cleared her throat, and said, "Of course Michael, there is no problem at all, you do what is best for you."

Michael left and went home. It was funny Maria hadn't been around for months but now she was gone the place felt really empty. Michael looked around and wondered where to start. He had never looked in his mother's cupboard, never thought about it before, but now he had better check what needed throwing out. The small cupboard by her bed was full of bits and pieces. Amongst the fluff that inevitably invades unused areas there was makeup that had gone dry, hankies, some cents and dimes, and cheap perfume. He found a dried small posy, the flowers crumbled as he picked them up. He found an old paper bag and just slid all the contents in for disposal. At the back of the cupboard he found an old cigar box. On opening he found a crucifix, some small prayer cards which he thought were quite pretty and a photograph. It was of a class of what looked like twelve to fourteen year old youngsters, with a nun and priest standing guard at each side of the set piece. The youngsters Michael reasoned must be standing on planks one above the other. He counted thirty youngsters in the picture. He peered closely at each face to see if he recognised his Mother. There in the middle row stood a beautiful girl with long dark hair smiling. She looked so innocent, her smile looked so easy and natural. He knew this was his Mother, what a waste of a life. The tears that felt buried deep inside launched a surprise attack and overwhelmed him. He surrendered to their onslaught and sobbed for several hours, finally falling asleep curled on his bed holding the photo. When he awoke he felt like he had a cold, his nose was blocked, his eyes were red and sore but a weight had been lifted, and he set to work to clear Maria's belongings. Her clothes were bundled in the middle of the room and tied in a heap. All useless bits and pieces were collected in the paper bag. He was going to burn the lot in the yard. The picture he was going to have framed.

He made a lot of important decisions last night and today he walked with purpose to Mrs A's house. Johnny had been good to him and said to take a few days off to sort everything out. Mrs A. opened the door and saw a much brighter looking Michael than she had seen for days.

"Well Mrs A, I said I would let you know today. I'd like to stay with you if I may. Perhaps we can talk about the costs. I would like to get rid of my place as soon as possible. Don't want to stay there at all if I can help it."

"Michael," Mrs A was pleased and surprised at the same time. "But I thought you would prefer to stay with Jimmy and Stella."

"Mrs A. I feel comfortable with you and besides, you are the best cook in Chicago. How could there be any other choice."

When you make decisions like this you do not always go into every detail. Michael would not have analysed his choice that Stella was different and bossy and as much as he liked them both, their home would not feel like his home. Mrs A. had known him as a small child, and he knew how to get round her and to some extent, she needed him. Michael was used to being needed and he did not want to lose that as well. Mrs A. feeling good and knowing the decision had been made started to mildly rebuke Michael. "Well I don't know. You're giving up a fine home with them, I don't understand it." She looked at Michael and smiled, "Yes you are right, my cooking would be hard to beat now I'll show you the room that will be yours and then we can discuss money." Mrs A. had quite a large apartment. She had two bedrooms a parlour and a large kitchen. The room she showed Michael was not far off the size of the entire basement he was used to. Well that may have been a slight exaggeration, but it was a whole room just for him. Mrs A's four children used to sleep in here, all in one bed. The big double bed was now all his.

They agreed after much bartering, Michael would pay $6 per week for the room, all his food, and all his washing and ironing done. Mrs A. might have wanted him to stay but it would not get in the way of her earning some money. They both knew the score and understood each other, it felt very comfortable. Michael spent the morning moving his belongings to his new room. Mrs A. came and looked at the basement to see if there was anything she needed. Apart from taking some spare sheets that would not fit any of her beds, waste not, want not, she told Michael to leave it all. Quite honestly she did not understand how they had managed with such rubbish.

That afternoon Michael went to see Stella. She was out but he hung around for several hours. It was definitely a classier area, he noticed stares as neighbours wondered why that lad was hanging around the entrance to the apartments. He was feeling rather uncomfortable and uneasy, he could feel eyes on him for the two hours. No one asked who he was but he felt sure if he had been up to no good, the cops would have been called. He was not used to this. At home, someone would always walk up to you and ask what you were doing, if you did not give the correct response you risked a hard clump round the head.

Stella returned about 5 p.m. She looked tired. "Come in Michael," Stella was breathless and busy hanging her coat and putting away her shopping. "Would you like a coffee?" Michael said he would. "I'm just putting something on the stove for Jimmy. He comes home for a couple of hours about six and I want to make sure he has a good meal and a rest before going back to work. Coffee will be ready in five minutes." She shouted this information to Michael who was sitting uncomfortably in the parlour. After what seemed a long time Stella came in with a tray of coffee and biscuits. When the coffee had been poured, milk and sugar sorted out, and biscuits offered, Stella asked how things were.

"Stella, I have decided to stay with Mrs A. I hope you don't mind. I think she needs me and, well I hope you don't mind." Michael was not doing this very well.

He was worried Stella might be hurt or misunderstand. Stella did not mind. In fact her emotional outburst on the day of the funeral had not been thought out very well. She valued her time alone with Jimmy, they did not get very much with him working such long hours. She had her life in an order that was rewarding. Her free time was totally focused on expanding the laundry business. Yes it was selfish, but Michael was not a part of her overall plan. She was relieved he was with Mrs A. Michael was maybe a little disappointed in Stella's reaction. He did not want to upset anyone but he thought Stella might fight for him a little. Michael was developing a ego.

It was agreed that Michael would come for dinner once a week, Monday was the day settled. Stella thought she would at least work on his table manners. Michael returned to his new home in the certain knowledge that Mrs A. would have something tasty for his supper and he would have a comfortable room of his own to stay. On the way home his mind wandered to this and that, when he looked up he was at the door of his old basement home. Feeling tearful again and a little strange he turned and headed for Mrs A's apartment and his new home.

CHAPTER FOURTEEN

As Good as it Gets

During the next two years Michael's life took on a contented pattern. He had found a new hideaway in his bedroom for his money. He had saved through being careful, $300 which he looked at and counted most nights. During the day Mrs A. took much pleasure in counting the money for she had found his hideaway. Mr Sabetti had changed his round many times because as it was explained to him, there were always the small time hoodlums about who might jump any of the runners for the money they had collected. Mrs A's food was good and he was getting fatter. Mrs A. had taken to eating candy all day and she was defying nature by getting even bigger. She now found it hard to walk very far, even in the apartment. Michael had told her to be careful but now she had more money and time she listened to the radio and ate candy.

Stella did not come around so much now that the laundry had got up and running. True to her word and against Mrs A's original wishes, Stella leased a warehouse in East Chicago not five minutes from Mrs A's house. It took two whole days for Stella to convince

Mrs A. that this was the only way forward. Stella's temper exploded a couple of times, but she was quite proud of the fact that she contained most of it. Mrs A. was a stupid woman who could not think further than today. Armed with a case of papers explaining her plan she sat at Mrs A's table and went through everything with her. It meant nothing to Mrs A. Finally Stella said just answer yes or no to the following questions.

"Have I been right from the beginning about getting more business?

Is it true you have fifteen women working for you?

Is it true you do not have to do any washing yourself?

Is it true you are making more money now than when you were doing the washing?

Is it becoming difficult for the lad Timmy to collect and deliver from all the different houses?

Is it true that it is getting difficult to maintain standards of washes with so many women working in different homes?

Wouldn't you like to see your name above a building as the owner of the business?"

Well Mrs A. had to answer yes to all the questions. Stella explained she would organise everything, Mrs A. wouldn't have to worry about it and she would get more money within a year than she thought possible. At the end of two days, both women were exhausted. Mrs A. agreed to Stella's partnership and each woman put up $200 each for work that needed to be done to turn the warehouse into a laundry. This was a big outlay for both but, as Stella said, the money would be repaid in no time.

Mrs A. signed the official papers making them partners. Mrs A. told Michael later. "It was not necessary but Stella had to make such a song and dance about everything. Perhaps that woman will leave me in peace now." Michael kept quiet. He knew how hard Stella was working and he thought it was a good move. Stella being a modern woman was determined that the laundry would be fair to the women workers. No way was she going to expect the women to work ten hours or more per day, as seemed to be the normal working day for laundry workers. She told the women the job was for only eight hours per day and there would be two shifts so the laundry was open from 7 a.m. – 7 p.m. Five workers would do 7 a.m. – 3 pm. and five from 11 a.m. – 7 pm. Each shift would have a half hour break. Each week they would swap shifts so the early turn did the late turn. Not only did Stella think this would be fair but it made sense. Eight hours per day is the most you could expect for quality work. As she was paying an hourly rate she wanted her women to be in good working form. She had also read a few years ago of a fire in a shirtwaist factory, where 150 women died because there was no fire escapes. This was not going to happen here so Stella made provisions for fire safety in the plans.

When the grand opening arrived Mrs A, Jimmy and Stella together with Michael went to view the finished premises. The sign outside impressed Mrs A. "The Chicago Laundry" Proprietors B. Arkinshaw and S. Cane. She stood and looked at it for ages, a misty look in her eye. Stella had learned a few tips over the years and whispered to Mrs A. "Your name first Mrs A, you started this." Mrs A. hugged Stella and thanked her through snotty tears, not a pretty sight. After noses had been duly blown and composure regained they entered the building. Ten women had been employed to run the laundry. As Stella explained, we do not need so many women if they are all in one place. The other five workers had been promised first refusal when business expanded as it would with Stella at the helm. They saw the big coal boiler which provided all the hot water necessary and the heating for the, and this was the showpiece, the drying room. A huge room had been constructed with row upon row of lines for drying. No more worrying about the weather. It had large hot pipes that kept the room very warm indeed, with ventilation to get rid of the damp air. Everything was on a huge scale with sinks so enormous and vats full of starch, irons and ironing boards and a press. Stella rushed around laughing with delight pointing out how things would work, how it would save time. Mrs A. sat in the middle on a chair that was hastily brought for her, she looked overcome and in need of a rest. Not in her wildest dreams could she have thought all this up. It was impressive. After a few minutes of thinking Mrs A. got worried. "Stella, Stella be still, how on earth can we pay for all of this? The coal will cost a fortune to maintain that boiler. The running costs, we will never make any money." Stella held her temper, she had explained everything before to Mrs A. The woman will not get pleasure out of anything.

"OK one more time Mrs A. If you remember our conversations and the papers I showed you to back up my plan, I have costed out everything. Even if we do not get more business, which we will, this is more cost effective. We are paying the women less per hour because they do not provide the heating from their own home. We start here with additional business from the KitKat Club. If you remember, we undercut their present laundry and we now have the business. If nothing else that will pay for our overheads. I have six restaurants around Chicago that are seriously thinking of using us. We can't fail Mrs A. Trust me!"

Over the next six months Stella proved to Mrs A. she could be trusted and business improved. Mrs A. visited the laundry every week by cab. She bought a suit and a new coat to ensure everyone knew she had stepped up in the world. For two years Stella worked hard and her time with Jimmy was limited. Jimmy was so proud of her. He knew she was bright but even he did not realise what she was capable of. He supported her in her work by never complaining she was not at home when he was. He missed her, and asked when things would calm down. Stella knew a good business should never calm down, but it got to the point when decisions had to be made and Stella made it. She appointed a Manager to run the laundry. Business was very good and of course, Stella opened a bank account for the business. As much as she tried, she could not persuade Mrs A. to pay her money into the bank. Every month Stella would have to bring Mrs A her money in cash. She argued that this was stupid and dangerous but Mrs A. would have none of it. Her money stayed with her not with some stranger in a suit. Stella was finding Mrs A. very difficult and as much as possible did not involve her in the day to day running of the laundry. She had enough to do without having to cope with this backward, visionless, stupid woman.

So after two years both women were earning enough money to feel suitably rewarded. They had the addition of a Manager's wage to find but with Stella concentrating only on new business, she reckoned this would maintain and improve their financial position. Stella still had her list and she was still ticking off each stage. She hoped in maybe a year, they could afford their own petrol van to do the collections and deliveries. As she tried with patience to explain to Mrs A. "It will be free advertising with our names on the side of the van and make every collection and delivery quicker. We've got to keep up with the modern times. Mrs A. poured scorn on the idea but Stella had got used to ignoring her.

It was Jimmy's idea. He told Stella they needed a holiday. They had never been away and now the money was coming in why not treat themselves. Stella had been putting the idea in his head for weeks but finally he had cottoned on to the idea.

"Where shall we go?" asked Stella much too innocently for she already knew.

"Somewhere different don't you think Stell. We can take the car and drive to Niagara Falls. I've heard about it but to see it would be wonderful. We can book into a hotel and have some fun. We both need a holiday, but especially you Stell, you've worked so hard for so long."

She kissed him and hugged him. He was so wonderful. OK she had planted the idea of a holiday, but it was his idea she needed the break. What a wonderful man he was. "Leave it to me Jimmy, I'll plan it you have got just too much work on to be bothered." So the route was planned carefully. The thought of leaving Chicago in August for a cooler place sounded wonderful. When she told Mrs A. that she would be away for about three weeks Mrs A. thought it was a waste of time and money. Who would watch the laundry. Stella now well used to Mrs A. kept her thoughts to herself and told her everything would be fine. The Manager Charles O'Toole was well capable of keeping everything in good order. During Stella's absence Mrs A. was to find out just how much work Stella had put in to the business from Charles, who she liked. Mrs A. decided it was about time she learned to be more grateful to Stella. At supper that evening Michael was to hear a very different Mrs A. talking about Stella. He had endured many an evening with Mrs A. finding fault with everything Stella did down to her style of clothes. He was 16 years old and had come to realise Mrs A's unjust criticism was pure jealousy. He had cottoned on to the tenuous thread that caused it. Mrs A was infatuated with Jimmy and Stella had compounded her dislike by proving how clever she was and how much she loved Jimmy. He found jealousy an emotion that could not be argued with. He had noticed how Mrs A. played up to Jimmy and laughed inwardly at the thought that she could in any way attract Jimmy. Mrs A. was a wonderful woman but attractive? Never, you could roll four Stellas into Mrs A. So he was very surprised at supper to hear Mrs A. change her tune. Mrs A, who had taken to telling Michael everything that was on her mind, looked at him rather sheepishly. "I realise I have been a little critical of Stella over the years."

"And how," thought Michael whilst trying to look intensely interested, a look he had cultivated through many mindless conversations with Mrs A.

"I hope as a good Christian woman I can admit it when I have done wrong."

"A good Christian woman! Never knew she was religious," thought Michael.

"Michael, I want to make amends for what may or may not look like I've been ungrateful to Stella. She has you know made my life so much better and she worked hard to make it happen."

"Tell me about it," Michael again answering in thought only.

"I've been to the laundry and Charles has told me what is happening. I don't think I realised just how much work Stella has put in to the laundry. What can I do to make amends?" Michael was watching Mrs A. talk and eat at the same time. He found it quite gruesome and fascinating watching the food swirl round in her mouth and odd morsels would go flying in his direction, which he had the good grace not to dodge. He figured his own table manners were improving under Stella's nagging and Mrs A's were going to the dogs. "Well Michael!" Mrs A. was impatient for a reply.

"Mrs A, you are the wisest woman I know. You will know what to do. I wouldn't presume to advise you." Michael was not stupid. No way was he getting into this one. Whatever he said would be looked on as a criticism of Mrs A. Annoyed yet pleased with the answer, it left her with a dilemma. Then it came to her, but it would be her secret, she would not even have to tell Stella or

Michael for that matter. When the meal was finished and washed up, Mrs A. turned on the radio and got the sweets out of the cupboard, Michael went to his room, where he quite liked the peace and quiet.

CHAPTER FIFTEEN

The Devil's Sidekick

Tony "Spit and Bones" Pirrelli had been having a bad time over the last two years. He felt misunderstood, undervalued, and angry. When he had been forced to work in the kitchen of the KitKat Club as a wash up boy he was ready to leave. Only his Mother, who had burst into tears and promised him a new car if he stayed, persuaded him to even consider it. Well he toed the line, kept quiet and did his job. At least his time off was fun. He had got in with a crowd of men who knew what fun was and did not take any lip from anyone. They liked Tony and without any protests from him, took him to the clubs in the North part of Chicago. His Mother still paid him an allowance to supplement his low wage, enabling him to buy champagne for his friends, and pay for hot, classy, women. He had standing with this group. They appreciated his drunken boasts, they roared with approval when someone looked at him in a disrespectful way and he took them outside for a thrashing, if the victim looked too much for Tony they all pitched in. They were known as the "Creeps" by the clubs they frequented but their money was good. The "Creeps" preferred to be known as the champagne boys. Yes, they appreciated Tony, he would do things they would only think about. They admired the time he knocked a tart out because she did not want to be fondled in public. OK, they got thrown out of that club but as Tony said, "I don't want to buy the girl until I have felt the goods." They had staggered and giggled all the way to the next club for a bit of roulette. Tony liked a bit of gambling.

The Champagne boys established themselves in Chicago as loud, drunken womanisers with plenty of money. By the time Michael had turned 19 years old everyone knew who they were. Tony's Mother who seemed to have aged considerably, was a regular caller at the station to bail Tony for being drunk and disorderly. Twice he went before the Judge for violent behaviour and twice he got off with a fine. His Mother pleaded for him. She was told by the Judge that if he came before him a third time he would send him to prison to teach him a lesson. Tony calmed down enough to avoid getting caught. A room was found in a club uptown where they could drink and whore all night. Once again, Tony felt invincible, he was with the kind of people who appreciated him.

One drunken night when the whores had left, no one wanted to go home. Someone suggested they played a game of who had done the most evil thing in their lives. The winner would get the whore of their choice and the others would pay for it. The deeds described in lurid detail and cheered by all during the confession ranged from wildly exaggerated stories of rape, to theft. Tony was left to last, all convinced he would have something spectacular to tell. He was always boasting of deeds real and imaginary. Much the worse for drink, he told the story of the girl he had raped and cut an X on her stomach. Everyone cheered but one shouted not good enough, they had heard that one before. They all giggled and swayed, and chanted, "We want more, we want more." Tony was too drunk to make up a story, and he was too drunk to keep his mouth shut. "OK, OK, I've got one for you. I've never told a living soul this. You've got to promise me you'll not breathe a word of what I'm about to tell you. I'm done for if it gets out. Can I trust you all?"

The look on Tony's face and the urgent way he spoke made them all lean forward and nod in unison. While Tony composed himself the silence was deafening. All eyes were on him.

"Well, my Father died in a car accident when I was sixteen. He was a miserable shit. He never liked me. Always on my back, don't do this, don't do that. He landed a few punches many a time. Well, he was ruining my life. My mother was always in tears. Finally he threatened to throw me out of the house, disown me, said I would have to scrape a living in the dirt and it would do me good. I hated him." Tony paused, his mind felt very muddled, something told him he should not be saying all this but what the hell, it's between friends. "So I killed him."

There was a sharp intake of breath then they all laughed. "Not a good one Tony. Not realistic." Tony looked at them seriously, "You think not?" It was the way he said it that made them look at him with interest. One of them said, "How did you do it?"

Tony was miles away, thinking. They prompted him again.

"It was easy. I drained the brake fluid on the car. When they had both gone to bed I got up and crept down stairs and went to the garage. I cut the pipe under the car, collected the brake fluid in a bowl and tipped it down the drain. When he went to work the next day, bingo! No brakes. He must have been going fast when he hit the brakes because there was not a lot left of the car when they found him. He hit a truck, the truck driver was a goner as well."

"Gee, are you making this up?" asked Paulie the tall one in the group.

"Nope."

The group sat and digested. They were into most things but murder, and murder of his father was out of their league.

"Well, do I win?" asked Tony not aware of the impact of what he had told the group.

They all nodded, still wondering if it was true. Paulie, George, Stefan, and Bradley were to remember this drunken evening and treat Tony with kid gloves. None of them quite trusted him again. On looking back on his antics they saw not the daredevil they once thought, but signs of a psychopath. Tony misinterpreted their unease and assumed they were in awe of him. He was walking tall and loving it.

After two years in the kitchen, Johnny pleased with his apparent display of settling down into something nearly sociably acceptable Tony was given a new job. For the past year he had been chauffeur and driver for the club. Ted had retired having had enough of the long hours. He'd stashed away some money over the years and was going to California to relax. California was slowly becoming the place to go.

Tony became chauffeur at an exciting time. There had been talk for some time that the government were going to prohibit the manufacture, sale or transport of liquor. Alfredo and Johnny had many discussions about it. It finally happened in 1919 when the eighteenth Amendment to the Constitution came about. He drove Alfredo and Johnny to secret meetings with the Leone boss. Alfredo was not big enough to import liquor for his club with all the networking that would be needed. An uneasy and lucrative trade was set up between Leone and Alfredo. The meetings took place in secret with each side having at least five heavies standing eyeing each other up. Alfredo could just about manage five including Tony. The cops did not bother the KitKat Club, and if they did, Alfredo was given advanced notice of a raid. Several top ranking police officers owed their comfortable lifestyle to Alfredo.

Prohibition was the best thing that had happened to the KitKat club. Prices went up, the club was altered to protect them from lightning raids, with bars that could be turned round and hidden, two sets of locked doors to get through to ensure adequate time to hide any incriminating evidence laying around if the cops stormed the club. Alfredo was always saying that you can keep the cops in your pocket but never trust the bastards. This all cost a lot of money that was soon recouped. All the alterations meant the whole place needed a face-lift. It was looking quite classy. More and more people were booking an evening at the KitKat. The takings in the casino out the back climbed steadily. Alfredo was content for the moment.

Tony worked such long hours these days that he had very few days off to join his friends. The four men, if truth be known, were having a much better time without Tony. Prohibition had made all the clubs wary of troublemakers; no club wants to draw attention to itself with rowdy drunken customers. The four, all from good families, had sown their wild oats and were ready to join family businesses and eventually find a wife and live a respectable life. Tony made it clear that he would never settle down. He was working for a family business but drinking, whoring, and gambling was what made life buzz. As a group, they fizzled out as Michael turned 21 years old. Tony was not too worried, he had made other friends who had more guts than the champagne boys. He had only just met them, they were always at the same casino he frequented in North Chicago. These two hard men Gino and Vincent asked about Alfredo and the set up at the KitKat Club. They laughed when Tony told them how the place was run and he had to agree with them that Alfredo was a loser and Tony was wasted there. They had promised to teach him how to use a gun effectively. They roared when Tony told them guns were not used by anyone at the club. The mickey-taking was meant in good fun and Gino and Vincent were careful never to aim it at Tony but only at the others at the club. Vincent asked, "How does Alfredo keep everyone in order? A slap on the wrists?" Gino added,

"What a pathetic bunch. How could you work for them Tony?" Tony was beginning to ask himself this. They had never done him any favours. Even the midget had a better job and more money than him. The seed was sown in fertile ground. Tony raked up all the old grudges that were partly buried. He would show them, just wait and see. At least he had two good friends that understood him.

CHAPTER SIXTEEN

Step Up

Michael's fortunes had changed over the past years. As Tony was made Chauffeur Michael was brought into the KitKat Club to learn the job of Manager. He came under the guidance of Marcel, or that was the name he used. Marcel was getting on now and was due to retire within one year. He did not think it possible to train this upstart in such a short time, and he made a point of telling Alfredo and Johnny this. Whenever they asked how Michael was doing Marcel would suck air through his teeth, shake his head, and forlornly tell them how could he make a masterpiece out of inferior goods. They worried at first, but having watched Michael at work, realised Marcel was just being Marcel.

Over the next 9 months Michael watched and learned from Marcel. He found him a peculiar person, not sure what he was. Marcel had an effeminate wiggle and he flopped his hands in a most disconcerting way. His voice was strange too, very unmanly with a hint of a lisp. Michael was not sure if this was Marcel or part of his act, Marcel loved to play the crowds and they adored him. Michael's questions were answered when he met

Marcel's boyfriend, an ordinary looking guy, obviously in a respectable job as his suit implied. He still was not sure until he saw them kiss each other goodbye one day. Michael liked them both but made sure not to stand too close to either of them. Marcel's training took on some basic standards intermingled with plain fussiness. He taught Michael some valuable lessons on paying attention to small details, often this meant a minute movement of the position of a plate on the table. It took Michael nearly two days of practice to satisfy Marcel on how to open wine and pour it properly. Marcel was always saying, "Remember Michael when customers arrive it's show time."

Michael understood. The wine, for instance, was gut rotting stuff with a fancy label. Michael's theory was Leone was making it in his bath and selling it to Alfredo at exorbitant prices. To serve this rubbish with style and class made the customers think it tasted better than it did. By the time Marcel left, Michael had learnt and practised everything from kitchen work to booking arrangements to hiring entertainment. Marcel was going to be a hard act to follow, he was going to miss him. He had a soft spot for the strange man. At his leaving do Marcel was quite overcome, he hugged and kissed Michael who took it with good grace. In his overwrought state, Marcel wanted to kiss everybody. He rushed towards Jimmy but caught the warning gleam in Jimmy's eyes and changed direction at the last minute to rush up for a farewell hug with one of the girl dancers instead. Michael wondered if Marcel realised if he had gone through with his intention, Jimmy would have beaten the crap out of him. He left the club on a flurry of tears, blown kisses and a huge bouquet of flowers that some bright spark had organised. Marcel loved them all and caressing his bouquet, which he thought was so kind of everyone, he rushed sobbing into the arms of his understanding man friend. When he had left, all breathed a sigh of relief and stiff shoulders visibly sank to a more comfortable stature. Jimmy broke the silence. Rubbing his hands together and walking resolutely to the bar he shouted to everyone present, "I need a drink, don't know about you lot." Everyone laughed and joined him. Within the hour the club area was empty leaving Michael to survey his club, his excitement was tinged with an undercurrent of apprehension. It was now his to run as he saw fit and he could not wait. It would actually be run the same as Marcel with one big difference, no flopping arms and wiggling.

At 22 years old nature had taken a perverse turn. When Michael was young he always looked at least 2-3 years younger and this had worked very well for him. Now when you looked at him you saw a slightly receding hairline around the temples making his forehead look much larger. He had taken to slicking his hair back with grease to look like Johnny and Jimmy, definitely the in-style. This lost him the curls that were once admired and made his nose, which had developed the bump in the middle and hook on the end look enormous. He never grew any taller and stayed at 5' which made him shorter than a lot of the girls working there but his rotund figure made him look even shorter, he blamed Mrs A's cooking. If someone had to guess his age, most people would say 30 years old. Michael was certainly no oil painting, but nature did compensate by making his eyes even darker looking and deep enough to drown in. Over the years he had developed a confident, comfortable charm and an aura, a presence about him that women found irresistible. His latest girlfriend Maude was a dancer that had just joined the group. Dancers came and went frequently. Maude had thought Michael from a distance was ugly. When they spoke for the first time, within ten minutes Maude was hooked. She told the other girls that when you looked into his eyes and got to know the real him, he was the most beautiful person in the whole world. Michael had been out with most of them and they knew what she meant. He might look a womaniser but each one of them knew he was still there for them. He was their lover, confidant, and friend. Michael knew more secrets than any priest in a confessional and he never told.

He ran the club as if it was his life's mission to make it a success. His style developed quickly and he made it part of his job to escort customers to their tables. He fussed over the women and in a short while got to know their names. It was usual for customers arriving to wait to be shown to their tables by Michael. The women would say, "No we'll wait for Angel. He knows where we like to sit." Angel had been informed that Mr and Mrs Dagenhart were waiting for their table and Michael as was his habit would open his arms and say "Show Time," and leave what he was doing to escort them to their table.

"Mr and Mrs Dagenhart good evening. I'm so sorry not to have been waiting for you to arrive. Someone has to pacify the chef. He is so temperamental but his cooking is exquisite so we must keep him happy." Michael wondered if this sounded a little like Marcel, he hoped not. "Mrs Dagenhart you look wonderful tonight. The dress, is it new? It's so gorgeous. The new bracelet, a present? It looks expensive, you've got good taste Mr Dagenhart. Was it for an anniversary, birthday, or just for being wonderful you?" No-one could get a word in edgeways but Mrs Dagenhart was lapping it up. "I'm going to seat you where everyone can see you, you look too divine to sit out of sight, is that alright?" Michael never waited for an answer and none was given, it was accepted that he knew best. He seated the couple, fussed with the table just to ensure that they knew he was concerned everything was perfect and called a waiter to bring the menu. "Have a wonderful evening, and Mr Dagenhart, watch Mrs Dagenhart, I fear someone will try and steal her if you don't." Michael left them with a nod of the head that was nearly a bow and a smile. Mr Dagenhart thought he was a nancy boy but Mrs Dagenhart loved him.

The secret, if that is what it was, of Michael's charm was his ability to sense how a woman was feeling and what at that time she wanted to hear. His charm was always based in a truth however thinly stretched. He reasoned that even a hideous dress that did nothing for the wearer, had a beauty and charm that a less sensitive soul would miss.

The club was fully booked most nights. This had the

effect on customers of panic booking. Most bookings were for one month ahead. Solid bookings for a month was a big step up. The entertainment improved and Michael was auditioning for singers and comedians. At the last meeting with Alfredo and Johnny it was decided that the KitKat Club was pulling in trade from all other areas of Chicago and a better class of cabaret was needed. The dancers got new costumes that were skimpier but tasteful, but a classy singer was needed, preferably a man as the male customers had the dancers to watch. Michael spent many boring hours listening to so called professional singers, none had come anywhere near the standard he was looking for.

Michael was eating at the club most days. He had very little time off. He started at noon and finished about 1 a.m. His days off were spent with whoever was the girl of the moment. He had taken to asking tailors to visit him at work to measure and fit new suits because he had little time. He wore only the best cut suits in the best materials. He knew his shape was difficult and a good suit made the best of a bad job. Sometimes there was a procession of people coming to see him at the club, his manicurist, barber, shoes were brought in to show him and anything else he needed. His bedroom at the new apartment now had three wardrobes for his clothes. Jimmy poked fun and took to reminding him of his past and the state he used to dress in. "Think you got too close to Marcel Angel, some of his ways have definitely rubbed off." Michael laughed, "Well give us a kiss big boy." Jimmy gave him a good natured punch on the arm and reminded him, "Talk like that and I'll kick your head in." Everyone knew Michael's reputation with the girls so no worries on that score.

Mrs A. and Michael had moved apartments. A two-bedroom apartment around the corner from Stella and Jimmy was found. Mrs A's fortunes continued to improve and she could afford to buy new furniture. . She told Stella that Michael's new job deserved a better place in keeping with his position. She had taken to talking about Michael as if he were her son and she somehow was responsible for his rise in status. "Well as a young boy I always said he would do well. Wholesome food is good for the brain and Michael has always had the best." Mrs A. was very proud of Michael. Every week she was invited to join him for a meal at the club. She had bought some special dresses for these occasions. Michael knew how to put on a good show for her. She was taken to the club by cab and escorted into the club whereupon Michael showed her to her table. They never had less than four waiters fussing over them. Customers in the club would turn and stare wondering who this important lady was. Mrs A. seeing the interest would wave regally at all those staring. For her it was the event of the week and she would plan her clothes and hairdo in readiness. On her birthday Michael arranged for a particularly popular and handsome singer to announce her birthday and lead everyone to sing Happy Birthday and then presented a bouquet of flowers and a kiss. Mrs A. would always try to look coy and embarrassed by the attention but failed miserably. She wallowed in it. Michael was the most precious thing in her life, which was pleasant but had its draw backs. She soaked up every detail he gave her about work, amusing stories of customers, new entertainment, even down to buying new table clothes. Mrs A. would always give her opinion on what she thought was best for the club and Michael always listened with interest and then ignored all suggestions. Michael stopped telling her about his girlfriends. Mrs A. did not like any of the girls he had been with. She was always telling him, "Michael, they are sluts, you could do much better. Why do you need them? You're happy here with me aren't you?" Michael realised it had been many years since Mrs A. had been with a man but how could she have forgotten so much? With time on her hands she had got wily in her old age. He started to get the breathless, I'm not well treatment.

"Michael, please stay in today. I know it's your only day off but I've got a pain in my chest and I'm frightened to be alone."

This worked for a while but she cried wolf many times and Michael had his life to get on with. Her temptation of preparing a nice meal for him did not work either, it did not hold the same allure as the girl waiting to enjoy his company.

Tony and Michael rarely crossed paths. If Michael saw him at all it was funny but his scar would itch. They had not spoken since that night. Alfredo and Johnny ensured he was not around the club and its customers, they still did not trust him. Tony obviously still hated Michael, even from a distance the glowering hateful eyes bore into him. Michael could handle that. Tony was a psycho and best ignored.

CHAPTER SEVENTEEN

Sting in the Tail

It was a Monday night, the night Mrs A. was expected at the club for her weekly dose of stardom. As usual, Michael had saved the best table for her. He had chosen Mondays as the slackest night of the week but fortunately the club was always 90% full. As usual, the table was laid with special flowers, she loved roses. The waiters were primed. Michael always ensured she had waiters, men still gave her much pleasure, even if she had forgotten what you are supposed to do with them. "Poor old girl," he thought, "she loved the fuss they made over her." Michael often thought how unfair her life had been. A good woman like her should have had the type of husband who stood by her and loved her. He knew all she wanted was to be loved. Well he loved her very much and would ensure she felt loved by everyone, even if he had to get hired help to create the illusion. It cost Michael every Monday to ensure she had a good evening. The waiters were tipped well, the singer who made a point of singing a song to her was given a good tip, not to mention the meal itself. Mrs A. had never been one for stinting on food but for many years now she had indulged in many culinary delights of a sweet and creamy nature. At the club she would always have a starter and a dinner and after a ten minute break she would order what she said was the best part of the meal, the sweet. She had access to the full range of all sweets on offer and always would be quite perplexed to decide which one she would have. The same game would be played every week with the waiter, as usual, agreeing the choice was impossible. The problem would be solved after much heart rending when she would decide to have three different ones. "Don't want to show favouritism do I?" she would say. Michael ensured the chef had some of her favourites on the menu, this also cost him in a backhander. All in all the evening was very expensive, but so worth it for the pleasure it gave Mrs A. and Michael as well. It was wonderful to see Mrs A. pink cheeked, enjoying the attention. He often wondered about the past and how he would never have been able to imagine himself in this position. It felt good to share his good fortune with someone. The Monday night with Mrs A had been happening for one year now but standards were never allowed to fall. Everyone working there knew how special Mrs A was to Michael and everyone knew how important Michael was becoming. This ensured no-one let the side down. Everything was timed and worked like clockwork. It was 8 o'clock and the cab had been dispatched at 7.30 p.m. Mrs A. would arrive at 8.10 p.m. Everyone was on cue to play their part in her evening.

At 8.30 p.m. Michael was feeling irritated. "If the fucking cab has fucking let me down, he's fucking sacked." By 8.45 p.m. Michael sent someone else to check what had happened. Michael may be joining Mrs A. for a meal but he was still on duty and would not leave the club. At 9 p.m. Stella rushed in and took Michael to the kitchen to talk to him. Michael was strutting up and down by this point. All his well oiled plans, which had been played out every week for a year, and this happens. He knew how much the evening meant to Mrs A. and he felt humiliated. He said in Stella's direction, "If I can't get one old lady's evening right, how can anyone have confidence in me to run the whole place. Heads will fucking roll somewhere."

Stella sat him down and asked him to calm down and listen. "Mrs A's been taken to the hospital." Michael sat not taking everything in but getting the gist of the odd words such as heart attack, alive, dangerous condition, will know in 24 hours. He nodded at every word that Stella uttered. When she had finished Michael got up to walk out.

"Where are you going?"

"The hospital of course. She needs me there." Michael was too calm. Stella grabbed her bag and rushed after him.

"You're not going by yourself young man. I'll take you there." On the way through the club, Stella grabbed a bemused waiter and pulled him along, urgently whispering to him that Angel was going to the hospital and find someone to take over. Michael did not alter his stride and looked at no-one, Stella had a job to keep up with him. She grabbed him at the front door and led him to her car. He said nothing on the journey there, looking straight ahead with unfocussed eyes. Stella told him again Mrs A. was still alive, she was getting the best of treatments and all the usual things of she'll be up and about before you know it. Michael said nothing. At the hospital Stella led Michael to Mrs A's room. She was not on a ward but had a room of her own. Michael sat down beside the bed and just looked at her. Stella left them alone and sat outside in the corridor not knowing what she could do. After a while Michael came out looking his usual self. and obviously in control. "Stella please get the Doctor now. I want to know her condition. I'll telephone the club while you do that, I want flowers in here. When she comes round I want the room to look beautiful. Why isn't a nurse with her the whole time?" Pleased to be doing something and without questioning him, Stella went to find a nurse and the Doctor.

Irritated, Michael listened to the Doctor telling him Mrs A. was critical and they would have to wait for the next 24 hours to see how she responds. "Can't you do anything else? Have we just got to sit here and wait?" The Doctor was tired but patiently explained everything that could be done was being done and would he please keep his voice down. Michael sat and held Mrs A's hand through the night. At 5 a.m. she died without regaining consciousness. The Doctor was on hand and pronounced her dead. Michael swiftly turned on the Doctor, his voice was full of anger but his eyes were pleading. "Why didn't you do more? She can't die!" The Doctor took Michael by the arm and led him to an empty office and sat him down. He could see Michael wrestling with every emotion and losing. For a few minutes the Doctor looked at Michael and with a sigh leaned forward and gently explained, "Mrs Arkinshaw's heart was worn out Mr Angelo. How long has she been such a big woman? If she had been like that for many years her heart had gone into overdrive to cope." Michael slumped forward, all the anger that had kept his body stiff and his back ramrod straight had given way to defeat, dejected and defeated he said, "She had always been a big woman but had got bigger over the last few years."

In kindness, and with an element of truth, because Stella had been giving Mrs A's history to the hospital, the Doctor said, "Well, I'm surprised she lasted this long. I understand you have been taking care of her, I would say you gave her more years than she would have been entitled to, and very happy ones at that from what I have been told." He got up and helped Michael to the door and said, "You need some rest so go home and get some sleep Mr Angelo." Michael nodded and abstractly thanked the Doctor and left, all the fight had gone out of him.

Stella had waited all night in the corridor. She was very fond of Mrs A, they had got a little closer over the past years. With all night to reflect Stella pinpointed the change in Mrs A. to when she and Jimmy came back from holiday. She smiled to herself when she remembered that when they got back Mrs A. had arranged for flowers to be delivered as a homecoming surprise. The romantic holiday had continued with Jimmy sweeping her in his arms and carrying her to the bedroom as soon as they arrived home, only to be interrupted at a delicate moment by the delivery boy ringing their bell with Mrs A's thoughtful gift. Yes, she continued to be annoying, but Mrs A. had softened towards Stella and allowed her to see the real person underneath. They had become the friends Stella had always wanted.

Stella grabbed Michael as he left the Doctor's room, he may not know what he was doing but Stella did. She took Michael home and made some coffee. They both sat and cried and consoled each other. This hurt him more than his mother dying. He was not sure how he would get over it. After Stella left he went to bed to escape into sleep. He slept fitfully the rest of the day and some of the following night. He went to find Stella the following morning. He was fully in control again. " I found Mrs A's money stash. Do you know she had $600 under a loose floorboard?"

"Michael, I tried to get her to put it in a bank but she would have none of it," Stella tried to excuse herself as if it was her fault.

"Please, I know what Mrs A. was like. She was a stubborn old lady," Michael found himself laughing. "Never did what she didn't want to do." It was good to see Michael more his old self and Stella was pleased to see it.

"I'm going to arrange the best funeral this money can buy. You leave everything to me Stella. Her kids have never contacted her or that bastard of a husband, they'll never get a nickel of her money. She is going to have a funeral in the style she would have liked."

True to his word, on the day of the funeral Michael had ordered the most expensive funeral cortege in Chicago. A black hearse with gold carriage lamps and four of the blackest, sleekest, proudest looking horses to pull it. He had chosen the most expensive coffin with gold handles. The flowers were the finest roses of every colour to be found in Chicago and so many of them that it took the four other carriages to hold them all. The laundry was closed for a day of mourning and all the workers attended the funeral. The pall bearers were dressed in the finest black outfits, with top hats and four led procession on the mile walk to the church. Such a show had not been seen before. The solemn pall bearers walking in front of the hearse, with the proud horses walking in perfect unison following, the blooming array of so many perfect roses in vivid and pastel colours created an impressive dignified sight. Neighbours stood on the street to watch with heads bowed but with eyes looking at such a magnificent parade much to Michael's satisfaction, "They are all paying their respects to a fine lady Mrs A," he whispered as if she was there. The priest had been well primed and said some wonderful things about Mrs A all of which Michael knew to be true. The coffin was lowered and the flowers were arranged around the grave. In six months time, when the ground had settled, Mrs A. would have the biggest tomb stone with Angels carved in the marble and she would rule the graveyard. In years to come when people visited the cemetery their eyes went immediately to the tall stone. They often wondered who warranted such a monument, they knew she was greatly loved by her son Michael, the inscription said so.

A day after the funeral Michael and Stella were called to the Solicitors Office. Messrs Davis, Davis and Penman were Solicitors for the Laundry business. They were surprised to learn that they had been called to hear the last will and testament of Mrs Beatrice Arkinshaw. Stella and Michael looked at each other, "Did you know about this Michael?" Stella asked. Non-plussed, Michael shook his head. Mr Davis left out at that point all the legal paraphernalia and quoted Mrs A's words. With great dignity, he told Michael and Stella, he remembered sitting with Mrs Arkinshaw to compose the will and how he had to argue about some of her wording. He informed them Mrs A. wanted to use words that were not dignified and not appropriate for a legal document. He continued and quoted Mrs A's wording that she had said that her husband and children had deserted her and had not been seen for many years and therefore her beneficiaries were to be Stella Cane and Michael Angelo. Stella and Michael had laughed at the mention of her husband, they both knew the word Mrs A. would have argued about. The will went on to say that Stella had been the driving force in the Laundry and Mrs A. wanted her to inherit her share of the business. She thanked Stella for putting up with her ways and acknowledged she owed her so much and had changed her life for the better. Michael was left anything else that Mrs A. owned, which was her furniture and bits of jewellery she had started to acquire and any money, found in the apartment. Her last sentence was to Michael that read, "I wish more than anything else I had been your real mother. You are the son I wished for. I love you." Stella and Michael sat numbed. Mr Davis excused himself and gave them time to talk. Stella was the first to start. "How did she manage to make a will by herself and why? Why would she do such a wonderful thing?" Michael thought, and remembered, he turned to Stella, smiling and tears in his eyes he tried to control the quiver in his voice.

"A few years ago she said she wanted to do something for you as gratitude for your hard work and to make amends for her thoughtlessness," Michael was still as tactful as ever. "This must have been what she came up with. I think this is so Mrs A, I am proud of her for doing this. Michael struggled to continue, the tears getting in the way of his vocal cords. "You know she was a generous woman but sometimes she didn't want anyone to know how kind she really was." Stella agreed, she had recently got an inkling of the real Mrs A. In unison they reached for their hankies, blew their noses and coughed to control the emotion.

Mr Davis returned and brought a business like attitude to the room. He concluded the meeting with an instruction that he would see Stella in a few days to sign papers making her the sole owner of Chicago Laundry. He wished them farewell and they left to talk some more about Mrs A's will. Stella offered to help Michael clear out Mrs A's clothes and anything Michael did not want to keep. He readily took her up on that one and they agreed to sort it out within the next few days. Michael took over the rent of the apartment and moved himself into Mrs A's bedroom which was bigger than his and he would leave his wardrobes in his old bedroom, giving him room to order a large double bed.

No one except Stella knew how much Michael missed Mrs A. She made it her business to spend at least a few hours a week alone with Michael to chat and go over old times, good and bad. Many tears were shed, much laughter over incidents and sayings of Mrs A, but all good stuff and very therapeutic. No one but Michael and Stella really knew Mrs A. At work, Michael was his old self, nothing got in the way of good business. The only difference any one could see to Michael was he became a little insular and instead of pursuing any girl of interest, he gave them all a miss for quite a few months. Jimmy was still pulling his leg at every opportunity and was of the opinion that maybe he was becoming another Marcel. Michael adored Jimmy, but could not tell him that at the moment he was of no use to any girl and his equipment had gone on strike in mourning for Mrs A. He knew this was temporary but all the girls he had dated, gorgeous as they were, and as comforting as they were, had no brain and would not understand how he felt. He was feeling restless and wanted a relationship in the future that offered more than just bed. He found it hard to believe he would think this way but he knew he wanted a soul mate, someone to talk to who could discuss things other than clothes or the latest hairdo. What he had with Mrs A. was something undefinable. They were easy with each other, they understood each other. He wondered if he would find that in any girl, he wanted something he could not put into words very badly. If he could not have this with a girl he did not want any of them. Work, that was his love, he would be the best in the whole of Chicago, nothing else mattered.

Michael was to bury everything in his work. Stella sensed a striving that was not fulfilling in him and she did not know what to do to help him.

CHAPTER EIGHTEEN

Trouble and Strife

Stella had problems of her own. The business was doing great. They now had twenty women working shift work through the day and night. Charles was running the Laundry and she had no problems there. Stella had worked hard to get more business and they now had a good percentage of hotels and clubs on their books, these were the mainstay of the business. Stella's input into the business was easier now. They had got the delivery van and Stella insisted it drive around Chicago even if there were no deliveries to be made. Charles was finding it hard to keep her satisfied. With more time on her hands Stella could be a pain in the neck and wanted to interfere with his side of the work. At times Stella's old temper would raise its ugly head and cause Charles to smooth ruffled feathers with workers and sometimes with customers. He did not understand why sometimes she was very business like, and other times a total bitch. He walked a fine line most of the time and considered leaving the laundry as an option on more than one occasion. If Stella had known she would have been devastated. She had come to rely on him totally. He was an excellent manager and was running the laundry with the precision of an Army General, but the women working there respected him and he maintained a high standard.

Only Stella could explain her mood swings. She had many worries to carry. She was now in her thirties and many questions were being thrown at her by Jimmy, the main one being why no kids. She had examined her feelings many times and came to the conclusion that the only person she really wanted was Jimmy. Jimmy had other ideas. He had always wanted children but this had never happened, despite his many efforts in that direction. He loved Stella but wanted more. She had been to all the recognised Doctors in Chicago to find out why she had not fallen pregnant. Nothing could be found amiss with her. All Doctors had come to the conclusion that Stella was either not relaxed enough, or not having sex at the right time. What ever the reason, she should have been able to become pregnant. Jimmy was not asked to have any tests because, as he said to Stella, there was nothing wrong with him and he was ready willing and able at all times. Specialists were advancing their knowledge but they still had far to go. If no children were conceived it must be the woman's fault. In the later decades they would have found out that the man could have a low sperm count and this was the problem, but not in the 1920's. Stella carried a big disappointment that it was her fault. It had caused a small but deep chasm in her relationship with Jimmy. As he always was saying. Marriage is about family. Without children what is a marriage. He would always finish this much used statement with a kiss and hug for Stella, telling her she was the most important thing in his life, but the dye was cast. Stella felt useless. It was her fault they did not have children and there it was, nothing else to be said. Her whole being was set in pleasing Jimmy and she had let him down. All her motherly instincts and love was geared and generated towards Jimmy. She did not feel the need for children, she had no maternal instinct towards them at all but she wanted them for Jimmy. All the tests had been embarrassing, humiliating and worthless. After many years of wanting children for Jimmy she realised she had to find something else to please him. Her long term plan had been for his early retirement but he was still only 45 years old and she would work to allow him to retire even earlier. What else did she have to offer?

Stella had started putting the idea in Jimmy's head. "You know, it might be worth thinking about honey. If you left the club and came to work at the laundry you would be such an asset to the business. There would be no more late nights or working such long hours, we could have more time together." Jimmy ignored Stella's suggestions. He did not want to leave the club. He liked the work, they were all his friends there, the girls were nice to watch. He had respect and was comfortable in his work. The club had a buzz about it, prohibition added a crackle of risk that was exciting. The laundry was women's work and deadly dull at that. Stella kept getting no response and finally pushed Jimmy too far. After months of being ignored and pushed aside with throw away comments of later, not now, and I'll think about it,

Stella became insistent, "You've got to leave Jimmy, it's getting dangerous and I want to protect you."

"Protect me?" Jimmy's voice boomed, "who are you Stella? I'm the man of the house and I do the protecting. I'm sick of hearing about the laundry. I have a job, and I will leave when I say so. You don't order me about like a little laundry woman! I do the men's work and you should be doing the women's work, so leave me alone."

The women's work stung and reached home. The only work Stella knew he was talking about was having children. The red mist started to film over her eyes but before she opened her mouth, incensed and misunderstood, she became overcome by tears that would not stop. To escape the frustration, she fled to the bathroom and locked the door. Jimmy angry with himself and Stella left the apartment and slammed the door, the vibration shook the bathroom walls.

Everyone noticed that Jimmy was not his usual affable self at the club but men do not interfere in each other's problems unless asked. They hoped he would sort out what ever it was and be his old self again. The women, being more inquisitive would ask if something was wrong, any such conversation going along those lines would be cut dead with him saying he was fine. Stella on the other hand would have loved someone to talk to, but there was no-one she trusted. So her work life revolved around being a cold, sharp, business woman to exploding into rage on the whim of trivia. She was becoming known as "The Bitch" by the laundry women who interpreted her moods as, "The Bitch getting above herself." She was treated coldly but respectfully by the laundry workers but she knew she was not liked and did not understand why. Stella was having a hard time, she knew she was a decent caring woman, she did not understand why she was so misunderstood by everybody. She reacted to all outside hostility, including Jimmy by retreating into herself. For nearly a year life was miserable and lonely for Stella and Jimmy. Neither knew what to do about the situation, and neither had any one to talk to. Jimmy was spending more and more time at the club, he and Stella saw each other less and less. It had to come to a head.

Strong as Stella was, she could not cope any longer with the situation. It felt to her there was hostility everywhere she turned. Jimmy was distant and she hardly ever saw him. Her head gradually filled with pain and anguish until it felt ready to burst. She wondered what the point of everything was. Even Charles at the laundry seemed hostile. Life was flat and grey and why continue, no one would miss her she reasoned. Even Angel was too busy to see her with working in that club. After 10 months of losing weight, losing confidence, and losing rational thoughts something had to change and quick. Jimmy being Jimmy, stayed miserable but did nothing to make the situation better. He did not understand what had happened or how things had got so bad, he buried his head in the sand and hoped it would go away. He had a few distractions that helped, like Gina, one of the waitresses. She had been flirting with him for a while which he enjoyed. He had neither the brains nor the sense to see what was going on. After working around girls for many years, one would have expected him to know a little of the feminine ways. Michael had been watching Gina play her games with amusement, but the smile was wiped off his face when he saw Jimmy encouraging her and she was taking this as an invitation for more. Flirting was fine but what would be the next step? Michael knew that one only too well. It was a step he did not think Jimmy saw coming. When they next met for a beer in the club they chatted about the girls as usual, Michael mentioned Gina and how she was coming on to him. Jimmy shrugged and said that it was just a bit of fun, no more. Michael knew there were problems with him and Stella and before the idiot did something he would regret he decided to talk to Stella.

He had not seen Stella for some months. Well the club was going great guns and with everything else, he did not see anyone much outside of the club. He was surprised when Stella answered the telephone, he thought she might be out as usual. He arranged to see her tomorrow morning before he went to the club. He was not sure, but he thought Stella was not herself. She sounded distant, not like her at all. Perhaps she was in the middle of something reasoned Michael. The next morning, feeling a little guilty, Stella was literally just round the corner, he could have visited before. He was not sure what he was going to say, but decided to play it by ear. Stella opened the door, it was 9 am and she was still in her dressing gown, not like her at all. Her hair was a mess and she obviously had not washed yet. Embarrassed, and with one hand trying to stroke her hair into shape she let him in.

"Sorry I'm still like this Michael, bad night, haven't got going yet. To tell you the truth I forgot you were coming."

He thought this strange because "Miss Efficiency" always remembered appointments, she was a neat and tidy person which he had always admired. Stella always had everything in the right place. Now she looked as if she had forgotten what the right place was.

"Stella what's up with you? Are you unwell?" Michael was worried. Stella mumbled as if everything was an effort, "No I'm fine, don't worry, I'll make some coffee – have you got time?"

"Sure, plenty of time thank you," Michael thought he would make time, this needed sorting out. When the coffee was made and poured and they were comfortable Michael started.

"I don't know what the problem is between you and Jimmy. I know he is not himself, he is miserable and short tempered. You look dreadful. What I mean is I can see you are really unhappy too. You have got to get something sorted Stella." Michael hated to see her so down and wondered for a split second if he should talk about Gina. On quick reflection he reckoned it might do the trick. Leaning forward and taking Stella by the hand Michael gently started.

"I know Jimmy loves you very much." All he got was a resigned, "Huh," out of Stella. He was not going to be put off, "do you still love him?" asked Michael. Stella looked up at him from her lap. Something clicked and she did not like this. He was a kid! talking about her marriage.

"I'm not discussing this with you Michael. You're just a kid and this is for grownups to sort out. It's personal and does not involve anyone but Jimmy and me."

Michael sat back and laughed.

"Stella I'm 24 years old, not a kid anymore. I care for both of you, you know that. You were the happiest married couple I have ever seen. You two are good together, you're the beauty and the brains and Jimmy is the brawn. Perfect!"

He sat forward again talking in earnest. "Now someone has got to do something to put this right and Stella it's got to be you. You are the strong one."

Stella nodded at these words but was not convinced she wanted to do anything, she could not forgive Jimmy for letting all this happen and not trying to put things right. Michael could see Stella was interested, but only just, so he carried on in a soft whispering tone.

"You know what Jimmy is like. He doesn't understand women at all. There's a girl."

Stella leaned forward, nearly clashing heads with Michael, he could see her eyes misting over for a fight.

"Listen Stella, just listen before you say or do anything. She is flirting with Jimmy and he flirts back, always has done, means nothing to him, just harmless fun. I've been watching and I can see the girl is taking it further and she is very keen to have him.." He paused for breath and held his hands up to Stella, shaking his head.

"Nothing has happened, I swear to that. I know he doesn't even think past flirting, that's the God's honest truth."

Stella was watching him very closely, just about keeping herself in control. Michael paused for effect and checked how Stella was reacting.

"If you want him, I think you had better do something to keep him. I can tell, she is going to fight you for him given half a chance."

He had exaggerated a bit but he needed her attention and he obviously got it. Stella looked more animated now, the colour was in her cheeks and she started bobbing about in her chair.

"How dare she! Who is she? I'll sort Jimmy out don't you concern yourself about that! I'm coming to the club with you and I'll get this fucking sorted!" He had never heard Stella swear and he definitely had not planned for her to go to the club. Michael did not want Stella's temper spread all over the place. He needed to get control of this.

"Why don't you get yourself sorted out here and I'll ask Jimmy to pop home about, what do you think, 1 pm for lunch? It will give you a chance to talk in private. You know Jimmy, he means no harm, he's just a big bear that needs you to protect him."

Stella thought about that and he caught a glimmer of a smile on her lips.

"It's working," he thought smugly. He said his farewells to Stella and left for the club to tackle Jimmy.

As usual, when Michael walked into the club first thing he was met by a queue of queries waiting for him. Suppliers wanted to see him, he got notice of waiters/waitresses who would be in late, off sick and the arrangements that needed to be made. There were always kitchen staff complaints, all of these were nothing out of the ordinary but all insisting on being dealt with immediately. Michael sorted all the trivia out and disappeared quickly to find Jimmy. He wanted to put this right as quickly as possible. He found out that Jimmy had gone on an errand and would be back by 12 noon. After all the rushing, Michael was fired up and raring to go, it was an anti-climax to have to wait, but wait he would. Stella was geared up and now he just had to work on Jimmy. He sat and thought about what he was doing and chuckled, what did he look like sorting out marriage problems. He reckoned if he was not careful Jimmy would give him a left hook for poking his nose in. He needed to think carefully what he was going to say to Jimmy.

At 12.30 am Jimmy arrived in a dishevelled state. He had a cut above his eye that the handkerchief held to his head did not stop the bleeding. His face had developed red marks that were threatening to turn into bruises. Jimmy was busy re-arranging his clothing. The jacket would need sewing on the sleeve he noticed. Out of the corner of his eye he spotted Michael.

"Just a little scrap with some tough guys. Think I look bad! You should have seen them," he laughed.

"Are you OK?"

"I'm fine. Part of the job Angel. They won't bother us again."

"Leone's boys?"

"Yea."

Michael had been hearing rumours that Leone's henchmen were leaning a bit, but this was the first time he had realised physical contact was being made. Jimmy had told him that some of their clients needed protection from the Leone lads who were getting a bit out of hand.

Apparently Leone and Alfredo had had meetings about this and Leone had apologised for his lads saying they meant no harm and were just being lively. Of course they both knew this was not true, but at the moment there was just a bit of pushing and shoving going on. Jimmy could handle that.

Michael took Jimmy for a beer, it was early but what the hell. Stella had been tricky but Jimmy was going to be even harder to handle. Michael leaned closer and in a quiet voice tested the water.

"I've been to see Stella today."

"Oh yea," Jimmy sounded cautious. Michael licked his lips, still not sure what to say but gave it a go.

"I think she needs you Jimmy. She looks terrible. She heard about Gina you know, don't know who told her."

"Gee, what low life would cause that sort of trouble. There is nothing between Gina and me, never will be."

Michael shrugged his shoulders and said, "There is always scumbags in this world. Stella really misses you, she said so."

Jimmy looked interested, "She said that?"

"Yea. I think she doesn't believe you would go off with another girl but she needs to hear it from you." Michael hoped he was on a roll, "She asks will you come home for lunch. I think she wants to put things right between you."

"She say that?"

"Yea. I think you will be pleasantly surprised."

"I'll go now shall I?"

"What a good idea Jimmy. No holding you when you make up your mind."

Jimmy left in a hurry. Michael sat back and took a sip of his beer. "God" he thought, "wait 'till he finds out who the scumbag is. I'm going to be in trouble."

Jimmy arrived home full of hope. He was greeted by a carefully made up, coiffured and beautifully dressed Stella. His appreciative smile left his face as Stella ran up to him screeching and slapping and crying. He definitely was not expecting this and was caught off guard. After much scratching, slapping, grunting and grappling, Jimmy grabbed Stella's hands and tried to calm her down. She was not going to be stopped and in a tornado of fury she kicked and bit him. One kick hit target and he let go of her to grab his crotch. Stella stopped, looked, and shocked at what she had done, plonked down in a chair watching him open mouthed.

"Oh God Jimmy, what have I done. I'm sorry."

Between wincing and gasping, his huge frame doubled up in front of her, he looked up with such bewilderment she wanted to hug him but she stopped herself.

"Why? What's going on here? What's got into you Stella?"

She helped him sit down beside her. The tears started and she gasped, "You don't want me any more but you take up with that tart Gina. How could you!"

He wanted to laugh at such a silly pathetic reason for all of this but had the sense to contain it. In his softest and gentlest voice looking straight into her eyes he said, "Stella, Stell, I love you. I don't want anyone else."

They spent the afternoon talking, crying and kissing and reassuring. Jimmy reassured in the best way he could. He took Stella in his arms and carried her to the bedroom. Tenderly he reaffirmed his deep love for her and she received him deeply, willingly, and truly. He took the rest of the day off work. This caused speculation amongst the staff because Jimmy never took time off without good notice. Michael laughed when anyone mentioned it to him. He knew things were going well. He felt a little smug the rest of the evening and had more of a stupid grin on his face than usual.

Next time Stella saw Michael she scolded him for interfering. She looked at him like a little kid and even pointed her finger as you do to children. "Remember this young man, adults sort out their own problems and your meddling could have made things worse. I forgive you this time, but in future keep out of it."

Jimmy was no better telling Michael his gossip had caused him no end of trouble with Stell, but he had sorted it. Next time he was told very sharply to mind his own business. Michael did not expect thanks but he thought, "Fuck 'em! Next time he'd leave them to it." Still, it was good to see them both back together. Stella was busy being her bossy, chirpy self and Jimmy felt in control.

CHAPTER NINETEEN

Fallen Angel

The meeting of Michael and Clementine Desserie was
not blessed by heaven. Sweet music, birds singing and
fireworks it was not. But it did start with a bang.
Michael was working as usual and backing out of the
kitchen with a tray full of bits and bobs to put on the
restaurant tables he backed straight on to Clemmie. She
went down like a ton of bricks pulling Michael and tray
on top of her. After an unbelievably long silence, both in
shock and clearly shaken, they got up off the floor.
Michael careful to remove his hands from her chest as
delicately as possible, she glad to get his weight off her
and was careful not to bend her knee until he was up.
They both stood, looked, adjusted clothing and then
Clemmie in temper, went for him.

"You mother fucking fucker, what the fuck are you
doing?"

Michael was incensed and a little shaken himself, he
was not used to being spoken to in this manner, replied,
"Who the fuck are you talking to you fucking bitch?"

"I'm talking to a fucking fat, hook nosed midget.
Who the fuck do you think I'm talking to?" Clemmie

screamed in his face. Well this introduction went on for a while, each getting more angry and each out doing the other for shouting. The air was not exactly blue, more a putrid, maggot infested yellow. They eventually ran out of suitable adjectives and air. Clemmie took a deep breath, calmed herself and tried to find some semblance of dignity and said haughtily, "Midget! I'm here to see the Angel, pray tell me where to find him."

Michael, triumphant, and feeling oh so good, kept dignified and in his softest voice said, "Well honey, your prayers have been answered." With a sardonic smile he asked, "What can I do for you?"

The one minute silence was invented by Clemmie.

Various staff members were hanging around watching at this point. It was lucky the club was not open yet although the casino was, he hoped the punters did not hear the racket. Michael had found the whole incident distasteful. He blamed totally the girl for making him lose his cool.

Clemmie, flustered now, embarrassed to see the small group of people watching her, asked Michael if she may use the toilets to tidy herself up and perhaps they could start again. Michael agreed and watched as she grabbed her bags, straightened her back and walked off in the wrong direction. He sent someone to redirect her and smirked as she had to walk past him again going in the opposite direction. He thought she was handling herself with great dignity. Jimmy had been standing there and nudged Michael. "Hey Angel, nice looking girl, but gee what a mouth."

Michael hated women who swore, he thought they

looked and sounded like whores. This one was definitely a tart, her mouth was fouler than anything he had heard before. He would get rid of her as quickly as possible. He did not need any more waitresses or dancers. It was more than half an hour before she appeared again. Michael had gone back to working on organising setting up the club and had almost forgotten she was there. He turned from what he was doing, sensing someone watching him and he saw her. She had on a long dress which fitted in all the right places, and what places they were. Her hair, which had looked a mess, was now sleek and combed and tumbled over her right shoulder. She looked stunning and she knew it. With her head tilted down but her eyes looking straight at him she walked towards him slowly. The walk produced a roll of the hips that was only just contained by the dress, her breasts moved rhythmically giving the watcher plenty to imagine and dream about. She could see the walk was having the desired effect.

"Mr Angel, can we please start again?"

Michael had never been given this treatment before and was quite stunned. Manners won and he pulled himself together.

"Call me Angel, everyone does."

"Well, Angel, I came to audition as a singer. Would it be possible to sing for you now?"

Michael could think of a lot of things he would like her to do for him but singing was not one of them.

"I'm not actually auditioning for girl singers. What's your name by the way?"

"I'm Clementine Desserie, Angel."

The way she said Angel in a deep, chestnut voice held promises he wondered if she would keep. He knew he was not feeling very business like at the moment and pulled himself together.

"Look Miss Desserie …"

"Oh, call me Clemmie, everyone does," she interrupted. A smile played around her lips. Michael felt she was taking the piss out of him in a very gentle way. He was feeling decidedly off centre, a little flustered perhaps. He was the boss he reminded himself and regained his composure.

"Look, Clemmie, the band will be here in a short while, if you hang around, seeing as you have gone to so much trouble with the outfit and everything, I'll listen to you, but no promises. Ok?"

"That sounds very fair Mr, oh sorry, Angel."

"There she goes again," thought Michael, he was feeling even more sure she was taking the piss. He did not want to leave her, but he should not stay, he had work to do, he was a professional after all. He decided as the boss he must make a decision on where he was going, work was his priority.

"Would you like a drink while you wait, Clemmie?"

"Why Angel, thank you, yes please. A coffee would be nice."

Michael had sussed her game, she was playing with him. "Nice to meet another con artist," he thought. He was enjoying the game and hurried to get the coffee for them both. Michael came back and sat down opposite Clemmie. He took a sip of his coffee and watched her with hooded eyes. He put his cup and saucer on the table and leaned back. He relaxed and gave her his most charming smile.

"Well Clemmie, I must say you look good, and if I may say so, you are being most courteous. Tell me, what happened to the foul mouthed bitch I was talking to earlier?" He thought that might rattle her a little. She did not flinch, she put her cup and saucer down and leaned back in her chair. She looked down into her lap and slowly raised her head and gave him a stunning smile tinged with embarrassment.

"I was about to apologise for my behaviour, Angel."

"She's doing it again," thought Michael. "How can anyone make the name Angel sound so, so full of sexual promise and at the same time give the feeling she is making fun of him." He liked it.

Clemmie hesitated for a few seconds seeing the effect on Michael. With her most sincere look she said, "I can't apologise enough for the things I said. I was frightened and it was all such a shock I said things that I really didn't mean. Can you forgive me?" She knew he would, and he did. Clemmie felt a spark of something flying between them. She could not believe it, she had never felt particularly attracted to any man in this way. He was ugly and short. What did he have to make her feel this way. Michael was asking himself the same question. She was a looker alright, but she had something else, he could feel it, and he did not want it. He still thought she was common and all this come on she was giving him was an act to win him over, he knew that. "You can't con a con artist," he thought. They both sat and drank their coffee psyching each other out by looking relaxed and smiling at each other as if each were totally in control of the situation. Clemmie was enjoying this. Normally she could reduce any man, when worked on, to her way of thinking. It could be boring, no fun at all, it was too easy. Angel was parrying with her and she liked that. Michael heard a noise behind him and saw the band had arrived.

"Shit!" he thought "Is that the time already." He was way behind in his work. The kitchen staff had been sneaking looks at them in the club. Normally Angel was on their backs to get their act together for the evening meals. Someone had started a book on whether Clemmie would be hired or not. All those who witnessed the earlier collision reckoned not. The kitchen staff were getting a different idea. Jimmy appeared as usual. He liked to be around when the band arrived. Sometimes the dancers went through their routines with the band instead of just piano, and sometimes there were auditions and he enjoyed them. He was surprised to see Clemmie sitting with Angel. He thought Michael would have sent her packing. Jimmy saw her as nothing but trouble. He sauntered up to Angel and asked what was happening. Michael told him Clemmie was auditioning with the band. He invited Jimmy to stay and watch. The band had set up and Michael had a word with them. After much nodding of heads Michael shouted to Clemmie, "OK honey, let's see what you can do."

Michael and Jimmy sat at the table while Clemmie talked to the band. The music started and Clemmie took up her position in front of the microphone. She looked stunning but when she opened her mouth she had the voice of an angel. That was wrong because no angel would arouse such feelings. Her deep voice was like covering your naked body in velvet – deep, plush, warm and sensual. Her movements were slow and rhythmical and did something very disturbing to both men watching. They did not know what song was being sung, what ever it was, it was to them only and everything about her promised more. When she had finished and was thanking the band both Michael and Jimmy exhaled as if they had held their breath throughout the entire song.

"My God Angel, that girl is something else. What a voice, what movement. You have got to have her here."

Michael took another deep breath, relaxed and sat back nonchalantly, "You've changed your tune Jimmy. I can see what you mean though, rather good I thought, has potential I suppose."

Jimmy gave him a sideways look as if to say, who are you kidding!

Clemmie knew she was good and had seen their reaction so the job was in the bag.

"Well, Angel, do I get the job?" she asked coyly, already knowing the answer.

"Honey you are good, real good, but we are looking for male singers not female singers. I'll see what I can do. How about you contact me in one weeks time, and I'll let you know then."

With more good grace than Clemmie felt, she thanked Michael and said she would see him next week, and left.

"Angel, are you mad!" exclaimed Jimmy. "She's the best singer I've seen here for a long time. She'll do wonders in the club. Why did you do that, why let her wait?"

"That one has got a very high opinion of herself. Won't do her any harm to wait a week. Let her know who's boss." Michael laughed to himself. Jimmy was confused and did not see any sense in what Michael was doing. "What if she went elsewhere, another club would take her like a shot."

"I know her Jimmy, don't worry. She is hooked on working here. She thinks she has the measure of me, but I have the measure of her."

Jimmy still thought it a stupid way to work. He didn't understand the games they were playing, but Angel and Clemmie did.

Time was dragging. Michael counted it was another 5 days before he would see her again. For two days he had cursed himself for leaving it a week, he doubly cursed himself for not taking her address or telephone number. By the 5th day he was convincing himself she would not come back and he had run out of curses, he just felt stupid and such a fool. He remembered the way she had looked at him, her eyes glistening with the word play games, the hint of a smile, and oh yes, when she smiled well, the warmth just covered and enveloped him.. He was certain she was interested in him, but then, she was not like the others, she seemed to know him. She had touched a part of him that was locked away. Jimmy had noticed Michael's distraction and had put it down to lust. What he failed to see was Michael falling in love. By seventh day,

Michael was asking himself who the fuck was he kidding, she had found nothing attractive in him, after all, he was a short, fat dwarf, she said so herself. Any woman with her class would be furious at the way he had treated her, and gone for good. He would get to the club no earlier, maybe even later, he did not need the disappointment.

At 12 noon precisely Clemmie arrived at the club. She had angrily told herself not to be early, in fact, it would have been better not to come at all. Who needs this kind of aggravation and humiliation? Not her she kept telling herself. But here she was and fucking early too. She looked around for a table and picked one near the back. After fiddling with her hair and adjusting her hat she took a deep breath and sat down. An hour past and she was still arguing with her conscience about leaving now. In the end she told herself to shut the fuck up or she would scream. That seemed to do the trick.

At 1 p.m. Angel arrived, he gave a cursory look around and missed her completely. He gave an inward sigh and walked towards the kitchen.

"Angel, I'm over here," whispered Clemmie. Angel stopped, and before turning around, adjusted his face. Relief, pleasure, triumph all fought for supremacy.

"She came, she fucking came back!"

He turned to see her, his face might be adjusted but she saw the pleasure in his face, and he saw hers. She was really happy to see him again. As they both walked slowly towards each other, each was frantically promising themselves not to screw it up this time, no more games. After deep breaths and flapping and waving of hands, they both sat down opposite each other.

"I, eh, want to, eh, apologise for my treatment of you last week." Michael was finding this hard. Triumph could have been hers for the taking but, restraint and good manners must prevail, and she had promised herself to behave.

"I, think I most probably deserved it Angel. It was a difficult meeting for both of us."

Michael nodded, once too many times. "Let's go back and start again, what do you think?"

"Fine, I think you are right," she nodded with intense meaning at this profound statement. Clemmie was feeling very awkward. This conversation was stilted, and unreal, but at least he was trying.

"You have a wonderful voice and the club would be pleased to have you here. How about starting Friday?" He studied her reaction and it was favourable. "Why wait until Friday?" she asked.

"Well, I hoped I was being fair to you and giving you some rehearsal time." He was studying her closely, the glistening eyes were not far away, although they were being held at bay by a professional and understanding mask. God! she was beautiful he thought. He licked his lips, unsure of his next move. "I thought it would be good to get to know each other better," he hesitated slightly, "professionally speaking of course."

"Of course," she echoed. He sensed the joke was not far behind her words. Nevertheless, he limped on, "I figure the best way would be over dinner. What about tonight?"

"I'd love to," she replied, a tad too quickly for her liking. He exhaled and relaxed, he hadn't realised until then how tense he had been. What the hell was she doing to him, he hardly knew her. It was arranged that she would come to his apartment at 8 p.m. for supper. They had both agreed that a quiet dinner at his place would allow them to talk undisturbed. They kidded no-one, each knew what would happen. They said goodbye, they even shook hands. Both felt this was peculiar but appropriate. Michael went back to work. The kitchen staff noticed his distraction. No shouting orders, nitpickingly watching them work just Michael in a trance-like state, humming some unknown badly composed tune. They reckoned it was the girl, they had watched the performance of the two in the club. A new book was started on the odds of how long it would last.

At 7 p.m. on the dot a slinky dressed and heavily perfumed Clemmie pressed the bell of Angel's apartment. She liked the area, she noted it was a lot classier than her area. Before she had time to adjust her hair for the umpteen time, the door opened to an excitable, nervous, and much more amenable Angel.

"Thank you for coming, come in, and welcome." He ushered her into the apartment, helped her with her coat and asked to be excused because the food was at a crucial stage. "Make yourself comfortable Clemmie, I won't be a minute," he shouted from the kitchen. Clemmie was not a nosy person, but she was a woman after all, she liked to note the touches that people made to homes that made them unique. She gave the parlour a wide scrutinising sweep. The place was confusing. It looked like it belonged to someone else. It was far too feminine for a man, with chintzy curtains and doilies everywhere.

The furniture was comfortable but really heavy, like older people have. She noted it was very clean, and everything was just so, the angle of the pictures on the sideboard was perfection. She reckoned a ruler would have been needed to make them so straight and each space between was identical. The pictures caught her attention and she went to look picking each one up to study. They were all of the same woman. Perhaps his mother. She was a large lady with a kindly face. He obviously adored her because a small vase containing a fresh rose stood in perfect symmetry between two of the pictures. "Shit," she thought, "I've messed his arrangement of pictures up." She tried to put them back as she found them but failed. Clemmie was not one of life's tidy people. Michael appeared as she was trying to rearrange the photos, he had two drinks in his hand.

"Don't worry about them, come and sit down and have a drink." Michael realised it had been a long time since anyone new had been to his apartment. "They are pictures of my mother, Mrs A."

"Why do you call her Mrs A?" Clemmie was intrigued.

"Long story, I'll tell you later if you are interested. Now, let's talk about you." Michael settled himself down and waited.

"Gee Angel, what do you want to know? When I was born, or where I have sung before, or something else?" She felt a bit prickly, this was not what she hoped the evening would be, it sounded like another interview. They settled on talking about the KitKat Club first. Michael explained how it had risen in popularity over the past years. He told her about Marcel and she laughed at Angel's description of him. He told her about some of the customers who came and the funny little anecdotes that were associated with them. Clemmie laughed and laughed. She had a throaty warm infectious laugh that made him dig deep for any anecdote that would keep her laughing. By 9 p.m. the food was near ruination but neither wanted to stop the intimate pleasure. Reluctantly Angel stood and offered Clemmie his arm.

"We've got to eat, I've been slaving over a hot stove for you, so please let me escort you to the table." She nodded gracefully and proffered her hand. He led her to the adjacent dining room. The table seemed full of flowers. All colours of roses she noted. The crystal wine goblets glistened and twinkled as the candle flame flickered with the movement of the air. The room was bathed in a warm glow. She was captivated by the scene and looked at Michael agog. "Did you do this?" He nodded. "It's beautiful and," she hesitated, she was going to say romantic but thought that may be forward of her, instead she said, "artistic." He nodded his thanks. He was pleased she liked it. It had taken him hours of arranging and rearranging to get that feeling. He helped her to her chair and excused himself while he fetched the dinner.

They ate in a comfortable silence, each stealing glances at the other. He not believing his luck and she, well, she wondering what it was about him that made her feel so good, sort of comfortable, warm and protected, he felt like the big sofa in the other room, she choked slightly at such an absurd thought.

The evening ended late. It was 2 am and neither knew where the time had gone, or what they had talked about.

"You can stay if it suits you," Michael offered. Clemmie gave him a wry smile. "I don't think it appropriate do you?"

"Course, you're right, just trying to be helpfu,l" Michael was seriously backtracking, kicking himself for saying it. "God what a fool!" he thought, embarrassed and furious at himself. She actually would have considered the proposition under different circumstances. He felt special, but tonight was not the right time. She called a cab and left with the promise of seeing him tomorrow at rehearsals. He washed up and tidied away hardly noticing what he was doing. He had not felt this good, ever. A thought sprang to mind and he stopped and laughed out loud, "Fuck me, all this work and I didn't even get a kiss goodnight!" He went to bed still laughing. He knew the joke was not that good, but he could not stop.

Angel arrived early at the club. He told himself he needed to get things organised, he let the kitchen staff get away with murder yesterday. It also occurred to him if he got everyone properly organised early enough he could sit and watch rehearsals. Clemmie arrived at 2 p.m. She had to be finished by 3.30 p.m. so the band and the dancers could rehearse for the evening. Angel watched as she goaded, flattered, and flirted with the band until she got what she wanted. He saw they gave her everything she wanted and more. The final piece was perfection. She kissed everyone on the stage and they loved her. Angel admired her style. They only had to play for her, he had cooked her a dinner and they got a kiss, life's a bitch! He laughed.

CHAPTER TWENTY

Smoke Screen

Alfredo Tarrantinni and Johnny Sabetti had another of their "Board Meetings." The style and pomposity of Alfredo had been chewed up and he was left a worried man.

"Any news boss?" Johnny always started any meeting with this. No point talking about mundane things until all local information had been assessed. Alfredo chewed on his cigar. They were more chewed these days than smoked.

"Not good Johnny, not good." Alfredo leaned back in his gigantic chair, more in resignation than relaxation. Alfredo rubbed his bald patch. Johnny noted it was getting wider, not far to go until it reached his ears, the pathway of hair that bordered his ears was bravely holding the tide back but it wouldn't be long before they were consumed.

"Capone is marching. He got most of the South and West and he going to be looking North to Leone or East to us, either way we're in trouble." Alfredo was out of his depth. He'd spent the last 5 years keeping Leone at bay. Leone was biding his time, Alfredo knew it would come to a head some time soon. This was planned for. Alfredo had been stashing huge sums of money for his early retirement. The club was making a fortune, and even after paying Leone for the booze, protection, and all the other areas that were being loaded on him. He had feelers out and would know when it was time to get out quick. That wasn't the problem. Capone was the only problem. Apart from Leone and his lads being jumpy and causing the frequent misunderstandings and fights that were happening on his ground, Capone would be looking at Leone and his ground, which would include the East side. To all of Chicago Leone owned the East side, and in all but name he did. Something kept telling Alfredo to get out now, but it did not feel necessary quite yet, soon maybe, yes soon. Everyone was scared shitless by Capone. The man was power mad and had shown he was prepared to take at all costs. The shootings had not been a concern in the early days, these things happen, as long as they happened away from his area, so what. A lot of the names that were known were now dead and to even up, the fights in retaliation had got bloodier. Alfredo had lost a lot of his contacts in the South. No one was prepared to cross Capone, everyone knew what happened to those who did. He had got very powerful. Even the "untouchables" were too busy to sort him. They had their hands full in New York. Chicago was a powder keg.

Johnny knew all this. He could see they were piggy in the middle, if fighting between Leone and Capone really got going, they could get caught up in it as well.

"We've got to support someone Johnny, we can't cope on our own. We need Leone's protection. If we went to Capone, Leone would have finished us before we shook hands on it. As you well know, I hate that fucking Capone! Leone's a match for him. Leave him to sort it. We'll keep our heads down and let them fight it out."

Johnny had heard this crap for months. Alfredo had been a good friend, they had known each other from childhood. His loyalty had always been for Alfredo but he had lost it, all good things come to an end and Johnny did not want to be there at the end. It was a matter of time, and not much of that before they were finished, if not by Leone, then by Capone. Johnny's money was on Capone. Chicago had lost its appeal, California was beckoning Johnny. He had money. Alfredo had always been generous. Johnny was not quite a partner, at least not on paper, but everything including money, power and standing had been handed to him. Alfredo was a fool! A kind, generous, loyal friend, but a fool who will get us all killed. Johnny felt his frustration rise and pushed it down back into the depths. He did not feel proud of himself but soon, very soon, he would go, quietly and without notice.

"Ok boss, we'll see how it goes." Johnny did not want to hear any more waffling from Alfredo. "So what else is on our agenda for today?"

Alfredo was back in his element, talking business. "I've invited Leone to the club for an evening. The new girl, what's her name? Clemmie?"

Johnny could have laughed "What's her name?" he thought. Alfredo had been like a lap dog always following her around but getting nothing more than a pat on the head from her.

"I reckon Leone would like to hear her, and it will give me an opportunity to talk in less, shall we say, threatening surroundings."

"Good idea boss. As long as Leone's men keep their distance. Remember the last time they came? We don't want our customers put off spending their money by their rough tactics."

Alfredo was getting impatient with Johnny. Always looking on the worse side of everything. With an air of resignation born from repeating the same thing time and time again, he sighed and looked at Johnny with pity.

"There you go again! I told you I sorted that. Leone was full of apologies at the time and said it would never, I repeat, never happen again. I happen to believe him. So lets leave it, OK?"

"Yes boss." Johnny knew he was a fool, but where was his brains. Where ever Alfredo was hiding his senses it sure was not on this planet. It was the same with Tony. That little bastard was up to something. Johnny had a few contacts around and kept track of Tony. He had never trusted him. Oh yes, he was Mr Nice Guy to Alfredo, he did as he was told and never complained but if you looked at him you could see the contempt he had for everyone at the KitKat club. When Johnny told Alfredo that he was seen hanging out in clubs with a couple of Capone's lads, Alfredo got Jimmy to find him and get him to the club now!

A very frightened Tony had been hauled none too gently before them. Alfredo had been his old self. Tony thought the end was nigh, but the kid had obviously learned over the years a bit of diplomacy. Much to

Johnny's disgust, Alfredo bought the story that he was just having fun. That Capone's lads did not know who he was and that he could pass to his uncle any information, titbits he picked up about what was going on with Capone. To prove his point, he mentioned that he heard that Capone was going to make a raid on an out of town distillery. Tony, with a pathetic pleading look, said that he would never do anything to hurt his uncle, in fact he was sure he could help him. Johnny wanted to pin him against a wall and beat the hell out of him, but Alfredo believed him. Johnny snorted with disgust at the memory. Another nail in the coffin of a dead friendship.

Alfredo was in his stride, "Make sure that Angel gives us the table near the front in the corner, we want some privacy. Tell Angel to get Clemmie to sing to Leone and come by the table when she is finished."

"When is this all happening boss? "

"Three weeks Saturday. Leone has got things happening till then." Alfredo ignored Johnny's look of "know your place in the scheme of things little man" and continued, "Make sure Angel gets everything just right." They moved on to another item on the agenda.

"Guns. Have you got Jimmy carrying one yet?

"No boss, he doesn't like them. Says he is faster with his fists."

Alfredo was getting exasperated with them all. "Is anyone in this place carrying a fucking gun?"

"Yes boss, everyone else, including me."

"With what's happening in this town, am I the only place that is run like a kiddies playground?" Alfredo, who did not carry a gun, was getting into his stride. "Does Jimmy know what is happening out there? Any fucking man on the street could walk in here and bang we'd all be dead."

"Calm down boss, as I said, everyone's got a gun who needs to have one – it's only Jimmy who won't and there is no shifting him, we're covered."

They talked about supplies, they talked about the casino, the staff and finished after two hours both feeling things between them had got worse, but neither able to start a conversation that would clear the air.

Johnny called Angel to his office and relayed the information about Leone's visit in three weeks time. Angel rolled his eyes and moaned about the last visit, and all the clearing up that needed doing after they went. Johnny snapped and told him to shut the fuck up and get on with it. This was not like Johnny. Over the years they had got quite friendly, Angel wondered what had upset him.

Johnny was going to wait a few months before going but, enough was enough. He had a few more things to settle, firm up on his business plans and organise transfers of money for California which should take no more than a couple of weeks. In three weeks he would be off. That suddenly made him feel good. Any regrets he may have had were lessening by the hour. He'd go tomorrow but Sonia couldn't leave that quick. She was going to be his new business partner. Sonia was an old friend and lover. Over the last year he had found that he turned more and more to her. Chicago was not a place to trust anyone, too many people had been quick to help

Capone, and Leone, and anyone else if it meant they were left alone, or worse, paid. Johnny hated such disloyalty, a smiling friend one day could be your enemy the next. So many friends and associates of Johnny's had died over the recent years. Given half a chance he reckoned he could line the walls of Main street with people he'd like to shoot. He trusted Sonia, he knew she'd do anything for him, come to think of it, she had done many little things for him over the years, he smiled at the thought. They had been talking in an off hand way about starting something in California. California was the golden land, and still, from what they had heard, had not begun to be harvested. The talking had started as a bit of fun, a distraction from what was going down in Chicago. The more they talked the deeper they got into planning. Over the last year both he and Sonia were worried about what was happening in Chicago and the plans went from pie in the sky to a reality. The clandestine meetings gave them both a tingle of anticipation that was addictive and all theirs. They would open a high class establishment with only the best girls, Sonia was the expert on organising and running that and Johnny would open a small club, for starters anyway. Sonia knew he would do well, he was always the brains at the KitKat. His plan was to have his own business and live the good life, her plan was to finally get Johnny. He knew what she wanted and played along, she did not need to know his final plans did not include her.

Johnny left the club, his mind mulling every detail. He knew the bad taste in his mouth would not go until he left this God forsaken town. He could push his plans forward a little without bringing himself to anyone's attention. He did not trust the bank either, shifting his money should have been easy, but what if anyone got to hear of it. If he was not so worried, he would have laughed at himself. Who would be interested in him. He was sick of the paranoid feeling that he was being watched. He would see Sonia today and see if she could move her business a little quicker. Call it a premonition, a feeling, or something, he knew he had to move fast, three weeks was too far away. He quickened his pace, something akin to panic flooded his head, he had to be gone in two weeks, three weeks was too late. The man leaning against the wall opposite, bored but working to look inconspicuous, followed him along the street with his eyes.

CHAPTER TWENTY ONE

Deep Understanding

Some of the club staff would be celebrating. It was agreed by all that 6 months was long enough to run the book on whether Angel and Clemmie stayed together. Of course there were arguments, those who reckoned it would not last wanted it to run longer. The decision was made that six months was the longest they knew of that Angel had gone out with the same girl, and besides, they did not look as if they were about to split. The payout was not that much but would buy the winners a few beers and give the winners something to crow about. The kitchen staff worked hard in damp hot and stressful conditions, apart from the Chef, his assistant, and maybe the assistant assistant, it was the lowest of the low job. It ranked lower than the man cleaning the toilets. At least the toilet cleaner was left to work in peace. The kitchen staff were underpaid, treated like vermin by everyone, usually taking their cue from the Chef who referred to each and every one of them as "Little Shit." Kitchen staff were as disposable as yesterdays dinners. If you moaned about anything, or did not want to work a 13 hour day, or could not do two jobs in the kitchen at the same time, or minded being hit by the Chef or objects he chose to throw at them, or spoke out of turn, or God forbid, not jump when Chef said jump, you were out. There were plenty to replace you. They stayed because it was a job. To lighten their load they had bets on everything. The daily bet was how many minutes would it take the Chef to lose his temper when he walked into the Kitchen at the start of the day. This was so predictable that a small wager of a few cents amounted to very little for the winner but it gave them a little amusement. The Chef never knew why the kitchen staff scuttled around preparing for the evening meals nervously looking at the clock, hoping today they would be the winner. Bets were made on minutes not hours with Chef. Chef liked no one, least of all the customers who he referred to as illiterate bastards, which was why Chef was not encouraged to meet his customers. No one knew his name, always referred to as Chef, Sir was reasonably acceptable but not preferable. Angel was the only one who came close to being liked by Chef. Angel never found it hard to massage the considerable, and almost warranted ego that man had.

The kitchen staff and waiters and waitresses had found life a little easier over the past months. Chef was always Chef, but before, they had Angel to contend with as well. He was not on their backs so much, nagging and picking at every small detail. Of course, if Angel started so did Chef, and he had enough to say on his own account. This change could have occurred because Angel had them in shape and they knew what he wanted, or it could be because he seemed more amenable, laid back, and not quite distracted but something similar. They noted that instead of working seven days a week from 12 noon to sometimes 2 a.m. He now started at 2 p.m. and finished by no later than 12 midnight and only worked 5 days sometimes 6 days but never 7 days per week. This was quite a relief to all. Mind you, they realised they could not let the standards he had set drop, heaven forbid! If they did that he might revert to being there all the time and they all had got used to a slightly easier time.

Angel was very happy with his lot. Life was swell, grand, wonderful. He was getting ready for Clemmie. They had got into the habit of having an evening in at his place at least once a week. He would cook the meal, she would help wash up. Very domestic and homely he thought. Whistling a tuneless air, he fumbled with his shirt buttons, in thinking about Clemmie, he remembered when he had found out her real name. He smiled when he thought about it. Very new into their relationship he had kept on and on about her name, how beautiful it was and all that. With embarrassment, she had told him that was her stage name not her real name. He had not thought about it, it was so her, she was Clemmie Desserie, he could think of nothing that would suit her better.

"So, what's your real name Clemmie?" he was curious.

"Now don't laugh Angel, promise?" He could see she was feeling awkward and promised.

"It's Clara Dunn." He did what he promised not to, and laughed.

"So Clara, why did you change your name." He tried to look inquisitive but failed and just laughed.

"Your reaction is exactly why, you bastard."

"Now, now, Clara Dunn, that's no way to talk." He was enjoying this. He heard her whisper under her breath again, "Bastard" and she leaned forward to playfully hit him across the head. He raised his arms to deflect the slap and laughed some more. It was then he decided to call her Clemmie. As he explained he couldn't call her Clara because it was not her, she obviously liked the name Clemmie, so Clemmie she would remain. He had told her his name was Michael Angelo but had been known as Angel for many years. She thought his real name was wonderful.

"Do you know who you are named after? Do you know what a wonderful name that is?" Angel had never heard of anyone else called that, various people had thought it was familiar but no one knew.

"Michael Angelo was a wonderful painter. He painted the Sistine Chapel in Rome, it's famous." Explained Clemmie.

"Can't be that famous, cos I've never heard of it or of another Michael Angelo."

Clemmie realised at this point that Angel's life was very shallow, uneducated, and limited.

"Do you never read books, the papers, or anything?" Clemmie was amazed. Angel at this point felt decidedly put out.

"Now look, lady. I have worked hard all my life, while you were busy playing with dolls I was earning money to keep my mother and myself alive, so don't put me down. You know nothing about me, my life, or what I have achieved. I never had time for an education like you did. I bet you never knew what it was to be hungry, well I did! So stick your education and your holier than thou fucking attitude." Angel was a little surprised that he was so angry. There was a brief silence while both assimilated what had just happened and tried to make it right again.

"Look I'm sorry Clemmie, I mean Clara, shit, I'm getting everything screwed up here. I don't know why I was angry, I'm sorry. You seem disappointed in me or something, I don't like that."

Clemmie cuddled up to him and kissed him gently. She searched his face, and in a whisper said, "No, it's me, you are right, I know nothing about your life. You know, I would like to hear about it, through that I will know you better. I want to know you better."

Angel kissed her back, and apologised again, kissing each eyelid as he apologised. He proceeded to give her the back history of his life. He left nothing out, he was ashamed of nothing, and wanted her to see how he had got where he had from nothing, and the friends he had made that had given him so much support. She cried for him on many of the parts of his story. He felt touched by that and very close to her. Here was someone he could tell anything to. They cuddled and she kissed him gently at the end of his story, smudging his face with her wet tears. That was the night they made love for the first time.

The memory of that night still gave him an ache in his groin that rose longingly into his stomach. She had been so tender, so sweet. He was very experienced but felt all the usual moves were not applicable. He felt vulnerable, like the first time, hesitant, and nervous. She was different. He had Tangoed with a swarm of girls but with Clemmie he wanted to Waltz. Their lovemaking was gentle, keeping in tune with each others needs and wants, each touch felt erotic and unbearably exquisite, they danced in unison and when they finally climaxed together, it was as if their souls rose out of their bodies and entwined about them in an indescribable pleasure that felt both familiar and frightening. They had not just made love, they had bonded in a way both could not explain. Their lives together had entwined and could not be parted. Angel and Clemmie lay back unable for moments to understand what was happening, not sure each had felt the same.

It still amazed Angel, and was imprinted in his memory. There had been many times since, but that first time was an education. He noticed he'd been standing in front of the mirror for ages still trying to button his shirt collar.

"What a fucking idiot you are," he said to himself, and laughing, went to rearrange the cushions in the parlour for the umpteenth time.

Clemmie was at home doing the same thing. It was strange when she had talked to Angel how often they seemed to think about the same things at the same time, even when they were not together. She was getting ready to go to his place. She knew at some point she must ask him to hers but not yet, maybe soon. She remembered when he had told her about his life. She was heartbroken for him. What a guy she thought. He did so much, was so brave, she loved the stories about Mrs A, and would have loved to have met her. She heard about Stella and Jimmy. Of course she had met Jimmy, she liked him but what do you talk to such a dimmo about. Her meeting with Stella was difficult but she had been prepared by Angel and hoped, for Angel's sake, to win her over. She remembered that meeting had taken place when they had been invited to dinner at Stella's house.

Clemmie had dressed to perfection for the meal at Stella's house. Angel had been quite nervous and anxious that Stella would like Clemmie. Clemmie already had the impression that Stella was a bossy bitch. Angel, unusually tactless in his nervousness had suggested that maybe Clemmie should consider wearing something, shall we say, more ordinary. She had not taken kindly to that suggestion and proceeded to assure Angel that she would wear what she thought was appropriate and not what Angel thought Stella would think was appropriate. She did, of course, wear her most figure hugging and glamorous dress, the one that always knocked men dead, the one that showed a cleavage that was like a magnet to most men's eyes, the one she was sure Stella would disapprove of most. "Let's start where we mean to go on, and work it from there," thought Clemmie

The evening was not quite a disaster, although it could have been. Stella had heard from Jimmy about the new girl singer at the club and that Angel had the hots for her. Jimmy told it as he saw it, certainly not the way Stella would wish to see it. Stella was prepared to greet a whore, dressed in a way that was not decent, who had a good singing voice if you liked that kind of way of singing, who was foul mouthed and did not care who heard her, certainly not a classy woman. She was going to sort this one out. It was obvious to her this Clemmie Desserie was only after Angel because he was gullible, certainly not used to women, and she would be after his money and would like to be associated with someone who had such a position in the club. A whore would not get a decent man, Angel was still a boy and did not understand these things, but Stella did. Stella only had Angel's interests at heart, and she now made it her business to protect him from predators of the female kind. Stella still had bees in her bonnet and at the moment they were in protection of Angel.

Stella opened the door and was not disappointed, she saw too much make-up, too much cleavage and the look on Jimmy's face showed too much interest. Graciously she showed Clemmie and Angel in, she fussed over Angel, took his coat, straightened his tie and hugged him. Clemmie smiled to herself. She would not play the possession game. Jimmy felt awkward. He knew something was going on but what, he had no idea. The dinner was ready so they were shown straight to the dining table, Stella sat Angel next to her and Jimmy showed Clemmie to a seat next to him. Dinner was good and was eaten in stilted small talk. Angel was enjoying the attention and had not noticed Clemmie being left out of the conversation. Stella was running the show and she made sure the conversation was solely about the past, something Clemmie would know nothing about. By the time the dessert was being served Stella was ready to talk to Clemmie.

"So Clementine," she started.

"Actually Stella I'm known as Clemmie now, I kinda like being called it."

"OK Clemmie," this threw Stella somewhat, and she struggled to regain her thread. "Have you been in Chicago long?"

"No. My sister and I arrived about 6 months ago. We were in New York for some time but thought Chicago looked a good place to live and work."

"So where are you from originally?" Stella was not very interested but had to keep this conversation going.

"We came from Mississippi. Our daddy has a cotton plantation and we were brought up there." She knew she would hook Stella with this one, such a stuck up lady was this one!

"Oh, and did you work on the cotton plantation? Your hands don't look like they have ever picked cotton."

"Good Lord no," Clemmie gave a little laugh. "We had servants to do that. I was brought up as a Southern belle Stella. Southern belles learn how to be good wives, look pretty, and how to run a home, or rather instruct the servants on how to run the home. A Southern belle does not dirty her hands by doing anything menial. I have never cooked anything, I certainly couldn't have prepared such a lovely meal." Angel caught the irony in her voice but Stella was busy assimilating this information.

"So you came from a good background." The disbelief was there for all to hear. "May I ask why you left it for, for," Stella was trying to be tactful. "A job singing in a club?" Clemmie looked at Stella kindly but firmly, "No you may not. I do not wish to be rude, but I do not wish to talk about it."

Stella was confused, Angel was interested, and Jimmy was not aware of the very heavy silence that followed.

"So how about a coffee Stell, I'm sure we could all do with one."

"You're so right Jimmy, I'll get it now." Stella was glad of the excuse, where would the conversation go now? In her absence, Jimmy talked about the club and people there, and Stella came back with the coffee to find them all huddled across the table laughing and talking about things that had happened during the week. She now felt like an intruder, and poured the coffee in silence and watched. She noted the touching of hands between Clemmie and Angel and the look between them that was both comfortable and close. It was difficult for her to change her views on Clemmie but the woman certainly seemed a little classier than she first thought, but time would tell, she could not be that wrong about her.

CHAPTER TWENTY TWO

Once Upon a Time

Clemmie and Angel went back to his place. Clemmie was staying the night. Angel was curious, and somewhat ashamed of himself. He realised that during their relationship he had talked about himself but he really knew nothing about Clemmie. He had forgotten that everytime he tried to ask any leading questions Clemmie would change the subject, usually on to something about himself. She had managed to keep him at bay and now realised she had opened a can of worms. She cursed herself all the way home. She was going to be so laid back at Stellas, so what if the woman thought she was a whore, so what if she did not approve of her. So where did her resolve go. She let the stuck up bitch get to her. She knew Angel would want to know about her life, and perhaps, just perhaps, she conceded it was time to tell him. Perhaps, in fact, she had wanted to tell him for a while, but how do you broach the subject. Well the best way was to hint and then let Angel ask himself. She was cleverer than she intended to be.

Angel woke her the next morning with a kiss and breakfast in bed. When they had finished and cleared the food from the bed, Angel broached the subject and asked about her life and where she came from, and why she had never talked about it. Clemmie nestled her head into his shoulder and protested that she had wanted to tell him, and he was the only person she would tell.

"It's painful Angel. That's why I didn't talk about it. I have never actually talked about it, even with my sister. We just blanked it. That doesn't mean that I don't think about it every day. I will never, never forget." She sobbed and hugged Angel. With a deep breath she controlled herself. He kept stroking her hair to reassure her, wondering what in the hell she was going to tell him. After blowing her nose none too delicately, she began.

"I was born in Mississippi. My mother died in childbirth with me, so I was brought up by my father and my nurse, Betina. Daddy was busy running the plantation, I loved him very much, and although I didn't see him much he spoiled me. You're right Angel. I had a wonderful childhood. So many clothes, all the toys a little girl could want. I was an only child, apparently my mother was beautiful and very delicate, daddy always said I looked like her but was much stronger. Betina was like a mother to me. She told me wonderful stories and I played with her children until they got old enough to work and life was good. I felt loved by everyone, in fact I was totally spoilt. My best friends, were Joshua and Salome. We grew up together, in fact, I can't remember a time they weren't there. We were about the same age and just kinda stayed together. Joshua and Salome were Betina's children. We shared the same mother's milk. Betina was my wet nurse after mother died." Clemmie paused to blow her nose.

"So, everything was fine until I reached 16 years old. Salome became a maid in our house so I saw her every day and Joshua worked in the fields but I used to sneak out to the garden in the evening to meet him to talk. Then daddy realised I was becoming a young woman and must start to act like a Southern belle. He said I must stop treating the blacks as friends, they were servants, he especially did not like me mixing with Joshua. He said it was disgusting. I was not a child and mixing with Negro men was not allowed. They were animals he said, with animal needs and it was dangerous and unhealthy. Well, Joshua was my best friend and I didn't recognise Joshua as the person daddy was describing. He went on that I had to learn to behave in a manner becoming of a plantation owner's daughter. He said he blamed himself for not taking enough trouble in arranging for me to mix with other families. He said if I had been a boy it would have been easy, but said he wasn't sure what you were supposed to do with girls. He was worried that I had been mixing too much with the servants. I had to learn to act properly. He said I must stop treating Betina as part of the family, she was nothing. If only he had known the half of it. When we were alone, which was often, Betina would sing loudly, she was wonderful, at the drop of a hat she would start. It was infection and she taught me to sing all the black gospel songs and what she called soul music we would sway and clap and dance around the house. I learned everything I know today from her. She always said I had a good voice and if I hid behind a screen no one would know I was white. This was praise indeed from her. They were good times Angel.

Daddy was making plans for me by now. I found out at 16 years old that going to church on a Sunday was not just to pray but to meet other families. Daddy made it clear he wanted me to meet another plantation owner who had a son as yet unmarried, but he was 15 years older than me, and a more pompous person I have yet to meet. I hated him." She started to sob again, "Oh Angel, it was all my fault. I was so stupid, so childish, if I only knew then what I know now it would have been alright." Angel kept quiet, still stroking her hair. He still had no idea what was coming.

"Anyway," she continued, "I started acting like the spoilt brat I was. I told daddy I could never, ever marry any man who was like this Bradley. I flounced about the house in a huff saying I hated men I had met, except for daddy, that they were boring, cruel, and I would stay on our plantation for ever. Daddy did not like that and from then on he adopted a more serious and colder tone towards me. Betina scolded me for talking that way. She said I had to marry a fine white man so I could live the life I had. Betina was frightened, she said my daddy would blame her for the way I was thinking. She said he would whip her. I was shocked, my daddy never whipped anyone." She stopped and looked at Angel.

"Oh Angel, what a stupid fool I was. I was so sheltered, I did not see anything. I had never seen the plantation fields properly, never seen the people at work close up, only from a distance. I had never seen where Betina lived. The children were brought to me to play with in my garden. I knew nothing. I remember after a tantrum I was sent to my room by daddy. He changed from that day. He said he blamed himself for not seeing to my education properly, for allowing me to spend all my childhood with niggers. He told me from then on I would do as I was told by him, and, even though it would break his heart, he would send me away to a boarding house for young ladies. I had been taught the piano by our local Minister's wife. A gentle lady who taught me my lessons from books a few hours a week. I got my love of books and reading from her. I could twist her round my finger, she didn't know how to control me. I know now she and daddy had a talk about me and what to do for the best. Oh Angel, you wouldn't believe what a spoilt brat I was. Even so, with daddy so mad, I still didn't understand. I tried to talk to Salome but she just got frightened and started to cry every time I mentioned what daddy had said. So one night I decided to go and find Joshua. I hadn't seem him for a week. He hadn't been waiting for me in the evening. He would explain what was going on. I found where he lived, where they all lived. You know Angel, they lived only 20 minutes walk away, yet I had never been there. Betina was beside herself with horror when I turned up. She kept shrieking that they would all be killed, the master would burn their homes. I told her to shut up and calm down. I was incensed by her behaviour. My father would not harm them just because I had gone to their home I explained, but she carried on. Joshua took me outside and was very cross with me. I was hurt and confused. Anyway, he promised to meet me the next evening at the bottom of my garden and he promised to answer all my questions if I would just leave and go home, and not tell my daddy where I had been. I thought they were all stupid for acting this way, but I left. I remember thinking that night that the workers homes were horrible. Why didn't they live in something better, maybe not as nice as mine, but they lived in quite dirty places.

Well we met, and he opened my eyes. From then on, I could see everything. Until then, God forgive me, I had only seen me and what affected me. Daddy's white workers who had always been so respectful to me, looked through Betina as if she wasn't there. Every morning they would arrive for work, if I was in the kitchen they would thank me for the coffee that Betina had served them. They would compliment me on the way I was dressed, something I liked very much. I watched as Betina scurried around them. I noticed she moved out of their way very quickly, sometimes they would knock into her on purpose and she would apologise for getting in their way, they totally ignored her presence.

I made Joshua visit me every evening, he didn't want to, but I made him. He made me promise never to tell daddy or anyone. Even Betina knew nothing of these meetings. I loved Joshua, it was all innocent Angel. He was my brother you see, and Salome was my sister. Over the months I found out Betina did not have a husband, now I don't know why I never asked. He said, after much bullying from me, that daddy was his and Salome's father. Salome was 2 years older than me and Joshua 7 months older. That meant my mother was alive while daddy was seeing Betina. It was too much to take in and I blanked this information. I did believe Joshua, he had never lied to me but why would daddy do that? Joshua and Salome were my half brother and sister, it was hard to take in.

Over what was a six month period my eyes were opened to such things as I never knew existed. It took so long for me to understand the realities of life. Most things I heard I chose not to believe. Joshua became increasingly frightened. He told me he would be killed for going against my daddy and visiting me, and if he ever found out what I knew he would be doubly killed. I remember laughing, and saying how silly he sounded.

Around cotton picking time, I never saw daddy until it had all been harvested. It was always the same. Everyone was so busy. So he didn't get round to telling me about his plans for me until some time after. One evening, after supper, he sat me down and told me I was to marry Bradley, it had all been arranged. That's when I found out the Minister and his wife had been talking to daddy and they all felt that was the best thing for me. Before I could open my mouth, he told me in no uncertain terms that I would do this willingly. He threatened that if I did not, he would disown me. He had done his duty and brought me up without a mother, now it was my duty to repay his kindness by doing what he says. Bradley would one day inherit a nice sized plantation from his father, and eventually get daddy's plantation when he died. As he said our children would inherit one of the largest combined farms in Mississippi. He went on, if you had been the son I had wanted, this would have been mine. He was relying on his grandsons to carry on the farm. I realised then what a disappointment I was to my father.

I had taken a lot in during all these months. From a sheltered, heavenly life, I seemed to have been dumped in hell. I took to my bed and it was thought I had caught some dreadful illness that even the doctors could not diagnose. For three weeks I drifted in and out of a fever. I know now it was some sort of brainstorm. When I came out of it, I convalesced for another three weeks. I was pretty weak. During this time I knew I had to sort everything out in my mind and get strong. I loved Salome too, but she was like her mother Betina, prone to panics if I tried to talk to her about anything to do with daddy. I had to see Joshua. He loved me, I knew that. The only thing Salome would tell me was he had been very worried about me and asked Betina to tell him everything about me and how I was. Daddy was due to visit some old crony he knew one evening, and I told a very panicky Salome to give a message to Joshua to visit me in my room that evening. I was still too weak to get up. Salome told Betina and I had the pair of them screaming and crying in my room, saying the master would kill them if he knew Joshua had come to my room. The only way I could shut them up and do as I asked was to pretend a swoon and, God forgive me again, I said if they didn't get Joshua here tonight, I would tell daddy they were making me ill. With much shrieking and flapping they left…

Joshua arrived about 9 p.m., daddy had left at 8.30 p.m. so all was safe. He seemed ill at ease but concerned about how I was. He sat on my bed and held my hand while I told him blow-by-blow about how ill I had been. It felt very intimate and I cried. Then I told him about daddy and marrying Bradley. Through a waterfall of tears I asked him what I could do. His answer was swift and to the point. He said, marry Bradley and please your father. This was not what I wanted to hear. Joshua was usually so sensible, and he had always come up with good solutions to many of my silly problems in the past." Clemmie buried her head further into Angel's arm. "I'm ashamed to tell you I lost my temper with him. I accused him of not caring about me and he was not my brother after all, but he was as bad as my father. To my surprise Joshua let go of my hand and stood in temper. I learned a lot from our conversation." Clemmie gave an ironical smile, and Angel who was fascinated by all this shifted position and rubbed his numb arm. Nestling Clemmie's head back into position on his chest he said, "What did Joshua say then?" Clemmie closed her eyes and with that peculiar smile continued.

"Oh he said lots. To start with he told me he was as much my brother as the dogs outside were my brother. Daddy would and had always looked after me. Joshua and Salome were nothing but animals in his eyes that he fed and housed. He said we work for him like the dogs work for him. He asked me what I thought brotherly and sisterly love was. Was it, he said, terrorising his mother and sister into doing what I wanted. Was it endangering his life by making him go against the master's wishes. He told me they had all cared for me and loved me. Sometimes, he added, that had been very difficult. He told me what a spoilt brat I'd been all my life. Oh Angel, it was all true, and then he gave me some profound advice. He said we were all caged. Some had better cages than others. My cage was gilded but it was still a cage. Only the master has real freedom. Marry

Bradley and make the best of it. He had looked at me, with a really sweet look, I remember that, and said that I couldn't survive on my own, I wouldn't know how." Clemmie paused to try and swallow the tears that were welling again. "Joshua paused, I realise now he was wondering whether to say something, and then decided he would. He took my hand and gently asked me if I knew where my father was now. I said yes, he was at some friends house. Joshua laughed, there was nothing funny in that laugh. He told me that his "friend" was Salome. He said my mother is too old for your fathers taste. Salome is one of her replacements. He not only uses us for work but also for play." Clemmie had won her fight with the tears but Angel could feel her taut body. Every muscle felt clenched. Angel's mind raced "What the fuck could he say to that?" But Clemmie carried on, she did not want her story to be interrupted. "The Bastard, the fucking bastard, was sleeping with his own daughter. Only she was just a bit of meat to be used and abused when he felt like it. My own father could do this? The man I thought was the best person in the world. I remember crying and hugging Joshua and all I could say over and over again was sorry, so sorry. I think I was a bit hysterical. Joshua hugged me and tried to calm me down." Clemmie was talking in monotone, every word was becoming an effort. Angel got worried and gently and soothingly he said, "Clemmie, let's stop here. I'm so sorry I started this. I'll get you a coffee. We'll go out for some air." He tried to hug her, to reassure her but she wanted none of it. She pushed him away, none too gently, and sat bolt upright.

"I've nearly finished and I want to finish it." She looked at him with a determination and hardness he had not seen before. His mute nod started Clemmie talking again. With a determination that did not quite hide the waiver in her voice, she continued.

"We hugged and cried for some time. We lost track of time. I didn't know how late it had got until I saw daddy standing in my bedroom watching this blackman hugging his daughter on her bed. It all happened in slow motion. Daddy grabbed Joshua and hit and kicked him around my room, I have never heard such a terrible sound. There was such shouting and screaming and the sound of punches and kicks. I remember hearing a high pitched continuous scream and I realised it was me. Funny that, I hadn't realised till I heard it. Daddy kicked Joshua all the way down the stairs. Joshua was like a tightly rolled ball. I think he was nearly dead when daddy got him outside." Clemmie was talking very matter-of-fact, her staring, all seeing eyes commenting on events before her. "I hope he didn't feel the rope put round his neck. He didn't struggle much, even when daddy threw the rope over the bough of the tree and pulled. Not an easy thing for daddy to do. Where he got the strength I don't know. I watched in silence. I couldn't hear anything. Daddy's mouth was going the whole time, he was shouting but I heard not a sound. I could feel I was screaming but no sound came out. It was really strange. When I woke the next morning in my bed I was sure it had been a horrible nightmare. Betina would bring me my breakfast soon and everything would be alright. Then I felt the soreness on my face. I sat up and looked in my mirror. I had two black eyes and a bruise the size of a fist on my cheek. Slowly I remembered. After what had seemed hours daddy had let the rope go and Joshua had fallen lifeless and unceremoniously to the ground. With one final kick to Joshua's head, daddy turned and walked towards me. He was shouting, I still couldn't hear the sounds, I watched as each word threw out a stream of spittle. I felt sure it was my turn to feel the rope on my neck, I couldn't move, I just watched as he came towards me with such a look of hatred in his eyes. The last thing I remember is an overpowering smell of sweat, and then I saw his fist coming towards my head."

Clemmie crumbled and sobbed so deeply and long that Angel thought she might never breathe again. Her body racked with sobs that came from so far down they barely reached her throat. Angel, confused, upset, and alarmed started to shake Clemmie, and continued until she took a deep anguished, noisy breath. Her lungs sucked hungrily on as much air as her open mouth could take in. She gagged on the air and he felt sure she was going to throw up. It took several minutes for her to win some control over the fight to breathe, sob, and gag simultaneously leaving Angel in a state of panic and distress. He started to shake her again. Eventually she controlled it, and sobbed and breathed in the right places. Angel developed a thumping headache. He let Clemmie sob, he rocked her in his arms making shushing noises for about an hour, they both fell into an exhausted sleep.

Angel woke first, he looked into Clemmie's face, puffy from tears but calm in sleep, and decided to get up carefully to make some coffee. His head ached dully. He hoped she would sleep longer and give him some time to assimilate what she had told him. He had found the high drama of it all embarrassingly uncomfortable but fascinating. He knew there was more to come and hoped with sleep there would be a, he hesitated for the right word, a calmer talk. He also realised this story had never been told before and it was down to him to say the right things to make her feel better. What he was supposed to say or do he hadn't got a fucking clue, he reckoned it would come to him. Clemmie woke to the rattling of cups in the kitchen. She felt like someone had beaten her up. Her body ached, her head was thumping, her eyes felt like they had bloated to twice their size. She reckoned that she had ruined everything now. Not only did she look a mess but had confessed to Angel what a mess she was. Her carefully manufactured cover had been blown. The cool, sophisticated person she had cultivated, full of confidence, was now uncovered as the gibbering wreck she was. What had possessed her to tell him everything. A potted, sanitised version would have done.

Angel came in with the coffee and saw her sitting on the bed. She looked ashamed, dishevelled, and so vulnerable. Oh yes, Angel knew exactly what to do, he had composed in the kitchen some soft gentle words. He put the cups down, sat beside her, looked into her eyes and before any of the prepared words broke forth, he burst into tears. He babbled and a string of incomprehensible words flowed with the tears. They ended up hugging each other, both saying sorry over and over again. Then through the tears Clemmie started laughing, and laughing, she coughed and choked but carried on laughing. "Oh Angel, that was just what I needed. You are wonderful. You look fucking worse than I do. The stress and strain released, Angel laughed with her. After hankies had been found and noses and eyes had been suitably mopped. They both took a deep breath and relaxed. Angel stroked her red and swollen face, "What a terrible story Clemmie. I don't know what to say to make it better, except it was not your fault. How have you kept this to yourself for so long?" Clemmie just shook her head. Angel hesitated and then continued, "Something wonderful must have happened for you to get from a spoilt brat to the person you are now. I have heard the lousy part of the story, the next bit has to be a success story." She squeezed his arm in gratitude. She thought him so kind and sweet and yes, so right. She sat bolt upright in a panic, "What's the time for Christ sake"! We have got to get to work." A calm if not a little smug Angel answered, "Have no fear my dear, I phoned while you were asleep and booked us off for tonight. This is not finished yet, we have all evening to finish our conversation." Clemmie was relieved, she reckoned she needed another night to get her face straight, no amount of makeup could hide the swelling of her eyes. She hugged and thanked him. They drank their coffee and showered and dressed. They needed a little time before starting again. Angel got in the kitchen to rustle up some ham and eggs. They were both surprisingly hungry, even though it was 3 p.m.

By 5 p.m. they had eaten and were now comfortably

sitting at the dining table having another cup of coffee to wash the ham and eggs down. After clearing the table, Angel enquired if Clemmie needed any more handkerchiefs before they started. She laughed. "The worst is over it's all downhill from now." She smiled a little self-consciously, "It must have been awful listening to me earlier. I don't know about you but I feel better it's out." Angel squeezed her hand, "Joshua sounded a wonderful guy." The tears were not far away, Clemmie nodded her head, "Yes he was." "Well Ok then spoilt brat, tell me what happened next." Clemmie smiled, Angel was doing it again, making everything lighter and brighter. Feeling relaxed and in control, Clemmie started.

"Well, as I said before, I woke the next morning and realised all the previous nights events were real and not a nightmare. I sat on my bed not caring what happened to me. After a while, I realised Betina should have brought me my breakfast and helped me get dressed. I put my dressing gown on and went to look for her. My door was locked. For the first time in my life I felt frightened. What was to become of me? I sat in my room until the afternoon. It did me good Angel. It gave me time to think. After all that had happened I was still thinking only of me. It occurred to me, what about Betina, she was Joshua's mother, and poor Salome, how was she feeling. I got really frightened then. Betina was always crying and shrieking about daddy whipping them. I knew now he was capable of it. Were they safe? What had I done to them. I think I started to grow up a bit. Daddy entered my room late afternoon. He looked at me as if I was a servant, contempt and hatred in his eyes. He had the Minister and his wife with him. All three stood and looked at me. I sensed some pity in the eyes of the Minister's wife but only just. It had been decided I was being sent away to a girl's college to learn how to behave and conduct myself as a plantation owner's wife. When I come back I will marry Bradley. I thanked my father and said I would be honoured to marry Bradley on my return. It was good to see the surprise in daddy's eyes at such a compliant, meek, response. The fucking bastard didn't know I had other plans. I begged his forgiveness, and promised to return a dutiful daughter and would marry Bradley and he would be proud of me. I asked if he could tell me how long I would be away from him. He told me 6 months. The brat in me wanted to shout no, but I held it back and thanked him again.

The Minister's wife stayed the night to help me pack and accompany me to the college to ensure I settled in Ok. I was told it would take many hours of travelling to arrive so an early start in the morning was essential. I remember lowing my head and asking if I may dine that evening with daddy as it would be my last chance for 6 months. He looked at the Minister and his wife and I saw them give a slight nod in agreement. I had to get out of my room to see if Betina and Salome were around.

I dressed carefully for dinner that evening. I was starving, I'd had nothing all day. The Minister's wife accompanied me to the dining room. I looked around as we walked to see if they were around. I couldn't see them. I felt panicky, were they alright? At dinner, we were served by Alfred. He had a veiled look of fear in his eyes. I don't remember noticing that look before. Throughout the meal I looked for signs of Betina or Salome but there was none. I have to say I felt quite frantic. Dinner finished about 9 p.m. and I excused myself and said I would go to bed early in anticipation of the long journey tomorrow. I kissed my father goodnight and curtsied to the Minister and his wife and went to my room. I could hear them talking on the veranda below, they seemed to think I was reforming and how good it was to hear me talk like a good dutiful daughter. I wanted to shout what a load of fucking hypocrites they were, but of course I didn't.

At about midnight, the house was quiet and I had heard everyone go to their rooms and settle down for the night. I crept out to go and look for Betina and Salome. I found Salome by herself at home. In fact she was already asleep and I woke her with a start causing her to go into an hysterical panic. At midnight everywhere is quiet and I thought she was going to wake up the whole fucking county. It took ages to calm her and make her sit still. I was worried about the time and if I would be missed, I couldn't afford for my plans to go wrong now. I asked where Betina was. I was told by a sullen Salome who would not look me in the eyes that she was gone. It turned out daddy had sold her to someone for work on the cotton plantation. He first gave her a good whipping for encouraging me to act the way I did and told her she was lucky to be alive. Salome didn't even get the chance to say goodbye. No wonder the poor girl couldn't look me in the face. I was the bitch that caused it all. Now I had found Salome, I didn't know what to say to make it better, what to promise. I had to get back it was getting really late. I tried to hug her but she wanted none of it, I don't blame her. I told her I was being sent away for 6 months but would be back. I told her to be good, do everything as she was told, I wanted her there when I got back. Without a proper plan I said the only thing I could. I told her I was to marry Bradley when I came back and I would make daddy give me Salome as my maid. I promised her things would be better, and I would look after her. I said I would try and find Betina as well and bring her to my new home. I had to go and I said goodbye. She gave me a strange look Angel, it haunted me for the 6 months I was away. It was almost a look of contempt, something I had never seen in a servants eyes before. You'd never believe it, but it took me many weeks to understand how I deserved that look. I know what I would have done if I had been her listening to a 17 year old spoilt brat who had been responsible for her brother's death and her mother's whipping and then seeing her sent away to do hard labour in the fields. I would have punched her fucking lights out.

Anyway, I got back to the house and fell asleep very quickly. I was woken at 5 a.m. to get ready. I was real fucking tired I can tell you, but I slept a lot of the journey to this college. We arrived at 1 p.m. I was shown to my room, the Minister's wife fussed a little but wanted to get back that night so she left after an hour. The 6 months passed fairly quickly and I learned a lot. I was considered withdrawn by the tutors and the pupils.

The place was full of fucking spoilt brats Angel. I couldn't stand them. I did learn though how to behave in front of gentlemen, I learned a bit of charm which came in handy and I can rustle up a mean tapestry cushion if pushed." They both laughed and Angel kissed her, partly in relief that this part didn't seem so dramatic. "They taught me to walk properly, and if exaggerated, this can look very sexy, as you know. I took to writing to daddy every week. Oh Angel, I sent such sweet letters to the fucking bastard. Once a month I would explain that all the girls there had such lovely clothes and mine were looking worn, and how the latest fashion in shoes were so divine. I said I wanted to return home looking the sort of daughter he would be proud of, so could he send me some money. All in all, he sent me about $400, all of which I saved. I had a small allowance for the feminine bits and pieces I needed, I managed to save most of that as well. I didn't care what the other bitches there thought, so for 6 months I was not very elegantly dressed, so what. I had about $500 dollars hidden in my case. There was more freedom to move around and once a week we were allowed to go to town to shop. We were chaperoned of course, but I managed to slip away and head for the bus station. Over the months I found out all the routes out of Mississippi, the timetables, the cost, and how long it would take to get from Mississippi to up North. I knew that technically Salome wasn't a slave, slavery apparently had been abolished, but it was a fine line. I had found out through reading books, and surprise, surprise, there were not many books in the library about the abolition of slavery and the civil war and things, but the most important part was the North was freedom for all. I wanted to go there. I picked New York as the best place to go. Don't know why exactly, I think because it was so far away from Mississippi, and I heard it was full of new exciting people. I planned everything thoroughly. I had 6 months to do it after all. As luck would have it, I also knew what I would do to earn a living. Going to town every week and losing the chaperone for a few hours everytime, I wandered round most of the town. One day I happened to pass a not so grand bar and I heard a black woman singing. I peeked through the window and saw the most marvellous sight. This woman was standing on a stage swaying to the music and singing soul music. She had on a tight red dress that did wonders for her. All the men in the bar couldn't take their eyes off her. I could see why. She was glorious and so sexy. I had never in my life seen anyone make such small movements that said so much. I wanted to do that. I practised the movements in my room singing under my breath, it looked terrible for a long time, well it never looked that good but I'd got the basic idea, it was later I really understood how to move and feel the music.

I arrived home 6 months later a stronger person. My plans were all prepared, now was the hard bit. I charmed the pants off the bastard when I got back. He fell for it hook, line, and sinker. I managed to get the wedding postponed for 6 months. As I told the bastard, I needed time to go through a decent courtship with Bradley. It was only proper for a Southern belle to do things modestly. The corn was due for harvest within the next month and I knew daddy would be so busy, it wouldn't be right to put him under too much pressure with a wedding and all. He thought the college had done me a power of good. I took to going for a buggy ride every day. I was allowed to do this because, as I explained to daddy, the air was good for a young lady's complexion. The stupid bastard believed it. For the first week Alfred drove me, then I took Salome along as my maid, it looked good to the neighbours I explained. Whatever I did during the day, daddy came home to a beautifully dressed dutiful daughter who made him a drink and organised the servants with supper. He was very pleased.

When the harvest was done and the cotton sold, as usual daddy would put a large sum of money in his private safe. This was the safe Angel I had watched daddy open and close for years. Now I watched keenly to get the combination number. He would stash large sums of money in the safe, peculiar habit, but when it was quite full, and he had paid all his bills, he would take it to the bank. I knew it would be one or two more days before he would make the journey to town to bank it all. I had seen this happen over many years." Clemmie was getting more and more excited and the words were flowing faster and faster.

"Anyway, the next day was going to be the day! I had packed a medium sized bag in readiness. I just had Salome to contend with. I was going to kidnap Salome. Well it was no good telling her what my plans were, she still didn't trust me, and it was for her own good. That sounds like a spoilt brat doesn't it Angel? But truly it was for the best. So, the next day I told Salome to put on her best going out outfit and pack a small bag. The look on her face was amazing, she was very scared. I soothed her by saying I wanted to travel to Bradley's house to surprise him and we would stay over the night because it was a long journey. I said daddy had said it was OK but not to mention it because he might still not trust her to be away from his home and he could change his mind. She seemed to believe this. Alfred had prepared the buggy and the horses and was waiting for us as usual. I slipped into the dining room with an empty bag and opened the safe and took all the money out. I counted it later and there was over $2,000, a fortune. I'd got the $500 dollars I'd saved in my hand purse for ready money, loaded my two bags on the buggy, grabbed Salome and we were off. About 2 miles away from the plantation we came to the sign post that pointed to Bradley's route and the other to town. I told Alfred to head for town because I had to pick up a parcel from the post office. Salome looked wide-eyed, she knew we couldn't get to town and back and to Bradley's home during day light. Alfred knew nothing of the Bradley visit I might add. I told Salome to sit quietly and say nothing. I reckoned we would get to town about 4 p.m. and the bus left at 4.45 p.m., enough time. The long stretch into town was quite boring, there is nothing to see but fields. The harvest was over so no-one was working there, they were all busy elsewhere doing God knows what. About half way I asked Alfred to stop and go fetch some flowers that were growing wild in the roadside shrubs. A strange request, but he did it. When

I pointed to some further back down the road he started to walk towards them. I jumped in the front and got the horses whipped up and moving quickly. I could hear Alfred shouting and Salome shrieking but I felt good, real good. We raced into town at about 4.15pm, Salome helped me slow the horses to a more sedate canter, the poor animals were well worn out. We pulled up outside the bus station and I grabbed Salome and the bags and walked quickly to get our tickets. I can't tell you how tense I felt. The fucking bus was 15 minutes late and I tell you, I nearly fainted with panic. Salome sat shaking on the sidewalk frightened to do or say anything. Well, it arrived, we got on. Of course Salome and I sat separately, she was at the back with the coloureds and me at the front. The journey was going to be long I knew but boy it went on and on. We had a few stops to refresh and get something to eat. As my maid, Salome could get my food from the counter but collected hers and ate outside as was fitting for coloureds. It was very lonely that journey. Salome seemed to have given up, she said nothing just sat and looked frightened. Everytime we stopped I expected to see daddy come storming in. The further we got away the more impossible that was but I never felt safe until we hit the North. It took a week of hard riding, of sleeping in the bus, of not being able to wash properly, of aching in every muscle and bone but it was worth it. When we changed buses for the last time to make the trip to New York it felt freer. We arrived in New York looking as dishevelled and dirty as the city itself. We found a small boarding house that had hot water and two very comfortable beds. We both felt we were still moving on a bus, and felt quite giddy. Salome, as my maid was able to share my room and we both washed and just laid down on those wonderful, soft beds and fell asleep. We were free, we had money, what more could we have wanted then, nothing I can tell you.

The next day was harder. I found out we were free but the whites still did not allow the coloureds to eat in the same place as them or travel with them. We looked around New York for more amenable places to stay. There was a small black part of town and I decided we would live there. I can tell you, I was not that welcome but they couldn't stop me entering their restaurants like they could stop Salome entering white ones.

We found rooms to rent that were not very nice at all but for the time being at least we could be together. We had plenty to talk about. I had a lot of explaining to do." Clemmie paused. "Can I have another cup of coffee Angel? I can't remember when I have talked so much. " She realised she was giving him a blow by blow account and was getting worried he might be bored.

"Clemmie this is interesting stuff and I want to hear it all. Hold on while I get another coffee for both of us." He scurried to the kitchen and his enthusiasm made her smile. She couldn't believe her luck in finding a guy like him. The coffee arrived and Angel seated himself by Clemmie, his elbows on the table, he nodded his head and beckoned Clemmie to continue.

She was feeling very relaxed and could have given Angel a daily account of everything that had happened, it still felt very raw. She reasoned if she did that they would be there for days and she was getting tired of all her talking. With a deep breath she continued her saga.

"The first 6 months were hell. Horrible accommodation, I was viewed by our neighbours as an intruder so no one spoke to me if they didn't have to. Salome was very difficult. She adopted a slave mentality and would only speak to me when spoken to. She kept her head down and would only say yes ma'am or no ma'am to everything I said to her. She cooked and cleaned and looked after me but we lived like strangers. Meanwhile, I started visiting the clubs. Me being me, I went to the top clubs first." She smiled apologetically. "I was still a spoilt brat who thought a top club would welcome me. I was in for a shock. I got turned down by them all. Who would want to hire an unsophisticated 18 year old. I got an audition in only one of them, and they turned me down. The others just looked me up and down and sent me packing. Can't blame them Angel. I was a skinny kid then, wearing clothes that a mother would be proud of but not suitable for night-club singing. I am embarrassed to think about it now. Anyway, I started to look at clubs that were not quite so good. Still no luck. After 6 months I was getting worried about money, both Salome and I needed new clothes and shoes. I started experimenting with new hairstyles and make-up to try and look older, we still had our rent and heating and food to get. I could see my money slowly dwindling and I didn't know what to do. I got very depressed, and with no one to talk to, or advise me, I thought I had made a big mistake in coming to New York. I had ruined my life and Salome's as well. It came to a head one evening after I had been turned down yet again by a club. I knew there were only a couple left I hadn't tried and they were fucking sleazy Angel. Everything felt hopeless and I just sat down on my bed and started crying. I'd been quite strong up to then and once I'd started crying, everything crashed in on me and I couldn't stop. After about an hour Salome brought me a cup of coffee. She said she could help. I'll never forget those words Angel. She said she could help." Clemmie almost shouted these words at Angel. He saw the relief in her face and realised this was a big deal to her. "They were the first words Salome had spoken to me off her own back. I was so shocked I stopped crying. She looked so shy, and almost whispered. The shop on the corner are looking for a cleaner. I could do that and still be here to look after you." Clemmie reached for the handkerchief that Angel had pushed in her direction. He had seen the tears coming. "Wow Angel. I was so overwhelmed by this and I started crying again, and hugging Salome who was not ready to be hugged and pulled herself away. I thought then I needed to take one step at a time. Salome was thinking for herself and she was willing to take a job to help us survive. It was the start of everything Angel." It did not sound that momentous to Angel but as he thought to himself, what did he know. Clemmie was now back into the swing of the story and her words were once again coming thick and fast.

"Salome took the job and it helped pay for food. I carried on going to the few clubs left and found one willing to hire me. Well it was a dump, but so what.

They offered me a singing job as part of a backing group for their lead singer. A bastard of a man whose ego was far, far bigger than his talent. The club owner was very good to me and thought I had potential." Clemmie decided it was not necessary to tell Angel that the club owner saw potential in bedding her, something he made quite clear at the audition. He was a bit too old for her and much too fat, but as she told herself, if she had married Bradley it would not have been for love, so same thing really. She learned a lot from him both in work and out of work. She continued with the parts for Angel's ears. "He oversaw my career. He advised me on what to wear and how to move to the music. I did really well there. After 6 months he let me do a solo number and I never looked back." She wanted to tell him that having sex with this guy really liberated her, she discovered that music and sex went together and she sang with her voice and body. She saw the effect on an audience and honed her skills. But she wouldn't tell Angel this. Angel knew about clubs, he had spent his latter years in one and fully understood what had happened. He admired her for using what she had to get on. There was a brief pause while they both sipped their coffee, which had gone cold. Their eyes met for a brief moment and Clemmie knew Angel understood. On an impulse, she leaned across the table and kissed him as an acknowledgement. Again, she continued.

"We had a reasonable life for some years. I got better and better at my craft. Salome and I got on well. She had begun to realise what freedom meant. She made friends in the neighbourhood and could come and go as she pleased. For a while, she let it go to her head and was everlastingly scolding me for wearing too much makeup, unsuitable clothes for a lady, and swearing. I picked up the habit of swearing in the club. No one listened to you if you asked for something nicely, tell them to fucking move themselves, and they did. Salome became an ace nagger. We had a big row, cleared the air and started again. Salome has never seen me do my act in the club, and quite honestly I don't want her to. But I made her understand that is how I make my living. I was making quite good money, we moved apartments to somewhere a little better and I was able to give Salome money to get herself some nice things. She looks after me like a sister now, not a slave, and we share everything."

"We stayed in New York for quite some years. I got bored with the club and Sam the owner. I knew I could do better. I wanted to sing the kind of music I liked and I had been hearing about Chicago and rhythm and blues music. I stayed in the same club through loyalty to Sam. I was fond of him and would have felt bad to move to another club in the same town. Salome and I talked about it and we both decided we were ready for a change. So here we are." Clemmie took a deep breath. "Gosh I have never talked for so long." Angel just stared at her. After a few minutes Clemmie felt uncomfortable. "What's up?"

Angel, in shock, had realised how lucky he had been to meet up with Clemmie, that he could not imagine his life without her. "What if you had decided to stay in New York, I would never have met you. I can't believe just how far your life has been from mine. What an accident it was that you came to my club and not one of the others." The day had been full of emotion and Angel could feel tears in his eyes, he felt overcome by everything. It was Clemmie's turn to hand him a handkerchief. "I'll make you a coffee this time, I've put you through a lot today." She kissed him tenderly. In a voice that crackled with held back emotion she whispered, "Angel, I love you. Just remember this, I would have found you even if you were on the other side of the world." This made him worse and she left him blowing his nose and dabbing his eyes to make the coffee. All he could think was, "What a woman! She loves me. Christ, how did I get so lucky?" He could feel his eyes brimming with tears and hurriedly looked for a drier handkerchief.

They spent the rest of the day making plans for the future. Marriage was not exactly mentioned but that is what they were talking about. All their plans included Salome, Angel felt he knew her, even though he had not met her yet, nor she him. Clemmie promised that she would bring Salome with her to Angel's apartment for a meal so they could get to know each other.

They lay wrapped in each others arms for the night both exhausted but feeling unbearably content and at peace. As he drifted to sleep, her breathing in sleep was soft and gentle and he could feel each breath caress his cheek. He inhaled the air around her deeply trying to capture the essence of Clemmie. His arms closed tightly round her and he thought if this was the best it ever got, he would die a happy man.

CHAPTER TWENTY THREE

Sad, Bad and Mad

The young man in the corner was a regular in the bar. He tended to keep himself to himself. Instinct tells you who is approachable and who to give a wide berth. Only those looking for trouble walked his way. Only the stupid did not fuck off as suggested. Once, it was rumoured, a particularly stupid bastard refused to budge, apparently he ended up with a broken arm and a promise that the next time he would be grateful to escape with only a fucking broken arm. Obviously the cops were not involved. If you drink in illegal joints you watched yourself. There was no one around to protect you, and this man was known as a friend of the owner.

Women who frequented this dive wondered why such a handsome guy was always alone. The years had been good to Tony. The skinny lad had filled out. He had been compared to Valentino the huge star of the big screen. He had the dark looks and handsome features, and on the rare occasions he had spoken to a woman in passing, they had reported how charming he was. Tony dressed in the finest suits that Chicago could offer with gold cigarette box and lighter, cuff links that would cost an average street worker a years salary, the whole package was very expensive and very appealing to most women.

The years had also taught Tony the importance of self control, and patience. This place was not where he wanted to be. This place served one purpose only, as a meeting place. The people here were low life and not worth his attention. Once again, he was waiting, as many, many times before he had waited. When it got to 9 p.m. he would leave. He hoped tonight he had not waited in vain.

Deanos, as this place was called, was the little known bar at the other end of town. It had neither style, class, or for that matter any decent booze, but no one who knew Tony would travel to a dump like this. It was the ideal safe meeting place for Tony and Capone's right hand man Ricky. What had started out those few years ago as an exploratory inroad into Leone's part of town had developed into an interesting partnership.

Chicago was a large town but it had a small town close up feel about it. Tony had been known about town as a loose canon with a chip on his shoulder. Anyone who was anyone knew what was happening out there. His antics over the years had been well publicised and talked about. He was viewed as a nasty, empty headed thug who could be useful for information but that was all. Tony was going to be a short lived informer. It had never actually been decided but it was loosely known that he would be got rid of when his usefulness was over. Actually, his death would have a two-fold benefit, one to shut him up and two, to send Alfredo a message that Capone was not to be messed with. Tony never understood his role.

Tony told Capone's men everything he knew. It was quite a bit, even though Alfredo and Johnny made a point of never talking in front of Tony. Tony was smarter than they realised. His usefulness was drawing to a close when, as chance would have it, one of those events you could never plan for, or even seriously consider would come your way, happened. The Gods, but in this case, the devil certainly looks after his own.

Tony had spent the latter part of the evening with two of Capone's men. They had been instructed to babysit Tony for just a little longer, they knew what that meant. Jay and Pete as Tony affectionately called them were waiting for the call to waste him, until then they liked to know where he was, and they ensured he was with them. That night was a bit awkward, they had to go to a warehouse down town to knock about one of Leone's people and rather than lose Tony they suggested he came along for the fun. Jay and Pete arrived at the warehouse and muttered to the two men waiting outside. They nodded and got in their cars and left. Tony, who had been watching the exchange asked what was up. Jay and Pete looked at each other and shrugged. Without saying anything they found the open side door and beckoned Tony to follow them.

Inside was dark with a small bulb hanging precariously from the rafters by a long flex. It cast a little light, which just made the shadows deeper, it felt hot and claustrophobic in the hazy dull yellow light that had only enough energy to shine for two foot either side of the bulb. Tony craned his neck to see who was tied in the chair, he heard the men muttering something about a prominent rival gang member but he did not know who.

Capone's men were not known for their charity or sensitivity, getting information by what ever means had never been a problem. They were professionals, neither enjoying or hating what they did. A job was a job and the end result was what mattered. Because this time it was a woman, a good looking, young, woman at that, should not have made any difference, but it did! The bitch wasn't talking either. OK, they argued in whispers, perhaps she really didn't know anything. They slapped her around a bit but their heart was not in it. She screamed and cried and pleaded, making them feel uncomfortable and nervous. They slapped her harder, shouted and then turned on each other. Tony watched and read the situation. With a confidence he had not felt with them before he took an arm of each one and led them to the warehouse door he whispered. "Go get a drink lads, and leave her to me. I promise if there is anything to know, I'll get it." He gave their arms a reassuring squeeze as he guided them gently through the warehouse door. They went willingly. They looked at Tony and he screwed his face into a reassuring smile. "Come back later – in fact, give me a couple of hours." They looked and agreed. So what they thought, he can do no harm and at least she might be more amenable when they got back. With a curt wave to Tony they left for a bar they knew not far away.

Tony took a deep breath and went back inside. First

he gagged her. She was crying and pleading and he wanted none of that distraction. He wanted to do this well, no more panics of what if someone caught him, what if anything. This time it was all his and he was going to savour the moment. He walked slowly in a semi circle in front of the girl sizing her up. She followed him with eyes that got bigger by the second as she recognised that this one was going to enjoy what he did. She panicked for a second and tried to scream but the gag prevented any noise above a muted groan.

Her eyes followed him as he walked from side to side of her. Where he got the knife she did not know, but now seen, she dare not take her eyes off it. The knife lay relaxed in his hand by his side. His quiet words sounded as a jumble to her. Before his footsteps echoed as he walked, now she heard nothing. All there was, was the knife. Suddenly the knife moved. He waved it gently, almost seductively close to her face. She felt the fine hairs on her face straining to touch the knife as it skimmed caressingly close to her face. Almost hypnotically she followed the knife gently moving across her cheek, rising slightly and passing over her nose, she could almost feel the soft breeze of the blade, she followed the journey down her neck. She breathed deeply and calmly. A sharp move. A glint of metal. A stinging pain followed by a gush of warm liquid. She knew it was her ear. Pain, panic and pleading fought with every muscle in her body. She wanted to tell him everything, anything, she would do what was necessary and more to get away from him and all the horrors he implied. He watched for a minute, letting her calm down. Then he moved forward and removed the gag from her mouth. He did this gently, almost lovingly. She felt this, and it stopped her panic. Her words came out jumbled at first, but with Tony's reassuring caress, she calmed down and told him everything and anything, even what size collar Leone wore. When she had finished Tony kissed her and whispered his thanks for the information. She felt safe. She felt he would free her. Her body relaxed and she smiled at him. It was the last time she would smile. Tony's smile changed into a grimace and in a flash he put the gag back on her. Once again, every muscle in her body tensed and pulled and pushed against the restraints. The look in her eyes went from surprise, to questioning, to terror as she realised what was going to happen. It took nearly an hour for her to die, slowly, cut-by-cut. Tony, drenched in her blood, was stimulated, and felt so alive. He had sex with her neither caring if she was alive or dead. When it was over, Tony sat panting, his body tingling, and he felt satisfied. This was the best he had ever experienced. He wanted more.

Jay and Pete arrived back at the warehouse a little worse for drink but not enough to interfere with the job in hand. They opened the warehouse door, it looked not quite right and they called Tony's name as they walked cautiously forward. The girl looked strange from their angle. They inched forward looking around again, calling Tony's name. They heard him call, "Over here." They walked closer to the light. What they saw routed them to the spot. It was a bloody sight and on close inspection the girl had cuts all over her body, it was not so much that that shocked them. She had been arranged naked on the chair her legs were crossed and her arms were placed in her lap in a demure pose. Why all her fingers were missing they could not guess. It looked obscene and they could not make out why she looked like that. They heard a laugh and looked over into the shadows. Tony was sitting on the floor hugging his knees and smiling. He rocked back and forth and laughed. He told Jay and Pete everything she had told him which was lots. They told him he had done good and patted him on the back and told him not to worry, they would get rid of her and tell Capone what a help he had been. Tony went home happy. They got rid of the girl and went to tell Capone what they knew. Tony they agreed was something else, definitely a psycho.

It was decided to keep him around for a bit longer. Over the years he had his uses. His skill was honed over many such incidents, to the point where he had a skill no-one else had. He managed to keep someone alive far longer than anyone else, he developed a liking in hearing them scream so he was pleased when someone would not talk, it prolonged his pleasure. There had been regular occasions when his skills had been sought, his identity secret, his victims never lived to talk about him. This unholy game he was playing was heading surely and steadily towards a check mate. Capone was the chess player not Tony.

Tony was led to believe the reward for his support was the knowledge that one day Capone would give him his uncle's club. It would be soon he was told, but be a good boy and behave well towards your uncle and everything there will be yours. For now he knew Capone was grateful for his loyalty and in good faith Tony was supplied with a fresh young woman after every interrogation he undertook. Sometimes they lived and sometimes they did not. Tony needed nothing else. The urge to have a woman for sexual use or abuse drove him night and day.

Capone found him distasteful and a definite fruitcake but he served a purpose for now and was loyal. It helped Capone's reputation that no-one taken by Capone's men returned alive but so many secrets were told. He was greatly feared which was good for business.

It was coming up to the time when Tony would leave the bar, it looked like nothing was on for tonight. The thought left Tony feeling let down and frustrated. It had been weeks since he last had some action and a woman – it did not feel good. He was feeling twitchy and upset. He looked round the bar but the few people there avoided eye contact and hunched over their drinks to make themselves seem smaller. They could see his mood and wanted none of it. It was at the point when Tony was going to look for trouble that Capone's man entered the bar. After a curt exchange Tony left to attend an interview with Capone – something that did not happen very often. The customers watched him leave and the atmosphere visibly relaxed.

Tony travelled in the car in silence, frightened to ask why Capone wanted to see him but sure he had done nothing wrong. It still left him feeling worried. The wait outside Capone's office lasted almost an hour, by the time he was called in he was twitching with nerves.

Capone liked him like that. He always said it made the mind concentrate on what was said and taught the listener to obey without question.

Capone looked at the jumped up pervert before him. Nice clothes and grooming did nothing to hide the animal in him. Tony was feeling worse as Capone silently eyed him up. Capone's contempt was scarcely hidden. This was the pervert who did unspeakable things to others but stood before him a gibbering wreck. He was glad it would not be long before he would put down this piece of vermin. For now though, it was back to business. He gestured to the leather couch he was sitting on and pointed to the seat beside him.

"Tony, nice to see you, sit down. I need you to tell me about the club and help draw a plan of the building – you know, how to get in and how to get out. Tony my boy, my right hand man, your wish is about to come true. I promised you the club and the club shall be yours."

Tony visibly relaxed and ventured a smile and a nod of thanks to Mr Capone. Such nice words were good to hear.

"Tony," Capone put his arm around him and pulled him towards him whispering, "We have a little job coming up soon at your Uncle's club and no-one but you and me at this stage knows about it. That's how much I trust you Tony." Capone squeezed his arm as he said these words. "I can trust you can't I Tony?"

Tony was overwhelmed with fear and awe of this great man. This was the man who, on his say so, gunned down most of the big names in Chicago – who would not be afraid?

"Yes Mr Capone, you can trust me. I'd never do anything to upset you." He sounded like a gibbering fool but Capone let that go, he knew he would do as he was told.

Capone outlined his plans to Tony and got his assurance that if anyone so much as scratched their butt in the club, Tony would tell Capone. Capone's success was not just down to his ability to have anyone in his way killed but also because he was a meticulous planner: every raid happened after hours of ensuring everything worked according to a thoroughly thought out plan with contingencies for any situation. His visit to the club would happen in the same way.

Tony went home that night quite overwhelmed with anticipation and fear. A mixture he found hard to contain. He wanted a girl, but he knew he would have to wait. No finding his own now, he promised Capone to behave and stay clean until after the Club visit, he was too valuable to Capone to be caught by the cops. This thought kept him going – Capone liked him. Anyway, Tony had his own plans to think about, the club visit could even scores for him.

Tony was glad his mother was not well enough to realise that Alfredo, her brother was going to die. Since the stroke she could not leave the house and was cared for day and night by a nurse. He admitted to himself that he had been something of a worry to her in the past but now Tony made sure she wanted for nothing. Ok so she couldn't talk or move, still Tony knew she loved him and he had found to his surprise he loved her. No way was he going to let her have any sadness in her life, so much so, he stopped anyone visiting her. He could tell it was upsetting her, there was a look in her eyes. Besides she had him. She needed no one else. She was given the finest food, albeit mashed to a pulp and her room was always kept dark so her eyes were not strained. Various nurses employed by Tony had argued that this was not good for her, that she needed stimulation, but Tony knew his mother, he knew she wanted peace and quiet. He sacked every nurse until he found one who did not argue with him. What ever time he got home he went straight to his mother's room to kiss her goodnight. She was awake as usual. He knew she could not sleep until he got home. "Goodnight and sweet dreams ma," Tony whispered. Of course she could not reply but he saw the tears in her eyes. Yes she was pleased to see him, he knew that.

Tony sat by his mother with a far away look. One more week and everything was going to be very different. He would be the big man at last. He had bided his time, and worked hard for his chance at the club. All that being nice day and night, doing a belittling job, but no more. Everyone would respect him and with Capone's backing he would be feared. He felt good, anyone who did not show him respect would be finished. That bitch singer Clemmie had led him on and then turned him down. She wasn't his type anyway, far too sullen for him but she didn't turn Angel down did she, that was hard to stomach. That the bitch had bad taste didn't help. He would tell his mother all about it soon, very soon. He decided he would leave out the bit about Alfredo, she hadn't seen him for some time, and

Tony hoped she had forgotten him by now. She had him, her little Tony, so he figured no one else would be important to her. He told her about all the girls he had been with and what he had done to them. She always listened to him and he knew she would never tell. It gave him pleasure to explain all the little details, no one but her appreciated his art. Sometimes she just closed her eyes but he knew she was just concentrating on his words. Life was getting to be as perfect as it could. He went to bed still feeling edgy, but as usual, his mother had helped make him feel better.

CHAPTER TWENTY FOUR

Midnight Hour

Tomorrow was his last day in Chicago. Everything had been sorted and his money transferred. The relief that it was finally happening lifted a huge weight off his shoulders and even the paranoid feeling that had clung tightly to him for so long seemed to have lost its grip. Johnny allowed himself the luxury of good humour, something that had been missing for many months. Angel noticed the difference straight away. He had tiptoed round Johnny for months, every conversation was conducted in curt semi-whispers, Angel talking in tones of a conversational manner had caused nothing but irritation and shouting from Johnny. Angel had come to the conclusion that "Fuck it! life was too short to worry, Johnny was a Bastard" and he only crossed his path if absolutely necessary. This had worked quite well up to now. The Johnny before him now seemed taller, looser limbed, almost animated, and smiling. This sight, perversely, irritated Angel. He had got used to behaving in a certain way with Johnny, now he was acting different. With so much going on at the moment, he did not need this messing around. Johnny stretched his arm towards a chair and offered Angel a seat. Angel nodded and sat. He thought sarcastically "He'll be offering me a drink next."

"Angel, would you like a drink before we start?" Johnny asked with a laid back, all the time in the world, attitude.

"No thank you Johnny. Shall we start?" Angel was keen to get back to work, Johnny's attitude spoke of hours instead of minutes to go through what was booked in the club. Johnny was in no mood to argue with anyone and couldn't give a damn about what was happening in the club but he had only today and tomorrow to get through and then he was off. Angel could see that Johnny's interest was only token, but this suited him. He knew what he was doing and did not need any interference from Johnny. He went through all the usual stuff of bookings, menus, acts, etc. finishing with Leone's visit tomorrow and how everything had been arranged. Johnny thanked Angel, in fact he patted him on the back and Angel left to carry on his work, relieved that the meeting was so brief and had caused him no problems. About half hour later Angel realised that something was not right, not right at all.

This feeling once felt, opened Angel's eyes to more things that were not right. Johnny was not right. Alfredo had not been right for months either. He used to be the big boss strutting around looking important. No one saw much of him now, he stayed in his office most of the time. The other guys were not themselves. Angel realised it had been ages since they had all got together for a drink and a laugh. Why had no one suggested this, they used to do it regularly. Come to think of it, the guys hadn't hung around the bar for ages. Then there was Tony, where everyone else seemed to have got miserable he had developed an amiable way towards everyone. Although they did not talk and certainly still did not meet in anyway socially, it was hard not to notice someone around a club of this size. Angel weighed up all the facts and came to the conclusion that he was definitely paranoid and making a mountain out of a mole hill. That settled, he got back to harassing the waiters and waitresses.

Angel had enough on his mind without looking for trouble. The promised meeting between Angel and Salome had happened. In fact, it was over a week ago. The evening had left him feeling not quite right about it. What "it" was he had not defined. He arranged for Clemmie and Salome to come to his apartment and he cooked the meal as usual. Salome was not what he had expected. He had never met, to his knowledge, an ex-slave, if that is what he could call her. From Clemmie's description he expected to see a confident, talkative, young lady. What was before him was a sullen, quiet, woman with eyes that darted everywhere except directly at him. It became clear throughout the evening that Clemmie was living in "cloud cuckoo land." Angel came to the conclusion that either Salome did not like him at all, something Angel was not used to, or as was nearer the truth, Clemmie had over exaggerated Salome's progress. All of Angel's charm did not work on Salome who answered all questions with one word answers.

In frustration, Angel sat back and let Clemmie get on

with it. Clemmie expended much energy doing all the talking for Salome, laughing for her, and generally all but working her from behind like a dummy. The next day Clemmie told him what a great time they had both had. She confided to Angel that she thought Salome had a crush on him, and how she couldn't stop talking all the way home. This was not how Angel saw her at all. Clemmie was now suggesting they could all move in together, that there was no reason not to seeing as Salome was OK about them both. Angel would have preferred to bury his head in the sand and let it ride but Clemmie was now going to push him into saying it did not feel right. That something was very wrong with the way Clemmie saw Salome, that he couldn't move into a situation that looked more like a vaudeville show than real life. He could see big trouble on the horizon and maybe his first big argument with Clemmie. The thought depressed him and worried him.

Then, of course, there was the concern of the Leone lot coming to the club tomorrow. Once again, it was to do with Clemmie. He had instructions to make sure she was nice to them. Well, as he well knew, and he had to smile when he thought about it, she knew how to turn a man on and ooze that charm of hers. But he also knew how wilful she could be. If she did not want to play up to Leone then she would not. Angel knew she would need careful handling to ensure she acted right, but there again, did he want her playing up to Leone. It was not jealousy he told himself, it was more to do with knowing Leone and what he would ultimately expect if he liked Clemmie, and lets face it, of course he would like her. He just saw trouble through and through. Tonight though, was theirs. He would cook a late meal after the evening and enjoy Clemmie. Tomorrow was another day. Trouble could always wait.

Alfredo was looking forward to tomorrow. Quite honestly he had had enough. The club, his streets, his people, no longer felt his. He knew he was getting older but now he felt it. He always knew when the time would be right, and now was that time. He did not have the heart to tell Johnny, he did not want to face the look of contempt, or to be called a failure. Johnny had always been the strong one of the two, he knew that. Alfredo had the money and the flair, Johnny had the toughness and street savvy. Alfredo was going to move to the coast, maybe California, and very soon. He hoped Leone might buy him out, but if not, he had enough money stashed to set up something down south. He would tell Johnny when things were more settled. For now, he just had to keep going. He missed Johnny's company and advice. He often thought wistfully about the "*old days*" and wished they were still there. It was certainly a time when he felt a man, and was treated like a man. Now, well, he sighed and wondered what he was treated like, certainly not with the respect he was used to.

Jimmy wondered what had happened to the club in recent times. It felt like a pressure was pushing everyone down. No one got the jokes anymore, in fact he stopped playing jokes. There was only so many times a fella can take being told to fuck off before you get the hint. Stell had stopped the heavy hinting of him leaving the club and working with her, but now he wondered if, perhaps, she had the right idea after all. Work had stopped being fun. Johnny kept on and on about him carrying a gun, and that was getting him down. Even Angel, was not himself, he used to be pleased to see him, but now it was great Jimmy, can we do it later Jimmy, or love to, but no time now Jimmy. He would never have let Stell interfere in his time with the lads like Clemmie seemed to be doing. He had tried telling Angel to stand up and be a man but all he got was a puzzled look and a laugh with a good will pat on the back. Times had certainly changed. He never thought the day would come when he would want to leave the club. He thought he might talk it over with Stell that night and see what she thought.

CHAPTER TWENTY FIVE

Eye of the Storm

Saturday was here and Angel was at the club early. It was 11 a.m. and he was looking for trouble. He had words with Clemmie last night about Leone's visit. After a bit of arguing Clemmie agreed that yes, it was part of her job to be nice to Leone, and yes, if that is what the management wanted, then so be it. But – she was not and never had been a loose woman and although she conceded she might promise things in her attitude, she never delivered unless it suited her. Clemmie told him in no uncertain terms that she would not act a whore for Leone. God knows, this is what Angel wanted to hear but why, oh why, was Clemmie making it her mission to go deaf to all Angel was saying in agreement, and yet picking up on things he was not actually saying. The evening finished with Clemmie convinced that Angel wanted her to sleep with Leone and Angel wondering if Clemmie, despite all denials, really did want to sleep with Leone. It had been a rough night. Clemmie refused to stay and went home not happy at all, and Angel had tossed and turned until daylight. He got up feeling terrible, miserable, angry, and frustrated. He asked himself many times "why were women so, so different to men." He had made an uncomplicated request for tonight and she had turned it into something totally different and made him out to be a pimp. The headache that had threatened since getting up, jumped him from behind and punched him between the eyes, making him double up. He had to get something to ease it, even thinking hurt. He sat at the nearest table until the sharp stabbing pain eased.

He heard her behind him. Seeing him made her feel relaxed. She had not realised how tense she had been. On seeing his pain she slipped to the kitchen and got him some water and a powder, returning quickly and quietly, she sat beside him. Her hand on his forehead relaxed his shoulders and the pain diminished slightly. Her tears, wet and warm smudged his cheek as she kissed him lightly. Apologies and sorrys rang through the air. Nothing would part these two. They knew everything could be worked out.

Chef was shouting again. He was in a murderous mood today. The kitchen staff scuttled around the kitchen trying to avoid Chefs eye and tongue. No one knew what he did or with whom on his time off. They reckoned someone had upset him bad last night. They knew he was going to be bad tempered today, Leone and his lot were in the club and everyone knew Chef hated him. The first time Leone visited the club a great fuss was made and Chef cooked the best steak in a special sauce, a secret to Chef only. The marinade and sauce took hours of preparation, it was known as Chef's Special and only prepared for very honoured guests. When Leone sent it back saying it tasted disgusting and give him a proper steak, well done, Chef all but collapsed with rage and frustration. He did the only thing he could under the circumstances, he controlled himself long enough to cook a fresh steak, well done as requested by Leone. After it had been served, Chef, unable to contain himself any longer, proceeded to trash the kitchen, laying out several kitchen skivvies with well aimed pots on the way.

But even by Chef's standard, his temper was way over the top today. The shock waves of his temper spread throughout the club. The cleaners, who were just finishing their work winced at the screaming abuse coming from the kitchen, the waitresses and waiters who were already hard at work preparing the tables and dreading any necessity that would take them into the kitchen muttered oaths and curses. For the umpteenth time, Angel wondered if Chef was really so good as to be worth all the trouble he caused. Talking to him was a hit and miss affair. Sometimes, Chef would listen to Angel but mostly it made no difference. Chef talked to no one but Angel, which was how he knew that Chef was waiting for his wife to return from visiting their married daughter, she had been to visit for 4 months now. No one knew Chef was married, and he made it clear it was to stay like that. So Angel understood Chef's temper today. Chef's wife apparently was not very keen to return to Chicago and be with Chef, hardly surprising to Angel, if he was one tenth like this at home, then he didn't blame the wife for staying away, but Chef was convinced she was coming home today. Angel reckoned he had heard that she was still not coming home, hence the temper.

Angel had over the years received petitions of complaints from the waiters, cleaners, and even the dancers and the band about Chef's behaviour, the only ones not to complain to him was the kitchen staff, but they were nothing anyway, and Angel would never listen to them. But today, Angel had had enough. Chef was going to have to go. Angel reckoned if he were to add up the hours he had spent sorting out staff who had been insulted, disrupted, or maimed by Chef, he wouldn't get much change out of a week. He knew he could pick up a reasonable Chef anywhere, he'd wait until after Leone's visit was out of the way, Alfredo had said that everything must be perfect for tonight, and he was the boss. Then he'd look seriously to replace Chef.

She sat down beside him quietly and pushed a cup of coffee towards him. He gave her a tired smile and pushed imaginary hair off his face, "Where did you get that?"

She shot him a mock quizzical look. "From the kitchen, of course."

He thanked her, it was just what he needed. "How did you get in and out of the kitchen without that bastard shouting at you or throwing something at you?"

She laughed and tapped her nose. "We have an understanding does Chef and I. Besides, I could see you needed something to buck you up. Don't forget our walk in half an hour." With that she was gone. He felt more tired than he had for a long time. Perhaps he was getting old, he told himself. Everything seemed wrong in the club today, he hoped it would all pull together tonight , at least until after Leone had gone. A breath of fresh air would do him good. Clemmie had suggested earlier that it might be good for them to talk and walk. He couldn't remember having done that before, well not since he first started at the club all those years ago. A walk with Clemmie on his arm sounded good to him. He figured he could leave the club at 2 p.m. for an hour, but first he would ensure the waiters and waitresses had got things well under control and he would have a quiet word with Chef to get him to ease up a bit. There had been no sign of Johnny or Alfredo so far. The way things were going so far today, he didn't need their interference.

At 2 p.m. Clemmie came looking for him. She had found his coat and was making it her business to interrupt an in depth conversation Angel was having with a waitress about the position of glasses on a table. After 5 minutes of sorting, they left the club to walk, no where in particular, just a walk in the fresh air together. Clemmie held his arm and he immediately felt relaxed. What a good idea it was of Clemmie to just go out and be together. They walked slowly but confidently down the street, setting a slow rhythm, their feet in step with each other they sauntered, occasionally hugging each others arm, and just smiling at each other. The man on the corner watched them until they turned a corner, he then slowly followed, he knew they weren't going anywhere fast.

They got back at 3 p.m. Angel, worried about what was happening in the club, would not stay out any longer. Clemmie did not argue, she could not shake the feeling that someone was watching them. The walk was good but both, unable to put into words, were happy to return to the safety (a strange thought) of the club. Each secretly thought the other was edgy and restless and this accounted for their own feelings of unease. Today was not a good day.

Clemmie got ready for a rehearsal and Angel went straight to the kitchen, Chef was shouting. Johnny and Alfredo arrived separately at the club about 4 p.m. Angel was in the middle of a slanging match with Chef. The kitchen staff had all but stopped work to watch, if there had been time, someone would have opened a book to bet who would win this argument. As luck would have it, just at the point where Chef was close to punching Angel, and Angel was close to saying "Fuck it! We'll manage," and sacking Chef there and then, Johnny's intervention saved both from real trouble by shouting at them to cool it and get on with their respective jobs. They both took a deep breath and realised they could have gone too far. Once again, Angel could not shake the feeling that everything was wrong today.

Angel managed to grab a sandwich and coffee with Clemmie. She agreed it felt a flat day today, but with an effort to raise the tone she brightly said, "You've got to have the down days to appreciate the up days, I reckon tomorrow is going to be just magical." She nuzzled his arm in anticipation. They had decided to spend the next day in bed to make up for wasting last night. Angel was on a promise. He felt the flatness lifting, it was going to be a good one today afterall.

By 8 p.m. the club was buzzing with people arriving for the evening. Angel went through his routine of making everyone feel special, he had got it down to a fine art and could "flatter for America" with his eyes closed. Leone arrived at 8.30 p.m. Not being a modest sort, his entrance caused everyone to stop what they were doing and stare. Angel scurried over and showed all five men to the reserved table. Jimmy had been despatched to tell Alfredo and Johnny that they had arrived. Leone was enjoying the moment and ensuring everyone realised his importance. He sauntered to the table smiling and acknowledging everyone's interest with a nod, or a brief raising of his hand, even stopping to say the odd sociable word to a table full of people as he passed. He acted as if he owned the place and Angel thought he seemed over the top, but who was he to argue with him. After seating them at their table, Angel, with a flick of his wrist, something well practised, signalled 3 waiters to fetch drinks and nibbles, and generally make a fuss.

Alfredo and Johnny slipped into their seats 10 minutes after Leone. They had seen Leone's show of strength and did not want to be part of it. Alfredo knew this was the beginning of the end for him, Leone would never have acted so confident before. He thought himself lucky to recognise the signs and give himself a chance to get away, before Leone decided his presence was offensive and arranged for his disappearance, as he had done to many before. Alfredo reckoned, with a bit of luck, he had about a month to sort his affairs out and go. He did not think Leone would buy him out, oh no, Leone knew a cheaper way to get what he wanted. Alfredo's men seated nearby, watched as Alfredo let

Leone walk all over him, it was uncomfortable to watch, so they were glad when the cabaret started and they could look elsewhere. The dancers did their stuff, the comedian was funny and Clemmie was a hit.

After she had finished her act, Clemmie went over to say hallo to Leone. She certainly knew how to say hallo. Angel strained to see what was going on at the table. This was hard to do from a distance. Johnny had banished Angel to the reception desk, he could see he would interfere if he could and Johnny needed tonight to go smoothly and without any hiccups – tomorrow he would be gone, he would not give a shit what happened after that. Angel saw enough to distress him. From his awkward position he saw Clemmie sit far too close to Leone whose hands were wandering close to areas he did not like, while whispering in Clemmie's ear. Her laughter at his comments rang round the club and she looked much too interested in Leone. They seemed oblivious to those around them. She had eyes only for him as they whispered to each other. When Clemmie kissed Leone in a passionate embrace, Angel wanted to rush over and pull Clemmie off him and punch Leone in his smug, ugly, fat face. While contemplating this as a legitimate course of action, he saw Clemmie stroke Leone's face and get up and leave the table. He watched her go into the kitchen. He followed as fast as was decently possible without attracting attention to himself.

He found Clemmie sitting in the corner of the kitchen drinking coffee, and looking very pleased with herself. Tense, distressed, and angry, Angel grabbed Clemmie, spilling her coffee in the process, and pushed her into the adjoining store room. The kitchen staff watched silently out of the corner of their eyes as they tried to look busy. It would give them something to gossip about tomorrow. Clemmie tried to protest, but when they got into the store room, Clemmie looked at Angel and saw he was shaking and looking close to tears. She laughed, and hugged him. "It's Ok. Angel, I've sorted him." He shook his head and the only word he could get out was, "How?"

She kissed him, and in between planting kisses all over his face, explained that Leone understood Clemmie was mad for him, that she wanted him right now, that she could hardly keep her hands off him. She had told Leone that he was the only man in Chicago worth being with, and she had waited so long to meet him. Clemmie had gone so far over the top, Angel recognised a scam in play and relaxed. He was now very interested and curious to see where this was going; Angel waited for Clemmie to tell all. Clemmie continued, she told Angel that she explained to Leone about her visit to the Doctors, and how he had taken test samples to see if she had caught an infection. She had explained coyly to Leone that the symptoms were a bit personal, but she would know in a week if anything were wrong. With an impish smile, she told Angel she had suggested to Leone that to hell with Doctors, they could have a good time anyway. Clemmie giggled, then tried to look hurt.

"Do you know what Angel, he couldn't wait to get rid of me. I think I had him worried for a bit because I wouldn't go. The bastard didn't want me after all." She laughed, peered into Angel's face and gently whispered

"It's all a game Angel, and I won."

He could feel his eyes welling up again with tears of relief, pride, and love, he just kissed her tenderly, because there were no words to do justice to how he felt. She understood this.

They got a fresh cup of coffee each and went to find a quiet room to be together for a while, the basement storage area was not wonderful but it was quiet and they could shut the club out for a little while. They drank their coffee in silence whilst Angel was stroking her hand and gently nuzzling her ear. As the victor, she enjoyed his adulation. No words were needed, the silence said everything. After 20 minutes he whispered that he must go back, that he would be missed. She walked with him to the kitchen, they would leave their cups there and, as agreed, Angel would go back into the club and finish the evening and she would go to his apartment and wait. Clemmie was on a promise, he had assured her he would get there as soon as possible and make her wait worthwhile.

As they entered the kitchen they both sensed something was wrong. The kitchen was empty – it was never empty at this time. Angel checked the time, it was half after midnight, everything was still all systems go. He was getting angry now. He would check if all tables were being cleared, although he could see a stack of dirty dishes and cutlery in the kitchen sink. He would skin every one of the kitchen staff alive when he got hold of them. He saw the back door open and went to check if they were outside having a cigarette, determined to sack each and everyone of them. He crept outside hoping to catch them, he stubbed his foot on something soft and nearly fell over. As he looked down, it was then he saw it was Chef's body, as he looked in horror, he saw more bodies by the back door. They were all dead. Instinct took over from thought. He dashed back into the kitchen and looked through the round window in the door between the kitchen and the club. He saw and heard shots for the first time. He turned and grabbed Clemmie, he all but threw her into the storeroom, telling her in no uncertain terms to keep quiet, keep the door closed and stay put. Clemmie's face, full of fear, did as she was told, not aware at that moment that Angel was not going to follow her into the storeroom.

The gun shots had caused screaming and pandemonium and what looked like a stampede. Working still on instinct, Angel knew he had to get into the club to see if he could help. If he had been thinking straight he would have left quickly taking Clemmie with him.

On all fours, he opened the kitchen door just wide enough to crawl through. He did not go far. What he thought he was going to do he had not a clue. His first thought was Jimmy – was he Ok, and could he get him out in one piece? As he crawled to the first table, the noise of people screaming, furniture being overturned as they pushed and shoved each other to get out of the main exit was deafening and terrifying. At least the gun fire had stopped.

Angel caught sight of the reserved table, Leone, Alfredo and Johnny hadn't stood a chance. They had been riddled with bullets. If Angel's brain had been working right he would have been physically sick at the sight of so much blood and torn flesh. As it was, he felt like he was in a dream, it was unreal. Seeing what looked like Jimmy sprawled on the floor and being trampled by the hysterical mass of people nearly jolted him out of his trance-like state. As he looked again, he was grabbed by his arm and pulled into the kitchen. He looked up at what seemed his saviour only to realise it was his tormentor Tony.

Tony smiled, Angel tried to smile back, whilst trying to work out what was happening. He saw the gun levelled between his eyes, Tony's smile looked intense and evil. Angel watched the gun move from the middle of his face, down his throat, it hovered near his chest and finally stopped level with his stomach. The pain as the bullet hit Angel in the gut momentarily knocked him unconscious, but cruelly, the pain also forced him back into consciousness. For a brief while it was unbearable but with each throb it dulled, and Angel just felt tired. He found he could not see clearly and all the noise was lessening in the background. He felt Tony's breath by his ear and his voice saying smugly "Got you this time and no Jimmy to come to your rescue."

Angel's last thought was thank God Clemmie was safe. He passed into unconsciousness and forward to death, not understanding he was dying. Tony left Angel with a final swift kick to his head, but Angel felt nothing, he was already dead.

Tony turned on hearing the door move and caught sight of Clemmie frozen in shock and just staring at Angel on the floor. She seemed unconcerned that although she was going through the motions of breathing no air was getting past her throat.

Tony lunged at her and pushed her into the storeroom and up against the wall. He knew he did not have much time and would have to leave soon. As he ripped her clothes off her she stared vacantly ahead. Tony whispered, "Well, lets see what's so great about you Bitch!" His spittle sprayed her face, she did not flinch. He raped her urgently and violently against the wall. She did not care, she just stared, her head banging against the wall. Tony thrust harder in frustration. "Scream, plead with me Bitch," he shouted. It was not going to happen, as much as he tried, he could not make it, and he could feel he was losing his power. In disgust he pushed her to the floor. He went to walk away, he turned by the door and shouted, "You're a lousy fuck." He aimed his gun and shot her in the head. She was instantly and gratefully dead. Clemmie did not feel a thing, she had already died inside at the sight of Angel.

***

The silence as the film finished was filled with a stunned, agonising howl of realisation. He hadn't saved her. Clemmie was dead. He was consumed with a grief that took his breath away; he had lost Clemmie. He rocked back and forth in an agony of pain and grief that he was sure would maim and crucify him. He wanted out of this knowledge, he wanted Clemmie, he wanted to be dead and at peace with her. The burning hatred he felt towards Tony would come later, much later.

Part Two

Love as an object is often interpreted by heart shaped symbols. It transcends language and most cultures. What is love in human form? What would you call a being full of love whose only purpose is to give fully and unselfishly, whose powers, awesome in strength, were only used to aid and help others. They radiated calmness, happiness, love and care. They have been called many different names, but most Christians would call them Angels. Michael Angelo (Angel) had the name, but it would take many, many lives and lessons learned to become one called God's Angels. They served Him, the Creator. The five experienced Guardians had come together to help Angel. Most humans only need one Guardian, but the problems ahead would take courage and patience and they would support each other in their quest to help Angel.

The film had stopped running. All was silent. Angel sat sobbing quietly, just his shoulders convulsing with each quiet sob giving notice of his intense anguish as he buried his head in his hands. The Guardians watching surrounded him with warmth and care, as was their way. His soul needed help and it was their responsibility to protect and guide him. They welcomed the role they were to play. For Him, they would do anything, and He had asked them to care for Angel. Angel could see no one but he felt comforted. He knew who they were, they were the Guardians and they were on his side. He remembered vaguely a long way back, it still felt blurred, but the bit he remembered allowed him to accept their caring, hear their voices, and feel their compassion. The Guardians were pleased; he had been alone too long.

To restore order in the scheme of things they had to tell him everything so he would know what to do and move forward, as was his right. Angel felt ready, he had many questions but these could wait until they had spoken. They could see he was more receptive and hoped that now he would work with them. They started.

"When you left your earthly body you journeyed towards us, as all souls do. You had not accepted that you had died, in fact Angel, you were very difficult. You refused to move towards the light, we tried to encourage you but you told us in no uncertain terms where to go and turned from us. We lost you for some time and were concerned at your unhappiness.

When we eventually found you, we captured you to ensure we could bring you to this place. You may remember it was not easy, you were very stubborn and frightened and fought us the whole way. You have refused to understand what has happened to you, you denied knowledge of us, your friends, and chose to remain lost and alone. We had to bring you to this waiting area. We are so sorry, but we could not bring you to us, as much as we would like to, but to put things back in order we need you still earthbound. We needed to show you your previous life so you would remember who you are, and we needed you to recognise the essence of Clemmie in her new life."

This conversation was carried out in Angel's head, no words were physically spoken. So when he thought "Am I going to find Clemmie?" They responded immediately with a yes. They asked if they might carry on explaining for a little longer as they were anxious to ensure Angel had full knowledge of what was happening. Angel responded with a nod as he was now much calmer and in control of himself. His surroundings no longer looked menacing, but rather comforting. They asked in a gentle voice, hoping he would stay calm.

"First of all, we must ask you do you realise you have left your earthly body?"

Angel looked at himself, the question seemed stupid, but feeling a little confused at such a thing being asked, replied "Well, I'm still here, I look the same, no wings attached so far." His little joke felt pathetic and he wished he hadn't said that. He carried on looking at himself. "Well, I look the same, I think the same, and no I don't feel dead." That word caused him intense distress and panic. Every muscle in his body seemed to clench as one, his lungs felt as if they had tensed and refused to expand and let air in. He felt dizzy and felt any second he would pass out. They felt his anguish and tried to reassure him. Although this situation had occurred before, each one felt worried and perplexed on what was best to reassure and help Angel. They sent him waves of comfort and safety which enveloped and surrounded him and he felt calm, and able to breathe again. They continued, anxious to help him come to terms with his situation.

"We use the word dead because it is one you recognise. We would not use that word; death is not a concept that happens as you know it. Angel, we use your last earthly name because you recognise yourself as this, you have lived many times. You do not die; you merely pass from one existence to another. When you left your last life you should have travelled to us to spend a brief time with us to rest and feed your soul before passing to another earthly existence. We hope you will begin to remember your many past lives. The one constant has been that you have always been together with the soul you recognise as Clemmie. Think Angel, think, and you will remember."

He was beginning to understand and could remember a little. They noted this and continued.

"You have been brother and sister, mother and daughter, son and father, cousins, lovers. Your life whether good or bad has always been shared at some point with Clemmie. A bond that is far stronger than just earthly love ties you. You have both been tested and had lessons to learn in each life that at times, have been hard, but you were never expected to cope alone. When one was in pain the other was there to soothe, when one was happy the other was there to share the joy, you have never been parted in a life. Clemmie had to go forward without you and she has had to cope alone. She must complete her life, and we are worried that without you, she may at times feel unable to continue and fulfil her existence and learn the lessons she must learn to go forward. Remember Angel, think back and remember."

The tears were not far away and he remembered. He remembered the loneliness he felt in the wilderness of nothing. He remembered the unhappiness, the longing for something he could not understand, the fear and feelings of being trapped. He remembered when they, he knew them as Angels, had been with him at the end of each earthly existence and had helped him prepare for his next life. He remembered the person he now called Clemmie was a Joe, or an Elizabeth, or a Portia, but always his "Clemmie" in essence, in previous lives. The knowledge made him feel stronger; he had remembered everything and was glad.

They were happy he was beginning to understand and was now calm. They realised the next bit was a little unorthodox, although not unknown through the ages. They were there to care for not only Clemmie's soul, but Angel's as well. They must ensure he comes to no harm and protect him while he was still so earth bound and governed by feelings and actions that could be beyond his control. Concerns had been voiced by some of the Angels as to how he, Angel, would cope without the beatitudes offered as nourishment to a soul in rest before commencing a new life. They realised he had missed that essential ingredient that would help him feel as one with life and after life. All souls as they live their earthly existence know this feeling. Although never understood by most as an earthly thought, the soul continued to feel nourished and engendered hope and love and calmness for those in a new earthly existence and a deep routed belief in continuation and their part in the whole scheme of life. They all agreed this would be difficult for Angel but they would help him through this. They would continue, cautiously to instruct Angel on what his role would be in helping Clemmie. They agreed it would not be kind to tell him everything yet.

"The time will be strange to you Angel. Clemmie is living in England and the year is 1968. You will not recognise her; she has taken on another body. She is 20 years old and female. We are worried you will get confused because she is not far away from the age you met her in your last existence, she is a girl, and you may have expectations of her that is not fair in her present life time. Remember Angel, you do not live in her time; you are just visiting to offer her support, please remember that. We need to instruct you further so you are aware of how to support her, and indeed, how to cope yourself. Angel, we are worried about you going into a situation that is alien to you."

"Yes, yes," Angel fully understood what they were saying. He quickly reassured them that he knew what to expect now. He told them in an almost sarcastic manner, "Clemmie is not the Clemmie I would remember but her essence would be in the new body." He was bored with all the talk; they were going on and on. The earthly side of his nature was getting impatient and yearned to find Clemmie. He remembered how he felt when he was with her in their life together and he wanted to feel that again. The longing he had experienced in the wilderness had Clemmie written all over it. He wanted to rush them, to make them get on with it, time was ticking away. The Angels sensed this and tried to calm the situation, but found they were being pulled along by his impatience. The Guardians could feel him leaving them and rushed to tell him the essential information.

"Angel, first you need to know her name, it's Patricia Banks and she is an unhappy girl at the moment. Remember no one can see you but her, so do try and be discreet. All you have to do is think of her and you will arrive where she is, invisible at first but when you think visible, she will see you. To return to us just think of us."

They felt most disconcerted and perplexed. With all their experience, they let this earthbound soul dictate their pace and it worried them, they may not have said enough to help him. As soon as he had heard their instructions he was off, no thank you, see you soon, or goodbye, as he said, "Clemmie's lives have been fucked one way or another, I'm going to make sure she's OK."

It felt very uncomfortable; they were not used to dealing with someone like Angel. Earth bound souls were usually calmer, a little confused, and certainly more amenable to work with and help, but Angel had got his second wind and obviously felt in control. They all felt he would be back quite soon, they just hoped he knew more of how to handle the situation than he appeared to.

From being alone and knowing nothing Angel, with more confidence than was wise, and with less knowledge than he thought he had, he was going to find Clemmie. Everything would be all right as long as they were together. He understood his role and he would help her and be with her until they could be together again in another life. This was easy, he told himself.

They watched, prayed and hoped he was right.

CHAPTER TWENTY SIX

The Banks Family

Most London suburbs look the same. The East London suburb of Newbury Park was no different. The streets were mostly tree lined, the houses built just before the second world war. Just around the corner were houses built at the turn of the century and looking quite heavily set but with years of wear still in them. Many of the occupants were from the East End of London who had made good and bought their own homes, something that was new to many of those families. Newbury Park was considered quite up market, definitely a white collar area, not well to do, but respectable. What lived behind each net curtained window was not for public consumption and many secrets were kept from neighbours. The 60's may have been flower power, the pill, mini skirts and free love, but in the suburbs shame still lived quietly in the corner.

Mr and Mrs Banks were a respectable family. They had lived in their house for 15 years and were well established in the area. They had moved from a small flat in Leytonstone and buying a house in Newbury Park had been a big step up for them. Mr Banks had on the face of it a very respectable job. He worked for a family business, which sold wholesale cork. Cork was a very popular product and the business was doing well. Mr Banks, unfortunately, only worked for the family and thus did not share in the profits of a booming industry. In public Mr and Mrs Banks, as they were known to all in the area, no first name terms, kept themselves to themselves as was proper for their status in suburbia. No longer East End people, everyone who considered themselves respectable made sure that nothing of East End behaviour escaped into the streets.

Behind closed doors life was different. Mr and Mrs Banks had only one child, Patricia. Unknown to neighbours they existed on little money. Mrs Banks was not a well woman and for many years had suffered in silence, although it was not appropriate for her to work, she could not anyway have done so for health reasons. Mr Banks worked hard and was little appreciated and was paid a barely liveable wage. The house had been bought on the promise of good rises and with the aid of a deposit loaned to him by his uncle, the owner of the company. The repayments together with the mortgage allowed for very little else and the good rises had not happened.

Mr Banks was a proud, brave, man. He had after all fought in the Second World War, he had seen sights that he never repeated to anyone, his wife knew a little but most was left unspoken. He spent much energy and time on maintaining a look of survival. He repaired his shoes umpteen times before buying new; he grew his own vegetables, and kept chickens. Originally from the poorest part of the East End of London, Mr Banks had a love of the countryside and, given the choice, would have been a farmer. But, he had a wife and child to support. He lacked confidence in himself and his profession. His uncle, never said, but it was implied, that the family business had taken him on out of compassion, that he would not fare so well elsewhere. Now, with a family to support, and with no confidence, Mr Banks remained with the family business, and took all the petty minded "You are lucky to have a job" treatment. Something had to snap, you cannot treat a man with no respect without retaliation.

When Mr Banks walked in and closed his front door at the end of a working day or week, he was king of his castle. He expected and got an immediate cup of tea on his arrival home, his dinner was minutes after, never later than 10 minutes after he walked through the door. He gave a cursory inspection of the house after dinner to ensure it was clean and tidy and Mrs Banks had completed all her tasks. The evenings and weekends were spent in tense silence. Whatever Mr Banks shouted for he got double quick; where was the salt, the tea, his clothes, the paper, a handkerchief. Mrs Banks and Patricia would scurry to get the item as quickly as possible. All days were bad, but some, after a particularly difficult day at work, were worse. Meal times were frightening. All three would sit at the table to eat, in close proximity with no escape. The tension unbearable, is the meal good enough? Don't ask, don't chew loudly, don't clatter the knife or fork, and please don't let him look at me. It is hard to swallow when the tension is that bad, but you must swallow otherwise you will choke and cough and he will notice you. If you don't eat he will have the excuse you know he is waiting for. With eyes on their dinner, they sense he is looking, they sense his temper rising, which one was it going to be?

The eruption, although expected, always came as a shock. The swift movement, the beating, the hateful words, the total feeling of powerlessness that he could kill and no one could stop him. This time it was Mrs Banks, her fault for looking so pathetic. He was sick of her sitting so quietly, sick of her illness, and sick of her food, sick of her. He would storm off to the garden after such an incident. Then it was Patricia's turn to comfort her mother who was left on the floor doubled up from an agony of blows to her chest, arms, and stomach. Filled with hate for her father and guilt at her gladness that today it was not her turn, she retaliated in the only safe way she could, she shouted when he was out of hearing that she wished he was dead. She hoped he would get run over tomorrow by a bus, that she would dance on his grave when he died, that when she grew up she would take her mother away and they would live together and he could do nothing about it. Her mother, as always, was crying and pleading with Patricia to keep her voice down, she was terrified that one day his temper would exceed itself and Patricia could be seriously hurt. Patricia and her mother loved each other and took care of each other. Many a beating should have been for Patricia, who was too "lippy" for her own good, but Mrs Banks often stepped in the way and protected her.

Mr Banks sensed this alliance and hated it. The beatings were always to the body so that the neighbours never saw the bruising. The shame of the neighbours ever finding out was instilled into Patricia so all three kept the secret.

Mrs Banks had taken to her bed recently, she had always seemed weak, but now she could not get out of bed. Patricia at 17 years old, had given up her job at the GPO as a telephonist, to look after her mother and the house. Patricia loved her job, even though the money was very little. She enjoyed the company of the other women, but it was never a consideration to continue when her mother became sicker. For 6 months Mrs Banks became quieter and quieter until it became too much of an effort to breathe. Without drama or fuss Mrs Banks quietly faded away and died. Mr Banks just continued as before, expecting Patricia to take over from her mother and cook and clean. Mr Banks surprisingly took Mrs Banks death rather badly. Patricia could not be consoled on her mother's death, her grief turned into hatred of her father and disgust at his too late show of affection for her mother. The two settled down into an uneasy life of routine. After an absence of nearly two years, a different Patricia was accepted back at the GPO, it was a job she told herself, she still cooked, cleaned, and waited on her father. The beatings had stopped but she could not bear to be in the same room for long with him. They both still grieved for her mother, even though it was a year ago, but they grieved alone. Neither had friends.

Patricia took to spending her evenings in her room

after she had finished her housework and her father watched television downstairs. He had taken to drinking rum each evening; he said it helped him sleep. Patricia hoped it would choke him and he would die.

At 20 years old, when other 20 year old girls were out at dances and discos or coffee bars, Patricia spent her time at work and at home. She was quite short and nicely plump. Her mother had said that when she became nicely plump, she was just waiting to grow and when she had, the plumpness would vanish. When she reached 20 years old she thought she must have finished growing and therefore she would always be "nicely plump." She now realised her mother had just been kind about her looks. She sighed, the thought of her mother still made her eyes prick with threatening tears, how she missed her. No, she realised she was no beauty, in fact, looking in the mirror, all she saw was a short, fat, ugly girl. "So what!" she thought. Her mother had been very pretty and look what that did for her!! She needed no one, and certainly not boys. Patricia had, in fact, become a nice looking girl, although nothing spectacular, with hair that reached her shoulders, it had to be said though that the mini-skirt fashion did nothing for a short, plump girl. By pushing her hair behind her ears she managed to make it look lifeless and the natural kink that gave her hair some body was hidden from view by grips placed strategically to flatten her hair to her scalp. The one thing she could not hide was her peaches and cream complexion, but the overall effect ensured no one gave her a second look. Her mother taught her to walk straight with her shoulders back. As a result many people might be forgiven for thinking she had a lot of airs and graces. This impression she gave was not helped by her sullen look. Gossips at work speculated they had never seen her smile. Some surmised that if she did, it would curdle the milk. Behind her back, Patricia was the butt of many jokes. People could not understand why she was so stand offish. They concluded she thought herself too high and mighty for their company. Patricia knew the girls at the Telephone Exchange took the "mickey" out of her and so she hated them all. She had forgotten by now how she used to enjoy working there. She did not realise how much she had been changing over the years.

She was out of place working with women and girls who spent their time talking about clothes, boys, or each other, none of this interested Patricia. Clothes were for keeping decent and warm. Boys, well, they were only after one thing, according to her father, and her mother said sex was not something nice girls wanted to do anyway. Patricia also thought that boys, however nice they seemed, changed as soon as they got married into something like her father. She felt she would be better off without men. The only thing she could talk about was music but she did not want to do that with any of the stupid people she worked with. The Beatles, and The Rolling Stones were her favourites and she played her records every evening, and in the privacy of her room she would dance to the tunes. This was her secret pleasure, not something to be done in public where everyone might laugh at her. The Rolling Stones and their music caused her most strange sensations. Puberty does strange things to young women. Interest in boys is natural, but what do you do when the only man in your life is someone you detest. You find yourself left with strange longings that are constantly being repressed. She did not realise how isolated and lonely she was.

Her weekends were spent shopping and cleaning. She enjoyed the shopping. The shopkeepers always enquired after Mr Banks health, and comments were exchanged on the weather. She liked these nice and easy undemanding exchanges without any personal questions. Mr Banks had, at last, bought a fridge. They had been one of the last homes in the area to get one, but better late than never. With Patricia working, the shopping had become a problem so a fridge was necessary to keep things in for the week. As she was working again, there was more money in the house. Patricia gave her father £5 per week from her £9 per week wages, the rest was for fares and saving for clothes. Mr Banks had, at last, been given small rises and once again Patricia had hateful thoughts about her father thinking how her mother had seen none of the benefits of the extras that were now around. Patricia still shopped carefully, old habits die-hard, no butter for them, Mr Banks liked margarine so that is what they had. Minced beef and stewing steak formed the majority of their meals. Patricia cooked most meats the night before and put in the fridge for the following day. It did not occur to either of them that perhaps a steak meal once in a while would be a change. They never went out for a meal.

For a time Patricia thought her life was good, better

than it had been since her mother died. She was content because she knew no different. She could not put her finger on how, or when her state of mind changed. Maybe it was because there comes a time in mourning when you stop thinking every day about the person who had died. This happened to Patricia. For about 7 months after her death she thought about her mother regularly, then, perhaps not every day. After a year she thought about her much less often, as was normal. Then one day, while making the beds, her mother suddenly popped into her head. She remembered when she had tucked her mother in bed and for no reason they both started giggling. They never knew what started it, but they could not stop. Each tried to tell the other it was silly, there was nothing funny to laugh at, but this just made them giggle more. Patricia remembered they both held their stomachs. However, the pain of giggling just made them giggle more. It was a really funny, happy moment. Patricia smiled briefly at the thought. Then for no reason a black ominous cloak seemed to cover her brain and she burst into tears. When the tears had passed she felt a black void had descended blotting out her contentment.

Patricia wondered what the point of anything was. She would tell herself to buck up and she carried on. She did not understand what was happening. She did not know why she felt like this, or what she could do about it. She knew she would be better off dead, she could be with her mother then. It made sense, if she was dead she would not feel the horrible anguished pain she realised now she always felt. Everything felt black and so heavy. It took effort to do anything, in fact why bother doing anything. She saw how lonely she was. She had not noticed before, but now, she asked herself when she last had a decent conversation with anyone. Silly really because she did not want to talk with anyone anyway. She did not want to laugh with anyone, she just wanted to be dead. Patricia endured, no one noticed or realised how she was feeling. Now she spent her evenings in her room listening to records and plotting how to kill herself without pain. She was not ready to do it yet, but in the near future she knew she would be, and she looked forward to that day.

CHAPTER TWENTY SEVEN

A Guardian Angel

Angel arrived in Patricia's room. He was glad she could not see him. Now he was here, he realised he had come totally unprepared on what to do. He knew this was so unlike him. He sat on the bed and looked at the most unglamorous young lady he had ever seen. Had no-one taught her to do something nice with her hair, she had it pinned close to her scalp and the rest hung in wavy rats tails. Her clothes, well, she wore a skirt that was far too short, "Ye Gods!" he thought. "What has the world come to when a fat girl wears a tight skirt up to her backside in a small top that looked like it had shrunk in the wash?" The music playing was not recognisable to him, it was definitely not his cup of tea. He was used to people that could sing and play properly. He felt the starts of panic and pushed it away. Everything was so different here, did he really expect anything to be the same, well, yes, I suppose he did and it was a shock.

He sat staring at the girl trying to see Clemmie in her but he saw nothing of her. She was just lying on her bed staring at the ceiling. He felt disappointed, he had hoped for something that resembled Clemmie, something he could hold on to in his mind. Still, he felt there was nothing else for it but to speak to her and hope she would recognise something about him. He desperately, urgently, needed her to recognise him and let him feel he belonged somewhere with someone he loved. He got off the bed and stood back, no need to scare her. He was nervous and wondered if, perhaps, he arrived too soon and should have waited with them a little longer.

Something distracted her and made her sit up, she thought often later as to what it might have been but could not remember a sound as such. She looked to the end of her bed and jumped with shock. A funny little fat man dressed most oddly in a suit stood there. The suit was not quite right, not like one her father wore. He was bobbing from one foot to the other and looking decidedly red in the face. He was screwing his hands together and looked as if he was trying to speak. After the initial shock, she did not know why, but she was not afraid, he looked actually rather funny. For some unknown reason she did not think it strange for him to be standing in her room. She realised she had not screamed.

He could not call her Clemmie, in his panic he could not remember her name, something like Penelope, or Patrick, or something. He realised she could see him and that he must say something. The silence was frightening him. He could see her open mouthed just looking at him. He had to fill the void somehow. In a voice that squeaked, and after clearing his throat, Angel stepped forward to the end of the bed. She instinctively pressed her head back against the wall but relaxed as he started again to sway from one foot to the other in a most odd, nervous, motion. She watched him clear his throat again and say

"Hallo sweet fuck, it's your Angel come to see if you are OK."

He smiled at her. He felt quite good, he did not have to use a name. Their little pet name for each other popped into his head and he was sure she would remember that. He looked at her expectantly. She just sat there with her mouth open saying nothing. He did not know what was wrong with this broad. Perhaps she was deaf he surmised. He was just about to repeat loudly what he had just said when she started, quietly at first and getting louder by the word.

"You foul mouthed pervert. I'll call my father who will beat you up. How dare you use such language in my presence. I have never, never, been subjected to such words in the whole of my life."

"Well fuck me lady, you've never lived!"

Angel was quite worried by this attack and had retaliated without thinking. Patricia was in shock again and bursting with indignation.

"You used that foul word again, you are nothing but a low life who should be dead."

"Well lady, I'm no low life, but I sure am dead!"

The gasp of air from Patricia was most satisfying. That shut the bitch up! It was silent for a moment, then Angel began laughing, he could not stop. Patricia became totally bemused and did not know what to do.

"Honey, when we last met for the first time it was just like this. We argued, ranted and raved. It was great."

As the words left his mouth he stopped and realised

what he was doing. Angel could not believe he had acted in such a low manner. He was terrorising this poor young girl, what must she think? All his previous life experiences told him this was not the way to get on the good side of this woman. He needed to calm down. He did not know what was the matter with him. He had never acted like this, not even when he was a kid. Angel was distinctly rattled. With a smile that had sorry written all over it, Angel looked deep into her eyes and asked, "Can we start again? I would like to introduce myself, my name is Michael Angelo, Angel to my friends."

"How do you do Mr Angelo, my name is Patricia, not that disgusting name you called me."

She thought he had a nice smile and relaxed a little.

"I am so sorry for using such bad language in your presence, Patricia. I will endeavour to behave in a more respectable manner."

He wondered why he was talking in such a fancy-assed way. He presumed it was her toffee-nosed accent. He had never heard a British accent before and thought it fucking stupid.

She was getting more confused by the minute and wanted to know what, how, why and when. He explained he had come back to help her. That he had always been there for her and she for him. He asked if she was having a bad time now and she replied very primly that it was none of his business, but she was fine thank you very much. He could tell this was not true. It had been a long time since anyone had asked her if she was OK, it felt rather nice. She kept asking him if he was really dead which not only gave her the creeps but gave Angel goosebumps, he did not like it at all. He changed the subject and asked her about the music playing, where did she live. What was England like. They both felt this was really a strange conversation but they were getting to know each other. She wanted to know why he was here. He kept saying to help her, but of course, he did not know in what way yet. She let that pass for the moment. She wanted to know what it felt like to be dead. They both shuddered at the word dead, and Angel changed the subject yet again to what she did for a living. Patricia would not yet admit it, even to herself, but the bit that felt dead inside her was beginning to stir. She was quite interested in this funny little guy but she would make sure he did not know that, although he seemed quite nice in a disgustingly American way, she did not trust him. She felt sucked into this almost dream-like situation. Everything seemed relatively normal but she knew it was not. She wanted to fight back, to gain some control on the situation.

"So if you are dead," she got pleasure out of seeing him squirm when she said that word, it no longer worried her. "You must know lots of dead people?"

Angel answered curtly "No."

"But if you are dead," she paused hoping for a good answer, "how is my mother, and does she have a message for me.?" She felt the prickly feeling of tears as she thought of her mother. He could see she was getting upset.

"I am sorry, but I do not know anyone on the other

side yet." For the second, he felt very sorry for her and wished he did know her mother. "I will try and find out for you when I go back."

Patricia was back on course. Yet another promise unfulfilled. He was supposed to be dead, there to help her, and the first favour she had asked of him, to give her news of her mother, and he knew nothing. She never asked favours of anyone. The last time she asked for anything was when her mother was dying. She prayed, begged and pleaded to God to save her mother but he did nothing. She damned God forever. He had taken the one good thing in her life and left the worst, her father. She could feel the old rage swirling within her and was pleased. She felt much more comfortable angry. She spat hateful words across the bed at Angel about when he got back to wherever dead people lived, she told him to tell God how she hated him and all those around him. That she did not want Angel there, she wanted her mother. If he could come to her room so could her mother. She raged for 30 minutes and Angel sat listening to the tirade and did not know what to do for the best. When she stopped, out of exhaustion Angel thought, the room went quiet, only the LP playing could be heard. He felt it inappropriate to say anything, realising she needed to calm down. Her heavy breathing, returned to normal as she rested. She closed her eyes for a few minutes and he wondered if she had fallen asleep. Just as he was wondering what he should do, she opened her eyes and in a most conversational and pleasant manner asked, "So you are my Angel then?" Does that mean you are my Guardian Angel?"

Angel noticed her tone had changed for the better and he hoped they may be on better terms. He answered hopefully,

"Yes, I suppose I am."

Patricia thrust her face forward towards Angel and the conversational tone changed dramatically, Patricia triumphantly spat the words loudly, "My rotten luck! How come I got the ugly, short, fat, filthy mouthed American."

Angel was hurt, he knew he was no oil painting but the ladies had always appreciated his qualities, not this miserable bitch.

"Well bitch! You used to find me attractive enough"

"Never!"

With a smile, he goaded her quietly.

"Do you want to hear about the many times we slept together, and how we made love?"

She pulled a sickly face and screamed at him, "I'd never sleep with you, you disgusting little man, the thought sickens me."

She shuddered to emphasise her feelings and burst into tears. She had not cried for a long time. This little twerp had made her cry and she was cross with herself, but once she started, she could not stop. She cried for her mother, she cried for her sadness, she cried for her loneliness, she cried for everything. Angel watched and felt great alarm. What had he done to this young girl? He was supposed to be the sensible one, the one who showed the way, the holy type person. He stopped the thoughts right there. Christ! he thought, I'm not sensible and certainly not fucking holy, what am I supposed to be? He looked at Patricia, then stared into her puffy eyes, he looked past the hurt, misery, loneliness and bitchiness. He saw curled up in a dark corner the essence of Clemmie. An overpowering feeling of sadness smothered Angel, he realised just how unhappy the poor girl was, and he had just made her worse. He felt really bad, he could not believe he had been so petty and made such cheap comments. The sight of her sobbing her heart out got to him. He knew he was responsible, they had trusted him to help, and he wanted to. He wanted to say something that would make it all better, but his feelings got the better of him. As he tried to speak, he was overcome by tears. She looked up at the noise and was shocked and surprised to see him in such a state. English men do not cry. Patricia had never seen a man cry, including her father at her mother's funeral. She was fascinated and embarrassed. In a brisk tone, prompted by her embarrassment, she told him to, "Get a grip on yourself." This was so weird and bizarre, she was sure this must all be a dream. Guardian Angels were supposed to be beautiful with wings. They were supposed to have wisdom, and say nice things, and certainly talk the Queen's English in deep booming voices. She doubted they would come in the form that this one apparently had, and she had never heard of an Angel crying. It was all so unpoetic, so disappointing. Not many people she thought got to meet an Angel, so why had hers got to be like this.

Angel looked at the situation. He saw a distraught girl. He did not even know himself or how he felt about this situation, let alone be understanding for this girl. What had happened to him? He had never, ever, been like this in his last life. He wondered if perhaps instead of being an Angel type person, he had turned into a devil type person. This scared the hell out of him. He needed to talk to them. He knew they were good, they would tell him what was happening. He was so ashamed of what he had done to Patricia, she was not happy before, but at least she seemed in control, now, well, now he did not know what he had done. He gently called her name as she faced away from him. He knew she did not want him to see her tears. She registered she heard him and he asked her if he could go away and come back, maybe tomorrow and start again. She told him to do what he liked, she did not care. She did not want him to realise for one minute she cared that he came back. Although she was not fully aware of it, this was the nearest to a relationship she had since her mother died, and he did say he was there for her. No one had ever said that to her, except, of course her mother.

It was an awkward goodbye, she realised she had driven him away and felt she had not given a good impression, this did worry her, why, she could not work out. She would fall asleep and question for days whether any of this really happened. Angel left feeling not just a failure, but dangerous. What had he done? He told Patricia as he left that he would be back. As well as apologising again, he tried to explain that he was new to this and did not mean to make such a mess of everything. He could feel the tears rising again, he knew this embarrassed her so he just reminded her that he was there for her and would do better next time. With an awkward goodbye, Angel disappeared.

CHAPTER TWENTY EIGHT

Waiting Room

Angel arrived back in the waiting room. His chair was there ready for him. He sat down heavily and with a sigh he asked them to forgive him for seeing Clemmie and making things worse for her. He asked them if he was an evil type person. They reassured him he was not. They did ask him to think about why he was acting so out of character they said they would talk later to help him understand.

"I know I should have stayed longer with you and understood what on earth I was supposed to do. I promise to do better and listen more."

One again, in despair, he held his head in his hands and sobbed. He sobbed for the life he had just lost with Clemmie, he sobbed for the Clemmie who was trapped in a dark corner in the girl Patricia, and he sobbed for what could have been. They let him cry, he needed to do that, they just quietly surrounded him with love and care. He did not need to sleep but the earthly part of him wanted the comfort of curling up on the floor and sleeping. They left him for a while so he might rest and feel refreshed.

When he awoke they were there waiting for him. He

knew they would not let him feel alone again. He understood why they kept him here and how worried they were about him. The warm feeling they gave out had got into his bones. He knew he should have given that same warm feeling to Patricia.

"Thank you guys for being here," was all he could think to say, he felt calm, grateful and ready to work. He had many questions and they told him to ask what he needed to know. He started with a question he dreaded to ask but needed to know.

"What happened to Jimmy? Was that him I saw being trampled?"

They told him it was, and that Jimmy was now in a new existence. They added he was doing well and was happy. Angel was sobbing again for his friend. They told him that was the earthly part of him, he must think bigger and realise Jimmy had moved on. In response to his question they would not tell him where. As they said, it was not important. Angel accepted this, but suddenly he realised Stella was alone.

"Christ Almighty, Stella! What happened to her? She couldn't cope without Jimmy."

Angel felt a deep dread, "Please, what happened to her."

They told him, yes, Stella found it very hard at first to cope without Jimmy, and they added, that she had mourned deeply for him, Angel as well. They told him that Stella had genuinely loved Angel, but she had not realised how much until his death. She coped in the end by returning to the church. She had turned her back on religion when she met Jimmy, but a local church and new pastor revived her faith. They told Angel that he would be pleased to know that Stella fulfilled her destiny, learned all lessons set her and died much loved by the community she worked to help after Jimmy died. She never remarried, and in fact, died recently in earth years. She was with them for a while. Angel's eyes moistened at the thought. But he wondered on reflection why Stella and Jimmy were not together in a new life. They told him again that he was thinking earthly thoughts. They each have other people they will love and will love them. But yes, in further lives their paths will cross, just as yours will cross with them. Remember Angel, all important people you have loved will return at some time in other forms to be with you.

"So what about that fucking bastard Tony? What happened to him!?"

In asking this, Angel's body became tense, his fists clenched and his breathing came in heavy snorts. They realised this was going to be the most difficult matter to talk about. They would only tell him enough to answer his question. They could see Angel was distressed and feeling quite violent.

They told him that Tony died in a hail of bullets 3 hours after Angel and Clemmie. He was killed on Capone's orders. He was never intended to live long. He had now moved to another existence. Angel, desperate for revenge, urgently asked where he had gone. They would not tell him. Tense and more angry than he could remember ever having been he shouted, "Where was the justice in allowing that fucking evil, murdering bastard to live again?"

They answered that lessons have to be learned in future existences and the soul called Tony must learn them. Angel was not happy with that answer. He knew his present existence had no place for the anger and hatred he felt for Tony, but revenge is a very strong earthly emotion and one Angel would find hard to let go. They tried to calm him and help him to understand. They needed him to accept.

In answering all his questions, Angel was left feeling hopeless and alone. Everyone he knew and loved had gone. He raged at them, and asked why they had shown him his past existence, it was cruel, he didn't want this, he wanted his old life back. In a little madness, Angel pleaded to them to return him to his old life, to turn the clock back. He knew they could do it. He promised sincerely and loudly to lead a good life with Clemmie. He could stop the killing, and he reasoned, he would die with Clemmie when the time was right and they would go on together as they should to the next existence. As a last thought he threw in the fact that they would be spared all the problems they have now, it was a good plan he told them, everyone would win. He begged them to consider it.

They were surprised at this sad, unrealistic plea and rushed, a little unseemly for them, they preferred to ponder and reflect on decisions, to stop him thinking this way and get him back on track. He did not want the miserable bitch where Clemmie hid. He wanted Jimmy and Stella back. He wanted to feel safe, secure, successful and he wanted to belong again instead of feeling old, out of control and doing something he did not fully understand. He had cold feet and wanted peace and quiet and Clemmie, They knew that. The earthly pull was making him forget all that he knew and they needed to pull him back towards them. They needed to show him his past life – they needed him to remember Clemmie, to recognise her soul now in the body of Patricia. Angel, in his previous life had developed the skills to help Patricia. They all agreed it would be painful for Angel, but essential for both their souls to progress. But they also agreed to help ease his pain as best they could. They knew the soul of Patricia would recognise Angel and feel comfortable. Meanwhile, they had to look after Angel and they sent him pictures of indescribable beauty, showing him where they were, and where he would be in time. The sights were familiar and comforting. The earthly part of his brain, had, for the moment taken over and found it hard to interpret the beauty being shown him. The beauty of a rainbow and the colours, vibrant and alive within it was the nearest Angel would get to describe what his mind could see. It had the effect of making him think about what he was asking for and how stupid it was. Exhausted, the fight drained from him, the madness left him and they could see he was ready to listen. They would empower him with hope, love and understanding. It would take time, but they were confident it would be done.

They spent much time with Angel so he could recognise what had happened to him and accept his present situation. Everything he had done so far had been in a panicky, rushing and maniacal way. It would take time for him to realise why he was acting so out of his earthly character. They knew all his earthly life had been devoted to belonging and being needed. He would learn in his own time that this had started with his mother. Where he lived were so many poor children, all looked the same and were ignored and considered worthless, in fact as much of a pest as the rats were. Angel was always different and he knew he was needed by his mother and he belonged to her and her to him. She survived because of him. He earned the money for a large part of her life and cooked and paid the rent. He never saw himself as nothing, he was a needed someone and his whole earthly life was lived this way. Angel made a difference, he was important. They would help him come to terms with the word "Dead" and help him accept his importance and belonging in this new existence. They would empower him with his own strength to drive away the demons that told him he belonged to no-one, that he was lost and unwanted. It would take time. All valuable lessons have to be learned, often the hard way. He was learning his first lesson now. His pride had been hurt and he had only thought about himself and his needs. He was learning and understanding what he was required to do.

CHAPTER TWENTY NINE

A New Start

Time had passed since he first met Patricia. Angel had promised to come back the following day. That had been 3 months ago. Patricia had waited impatiently for the following day and was disappointed when Angel did not appear, she told herself it was to be expected, still what did she care. She had put on her best dress and done something with her hair, not especially for Angel she told herself, more so he could not say anything rude about her. After a month she began to think she may have dreamed him up, and she felt sad. The new hope inside her that had stirred when she saw Angel refused to go away and she was left with a yearning for something she did not know or understand. The frustration took the form of bitterness and came across to others as sarcasm or insolence. Before, she just ignored everyone, now she was on the attack. After six months passed Patricia was sacked by the GPO for gross misconduct. She had been warned many times for speaking to customers in a manner not becoming of a lady, and certainly not a GPO worker. In the early days her supervisors had agreed, that yes, some customers did appear to possess fewer brain cells than most household pets, but that was why she was there to help them with their telephone problems. After a while, they realised Patricia was just looking for trouble and if it did not come her way, then she started arguments. The supervisors were older ladies who looked on their switch room full of girls in a strict but maternal manner. As they used to say to each other, "Lord knows I've tried with her but there is no getting through to her." She knew she was hated by everyone there, they used to whisper behind her back or sneak looks at her while working on their switchboards to see what she was saying or doing. It would give them good gossip during their breaks. Before she would just ignore them, now she shouted across a busy switchroom, "Who the hell are you looking at bitch!" That sort of behaviour and language would never be tolerated, after one too many complaints, she was asked to leave. With no notice she went home that evening dreading telling her father she had been sacked. She felt the shame of such a thing, and quite honestly, did not think she deserved it. She decided to tell her Father the next day when she hoped she would feel more in control. When she got home she went straight to her room. Her father, sitting in his usual chair in front of the television with his early evening glass of rum shouted, "Oye Patricia, where's my dinner?" She shouted back, "In a minute dad," and in a voice that should have been quieter, she added "Then drop dead and do us all a favour." He thought he heard her say something else, but he knew he must have got it wrong, his Patricia would never say that.

After dinner that evening, Patricia went to her room as usual. She spent an hour accumulating all the self pity she could and the total came to enough is enough. With an unrealistic view of herself as the victim of the worst life anyone could possibly have with nothing to look forward to, she walked out of the house towards the main road that was ten minutes walk away. She preferred to believe Angel's visit happened, and was not a dream and it had served one good purpose. Now she knew for certain there was life after death. Her mother was on the other side, and she would be waiting for her, they could be together, this was all Patricia wanted. Without any further thought or discussion with herself, she walked across the two-lanes of heavy traffic and was knocked down and run over by a family saloon driven by a husband who thought he was going to be very late home and his wife would be waiting to serve the dinner, he hated heated up food. He later told police between tears that he did not see her, that she had just walked out in front of him. He sincerely wished he had left work on time and then this would not have happened. It would take him many, many months to stop seeing her face as she lay on the ground not moving. He saw blood trickling out of the side of her mouth and he thought she must be dead. The ambulance arrived quickly, the hospital was, fortunately, on the same road, just a few minutes away. Doctors and nurses worked hard to revive her, she kept slipping away, but they carried on bringing her back. They worked for hours to stem the blood flow and keep the heart pumping. They all saw a young girl and they were going to do the best they could to hold on to her.

He saw her standing about two feet from him. It was Clemmie. She had come to him. It was wonderful, but the voices kept telling him it was not right. He kept looking, he wanted to get closer but his feet would not move, he wanted to call her name but his voice would not respond. He wanted her so badly, to hold her, to hear her voice, to be with her. He shook with emotion and fought the voices who kept telling him to listen. This is what he wanted, what he always wanted, it had to be right that she was here. The argument raged between Angel and them for what seemed an eternity. They kept asking, "Who are you thinking of most, yourself or Patricia?" He told them loudly and clearly, "Fuck you all, this is between Clemmie and myself. She's here for a reason and that is to be with me! Do you hear! Clear off, go away, you know nothing." They gradually wore him down, he understood what they were saying, and with an inward sob listened to what he must do. He had realised that it was his fault Patricia was here, that if he had listened to them, it might not have come to this. He watched her hover in and out of life. He knew one word from him and he could keep her in death and with him. He could feel her pain and despair that brought her here and he knew he must stop thinking of himself and help her in what ever way she needed.

She opened her eyes and realised she was ok. That was not right. She remembered what she had done. She was slimmer than she remembered, she thought, funny what you notice first, it was her hair, it was longer and thicker. She felt calm and rested and at peace, it was wonderful. She heard a noise and looked over. He was standing there, all was clear, she was Clemmie again and he was her Angel. She smiled and stood and held out her arms.

"Angel, where have you been? I've missed you."

They spontaneously hugged and kissed. The feeling of love and happiness felt indescribable, neither wanted to let go. He had left her alone, he knew she needed someone, and he had deserted her. He must make amends. After a while, still holding each other tightly, Angel, fighting his emotions and winning, gently told her what she must do.

"Clemmie, honey, you can't stay here, you must go back now." She held him tighter and asked, "Why, when I have just found you again, I can't bear to live that life without you. He kissed her on the forehead and whispered, "You have a life to complete, I will always be with you and when it is the right time, we will be together always." She looked at him, and he recognised the defiant tilt of her chin, "No, I won't go back to that miserable existence as that miserable bitch, I'm fucking staying mister." Oh god! he had missed her. Such a strong character, such a beauty, how he loved her and everything about her, but he knew she had to return. He grabbed her arms and shook her gently. "Becoming quite a fucking madam aren't we?" He kissed her sharp and hard on the lips and continued tensely, "I would love you to stay," he paused, and took a deep breath "ok, ok, stay, but if you do, remember, we may not be together again because you would have broken the unwritten rule. If you leave a life before your allotted time, then you have to go back double quick to learn your lessons."

Angel was becoming choked up with tears and fought to say the words he needed to say, "Remember Clemmie, I will be with you always. Sure, we can be together for a very short while now, but I want you forever, not just a few minutes. You fucking go back, do you hear, I want you forever. It's the only thing that is keeping me going at the moment." She looked at him and realised he was serious. Clemmie contemplated life without him and knew that was not an option. Clemmie understood the cycle to eternity, as most souls do, each life whether good or bad is relished as lessons to be learned as part of the journey to everlasting heaven. In his panic, Angel had disrupted the soul called Clemmie and made her rethink her choices. After much thought, and with a sigh of resignation borne out by what must be done, she laid her cards on the table.

"O.k., I'll go back, but only if you promise to be there. Remember Angel, you know me as Clemmie who had all the gifts to keep her going. I had looks, charm, and all sorts of tricks, you know I would never have considered killing myself. Patricia has not been dealt any of these gifts, she is not particularly good looking, she has no charm or confidence in herself. She has no one to love her. I am Patricia without any of the tools Clemmie had to dig herself out." Her control left her momentarily and she cried, "Angel, be there, love me, give me your strength, help me get through." Don't leave me alone in that miserable existence." He agreed through tears. She looked at him and it was all too much. She wanted to stay with him, she pleaded with him, kissed him and hugged him, "Angel, find a way for me to stay. If you love me, really love me, you'll do this, not just for me but for you as well." It felt impossible, of course he wanted her to stay, God Damn it! but she couldn't and that was that! He had to persuade her. Overcome with love, fear of the consequences, and enough emotion to sink a continent, he grabbed her tightly to him. The tears stung his eyes and he closed them tight. His words coming breathless and fast, he whispered, "Clemmie, I love you, and because I love you, you must go back." It had come to him in a flash, and he spoke the words slowly and determinedly, "Clemmie, if you are Patricia, where is Clemmie?"

"What the fuck are you saying Angel?" Clemmie was tense and confused. Angel released his tight grip and caressed Clemmie's face. He whispered, "Honey, don't you see, Clemmie and Patricia, you are both the same. It's just that Patricia doesn't realise what a great person she is. I promise on my soul I'll be there to help her find the tools she needs to survive. She will feel loved, I will love her, I promise. I love you, I love her, you are both the same." She looked at him standing before her panting for breath, the words had exhausted him she could see, he looked so distraught, so lost. She understood what he was saying and agreed she would return, she knew he would not let her down again. He was so proud of her. Back in control again, Clemmie asked, "Before I go back, where the fuck is this place? Is this heaven?" He explained about the half-way area, and she agreed it would always be heaven to her because he was there. With a final gentle hug and kiss, she reluctantly let him lead her back. "Wasn't she fucking wonderful?" he said to them with so much pride he felt fit to burst. They had to agree, she was something else. Now Angel knew his role. He was to love Patricia and help her find happiness. He felt better. They were glad he had found a comfortable role for himself. They hoped when he was really needed he would have learned enough to cope and help Patricia through it.

"We've got her!" shouted a triumphant but tired doctor. Her heart beat was regulating nicely, she breathed at first in gulps, but that settled into a good rhythm, the bleeding was under control. They bandaged the broken ribs, set her left leg and cleaned up all her other superficial wounds, and cuts to stop infection. She did not look pretty, and the matted blood in her hair and blood smears would wait until she had regained consciousness.

CHAPTER THIRTY

The Awakening

He sat by her bed just looking at her. She slept, unconscious of all the to-ing and fro-ing going on around her with nurses constantly taking her pulse, her temperature and generally fussing round her bed. Apart from the black eye, the lump on her forehead and the bruising and cuts on her swollen face, he thought she looked beautiful. Her hair, still matted with blood, could be cut and shaped better he told himself. He looked at her cut hands and noted he would suggest to her some nail polish. He was going to make sure that everyone could see her beauty, she had hidden it for too long. A scraping noise made him look up from her face and he turned to see her father pull back a chair and sit down. The man was clearly upset and mumbling to what looked like his groin. Angel was intrigued.

"I know I've been a difficult father, but please don't leave me. I'll make it up to you, I promise. Please get better. I can't bear it. I love you very much. You are all I have, please get better." He looked up and stared at Patricia. Angel could see the tears in his eyes were ready to spill onto his cheeks, but he quickly wiped them away and with an embarrassed look, his head slightly bowed, glanced from side to side to see if anyone near was watching him. Angel felt kinda sorry for him. He looked very alone and lost. They sat side by side staring at Patricia, willing her to wake up. After about three hours Patricia started to stir. Her father leaned over to encourage her to open her eyes, in doing so he put his elbow through Angel's arm resting on the bed. A most odd sensation for Angel and one that for a few seconds made him realise he was really not there. Being an Angel for real still seemed very strange and quite upsetting. Apart from the obvious things, like not being able to touch her or move things, while he and Patricia were alone he felt alive, he realised it was other people that were making him feel dead.

When she opened her eyes, everything was slightly blurred, after blinking a few times she noticed two men sitting by her bed. She did not recognise either of them. She tried to say who are you but it came out as one long droning sound. Her lips were so dry and her tongue felt too big for her mouth. She could not be bothered to ask again, she was tired, so she went back to sleep. The nurse explained to the distraught father that this was normal, she would have concussion and be very woozy for a while. She would most probably sleep for a few more hours and the nurse suggested kindly that he might want to go home and get some rest and come back later, she added that it would be helpful if he brought some of Patricia's night clothes back with him and the usual toiletries that a young girl would require. Mr Banks was not sure what these things might be, but decided to go home and have a look.

Mr Banks walked home in 10 minutes. He sat down and had a glass of rum, it was still early in the day but as he told himself, it was for medicinal purposes only. It had been a tough night. After he had drained the glass, with a loud sigh he got out of his favourite chair and climbed the stairs to Patricia's room. He entered the room realising it had been many, many years since he had been in there, a long time even before his wife had died. It seemed a different world to him. The walls were covered in posters of young men, obviously pop stars, even he knew all about the Beatles and a little about the Rolling Stones who appeared to dominate the posters, although there was Joe Brown and a particularly nice picture of Elvis Presley, the picture was obviously taken in his younger days, not as he was now, all bloated and rhinestone suits. The room was a mess with bits and pieces of clothing, records, magazines and tissues everywhere. His eyes caught the shelf by Patricia's bed, he recognised what he saw, it was a little picture that his wife, Edna, used to keep in her bag of him and her when they were first married. He wondered where the smiling, young, very carefree couple went. Why had things changed so much. On the shelf he also saw Edna's favourite bottle of perfume. He hadn't seen the same type of bottle since, he couldn't remember when. It was called 'Evening in Paris' and was a deep blue bottle with a silver, slender top. He picked it up and opened it. Even though it was empty, he could still smell the happy times years ago when Edna used to wear it. He was always laughing then, so was Edna. He couldn't remember when they stopped laughing, it was so long ago. Patricia had a hanky with E embroidered in the corner beside the perfume and bits of lipstick that he supposed was Ednas'. The rest of the room was a mess, but this little corner of the shelf was tidy with everything neatly arranged. He sat on the bed, moving a mountain of papers to do so, and murmured to his shoes that he had no idea what had been going on in this room. He realised the child was grieving still, and doing it alone. A picture of Edna on the dressing table looked across at him, although she was smiling, he could see the disapproval of him in her eyes. It was all his fault, he knew that. How he had got into such a mess he did not know. He still missed his wife, but she had gone. With resolve he realised he had not lost Patricia and had time to make it up to her. He would change, he didn't know how, but he would try. He felt a little better and with a determination he had not felt for a very long time, he went about looking through the drawers of his daughter's cupboards to find something to take to the hospital.

She awoke again after an hour. It may have had something to do with the noise. The long ward was busy. The clanking and banging of beds being shifted from one end of the ward to other. New, very sick, or those coming out of surgery were moved nearest to the nurses station. As they recovered they were moved further up the ward. At present, Patricia was sited next to the nurses station but she was obviously going to have a change of company with a new admission being put in a bed beside her. The old lady who was there had done nothing but complain loudly of the noise caused by the nurses checking their sick patients through the night, she was obviously feeling better and the decision was made to move her further down the ward, so her bed, side cabinet, and any of her personal items were all shifted noisily to the other end of the ward. Patricia may also have been roused out of her sleep by Angel shouting at the old lady to "Shut the fuck up" when she complained again, to the nurses and orderlies pushing her bed, about all the noise and disruption she suffered during the night when Patricia was moved in to the ward. He knew she couldn't hear him but it made him feel better, he should have realised that Patricia was the only one to hear him and as she roused out of her sleep he felt bad that it may have been his fault, although he was getting anxious to see her awake so he could talk to her before her father came back.

She opened her eyes and looked at him. She felt limp and faint. She wondered who the funny little man was sitting by her bed.

"Hi, who are you?" she asked. She felt so dry every word stuck to her teeth.

"Oh God!" he thought. "Here we go again." He envisaged starting from scratch and hoped they would not argue like they did last time. Before he could answer, she asked for a drink. He was about to get up and ask a nurse but remembered they could not see him. Embarrassed he asked her to press the button near her hand. She was given a very small drink by the nurse and told she could have more later. The nurse decided she would watch her closely because her focus was off. She seemed to be looking at something close to the bed instead of at the nurse at her side. Concussion she knew could cause strange focusing but this one was new to her. She would ask the sister when she came on the ward.

There was no talking to Patricia who still went in and out of sleep for the next hour or so. By the time she awoke again she seemed a little brighter and looked at Angel as if she might know him from somewhere. He explained again who he was, that she was the only one who could see him, and that in a little while he felt sure she would remember everything. Patricia just looked at him, seeming to take in all the information but not acknowledging she fully understood. Angel left and said he would be back later. It was at this point her father arrived back. He was happy to see her fully awake and asked how she felt. She remembered him and suddenly remembered where she was, it all seemed to suddenly make sense and she felt deep embarrassment. Neither her nor her father alluded to the suicide attempt, but rather called it a careless crossing of the road. A whole conversation was built up over the fact that she should have been more careful and that it was, of course, an accident, and how the cars of today go far too fast etc. Both knew this was not true but felt more comfortable talking about an accident. Neither felt very close to each other, but that was nothing new. Mr Banks was the only one to find that unsatisfactory.

Her father stayed a few hours but left after promising to return the next day with magazines, fruit, and drink and anything else he could think of. She was glad he had gone. It had felt awkward, and later she would realise that she had never been that long in her father's company for many years. She felt confused, she seemed to remember another man at her bedside but tiredness took over and she drifted into a comfortable sleep before she thought any more about him. Angel returned just as Patricia woke. He sat by her bed and quietly said, "Hi, how are you doing?" She looked at him and at first he could see she did not know him, and then he saw a light of recognition in her eyes.

"Hallo, I remember you, you are my Angel."

He was so pleased she remembered and she didn't look angry at all. Things were looking good. After a few seconds, she looked at him again and tried to smile, but the tears were streaming down her cheeks. Angel felt quite alarmed and wondered what she had remembered that had upset her.

"I remember a bit now," she said and in a small voice asked, "I died didn't I?"

Angel nodded and tried to hold her hand but, of course, she could not feel it.

"You led me back didn't you, I remember that. You made me return to here. Thank you."

"I'll always be here for you Patricia. I promise you that. Now you get better quickly because we have shopping to do when you get out of here."

She nodded, not quite understanding what he was going on about, but happy to have him around, why? Well she would think about that later. She was still not fully aware of what was going on.

Angel was busy working on his plan to get Patricia back to being a young woman. He would ensure her hair, nails and make-up was perfected and her dress sense improved on. He would boost her confidence and make her feel good about herself. He was good at that, he knew what to do. If he had only realised what he was doing, and who he was doing it for, he would have convinced Patricia to join a Nunnery. But with more good heart and no sense of foreboding, Angel was planning.

**

They let Patricia home after a week in hospital. Her leg would take a lot longer to heal but the rest of her had improved no end. When she got home her father carried her to her room. He said it would be sensible for her to stay in there because the bathroom was upstairs and she could manage to get there with a crutch. He opened the door to her room and she gasped. Mr Banks grinned in a self-satisfied way.

"Well, do you like it?"

She was not sure at first, he had decorated the room and put all her posters back up. All her magazines were neatly arranged on the table and everywhere was clean and tidy and smelled of new paint. There was even a bunch of flowers on the cabinet by her bed. She felt embarrassed, and awkward, he had never done anything like this for her before, ever. She found it hard to know how to respond.

"Well, um, wow, it's really nice. Thank you very much."

Mr Banks was very happy with the praise. He had been quite excited to bring her home and see her face. He had spent the week decorating and cleaning her room. He sat her on her bed and could not contain himself any longer. He had bought her a present. He rushed to his room to get it and came back with the latest transistor radio. It was really small and it had ear phones. He liked it very much and thought it fab. Patricia's excitement and embarrassment was rising by the minute. Her father had bought her a present, but not just any present, but a wonderful present, and it wasn't even her birthday. And had her father said "fab." She could not believe her ears, OK, it was not the in word now, but it was a few years ago, and for her father to say it, well, he was really trying to be nice. It felt all too much. There was no precedent on how to react. This had never happened before, she felt embarrassed, hoping he did not expect a kiss, she was not ready for that. Mr Banks would have liked a kiss, but it would have been an embarrassment for him as well.

"Dad, thank you very much. It is a wonderful present. It's really fab. Thank you."

They laughed at her using the word fab as well. Both felt quite happy with the situation. Mr Banks left to make a cup of tea while Patricia fiddled with the transistor radio. She laughed to herself when she thought of the word "fab". How embarrassing to hear her father say that. She put her red face into her pillow and laughed.

Remembering Angel showing her the way back from death had, as you might expect, a profound effect on Patricia. She played the scene over and over in her mind. It was the most wonderful feeling to have someone who cared so much for you that they not only showed you the way back to life, but also stayed with you to ensure you were OK. She also nearly remembered how she felt when he led her back. The feeling was not quite there, but she felt on the periphery of something like an intense love. She tried and tried to relive the moment but it would fade around the feeling and she was left with the view of Angel walking with her. She was happy. What a strange thing to recognise, but yes, even her father seemed nicer. She reckoned over the weeks, that bang she must have got on the head had done her some good. She said to Angel many a time, that it had brought her to her senses.

"I was so depressed, so horrible, so hateful. Why was I like that Angel? I don't understand what was happening to me."

Of course, Angel had got it sussed out. Well, he had talked with them, and they had explained to him and he explained to Patricia. He was now much more in control and getting to like this kid very much. He explained that she'd had a really rotten time. As he said, even he was not nice to her. Now she had someone to care for her, which was him, she could be the person she always was deep down. He added which was a beautiful, person on the outside as well as on the inside. She liked the way he talked, he said such nice things. At first she did not believe it, but he had a way of making her feel proud of herself. She was confined to the house for a further 3 weeks before the cast came off. In that time she got her father, on Angel's instructions, to buy some nail polishes as seen in a magazine, together with nail polish remover, a manicure set and tissues. Her father, a little bemused by all that, did as he was told, happy to make her feel he was interested. He didn't understand why she wanted things like that.

They talked for hours and hours during the day about her life, her mother, her father. Why she had been so unhappy. He spent hours telling her about his previous life. He did not tell her that she was Clemmie, it would have been very difficult for her to cope with. She accepted he was an Angel very easily he thought. She explained that there was no one in this life that had shown any interest in her, except, of course, her mother. It seemed to make sense to her that the only person who could like her would be dead. Her mother was dead, and she had accepted Angel's explanation that her mother had to move on and was not allowed to contact her. He told a small white lie, and said he had a message from her sending Patricia her love and asking her to be happy. This was obviously all Patricia needed to hear, she believed him, and he did not feel guilty about the lie. He knew if her mother could have left a message it would have been that. If she could have put into words how she was feeling, she may have said how that something that had been missing was now in place – her soul felt normal.

On his regular visits back to them, he kept asking why it had all become so much easier. Patricia liked him. They were not arguing and everything was great. They asked him if, perhaps, with his new, calmer way of acting might have something to do with it. They also wondered if perhaps the feelings of love he was giving out had warmed Patricia. He agreed, yes he was kinda getting to love the little brat. He told them it would not be long before she was proud of herself and getting her life together. They thought he was doing a power of good. He liked that.

Over the months Angel kept this promise. It took a few trips to the hairdresser to get the cut right but now Patricia's hair had been highlighted with blonde streaks to take away the mousy look. The shine was due to good shampoo and constant brushing. It started to look and feel thicker and framed her face with gentle waves. Clothes were a bit more of a problem, but Patricia had lost weight and together with better quality materials, she was looking quite sophisticated. She had always walked like a model with her back straight and head up, Angel told her she now looked like a model. They laughed about everything. Happiness had certainly put a twinkle in her eye. She could not imagine what it would be like without Angel in her life. She loved him, he had become her best friend, brother, mother and father.

She had recently got a job as a telephonist/ receptionist in an Insurance Company in London. She loved it. The staff there were quite young and would often invite her to join them for a drink after work. She had developed a social life as well. Angel felt a real success. He told them he wondered if his work was nearly done, what did they think. They just said they would see how it developed. Angel did not follow her to work or after work. He was not stupid, he realised she needed space to develop.

The next step happened quite quickly, they had asked if Angel was able to cope with that. Patricia got a boyfriend. Patricia was not Clemmie, he did not feel jealous, more like an older brother, he was happy for her. He had seen the fellow, his name was Steve. He seemed quite shy, kept going red in the face every time Patricia looked at him. Seemed a good sort Angel thought. A bit heavily built for a young man but Patricia seemed to like him. He had bright orange hair which Angel always thought meant he had a temper, but he could not see a temper in this very amenable young man. He watched from a distance whilst Steve courted Patricia. She led him a merry dance, testing him for temper, for patience, for caring. He seemed to pass all her little tests with flying colours. Angel had mentioned to her that she should not push any young man as hard as she had. Patricia pointed out that she knew what she was doing. She liked him a lot but wanted to make sure there were no surprises after they were married. Angel was shocked, married, you are talking married already, you haven't even slept together. And how long have you been going out, it only seems 5 minutes? She blushed and said they had been going out for 18 months and she was not a loose type of girl, she would marry as a virgin. Angel asked if her father knew of their plans. She told him she had discussed it with him but he did not like Steve and so she had decided she would marry him anyway, she didn't need his consent. Angel recognised the defiant tilt of the chin. He thought the lad looked OK, he had a good job and seemed to follow Patricia round like a lap dog what could go wrong. He was pleased for her.

Patricia married 3 months later in a registry office. The witnesses were two people from their work and the only other person there she knew was Angel. Only Patricia saw him blowing his nose and getting quite emotional. Steve asked why she seemed to be laughing, she explained it must be nerves.

Angel had wished her luck and said he would leave her to get on with her new life. It was an emotional moment. He was so proud of her, so pleased she had her life together and that he had something to do with it. He promised he would never be far away and if she wanted him to just call his name. Both were crying the night before her wedding. He said the last time she would see him is at her wedding then she must have time to live her life with her new husband. Angel said he was impressed by Steve's organisation of everything. He had found a rented flat for them both, it was quite nice, Angel reckoned it would do for a start. Steve looked well on the way to promotion in the Insurance Company so Patricia would not starve. He told them he was really happy for them both but why did he feel so terrible. This is what he always wanted for Patricia.

The earthly demons were gnawing at his soul again. He wanted to stay with her. Of course he told them angrily he wanted her to be happy but why with a dirty blonde haired boy who ok, looked right for her, but he, Angel, was the only one she really loved. They surrounded him again with warmth and caring, telling him they were proud of him, that no one else could have done such a good job, that one day he would be with Clemmie again and he must remember that. He did take a little comfort from that, yes, she was on track, she would live this life and then she would be his for eternity. That helped, he felt a little better.

Now he thought they would let him go where he

should have gone before and wait for Clemmie. But they insisted he wait where he was in case Patricia called him. They reminded him he had promised her he would come if she called. He thought they were being petty minded, he could only see a happy ending for Patricia.

CHAPTER THIRTY ONE

The Wake Up Call

The call came. 10 years later. To Angel it felt almost like a blink of the eye, time had passed quickly where he was. The call made him feel immediately confused, disorientated with what was going on and rather excited. His Clemmie/Patricia wanted to see him, he felt rather wonderful. They told him to be careful and mindful to assess the situation carefully. They reminded him of his first visit to Patricia, and he promised that would not happen this time. Once again, he was anxious to go to her. He wondered if she had changed much, the earthly side of him checked his clothes and pulled and straightened his jacket and trousers. He brushed imaginary fluff from his jacket sleeve and prepared expectantly to meet Patricia.

He went to where she called him and found himself in what looked like a hospital operating theatre. The person on the operating table was surrounded by what looked like two doctors and three nurses. In his alarmed state he shouted her name. He rushed forward to be by her side, unaware he had walked through the doctor and nurse at the end of the table.

He looked at a tired and sweating Patricia who, whilst awake, he could see was in a lot of pain. Becoming even more alarmed and knowing he must not let her see this, he took a deep breath, calmed himself and asked gently, "Honey, what has happened to you?"

She looked up at him, and instead of smiling at his arrival she spat in a tight whisper, "I'm having a baby you idiot!" With that she groaned and started panting and blowing as if her life depended on it. The doctor told her well done, and nearly there, and encouraged her to keep panting. He wondered why she had called him an idiot but, well, he had been called worse while helping women deliver their babies. Angel tried to take in the scene, and quickly realised this was no time to panic. He would ask all the questions he wanted to ask later, like where the hell was Steve? Back to the task in hand he would help Patricia through this. Once again, with a deep breath to calm himself he told her, "OK Patricia, honey, I know you can't feel it, but I'm holding your hand." He was in control. The contraction had subsided and Patricia could talk. "I can feel it Angel, I'm glad you're here." He looked down and realised he could feel her hand too. With tears in his eyes he thanked them, they had made this possible. Angel noticed the nurses and doctors looking oddly at Patricia. He nodded at the staff at the end of the operating table.

"Honey, I don't think you should talk to me while they are here, you're frightening the normal people." She gulped a giggle and squeezed his hand.

"Great idea Patricia, just squeeze my hand in reply." Angel winced as the gentle squeeze got stronger and stronger. He looked at Patricia and saw she was coping with another contraction. She squeezed his hand harder than any muscle bound man could. When the contraction had passed and Patricia had lessened her grip, Angel said with feeling, "Fuck me! Your pain is definitely my pain too." She gave him an apologetic smile and stroked his hand in apology. "No honey, if it helps, you squeeze as hard as you like, what do I need this little old hand for anyway, it's all yours." The contractions ebbed and flowed for another hour. Angel was getting worried and tired, and his hand hurt like hell. He was wondering if this should go on for all this time. She slapped his wrist to stop him loudly cursing and swearing at the doctors to fucking do something instead of just standing there. He apologised again to her and stroked her damp, dishevelled hair. She looked at him and smiled. She could not help herself, "I'm so glad you're here," she said. Angel stroked her face and whispered, "I'm glad you called me." Only one doctor remained with Patricia, the other being called away. He distractedly answered, "Course we're here. Won't be long now Patricia – you're nearly there." With that Patricia started bearing down. After another half hour of intense hand squeezing, Patricia delivered a beautiful baby girl. She and Angel cried together as they looked on what they both thought to be the most beautiful of babies. The baby was wrapped and placed in Patricia's arms. In wonder and excitement of witnessing a new life, Angel kissed the baby and then Patricia. "You did it, you just did it. Oh Clemmie, we've got a beautiful daughter."

"Who's Clemmie?" Angel shocked into silence at

what he had said and unbelievably sad to realise this was not his daughter, could not answer Patricia. The nurses came in that instance and took the baby away for weighing and all the other things they do with new babies, and proceeded to clean up Patricia and make her more comfortable. She was distracted and forgot her question, she realised she was very tired and wanted to sleep. Angel said he would come back when she had rested. He gave her a tender kiss on the forehead, relishing the ability to touch her, and with much reassurance that he would be back as she woke, he left her to sleep.

He returned distraught and tired and angry and incredibly depressed. He did not understand what had happened, and why did he feel so bad. They explained that childbirth heightened all the senses and the essence of Clemmie would have been very close to the surface. In his state of emotion he had got caught up with the essence of Clemmie and the baby had felt like his child. They understood his disappointment and realised they must help him through this because they knew he needed to be strong for Patricia, he would soon realise why he was here and they hoped he would know what to do to help Patricia through it. Time was short, but Angel was much easier to help now, he accepted their wisdom and they spent time helping him to understand and cope with his feelings so he would be ready to help Patricia.

A wiser, stronger, albeit a little sadder Angel arrived back at Patricia's bedside. She was in a room by herself. He looked at her but he only saw Patricia, the essence of

Clemmie had retreated back into the inner Patricia. Although a little disappointed, he knew he should be pleased because he realised he did not need any distractions at the moment. He knew something awful must have happened. It was not normal for a married woman to give birth alone without a husband, family, or friends around. Everybody has someone, or so he thought. What had happened to Patricia in the 10 years since she got married. He would find out soon.

She woke as he sat beside her, almost as if she sensed his presence. He held her hand, happy to note he could still touch her. "Hallo sleepyhead," he whispered as he stroked her face. She smiled lazily, her eyes not quite focused. He caressed her hand while she came round. He took his hand reluctantly away as Patricia tried to move. With a grunt she pulled herself up into a sitting position and re-arranged her covers, took a sip of water and grabbed Angel's hand back into hers. She needed his strength, he knew that. "Where is your baby?" Angel asked, not knowing when it would be a good time to ask what he needed to ask. "The nurses will keep her in the nursery for a few hours so I can sleep, I'll have her here when she needs feeding." Angel was impressed, "You know a lot about all this." Patricia smiled, "I should, this is my third baby." Stunned, Angel looked at her "You've been busy. I can't believe it, little Patricia a mother of three children." He squeezed her hand and asked their names. "Well," she composed herself, obviously very proud of her children, "My eldest son, who is 6 years old, very handsome is called Michael after you, and my youngest son, who is 4 years old, such a lively character, you'd like him, a cheeky little imp, is called James, Jimmy, after your best friend, and my daughter, as you know is one hour old, and so beautiful," Patricia's eyes misted at the thought of her, "I'm calling her Angela after you." Patricia felt embarrassed by Angel's stare, but all he could say was, "Wow." His eyes misted and threatened to flood. With a squeeze of his hand she told him how much she had missed him over the years. Her children, she told him, were her absolute joy, and somehow, they reminded her of him, Angel. He thought motherhood had changed her. She would never have talked so emotionally before. He asked her gently what had happened, and where was Steve. Why wasn't he with her and their beautiful baby and where were her boys, and why no-one else had been with her. She laughingly told him to slow down and then unexpectedly, she burst into tears. When she had settled and blown her nose, wiped her eyes, she sniffed, took a deep breath and started from the beginning, making sure she was holding Angel's hand tightly. He squeezed her hand reassuringly as she started.

"Well, we got married, remember." Angel nodded and squeezed her hand again, as if to say go on. "We were happy for years, Steve has done well in his job and we are comfortably off, got a nice house, everything materially I could want. Steve became very sociable, mainly to do with work. We went to some lovely events and we were having a great time." She smiled at the memory, then her smile changed to a look of apology as if to say now comes the nasty part. "When Michael was born, Steve carried on socialising and I stayed at home.

He was good to me and seemed proud of me, but would not stay at home because, as he said, his work and socialising paid for our life style. I sort of understood that, but it was hard. I never went anywhere after that, no baby-sitters you see. After Jimmy was born, real trouble started, I think I let myself go a bit, I was tired with two children to look after and never a break from them, but Angel, please don't think I didn't want them, I did, they are my reason for living, I just wanted a little break every now and then, I don't think that is too much, do you?" She looked at him for his reaction and he kissed her on the cheek and reassured her she deserved a break, every woman would expect a break, he added not helpfully, that he thought it should be the law to allow mothers to have a break. She laughed, and he realised he had gone too far over the top with that comment. Never mind, she felt tears in her eyes at his earnest caring, she had missed him. "Anyway, Steve was hardly at home and if I complained we would have terrible arguments. His language was and is disgusting. I was not brought up to allow swearing, you know that Angel." Angel nodded, he remembered how upset she got. "But at least your swearing was not directed at me personally. The punches didn't start until a couple of years ago." Angel could not understand how she could talk so matter-of-fact about this man who was her husband. He was getting ready to do him a serious injury, but he tried to keep his temper in check until Patricia had finished. "He treats me now like his skivvy. He says I'm a parasite and living off him so I must do what he says. He loves his children Angel, he really does.

He buys them lots of things and spoils them rotten."
Angel felt his temper rising again, his cheeks felt redder
and redder. "Why haven't you left him? Go home to
your father, he'll take you back." She smiled gratefully
at Angel. It was wonderful to have someone on her side.
It had been so long. "The children love their father, I
can't take them away. I couldn't survive on my own. I
am useless at anything outside of the house. Look at me
Angel, I'm good for nothing. I haven't earned any
money for six years, since Michael was born." Angel
wondered where the confident, articulate girl he left to
get married had gone. "Why isn't your father here?" He
could tell by Patricia's manner that she did not want to
answer. She shifted position, and looked at the ceiling,
he could see she was trying to compose herself, the tears
were not far away. In a hesitant, small voice she told
him.

"We had a huge, awful fight just after I got married.
He was cross I went ahead without his blessing, or
invitation. He was upset, I could tell, but that didn't stop
him telling me that Steve was no good and would, after
a short while, do me some harm. I thought he really
hated Steve. I lost it with him and my temper got the
better of me. I can remember every word to this day. I
called him selfish, evil and wanting me to have no
happiness. We said terrible things to each other, rather,
I told him everything I'd ever thought of him like how
wicked he was to my mother and how I wished he had
died and not her. By the time I had finished he was close
to hitting me, looking back now, I can tell he was really
upset. Anyway it finished with him disowning me and

telling me never to darken his door again. I was glad to leave and wished him a painful death." Patricia looked near to tears. "I wish I hadn't said that." After a short pause she looked at Angel and said, "He was right you know. He must have recognised something of himself in Steve." She was now in tears. "I miss him you know, but I said such terrible things, I couldn't contact him, I was too ashamed, besides he has never contacted me. He was right all along. I've burnt my boats there." Her crying had evolved into huge streaming tears and she let go of Angel's hand to search for a hanky or tissue.

Angel, who had been struggling between anger at Steve and sadness and comfort for Patricia had given in totally to comforting Patricia. When she had settled down and the tears had been stemmed, Angel cuddled her. She responded immediately and hugged him back telling him how he was the only one to love her truly and she loved him. She begged him never to leave her again. All the emotion had tired them both and Patricia laid down again and Angel laid beside her holding her hand. Without looking at each other, Angel asked her how she would feel if one of her children left her after saying hurtful things, would she forgive them, would she want to see them again and what if they had children, would she want to see her grandchildren. Patricia answered yes to all those questions. Gently Angel suggested that perhaps her father, as a parent, would feel the same. Did he even know he was a grandfather? Patricia thought about that and started to cry again. Angel went on, perhaps the birth of her daughter would be a good time to write to her father. He wondered if perhaps they would all benefit from seeing each other. He told Patricia what her father had said at her bedside when she was unconscious from the suicide attempt. Patricia responded to that by crying so loud a nurse popped her head in the door to see if she was all right. After blowing her nose she reassured the nurse that it was just the emotion of giving birth and she was going to have a sleep. Angel said when she was feeling better she should write a letter and he would go with her to visit her father. Patricia nodded her agreement and thanked Angel. But Angel wanted to find out more of what was happening. Once again he wanted to know where Steve was.

Patricia wanted to sleep but Angel kept asking her about Steve. At last she said what she did not want to talk about. The reason he was not at her side for the birth of Angela she explained was because he was with his mistress, fancy woman, whatever you want to call it. When she went into early labour she knew where he was but was not going to give her the satisfaction of calling him at her house. She had asked her neighbour to look after her boys and told her she would be fine going to the hospital by ambulance. She reassured Angel that she had been Ok about it until the labour got really started and she thought of Angel and called for him to be with her. He was touched by this and caressed her face in thanks. He wanted to know why she had never called him over the years. Surely, he reckoned, she could have done with his support and he told her earnestly that he wished he had been around for her earlier, that he could have helped. Once again, the ceiling seemed to have caught her attention. With a sigh that held a volume of tears, she explained how embarrassed she had been, how she knew he wished great things for her and what a disappointment she was. A useless wimp is how she had described herself. She was worried that not only had she disappointed him but that he would be disgusted by her and how she was. The call to Angel was a desperate spur of the moment thing that she was glad she had done. He promised he would never leave her again for so long. With tears welling in his eyes he told her how sorry, no mortified he felt at leaving her with Steve. He tried to assure her he had her best interests at heart and thought she would be happy with Steve and he was no longer needed. No fucking way he told her, was he going to leave her by herself. He was going to stick around for ever. She felt so good, the best feeling she had for a long time, a wonderful family and with Angel by her side she felt stronger. At that moment the door was opened urgently. Steve strode in slightly breathless and very red in the face. He looked around the room in desperate panic to find a suitable place to put down the very large bunch of flowers so he could hug his wife who sat stiffly and coldly upright in the bed. He explained he had just found out, and how was she, and where was the baby, a daughter he muttered quietly and proudly. The concern for his wife left his eyes when he saw her looking so well, now he wanted to see his baby. Coldly Patricia told him she was in the nursery. She answered all his questions about how she was feeling, and did she cope all right with one word answers of yes, no, ok. To Angel who stood in a corner of the room it looked like Steve was a caring considerate husband who was still in shock and dismay from missing the birth of his daughter and Patricia looked like the bitch from hell he remembered years ago. Confused, Angel left them together and returned to them. Could they explain what the fucking hell was going on.

They told him nothing but used their time with Angel to calm him and make him realise he had to see how things developed. Angel realised that no matter what Patricia had lied about, for he found himself believing that she had lied about Steve, he would always be there for her and try and cope with this new development. He realised that he loved Patricia, not like Clemmie, but more like a daughter. Patricia had some recognisable traits of Clemmie but was her own person. Angel reckoned that if he had a daughter with Clemmie, Patricia would be the result. The feeling of love was very akin to how he felt about Mrs A. and he was content to recognise the feeling and felt comfortable and reassured and strong. Patricia was going to be happy, he would see to that. They thought sadly, he was panicking again and not thinking straight. They asked him where he kept his magic wand. As he was about to, once again, go on the attack and put Patricia's world to rights as he saw it, he stopped in his tracks and smiled. He recognised the ironic humour of their comment. This time, he listened to them and realised he must help Patricia gently, and in a way that she wanted. To start with, he thought, he would keep a check on Steve to see what he was up to. He felt like a detective. In answer to his question, they had told him he could go anywhere he wanted if it was connected to Patricia. So feeling quite elated and excited at doing something, and with an attitude that he was playing a game, Angel set off to find Steve. They would wait and worry about Angel. They knew it would not be long before he was back.

CHAPTER THIRTY TWO

Home Truths

He found Steve at home. He looked around quickly and noted Patricia had done really well, her home seemed to have everything from lovely carpets, furnishings that looked expensive. He watched as Steve prepared a meal for the two boys playing in the garden, Angel stayed while they ate the meal and he followed them to the hospital to see their mother and new baby sister. He felt confused, Steve looked a caring husband and loving father. What on earth was Patricia's problem, he even wondered if she had made up the story about the mistress. Angel could see no signs in Steve of having a mistress. He knew men, and there was no guilty look, no apologies, or that furtiveness he had seen in other men during his earth life.

He decided to follow Steve back with the boys. They seemed to be going home. He did not know why he decided to do that. He had already come to the decision that Steve was an O.k. guy, he supposed it was because he could not bring himself to believe that Patricia had lied to him. He knew Patricia could be many things, bad tempered, and selfish, but lying was not something he had seen in her before. He watched as Steve put the boys to bed and went through what looked like a ritual of storytelling and kisses and tucking in. Angel was about to leave the scene, he was getting bored, and fed up with Mr Wonderful. Steve was beginning to irritate him. He knew he must have done something to cause Patricia to act like she was. He was going to go back to the hospital and sit with Patricia when someone knocked on the door. Angel followed Steve to the door to see who it was. A young lady of about 25 years walked in through the front door, when the door was closed she turned and stretching to put her arms around his neck, gave Steve a lingering kiss that looked both familiar and passionate. Instead of pushing her away Steve reciprocated with obvious pleasure. Angel knew she was no relative or neighbour popping by for an update on the baby. Steve took her coat and bag. She made herself comfortable on the settee in the lounge while Steve poured them both a whiskey and lemonade. They seemed to Angel to be very comfortable and at ease with each other. Angel fought hard to control his temper. Now he knew that Patricia had been telling the truth. The man had no shame, this was his wife and children's home and he had brought this fucking whore into their home. He stayed and listened, just to make sure he was not misunderstanding the situation, as if he could misunderstand what he was seeing he thought. They talked about the new baby and that Patricia insisted her name would be Angela. The whore's name was Janice, he thought that was the worst name he had ever heard and it suited the fucking bitch. At first he thought she looked quite pretty but on closer inspection he found she was an ugly bitch with a laugh that cackled stupidly. His hatred of Janice switched dramatically to Steve when he heard him call Patricia a snivelling bitch who was not a fit mother for his children. He was promising the whore that one day he would take the children from Patricia and go and live with Janice. The whore signalled her agreement by letting her hand slip further down his chest to his lap. Angel left in disgust, he knew he did not want to watch the inevitable outcome of such a move. He was hot, he was angry and incapable of facing Patricia feeling like he did. He hung around for what were 4 earth hours, he sat in the boys room watching them sleep. It calmed him a little. He watched their chests rise and fall with each breath, they looked so sweet and innocent. Both boys looked beautiful, they had blonde hair although the eldest, Michael, was going darker, they had long eye lashes just like Patricia, and a complexion that could only be described as peaches and cream. He felt stinging tears coming into his eyes, he understood why Patricia was so proud of them. The anger was rising again, and he told the boys that their cheating, two-faced bastard father was not going to take them away from their mother. He heard the front door close downstairs and went to see what was happening.

Steve was taking the glasses into the kitchen. The bitch must have left, Angel surmised. Angel followed Steve from the kitchen back to the lounge wondering what on earth had happened to his and Patricia's relationship and how on earth was he going to help Patricia through this. Steve sat down and was just staring into thin air with a smile on his face. He murmured softly, "a daughter."

Angel watched him, he found himself looking intently into Steve's eyes to his soul, trying to find a reason for his treachery. What he saw he did not believe. He withdrew quickly and massaged his throbbing temples. The pounding subsided slowly and he tried to assimilate what he saw but his mind refused to allow that to happen. His breathing was coming in gulps. It had been a long time since he had suffered such a shock. It took many minutes for his breathing to regulate and the throbbing in his head began to settle into a constant dull ache. He had to look again, he must have it wrong, this could not be right. Slowly, again he looked into Steve's eyes and, yes, he saw Tony, strutting as bold as brass. Angel withdrew again but this time a numbness of pure hatred had engulfed him and he was spitting nails and ready to murder. He lunged at Steve roaring like a banshee on heat. Each blow aimed at Steve's face and body was projected with all the venom of a force 10 gale. For about 10 minutes Angel staggered and fell through and against Steve as each forceful blow failed to connect sending Angel propelled forward and sideways with momentum of the blows. Exhausted, frustrated by the unharmed and unruffled Steve still sitting smiling on the sofa Angel, raged with murderous and vengeful curses. He tried to pick up objects to smash into Steve but however much he tried he could not. Eventually he collapsed in tears of frustration, not knowing what to do with all the murderous actions he could not produce. Panting and sobbing he tried to clear his mind. There must be a way to finish Tony, he had to put aside for the moment all his vengeful feelings and stop and think, he could feel the sweat dripping down his face with the odd drop stinging as it entered his eye. Absentmindedly, he wiped his face he had a plan. It was a wonderful plan. He went up to Steve, his face no more than one inch from his and shouted, "You fucking, murderous, bastard, I am about to get you. You are dead, but before you are dead, you will lose the most important things in your life – your kids. If I could get to you, I would have squeezed every inch of life slowly out of you, you." He had to stop there. The hatred had developed so much that Angel thought he might faint. He had to leave and work on his plan.

Angel could not go back to them, they would have stopped him. Besides, they were the last people he wanted to talk to at present. They knew about Tony, he was sure of that, how could he trust them again, he hated them as well. He needed no one else, he would see to Tony himself. A park nearby was closed, it was 1 a.m. after all, this would do for him, he would have no distractions while he planned. It was a simple plan, it had poetic justice in it, and it would succeed. The only person who could physically hurt Steve was Patricia. All Angel had to do was to guide Patricia to leaving Steve and taking the children, that would hurt him, then he would get her to kill Steve. It was justice. Tony had killed Clemmie and him and she would repay him by killing him in this life. He reasoned it was Karmic justice, in some ways, Angel reckoned this is what was supposed to happen all along, now he knew what his role really was. He spent the night working out the finer points. Patricia trusted him and would do what he asked. Again, he had no need of sleep, but for the remainder of the night he lay down and slept. The evening had exhausted him. The next morning he reasoned would be soon enough to talk to Patricia and start his plan of action.

Angel awoke to find himself back with them. He raged and screamed at them and tried to leave but could not. He cursed them strongly, accused them of treachery and betrayal. Revitalised with sleep he ranted on and on getting more and more tired. They let him, knowing now was not a good time to explain or help him. After what seemed hours, Angel ran out of energy and sat with his head in his hands breathing deeply and loudly, unable to shake the rage he felt, but unable to give vent to it any more. He tried another tack. He asked if they would give him the ability to touch anything on earth as he could Patricia. They refused. He knew why, he knew they were aware of his plan. He asked what was wrong with his plan. Why could he not kill Tony, it had to be justice for what Tony did. He pleaded with them for help. He quoted one of the very few parts of the bible he seemed to remember, "God helps those who help themselves. So that is what I am doing." In desperation, he sought to think of anything else he could dredge up from his limited knowledge of the bible.

"I seem to remember something about God being good but also a vengeful God. He must approve of this plan, go ask him, I'll wait."

They thought he was going quite mad and certainly did not understand the point of any of this situation. They metaphorically rolled up their sleeves knowing a lot of work needed to be done with Angel. Firstly, they said he could not see Patricia yet as he would disturb her soul with his ideas. Secondly, they knew he had totally worn himself out emotionally. Although it had never crossed his mind, they reminded him he had not eaten since joining them. It was, of course, not necessary, but they suggested it might give him some emotional nourishment if he were to eat a meal and have maybe have a cup of coffee with it. He told them he could not eat a thing. They laid a table and chair out for him and on it he found ham and eggs and fresh coffee and warm rolls and butter and some pancakes with the syrup he liked. The smell beckoned him and one mouthful out of curiosity led to the lot being finished in record time. He had to admit he felt better, warmer and more relaxed. They told him to look behind him, there he saw a door, the first door and wall ever in this place. They encouraged him to go forward and open it. He felt scared and did not know why. With much encouragement he tentatively moved forward and opened the door a little. From what he could see, it looked very familiar and he opened the door wider. It was his apartment, he went in and found everything as it was. The picture of Mrs A. was there with a rose in a small vase positioned close to it as always. He looked around smiled, and before he realised, he was overcome and crying like a baby. They left him in his familiar surroundings hoping it would help him feel at peace. They knew he had been through a bad time.

Angel awoke from sleep in his bed and for a split second wondered if he had dreamed everything. He got up and made some coffee and walked round his apartment touching lovingly everything, including the mats on the floor. He knew they had recreated this for him. The murderous rage had subsided enough for him to want to listen to what they had to say. After his coffee, he washed up, relishing this simple task, tidied his bed and reluctantly left his apartment to talk to them. Outside again, was the same. He thanked them for giving him his apartment back, apologised for the terrible things he had said about them and asked them to tell him what the fuck was going on.

They were glad he seemed so relaxed and hoped all would make sense to him. They explained that Patricia had lessons to learn and so did Steve. They told Angel very firmly that he must allow them to learn or make mistakes, it was in their karma to learn. Angel's role in all this is to support Patricia. They asked him if he thought getting Patricia to kill Steve would be supportive and help her karma? and what about her children, how would they feel with their father dead and their mother a murderer. Who would look after them. Did he want their lives destroyed as well? They also asked him why Patricia had not left Steve up to now if she knew he had a mistress. They asked if she hated him so much, why had she had another baby by him? Before he could answer they told him not to suggest Patricia had been raped, this was not the case and he knew it. She was making her own decisions, he was there just to support whatever she wanted to do. If he really loved her, knowing the consequences of disturbing a life and its lessons, he would ensure he did not influence her with his own feelings. They needed him to realise he would be destroying Patricia's life and her children's lives if he had gone through with his actions. He quietly realised they were right but, and it was a big but, why is Tony getting away with it again. Who is going to make him pay for his previous actions? They reassured him he would pay in his own way, not Angel's way. Angel left them to assimilate the information from them and make another cup of coffee. He found drinking coffee in his apartment very soothing and restful. He spent many hours thinking on what they had said and wrestling with his feelings about Tony. The winner of this match was Patricia. Angel realised he was always going to be there for her and must help her in whatever way she wanted. He would continue to wish Tony a painful death but would leave it to his karma to sort him out. Angel would not have to wait long.

They agreed he seemed to understand. They were pleased he felt more able to cope. It had been a worrying time for them, they were glad Angel seemed to have learned so much with them and coped quicker than they could have hoped. Angel wanted to see Patricia, he was worried she might think he had left her again, he reminded Them that he had promised her he would always be there for her, and he asked how many days had he been away from her. They agreed he was ready to leave them again and that two days had passed and Patricia was now at home. Once again, without so much as a thank you very much, goodbye, or see you soon, Angel had gone to see Patricia. They realised he may have learned a lot since being with them but he was still impetuous.

CHAPTER THIRTY THREE

The Real Stuff

Patricia was making up some bottles for Angela in the kitchen when Angel arrived. She sensed him more than saw him.

"Where have you been? I thought you had left me again," Patricia sounded down. Angel thought it must be his fault and wanted to make it better. He explained he could not come straight away but was here now for her. She in turn started to cry. The anger was rising as Angel assumed Steve had upset her but before he said anything she told him to take no notice of her, she was tired and had the baby blues. She saw the look on his face and explained about how a woman gets tearful a few days after having a baby and it would pass, something to do with her body returning to normal after a birth. He stayed with her all day and made her laugh and watched her feed Angela and look after her. He could not believe Angela had grown in two days since he last saw her. In passing, whilst preparing the evening meal, Patricia mentioned she had written to her father telling him about Angela's birth and the fact she had 2 boys already. Angel thought she looked a bit embarrassed. She asked whilst peeling a potato very carefully, if he thought her father would reply. Angel reckoned he would. He asked her where she was living now and was it far from where her father lived in Newbury Park. Patricia explained that although they lived in Loughton, which was either a two bus or two train ride from Newbury Park, she could get there in about 15 minutes by car, so it was not far really. She added that Loughton was a good class area and wonderful for children as it had Epping Forest close by. He asked if she liked it here and Patricia replied without hesitation, no she did not like it in Loughton. She went on to explain that all her troubles started when they moved there. Her neighbours she told him, although lovely, were not from her background and she had nothing in common with them, Steve had met this other woman since they had moved there. So, she felt lonely, isolated, unwanted and not classy at all. So, yes, she wished she lived back in Newbury Park somewhere normal where she could go in the garden in her curlers without the neighbours thinking she was dreadful, could invite someone in for a cup of tea without feeling ashamed of how the place was a mess and not that well decorated. Some days she told Angel she spoke to no adult except at the shops, where you still had to be careful because the local shop keepers were such gossips. Angel asked if she talked to Steve. She laughed a sad humourless laugh and said he often was not home until very late or he would go away for a few days, all work of course she added wryly. Perplexed, Angel asked why she was still there and had not left him. She could not answer him at first. After some thought she sited the children as her reason for staying, and when challenged that this was not a valid reason, she answered that she was not ready to leave him. As she said, he had loved her once, perhaps he would again, where else was she to go anyway, as she had said before, she was no good by herself, she could not support her children. Angel goaded her a little to say what she did not want to say and that was if she left Steve he would take the children and she could not survive without them. Angel thought that was unrealistic but Patricia was adamant that she would not want that put to the test. She could lose everything and she was not prepared to do that. At that point Patricia got very upset and feeling alarmed, Angel reassured her that she should do what she thought best.

About one week later, Patricia answered her telephone at about 11 a.m. and a hesitant voice asked if that was Patricia, on replying yes, the caller said this is your father speaking. She had recognised his voice but unable to say anything constructive she feigned surprise at his call. Both spent minutes talking utter nonsense about not recognising voices, it had been a long time, weather bad at present, etc. Angel had been listening to this utter crap, he told Patricia so in no uncertain terms and goaded her to say something. Patricia and her father were waiting for the other to speak first, to say something to mend the situation, each had far too much pride, neither wanted to feel rejected. Angel was getting madder and madder telling Patricia to say something nice. Just to get Angel off her back, Patricia suggested tentatively that she could call round to see him, and bring the children with her, if that is what he wanted, she added. Her father cleared his throat and said yes, that would be very nice. He asked a little too quickly for his liking when was she coming. Feeling a little apprehensive, but very excited, she said she could come tomorrow if he wanted. He agreed that yes, that would be nice and he would get some cake and lemonade for the children. They agreed they would come at 12 noon. He thanked her for ringing and finished the call quickly. He did not want her to hear the lump in his throat. The tears came as he put the phone down.

Angel was about to explode when she came off the phone, he wanted to ask her what the hell she was playing at. He was going to ask if that was supposed to be a "let's make it up" conversation, but of course he did not. He saw her face as she put the phone down and decided to hug her instead. When her tears had subsided, she wiped her eyes, cleared her throat and said to Angel to keep out of her way as she had lots to do. Perplex he asked what the fucking hell had she got to do that was so important today. Quite primly she told him as she bustled around the kitchen, that she was visiting her father tomorrow and she wanted to make sure the children had their best clothes clean and pressed. He looked at her as if she was mad. She turned, gave him an impish look and laughed. It had been a long time since she had seemed so happy.

It seemed to take Patricia all morning to get herself and the children ready to visit her father. The boys were quite bewildered by their mother humming and every few minutes cuddling them and saying they were going to meet their granddad. By the time they were ready to leave the boys were hyped up and behaving badly with the excitement of it all. Even Angela, who was too young to understand also seemed to do her bit by being sick on 2 outfits and needing to be changed in quite a panic. With much fuss and panic, they all got in the car. The boys were fighting and Angela was crying, Patricia realised she had hyped them all up too much and needed to calm them down. Angel had a headache and said he would meet them there, he could not bear all the noise.

Twenty minutes later Patricia pulled up outside her father's house. The boys were quiet and Angela was asleep. Angel did not know what she had done but he thought her bloody marvellous to have calmed them all down. If Angel had bothered to stay with the car he would have seen that all Patricia had to do was to sing to her children to calm them down. She had a terrible voice but her children seemed to like it. Angel watched as she got them all out of the car. The baby, still asleep, was carried in her arms. She managed to straighten the boys hair with one hand and usher them up to the front door.

As she took a deep breath, grouped the boys together and put a protective arm around them, the door opened. Mr Banks had been watching for their arrival, the sight of Patricia and the children had brought a lump to his throat and a desire to open the door as soon as he could. The embarrassed smiles lasted for seconds but felt longer. Michael looked at the old man in front of him, and prompted by his mother, boldly said, "Hallo Granddad." Mr Banks stooped and did something Patricia had never seen before, in a fit of emotion he grabbed Michael, lifted him, and hugged him burying his head in Michael's tiny shoulder. Feeling uncomfortable and wanting to fill the embarrassed silence that would certainly bring on those waiting tears, Patricia grabbed Jimmy to her and said, "This is your granddad Jimmy, say hallo." Jimmy, shyly moved forward and grabbed Mr Banks leg and hugged it saying hallo. By now Mr Banks was a little more in control and sniffed and smiled at Jimmy, grabbing him and carrying him in his free arm. The boys quite enjoyed that. He looked at his daughter, so grown up, so motherly and said in a soft, emotional voice that Patricia found hard to cope with, "Hallo Patricia, I'm glad you came."

Tears glistened in Patricia's eyes all afternoon. She watched as her father played with the boys. She remembered how good he was with children, how he used to play with her. She found it strange that she had forgotten what a wonderful time they had all had when she was very little. Even Angela seemed to enjoy her granddad's company, gurgling and kicking her feet excitedly when he cooed and played around her. Patricia noted how clean and tidy the house was, her father had obviously got fond of bleach as everywhere reeked of it. She had never seen her father do housework and was impressed that he had not let himself go. She pushed away the sad thought that if only her mother was here to see all the changes. Time went so quickly, before she knew it, it was 5 p.m. and she had to leave, explaining there was an evening meal to prepare, baths for the children and so on. Mr Banks quite understood and marvelled at how she managed to cope with three children, Patricia flushed at this praise from her father.

The goodbyes were less embarrassing and wooden, Patricia had seen a side of her father that was reassuringly nice. Nice was a plain word, but for Patricia, nice meant comforting and normal. On promises of ringing and arranging to visit soon, Patricia gathered all her children and left. After waving them goodbye and watching the car pull away until it had turned the bend in the road and disappeared, Mr Banks went back inside his deathly quiet house and surveyed the tortured remains of the cake and lemonade. The aeroplanes that had been launched by the boys under the guidance of Mr Banks and landed on the floor and chairs seemed, again, just bits of paper now. Cushions that previously sat stiffly on chairs were now pummelled into misshapen lumps of nothing and a pink rattle was carelessly lying on the floor under a chair. It had been many years since the place had looked such a mess. As he set about clearing up, the silence was broken by his whistling an old war time song long buried in the past. It had burst forth most unexpectedly, and put a spring in Mr Bank's step. He hoped their next visit would not be too long away. Next time he would show the boys some of his conjuring tricks. He felt happy, very happy indeed.

Angel had dipped in and out of the afternoon. He could see it was happy families and he was not needed. Still obsessed with Steve he had taken to following him everywhere. He had promised not to interfere with Patricia's karma and let her make her decisions, but that did not stop him still hating Tony and wanting him dead. With so much hatred still to get rid of, he spent days sitting beside Steve just cursing him and trying to pick up objects to smash into him. It was an exhausting time for Angel, and one he needed to keep hidden from Patricia. She was beginning to suspect something, his visits were not so regular and she wondered if he was tiring of her. He had to keep reassuring Patricia, he was finding it hard to go from hatred to love and did not know what to do with all the rage that billowed and cascaded as he went from Steve to Patricia. The hatred was festering and with no relief, was eating him up. He knew he was no good to Patricia as he was.

Over the years he watched as the children grew and the obvious pleasure it gave Patricia. He watched the relationship with Patricia and her father develop and when he died 7 years later, he was much loved and missed by Patricia and the children. Steve never got on with him but Patricia managed to keep all visits to her father separate from her married life. Steve hated Mr Banks and tried to stop Patricia seeing him but this was the one and only area she was defiant, she needed and liked the feeling of being loved. Mr Banks had discovered, first through his grandchildren, how to give and receive love again.

Steve was making Angel worse as the years went by. He was continuing to see the other bitch and treated Patricia like a servant. Angel left as soon as he arrived home, he could not bear to see the way he treated Patricia, and to see Patricia so cowed by him. Since her father had died Patricia felt worn down by the misery of her married life, she was near to having had enough. She still refused to leave Steve, although Angel sensed she was weakening a little, he hoped his subtle comments over the years were wearing her down. He did not think he was interfering with her karma, she was just seeing things straight that's all.

The Guardians watched and waited.

CHAPTER THIRTY FOUR

Reasons

There came a point, a catalyst in Patricia's and Angels' existence when something had to happen. The atmosphere in Patricia's house was unbearable. After another of their many arguments, Steve had threatened again to leave Patricia, that he had had enough of her, and was going to take the children soon to live with him and his girlfriend, who he added would be a better lover and mother than Patricia had ever been. The words, hateful and vile, had been spat at her. Patricia reacted and begged. In a flurry of panic and fear she cried and pleaded with him to stay with her, promising to be everything he could ever want. Angel thought he had plumbed the depths of despair and hatred of Steve but realised this injustice, this indigestible intense hatred would, if he had been alive, have killed him through a heart attack. Oblivious to the white hot hatred being hurled at him by Angel and uncaring of his wife's misery but busy with his plans, it was a week before Steve noticed a small lump had appeared on his upper thigh. He went to the doctor because it got bigger by the day and by the time he went for his appointment it seemed to have doubled in size. The hospital appointment was rushed forward and within 3 weeks Steve had a biopsy and the result that it was cancer. All plans went on hold. The word cancer had caused such a deep fear in Patricia and Steve that an immediate truce was called. To Angel's disgust, Patricia promised support Steve through this crisis. The doctors had said it was treatable and the tablets he was given would shrink the cancer in his leg and his life should be fairly normal. Angel made one of his regular returns to the Guardians. The hatred was eating away at him and he now looked gaunt and pale. He cursed them, saying why had Steve got one of the few cancers that was curable, was there no justice. They worried about him, but said nothing. Time would tell.

CHAPTER THIRTY FIVE

The Waiting Game

Over the next 6 months Patricia and Steve endured the cancer. Steve still expected Patricia to wait on him hand and foot without giving anything back to their relationship. Angel just couldn't help himself, he had to say it to her, for her own good and believing he was careful in not interfering too much with her karma, told Patricia in quiet, venomous tones, that Steve was ungrateful for all her caring. He was about to add that he should rot in hell but Patricia stopped him and firmly pointed out that he had cancer and that was that, she was there for him and if he treated her badly, well, that was up to her how she felt about it. Fed up with all the digs and sly comments from Angel, Patricia had enough and told him to go away and leave her alone, her voice raised to emphasise how she felt. Angel had taken to going off to sulk when things didn't go his way. He could not, never would, understand Patricia's loyalty to the fucking bastard who should be dead. Pleasures were few and far between, so Angel was glad to note that the bitch, for he could not bring himself to call her by her name, the fancy woman, had left Steve. He rejoiced at his humiliation that she no longer wanted him. It was a small victory to enjoy but Angel wanted to win the war, he wanted Steve dead.

All the pent up hatred Angel was storing, and he was kidding himself that Patricia could not see it, had, of course, seeped into their relationship. Angel had not seen how slowly, and insidiously their relationship had eroded. Each was so busy with their own misery that they had not noticed how distant and irritated they had become with each other. Angel was totally irritated by Patricia's cowering to Steve and blindingly angry that she would seemingly forgive him after all he had done to her, why she did not just wish him dead like he did, he would never understand. His frustration at not being able to say anything that would interfere with her karma had made him crafty and his hatred of Steve had driven him to make what he thought were subtle digs, that he hoped would erode any feelings Patricia had for him. But the stupid dame was not listening. Patricia, on the other hand, was getting fed up with Angel. Subtle comments he did not make, they felt like she was being jabbed in the side every time he opened his mouth. He made her feel a fool, and stupid for staying with Steve. Patricia endured Steve and Angel, it had become a way of life to put up with everything and not talk back, but sometimes, she wished Angel would just go away and leave her alone to cope. She felt very unloved and lonely. Each seemed to have forgotten their special relationship, over the years, it had become normal for Patricia to have an Angel with her.

After a particularly bad week with Patricia worried

about Steve, who was still working despite the lump impeding his walking, and the children who, caught up with all the worry of their parents and the distracted atmosphere, were misbehaving and fighting amongst themselves each running to their mother to referee their many fights. The final straw was Angel appearing at a time when she was looking forward to a bit of peace and quiet and time for herself, only to start, yet again, to question why she stayed with him and listing all the evil things he had done and said to her and how she just sat back and took it all. The bubbling held back hurricane of a temper that had tended to appear when Angel arrived just erupted. Enough was enough, she told him to go, sling his hook, sod off. She screamed that he was just making everything worse, she didn't need him, want him, or care about him. Angel, mortified that Patricia could talk to him like that, after all he had done for her, called her an ungrateful bitch and left.

The Guardians received him back to them and tried to comfort him. They needed him calm so they could talk to him and get him to understand. This is not what they wanted to happen. Angel had deserted Patricia at a time when she would need him. It felt to them that Angel had learned nothing over the years. They would let him rest and gain some peace in the apartment they had prepared for him, then they would set to work on Angel, time was short and they needed him back on track.

The time Angel spent with them was painful, home truths always are. It had taken a lot of time, tears, anger, and remorse before Angel let go of the hatred and started to listen, learn, and remember why he was there. As he said later, "I've been a selfish, childish bastard." They agreed and wanted to know how he was going to put things right between Steve, Patricia and himself. Angel did not know where to start so they suggested that it might be good for him to just observe Steve and Patricia for a while, to get the feel of the situation. They added that it had been two years since he last saw Patricia and Steve and things would be different. He knew what they really meant was they didn't want him to rush in and cause trouble again, he understood their concern and thought it a good idea to just watch first. Angel still found it strange that so much time had passed on earth when it had seemed like only a few days with them. He was anxious to see Patricia again. Talking with The Guardians about Clemmie and Patricia had made him remember why he was there and rekindled the almost forgotten feelings and yearning for Clemmie. They had helped him realise how destructive his hatred for Steve/Tony was. It frightened him to remember how he had behaved towards Patricia, he realised he had treated her badly, almost making her pay for not hating Steve in the way that he did. They had talked long and hard to Angel about Steve to get him to come to terms with his hatred. Angel agreed it was eating him up and hatred was so destructive. He had allowed the burning hatred to destroy his relationship with Patricia, and made him go back on his promise to her and them to be there for her. While he was with them he could feel the hatred leave him and he felt lighter and happier and more receptive to what they said. He knew he had screwed everything up and was, in fact, quite worried about seeing Patricia and Steve again in case he reverted back to the bastard he had been. A calmer Angel, more like he used to be, set off to find and watch Patricia, he had seriously let her down. He hated what he had become and was desperate to make amends. Would she forgive him, could he put everything between them right. He hoped he was not too late. He loudly, sincerely, and passionately promised them on everything he held holy, he would make it up to Patricia/Clemmie. They watched and hoped this time he meant it.

CHAPTER THIRTY SIX

Making Up is Hard To Do

He arrived in Patricia's home at what appeared a very busy time. He saw Steve just sitting in a chair watching the television whilst Patricia seemed to be running from room to room. She was dishing up a meal, serving it to the children, he noted how much bigger they were, all teenagers now and still the boys were fighting, nothing serious, just playful slaps that irritated Patricia who wanted them to eat up quickly so she could wash up and clear away. Angel thought she said something about the nurse would be there soon. Patricia obviously thought this person important because she was practically dusting and hoovering at the same time, she looked upset and close to tears. Still Steve sat and stared at the television. Angel could feel that old hatred start to burn. He saw all the fuss and commotion going on and it was obviously very upsetting for Patricia, and Steve just sat watching the television, without a care in the world, with no intention of helping. How could they expect him to have good thoughts about Steve when he acts like this. He felt more and more angry at the situation and decided to return to them, the sight of Patricia and Steve sickened him. As soon as he got back to them, they told him in no uncertain terms to get back to Patricia now. They had never talked so firmly to him before and he wondered what had got into them.

He returned to Patricia in a blink of an eye just in time to see the important nurse arrive. Patricia was sending the children out to the shops for something or the other, obviously from her manner, she wanted them out of the way. Angel, sensed something big was happening. The nurse busied herself opening her bag, getting out what looked like tubes and things. Once the children had gone, the house seemed much quieter and rather depressing. Angel noted Patricia started to cry as soon as the door closed on the children, and for the first time, Steve looked over to her and held his hand out for her to come to him. She rushed over to him and tenderly and carefully hugged him. Angel wondered what the hell was going on. The nurse sat down and spoke quietly and calmly to them both. What she said was very clear to Angel. Steve was dying, he had something called Lymphoma or something like that which could eventually drown him, his body would fill with liquid and eventually fill his lungs. Apparently the doctor at the hospital had told him that morning and the nurse was there to change his drainage that came out of his back in a tube to a bag by his side. She was going to show Patricia how to change it and how to keep the area clean.

This is what Angel thought he wanted, to see Steve die, but he got no pleasure out of this information, the look on Steve's face said it all. Here was a man, still fairly young, knowing he was going to die and leave his wife and children. He looked at Patricia and Steve and saw they were trying to be brave. He had never seen them so close, each supporting the other. When the nurse had gone Patricia sat next to Steve on the settee, she seemed exhausted but defiant. She grabbed his hand and in a voice bubbling with held back tears she told Steve that they were going to fight this, she had the strength for him and would help him. No way was he going to die, he was going to beat this cancer, she told him of stories she had read of people who had recovered from cancer against all the odds. Her voice felt stronger and she promised him he would survive. Steve looked at her and felt her strength and for the first time since getting the awful news, he smiled. He squeezed her hand as a thank you. They both knew the children would be back soon and had decided not to say anything at the moment about the advancing cancer, they would tell them when it was necessary.

Angel returned to them. It was a shock, he thought Steve had a curable cancer, what had happened he asked? They told him never to assume what was going to happen. He desperately wanted to talk to Patricia and asked them if he could, he could see she needed his support. They said not for the moment. Both Patricia and Steve needed each other and an undisciplined Angel could make things worse. Angel felt deeply depressed and remorseful at the way he had acted over the years. Once again he thought if only he had listened to them, he would be at Patricia's side now, helping her instead he would just have to watch and wait, the frustration of doing nothing felt painful.

He watched as they went about their daily life. The

children were boisterous but good kids at heart. They had all sensed something was wrong but did not know what to say so they handled it as best they could. The house had a cloud of dense gloom hovering over it and all felt it. Angela was always at her mother's side when at home, they talked a little about Steve's illness so Angela had an idea of what was happening. The boys did not know what to say so they just annoyed everyone with play fights, they should have known better, they were getting older, but this was the only way they could handle the tension. This continued for three years, and the visits to the hospital with the odd week in hospital followed by home visits by nurses became the norm. Steve got sicker and then recovered slightly, only to get sicker again followed by a slight recovery. Being so close to it all, it appeared to Patricia that Steve was winning the battle. She could not see that each time he made a slight recovery it was never as great as the one before. Patricia could not and would not see how sick Steve had got. Patricia and Steve firmly believed that he would survive, together they were winners. There had been so many panics and rushes to hospital, but each time Steve had recovered from the setbacks. They had become convinced he was invincible, and so the last trip to hospital came as a shock to them both.

A glum doctor told them that every treatment had been used to halt the spread of lymphoma but it still kept coming back. They had run out of treatments and time. The doctor had become quite fond of Steve and Patricia, recognising the fight they were putting up, Steve had survived more years than most people, and their strength was testimony to that. It was hard for her to tell them that there was not much more they could do, she desperately wanted to give them a different answer but had exhausted all her knowledge and avenues.

She left Steve and Patricia to their silence. There was nothing each could say to the other. The fight, the battle that had kept them strong seemed to leave them both and they visibly shrunk in their chairs. They sat and cuddled each other, Patricia started to cry and Steve followed her. They cried on and off for an hour until Steve pulled himself together and told Patricia that the children must be told and plans had to be made. The strength had left Patricia and she could not bear any of this talk. Steve gained in strength and started to organise and plan. Patricia arranged for a neighbour to look after the children, she told Steve she would not leave his side in hospital and would do everything for him.

The doctor still tried to prolong Steve's life by holding the lymphoma back by putting drains in his chest to clear his lungs, and drains in his side. He wanted to live and told the doctor to do anything that would give him more time. Angel waited and watched. He was reduced to tears on many occasions. The hardest to watch was on an evening when everyone else in the ward was settling down to sleep, the lights were dimmed and it cast a soft beam around Steve's bed. Patricia and Steve, as was their habit of late, sat holding hands in a comfortable silence. Patricia, would sit on a chair placed by the head of Steve's bed, she often read during this time as Steve drifted in and out of sleep. On this occasion Steve turned to Patricia and asked her forgiveness. She looked at him unable to say anything. He looked her in the eyes and told her he loved her, had always loved her, and begged her forgiveness for the wrong he had done her. He thanked her for staying by his side. He knew he would not have lived so long but for her strength. With death around the corner, his mind was concentrated on saying the words that needed to be said, and he truly meant them. She leaned over and kissed him gently on the lips. They both cried. She told him she loved him and had hoped to hear the words he spoke. She climbed into bed with him for the last time. They lay together holding hands, it felt as if a weight had been lifted from them. The nurses did not disturb them, they knew time was short and they looked so happy, asleep side by side.

Angel went back to them and asked if he could now go to Patricia, he could not bear to see her in such pain by herself. He felt truly sorry for Steve and thought he had endured his illness with dignity and strength. They told him no, Patricia needs Steve now not him. Angel felt they were punishing him for making a mess of everything before and begged to put things right now. They firmly said no, but added he could watch and wait and that was all, his time would come.

The next day Steve's condition changed dramatically, barely able to talk he answered the doctor's question of did he want them to continue to try and keep him alive. Worn out and at peace with himself, Steve said he wanted to be left alone, so much had been done to his body, there had been so much pain for so long, now he was ready to let go. Patricia witnessed this, and supported his decision through tears that ran down her face like a waterfall. The children were brought to the hospital by a neighbour and Angel felt their bewildered, painful realisation that their father was going to die. Patricia was no good to them she had eyes only for Steve.

All day Steve's life force slowly ebbed away, all could see him leaving, when he finally left his body it was gentle and painfree. Patricia, strong for so long, lost all sense of reality and began screaming. The nurses took her to a side room, she was frightening the other patients on the ward, and the children were taken by two nurses to another room. They were all in shock at the death of their father and stunned by their mother's reaction. The doctor arranged for them to talk to a counsellor in the hope they would be able to accept the situation. Of course, the children wanted none of that, they just wanted their mother. They were left to cry and cuddle each other while the doctor went to see Patricia and try and get her to calm down and comfort her children. Eventually after some comforting and then tough talking, Patricia pulled herself together enough to gather her children and go home.

Angel watched this and cried for them all. He had watched Steve die and his soul leave his body and ascend, it should have been graceful and beautiful as most souls are. Steve was now the essence of Tony, and his soul vomited out of his body and his aura crackled and fizzed like a pan of hot fat. Angel instinctively took a step backwards, away from the menace in front of him. He watched as Tony stood outside of his body. His black and red aura violently swirled around him the evil pulsated rhythmically in tune with Angel's panic breathing. He had never seen the devil's work in such rawness. Suddenly, a blue light encompassed Tony and it seemed to trap him within it. The black squall that was him fought and swirled and spat but the blue encompassed every strike and tortuous surge and gradually calmed and settled. Tony's soul was soothed and cleaned and calmed and the violent black and red shimmered into a pastel yellow. The glower in Tony's eyes faded, and Angel saw him change before his eyes into a gentle pulsating soul at peace. As Tony began his ascension to the Guardians there was a brief moment where he hovered in front of Angel and looked into Angel's eyes, no words were needed, his sadness emanated from him. After a brief heavy pause that encompassed a lifetime of regret, Tony looked upwards and carried on his journey to them. This small act had a profound effect on Angel and he said a little prayer for the essence of Tony, he knew he had paid terribly for all the wrong he had done in the last two lives. Only now did Angel realise what the Guardians had been trying to tell him. The love and goodness of Patricia and the forgiveness of Angel had neutralised the evil essence of Tony and allowed him to be with the Guardians and grow in their warmth and love.

Worn down by the emotion of it all, Angel returned to them and asked what they wanted him to do now. They noted how compliant he seemed and how he wanted whatever was best for Patricia, regardless of his own needs. They said now was the time for him to visit Patricia. A sombre and quiet Angel went to Patricia.

CHAPTER THIRTY SEVEN

Autumn

He found her sitting in the dark. The children had gone to bed, exhausted by the emotions of the day and they all wanted to escape into sleep to hold back the realisation that their dad had died.

He did not want to frighten her, and wondered how to say hallo without scaring the hell out of her. He need not have worried.

"Hallo Angel, I know you are there," she said in a flat monotone voice that worried Angel. She had sensed his presence, without looking round. He could hear in her voice that she was not bothered whether he was there or not, talking was a big effort. Softly and gently, in keeping with the atmosphere, he edged forward until he was right behind her.

"Hi Patricia, I couldn't stay away, I wanted to be here with you, I'm so sorry about everything."

He told her about seeing Steve leave his body and his journey to the Guardians. He was economical with the whole truth and told her how he had left his body gracefully and peacefully. He assured her he was going somewhere beautiful and he was no longer in pain. On hearing that, Patricia turned sharply and faced Angel.

The turn was so violent, he wondered what she was going to do and took one step backwards. She threw her arms around him and sobbed, and sobbed, deep, low and painful sobs. He felt good to be able to hug her and let her sob until she had no more energy. He sat next to her on the settee making shushing noises as she settled down and fell asleep against his chest. He sat shaking with the emotion of everything, he replayed Steve's illness, death, and Patricia in mourning, and vowed to stay with her forever. She needed his strength now.

They watched with pleasure and thought Angel might have, at last grown up.

Over the next week Patricia would not let Angel out of her sight, she was drawing on Angel's strength. He went with her to the funeral parlour, the church, the Insurance Company, the florist, and he sat with her while she talked to the children. Every now and then the situation would get too much for Patricia and she would give in to mild hysteria, asking for Steve to come back to her. Certain people thought she may have gone a little mad with grief, she was caught by many in conversation with her, looking to a blank space and crying for help, or asking a blank space what they thought of a comment made. No-one said anything, those closest to her assumed she would get over this crisis after the funeral. The children quietly watched all that was going on and found comfort in each other. They hoped their mum would be their mum again in a short while, not this out of control person she appeared to be.

When Patricia had buried Steve and everyone else's life had returned to normal, Angel set about getting

Patricia stronger and back to her old self.

For many months Patricia sat and talked to Angel about Steve, she went over the good times and the bad times. As she told him, she got what she had always wanted, his love back, but only for a very short time. She told Angel that over the years of his illness they had grown close, especially the last year. She asked him to explain why it was taken away from her, why couldn't she have it for longer. It was hard to accept he had gone. He had no answers for her.

Because she had recognised that people had thought her strange when she looked or talked to an Angel no one else could see, it was agreed by both of them that Angel would come to her of an evening when she was alone. The children had got frightened by their mother's odd behaviour of talking and looking at thin air, it spooked them. She was sufficiently recovered from her grief to realise that she was acting like a nutcase and did not want to add to the burden of grief her children were already carrying.

She got stronger and stronger with Angel's help and started to sit and talk with Michael, Jimmy and Angela about their father and his love for them. They talked about all the good times they could remember, no one wanted to talk about the bad times for they all remembered how their father had treated their mother. With lots of hugs and kisses the children settled and felt comforted to have their mother back as she used to be.

The Guardians watched.

Time marched on and Angel was there to cry at Michael, Jimmy and Angela's weddings. Angel had a very soft spot for Angela, having been there when she was born, so at her wedding service Angel caused so much emotion and disruption that Patricia had to ban him from the church. He had taken to standing next to the vicar at the alter and with tears streaming down his face was looking at Angela. He kept shouting, in between tears, to Patricia and telling her how beautiful Angela was, how she was near to tears herself, and altogether giving a running commentary on what she was doing. It was totally distracting to Patricia and she could not hear what the vicar was saying. At one stage she saw Angel blowing his nose and then putting his head on the shoulder of the vicar as if exhausted by the whole sight. Although no one else could see or hear this spectacle, Patricia was finding it hard to concentrate, torn between crying herself and laughing at the absurd way Angel was behaving. But they spent many an evening talking and crying over the wedding photos of all three children. The birth of each of her 8 grandchildren was greeted by Angel, again in tears. Patricia had grown to find this aspect of Angel to be the most endearing, she presumed it came from what he thought was his Italian ancestry, although he had told her he was not at all sure who his father was.

The children were settled in their lives and visited as often as possible, of course with children, jobs, and homes to look after they were not able to see her every day and so they worried that she was lonely or unable to look after herself. They nagged her constantly trying to persuade her to live with one of them, they told her she would be no trouble and would have company, otherwise who did she talk to during the day? They knew she had no friends in Loughton that she wanted to see. It was quite exasperating for them because all Patricia would say was she was never lonely, she had her Angel to talk to. Finally, after too much nagging, Patricia had had enough, she was adamant and expended more energy than she could afford in telling them that she was happy where she was, she thanked them for their concern but she would die in her now beloved Loughton and be with Angel.

Loughton was surrounded by Epping Forest and as she got older she took a great interest in the great Oaks, Ash and Elm trees that help to make up that majestic forest. She used to walk regularly amongst the huge trees but as she aged she wasn't able to walk without getting out of breath, so she watched from her window. It was calming watching nature take its course, there was much comfort from watching all the seasons knowing after winter spring would arrive again and everything was renewed. They gave up arguing with her, they could see it was making her tired.

They had all heard the stories about her Angel. Whilst not believing in the tales she told, they were content that she was happy and certainly not harmful to herself or anyone else. Her imaginary friend became a family secret, they would not share that one with the doctor who may not understand. Michael, as the oldest and most sensible, suggested they keep a discreet eye on their mother, just in case, well no one wanted to mention senile dementia, but that was a concern. Patricia knew they were getting together to talk about her, and trying to organise her life. As she told Angel, it was nice to see the children so close and doing things together.

With time to spare, they spent many an evening talking about this and that. One time in particular Angel had asked who had been President of the USA since he was there. She told him about Kennedy which upset him. She explained about how Nixon was nearly impeached. Angel laughed when told that Regan, an ex-actor had become President and then there was Clinton who had battled with the disgrace of a sex scandal and impeachment. He didn't want to hear anymore. He found it depressing to hear how his country had faired. Although it was good to hear that prohibition had ended. Good booze at last he muttered.

Over the years Patricia got frailer. In middle age she got bulky and developed a bit of a waddle in her walk. As she got older she slowly got thinner and thinner until everything she wore hung on her. She still looked the same to Angel who would stroke her liver-spotted bony hands whilst they talked. When she smiled at him she was in her twenties again, he told her so, and she smiled even more. She had recently taken to falling asleep in the early evening and Angel would just sit holding her hand and looking at her. He had developed a quiet, intense love for Patricia and wanted to be with her all the time. As she grew older and closer to the end of her earthly life, the essence that was Clemmie was very close, almost touchable and Angel could feel the stirring of feelings and longings that had been suppressed for a life time. When he returned to them, as he did regularly, they told him it would not be long before Patricia left her earthly body and the essence of Clemmie would be reunited with Angel.

CHAPTER THIRTY EIGHT

Understanding

Patricia could feel her life force ebbing away and felt frightened. Angel spent much time reassuring her of eternal life. His favourite saying was, "What am I then, a fucking dummy?" She always laughed at that. She worried about the children. Angel had to remind her that they were all in their late or early 50's, certainly not young children, even her grandchildren were in their 20's. It was natural for parents to leave their children in old age. Angel still stroking her hand told her how they would be together and although he could not remember being there, heaven, as it was known to Patricia, was a beautiful place, he added that he had this information on good authority.

Later that same month Patricia fell ill with pneumonia, the Doctors told the children this was common in older people, and they kept her in hospital. She spent most of her days sleeping, this was good the Doctors told the children. They did not believe this piece of information. They visited as regularly as they could but Patricia slipped in and out of consciousness for three weeks. Sometimes she was awake and able to recognise her children and they in turn had conversations with her.

Angel was always there, still holding her hand. She

knew he was there, she knew she would never be left alone and this comforted her. All her life she felt as if there was something on the periphery of how she felt about Angel. She could never quite reach that feeling. Now as she lay there looking at him holding her hand she felt closer to that feeling, still tantalisingly out of reach but closer.

The Doctor called Michael who called Jimmy and Angela. He advised that Patricia was near the end and they should hurry to the hospital if they wanted to be with her. They arrived just as Patricia opened her eyes. It was as if she was waiting for them to arrive. They all noticed her look to her left with a smile. She was looking to Angel to give her the strength to say what she needed to say to her beloved children. They may be in their 50's as Angel said, but to her they were her babies and she needed to do one final thing for them. She needed to reassure them that she would be alright and how much she loved each and every one of them. It was an emotional speech she made but one that made them all smile through their tears. Angel told her she was doing a wonderful job, he was crying, but kept squeezing her hand to give her the strength to say all that needed saying. She was not going to die until she had put their mind at rest. Her final remark was that she was going to be with her Angel and he would look after her. Then she fell asleep, having used all the energy she had left.

The children sat huddled together for support, intently watching their mother, they heard her breathing get shallower and shallower and knew it would not be long. They breathed in unison with her, almost willing her to keep breathing but after one hour she just stopped breathing. Her last breath was exhaled and sounded like a sigh of intense pleasure and her face, which for the last hour had seemed immobile and far away lit up with the most beautiful smile, her eyes opened and she raised her arms briefly to the space at the end of her bed. Michael, Jimmy and Angela all smiled at each other through their tears, they knew for sure that her Angel had come for her.

He held his breath and stood at the end of the bed waiting for her to come to him. She rose and smiled almost shyly. There were no words, what could they say, they held hands and gently kissed, shuddering with pleasure as their lips stung exquisitely with the current of emotion that passed between them. She turned to look at the children but Angel kissed her eyes and led her upwards. The only thing he could say was, "No regrets Clemmie, the children are fine." She smiled a brief sad smile and let herself be led.

They had an eye contact that could not be parted. Neither wanted to look at anything else, they drunk off each other, Angel marvelled that she could not be more beautiful yet she was, she glowed with a passion that was unrequited. He could not trust himself to say anything, the tears were forming and he felt giddy with a throbbing excitement that coursed through his body, making the hairs on his arms stand up and his finger tips pulsate. After all this time, at last she was with him. His mouth had gone dry and he tried to lick his lips. He wanted to hug her close but dare not, the feelings he had were too strong, he knew he must calm them. She kissed his hand and stroked his face, they would not be able to contain their feelings for much longer. It was unfinished business, their last life was ended far too quickly, they needed to say goodbye to each other in this form, for they knew they would be together in different bodies in future lives but at the moment they were still earth bound as Angel and Clemmie, who would fight for the right to have this short time together.

They arrived at what was the half way area with them. Both were surprised and a little wary. Angel asked, without taking his eyes off Clemmie why they had not gone on as they should. A feeling of foreboding overtook them and Angel and Clemmie tightly held hands. He tried to push her behind him, to protect her from what he had not figured out, but she would have none of that. There was no way they were going to be parted again. They both stood defiantly, ready to fight, they knew they had done enough, they deserved to be together.

Angel started before they could answer. They listened, unable to interrupt the tirade from them both. The pair of them were quite formidable so the Guardians let them get it all out of their system not interrupting any of the, "He said, They said" comments, punctuated with promises of how he and Clemmie would conduct themselves in future, they were pleased to hear how Angel and Clemmie were going to be Saints and save the earth with their good works. They thought this was a little unrealistic but appreciated the effort. Now was the time to stop Angel and Clemmie, they could see they were getting upset and definitely getting the wrong end of the stick and that was not the point of bringing them here. Both Angel and Clemmie were quite exhausted by now having given full force to their reasoning, there was a gap in their shouting, as they tried to get their breath so the Guardians jumped in quickly to tell Angel and Clemmie why they were here.

They made it quite clear at the start of their conversation that Angel and Clemmie were now reunited for eternity. They hoped this would keep them both quiet and listening to what they had to say. He looked at her and they both visibly relaxed, they were not going to be parted again.

Angel thought they sounded just a little pleased with themselves, they were clearing their throats in a manner Angel recognised as a cover for laughing. They continued and told them both that they had all agreed, that perhaps Angel and Clemmie would like some time together in the Apartment they had prepared for Angel. As all souls know, once in the place known to many as heaven, all earthly characters were left behind. They thought that perhaps Angel and Clemmie may like to renew their relationship for a while. Both Angel and Clemmie nodded and smiled in unison. But, they added quickly, if perhaps they would prefer to carry on with their journey that was fine too. Angel sensed the joke, and overwhelmed by their thoughtfulness, could only say, "Gee, you guys are great. I am really looking forward to seeing you later, much, much later I hope." They laughed.

During this time, Clemmie had found the door to the apartment and seen the familiar furniture and décor inside. She called gently, and provocatively to Angel "Honey, I'd come here quickly if I was you. I don't know what I'm going to do to you first, but I'll figure that out as we go along." She lowered her eyelashes and gave him a stunning, come and get me look. He started to move towards her and turned to them and said breathlessly, "God! What a woman. Isn't she just wonderful?" With that he rushed in to the apartment, mindful that he closed the door.

They sighed. This was so typical of him to rush off without a how are you doing, goodbye, or thank you. They all agreed, they were really going to miss him. Their work with Angel and Clemmie was now successfully completed. They were pleased Angel had learned such a lot. It was recognised by them that being a stand-in Angel was a hard way to learn life's lessons, but he had and so his future would be blessed. The Guardians knew this was not the end, so sadness was quickly replaced with a sense of joy at the thought that they would meet them both later.

In the meantime, He had another assignment for them. One of them sighed and with an impish smile said "No rest for the wicked." They all laughed at that.